Just Saying

BOOKS BY SOPHIE RANALD

Out With the Ex, In With the New

Sorry Not Sorry

It's Not You, It's Him

No, We Can't be Friends

SOPHIE RANALD

Just Saying

Bookouture

Published by Bookouture in 2020

An imprint of Storyfire Ltd.
Carmelite House
50 Victoria Embankment
London EC4Y 0DZ

www.bookouture.com

ISBN: 978-1-83888-132-0
eBook ISBN: 978-1-83888-131-3

Chapter One

Even though it was Friday, and my birthday, I only stayed in the pub for the one glass of wine. I know, right? A couple of years before, I'd have been all over the opportunity to have a wild night out on the town and get happily shitfaced with my colleagues.

Who knows, two-years-ago-me would have said to herself, *I might even meet someone.*

But here's the thing. I *had* met someone. Just weeks after beginning my training contract at Billings Pitt Furzedown, a London law firm that was almost, but not quite, in the so-called magic circle of the super-elite, I'd hooked up with Joe, who'd started in the same cohort of ambitious, naïve, sharp-elbowed, wet-behind-the-ears soon-to-be solicitors as I had.

It happened at what seemed like warp speed – yet also felt totally natural. Within weeks, I'd been spending almost every other night at his, and he'd been spending the rest of the time at mine, both of us heading back to our respective shared flats on Sunday nights to catch up with laundry, open our post and reassure our flatmates that we weren't disappearing into the vortex that sucks new couples out of their friendship circles, never to return.

But we both knew, even in those early days, that meeting each other was going to change both of our lives in a big way, for a long time.

It wasn't like some massive drama took place between us – like Joe declared undying love for me on date number three, or anything. If he had, I'd have marked him out as a potential psycho and headed for the hills as fast as I could. It just felt right, right from the start. It felt like we were two plants that had been put in pots next to each other, and as we climbed the same sunlit wall our tendrils reached out for the same things until they became intertwined, and we grew together with the same water and light, neither crowding the other out.

Cheesy as fuck, right? That's what my friend Heather said, anyway, when the lease on the flat I shared with her came to an end and I told her I was going to move in with Joe – and then right away she gave me a huge hug and told me anyone could see we were made for each other and she was going to be best woman at our wedding in a few years, just watch.

So Joe and I had been living together for a bit more than a year. In the beginning we'd shared the flat with a mate of his, but when Chris had been offered a job in Dublin we'd figured out that we could – just about – afford the rent by ourselves, and decided to go it alone, together.

Anyway, like I say, it was my birthday and I knew that Joe would have made surprise plans for me. My last birthday had been just a few days after we'd moved in together, and we saved up to buy a bottle of the most expensive champagne either of us had ever tasted, ordered a Chinese takeaway and ate it on the living-room floor because we didn't have any furniture yet. It had been perfect. This year, I guessed he might have booked a table at a local restaurant or something, and I wanted to get home and change out of my work suit into something prettier and more comfortable, and get ready to celebrate being twenty-seven.

But before I even walked into our flat, I knew Joe had planned something different – something special. Tied to the door handle was an enormous bunch of white heart-shaped balloons, and I didn't even have to count them to know that there would be twenty-seven. I carefully untied them and let myself in, feeling an enormous smile spreading over my face.

The curtains over the glass door leading to the garden were closed, so the flat was filled with a dim twilight, but there were candles lit on the table, which was laid for two people. On it were a little pile of carefully wrapped presents and a card for me to open. There was a folded piece of paper on one of the plates, with 'Menu' printed on it in a swirly typeface. I unfolded it and felt my smile grow even wider: 'Smoked salmon blinis, Fillet steak with mushroom sauce, Chocolate mousse'. The very same things Joe had made the first time he ever cooked for me.

Then I heard his voice from beyond the curtains.

'Alice? Come out here.'

'Just a second.'

I tied the balloons to the back of one of the chairs, pushed the curtains aside – and then I froze.

'Oh my God! Joe! What have you done? You absolute nutter!'

In the fading sunlight, our small patch of garden was filled almost from side to side by a huge inflatable hot tub. Steam rose from its bubbling surface, leaving only the faintest haze in the summer evening air. Fairy lights sparkled around its edges; a silver ice bucket holding a bottle of champagne stood next to it. And, best of all, there was Joe, wearing only board shorts, flip-flops and a delighted grin.

'I only hired it for one night,' he said, 'so you'd better get your bikini on, birthday girl. We've got no time to waste.'

I didn't need telling twice. Ten minutes later, I was neck-deep in the warm water, half a glass of champagne down, Joe's bare shoulder strong and smooth next to mine, the jets gently pummelling our bodies, the first stars visible in the ink-blue sky above us.

'This is so amazing,' I said. 'Who knew our weed-infested garden could be turned into romance central?'

'You know me, Alice. When you're here, everywhere's romance central.'

I laughed and squeezed his hand under the water, then ran my fingers up the ridged muscles of his stomach, feeling goosebumps pop up on his skin.

'When did they deliver this thing? I thought you had an early meeting today.'

'Yeah, I kind of made that up. I went and sat in a coffee shop by the station until I saw you go in, then pegged it back here in time for them to drop it off and install it at nine thirty. It takes ages for all this water to heat up, you see. And then I left the office at five on the dot to get all the food ready.'

'You're quite something, you know that?'

'I've got a girlfriend who deserves the best.'

He leaned over and kissed me, gently and affectionately at first, but then it changed into something more. I put my glass down so I could wrap both arms around him, pulling his warm body closer, our legs tangling together under the water. We kissed and kissed, and then – when we realised that if things went much further one or both of us would probably drown, which would be quite the passion-killer – we went inside to the bedroom, discarding our sodden swimwear on the floor along the way. We fell onto the bed in each other's arms, laughing and gasping with longing and pleasure.

We had the kind of shag that was passionate but also leisurely – the sort of sex you have when you know you've got all night to do it again, all weekend to do it some more, and the rest of your life to keep getting better and better at it.

And when we'd finished, we pulled on some clothes and finished the bubbly while Joe cooked our steaks, then ate our starter while they rested, which he insisted they had to do if they were to be perfect.

'Whatever you say, Marcus Wareing,' I teased.

'A Michelin-starred chef would be ashamed of himself, serving dinner at eleven o'clock at night.'

'Not if he'd done what you just did to me.'

'What, so back there you were thinking filthy thoughts about Marcus Wareing?'

'I admit nothing.'

We burst out laughing, and I wrapped my arms around Joe from behind while he stirred the mushroom sauce and opened a bottle of red wine. The candles were glowing, the room was filled with delicious smells – the most delicious being Joe himself – and I felt completely happy.

Then we both jumped out of our skins at the crash of the door knocker.

'What the hell?' Joe said.

'Could it be a neighbour complaining about noise?'

'We weren't making any noise.'

'Deliveroo driver at the wrong address?'

'Maybe. I'll get it.'

Still shirtless, Joe walked the few steps to the front door and opened it, and I heard a familiar voice.

'Sorry to barge in. My God, something smells good. I'm not interrupting anything, am I?'

My brother. What on earth was he doing here?

'Hello, mate. Your sister and I were just in the middle of dinner, but you're welcome to join us,' Joe said.

'Fantastic! I'm bloody starving. I just flew in from Penang, via Singapore and Zürich because I was too skint to fly direct. Couldn't even afford the train fare to Mum and Dad's so I got a bus here from City airport. I'm out of credit on my phone, or I'd have let you know. Happy birthday, Alice. I'm not interrupting anything, am I? Don't hug me, I've been in cattle class for almost thirty hours. Any chance of a shower?'

Looking at my brother's familiar, grinning face, I felt a familiar mix of affection and exasperation. Our romantic evening was screwed, that was for sure – but, at the same time, Drew's presence was like a bright light had been turned on in our living room, dimming the glow of the candles.

Compared to my brother, I'm pretty ordinary-looking. I'm middling height, not tall but not short either. I've got blonde hair that I help along with some highlights when I get time to go to the hairdresser, and greeny-blue eyes. A typical English rose, I guess. Sometimes I scrub up well, sometimes I look like I've been dragged through a hedge backwards, just like anyone.

Still, when I looked at Drew, I couldn't help feeling, just for a second, that nature could have been a little bit fairer when she dished out the looks in our family.

The features and colouring that were ordinary on my face had somehow been translated into something exceptional on Drew's. He was gorgeous. Taller than me, broad-shouldered and lean, his blond hair gleaming like a shampoo advert, his eyes managing to look warm in spite of being deep blue. His face was movie-star handsome. Girls reacted to him like cats to catnip. Okay, maybe they didn't actually throw themselves on the ground, writhing and yowling, but you could tell they wanted to.

If I let slip on social media that, right now, Drew was naked in my shower, there'd be a queue round the block like when Space NK opened and was offering free goodie bags.

But Drew had never quite got his shit together. After school he'd had a series of casual jobs – working in a supermarket, working in a call centre, working in a warehouse fulfilling online orders, doing a couple of courses in website design and social-media marketing. And in between them, he was out of work for months at a time, living at home and claiming benefits.

He said he wanted to be in a band, or go travelling, or be a poet. But he never did very much about any of those things. Actually, the travelling he did get around to – taking off for months at a time to New Zealand and Bali and Peru and other far-flung places, getting casual work in bars when he could, before eventually coming home and moving back in with Mum and Dad, back to unemployment and writing poems that occasionally got published in obscure literary magazines that didn't pay a fee.

'So how was Malaysia?' Joe asked, dragging me away from my thoughts.

My brother had emerged from the shower, and I knew from experience he'd have left at least three sodden towels on the bathroom floor and his backpack would look like a bomb had gone off inside it.

'Sick,' Drew said. 'The beaches are just amazing. There are loads of social problems, of course, and poverty. But the natural beauty is incredible. I volunteered for a charity that's working to protect their biodiversity, and I washed dishes in a restaurant to pay for my flight home. But here I am.'

I watched as Joe carefully divided the two steaks, cold now, into three and shared out the oven chips.

'Mum's been going nuts worrying about you,' I said. 'I had to show her your Insta feed to convince her you were still alive.'

'Oh shit. She didn't see the picture of me passed out on the beach surrounded by empty Tiger beer bottles, did she?'

'Yeah, I drew her attention to it especially. She said it looked like a fun night.'

Drew stuck his tongue out at me, looking like a twelve-year-old boy again.

'Anyhow, how about you guys?' he asked. 'What's up in the world of high-powered lawyering?'

I made a face. 'We're not exactly high-powered, you know. We're still trainees – the lowest of the low.'

'But Alice is all set with a job when she qualifies,' Joe said. 'Newly qualified solicitor in the intellectual property department.'

'And what's your plan then, Drew? Now that you're back?'

'God, Alice, I don't know! I'm still jet-lagged. I don't have a plan.'

'You never have one.'

'I don't need one,' Drew said. 'Plans are so bourgeois. Making it up as you go along is far more interesting.'

He pushed back his chair and glanced outside.

'Hey, is that a hot tub? Cool! Let's open another bottle and have a go.'

So Joe and I changed back into our damp swimsuits, Drew pulled off his T-shirt and put the bottle of duty-free vodka he'd brought into the ice bucket, and we all got in. The hot tub was a tight squeeze for three, but we managed it.

'Mind if I smoke?' Drew asked.

'Go ahead.'

Joe sloshed vodka into our glasses and Drew lit a fag.

'God, I'm knackered,' he said. 'I thought that flight was never going to end. It's good to be back.'

He stretched out his arms and legs, giving me an accidental kick on the ankle, tipped back his head and closed his eyes. I looked at Joe, worried he'd be annoyed at his carefully planned surprise being gatecrashed. But he winked at me and blew me a kiss, and I knew everything was all right.

Then he said, 'What's that smell? Like burning plastic.'

Drew's eyes snapped open again.

'Shit,' he said. 'Shit shit shit. I've only gone and burned a hole in the bastard thing. I'm so sorry.'

'I expect they'll be able to patch it somehow,' I said, although I didn't really have a clue.

'It's leaking like crazy,' Drew said. 'And kind of sagging.'

He tried to sit upright, but he must have slipped backwards, because the side of the tub where his back was dropped dramatically, sending a tidal wave of water out over the side and into the garden. Once it had started, it was unstoppable. The weight of the water forced down the side of the tub, its structural integrity destroyed. As the hot tub's wall sagged down, my brother's body followed it until he was almost horizontal, water streaming over him. Joe and I tried to hold up the now-deflated side, but it was hopeless – partly because we'd started to giggle, and our laughter soon became an unstoppable flood, too.

We helped Drew to his feet and watched as the whoosh of water slowed to a stream and then a trickle.

'Between you two,' I said, 'you've certainly given me a birthday I won't forget.'

Chapter Two

Joe and I were woken the next morning by the thud of the front door. As he'd promised, Drew – no doubt woken up by jet lag – had got an early start to head home to Mum and Dad's place in Reading, and Joe and I were left to deal with our hangovers and make our excuses to the hot-tub hire company alone.

'What time is it?' Joe mumbled, turning over and pulling me close to him, big spoon to my little spoon. I could feel his warm breath on my neck and the length of his body pressed up against mine, a perfect fit.

'Eight fifteen.' I had to crane my neck to see my watch, because my arm was trapped under his. 'God, I'm hungover. We shouldn't have opened that last bottle of wine. I don't know if I'm up for Parkrun today. Seriously.'

'Come on, Alice. Getting out of bed is the hardest part.'

'You get up first. Go on. Bring me a coffee. Please?'

'It's your turn. I made it last week, remember? Even though I was the hungover one.'

'I could make the coffee and we could have it in bed. Go on, let's sack it off, just this once.'

'Alice! You'll feel miles better afterwards – you know you will. You always say…'

'But it's my birthday,' I objected. 'We could go to the farmers' market instead. Get some breakfast.'

'Well, since you put it that way…'

I rolled over and turned my face up to his, feeling his hands start to caress my back, and I knew I was safe. There weren't many ways of persuading Joe that staying in bed was a better idea than getting up and running five kilometres, but this was one of them.

Two blissful hours later, we burst out into the morning. The air was fresh and clean, and I could tell that it was going to be a glorious, roasting-hot day.

'God, I'm starving,' Joe said. 'I hope the burger van will be at the market today. They do those killer breakfast butties, remember?'

'Or the place that does the lamb wraps.' My mouth watered at the thought. 'Or we could have hot dogs with fried onions.'

'God, stop. You're torturing me. I want all that stuff.'

'And cake.'

'Carrot cake, or salted caramel?'

'I vote for both.'

We turned onto a street lined with Victorian houses, flanked by tall chestnut trees, and we walked on, Joe's hand warm and strong in mine. Soon we were joined by a flow of people – young families with their babies in buggies, older couples carrying wicker baskets, pairs of twenty-somethings like us heading out for brunch in the sunshine.

Although it had only just opened, the farmers' market was already crowded. The organic vegetable stall had a queue snaking round it, people examining bunches of asparagus, peppers so shiny they looked like they'd been polished, bundles of dark leaves with rainbow-coloured stems and punnets of glistening strawberries.

'What do we need?' I asked Joe.

'I thought we could get a chicken to roast tomorrow,' he said. 'Maybe make a salad, and something for pudding. Apricot tart, maybe?'

'Sounds great. I guess I'll be on chopping duty, as per usual.'

'So long as you don't almost chop off a finger, like you did last time.'

'It was your fault. You pinched my bum and distracted me.'

'Your bum distracted me first.'

I watched as Joe pored over the table of fresh chickens as intently as he read through a legal contract on his laptop, before selecting one that, as far as I could tell, was no different from its poor, dead brothers and sisters.

'I reckon I'll be working late most nights this week,' he said. 'So I'll probably eat at the office. We could make some soup with the leftovers from this.'

'Sounds good,' I agreed, although I knew that I'd be working late most nights too, and also ducking out from the office at seven to grab a tub of noodles or yet another cheese and pickle sandwich – or, if the pressure was really on and I couldn't leave my desk, ordering a pizza on Uber Eats. And I knew that the leftover chicken would sit forlornly in the fridge until the following weekend, when one of us would guiltily throw it away.

I followed Joe round the fresh produce stalls, growing steadily hungrier and casting longing glances towards the line of food carts on the other side of the market. But there was no point suggesting we eat first and finish our shopping later: my boyfriend was on a mission. He chose seedy wholemeal bread, a bag of dusty baby potatoes that he said were Jersey Royals – and, considering they cost about fifty pence per potato, they should have been – a paper bag of golden apricots, a tub of fresh cream and a load of tomatoes in an array of colours that, as far as I was concerned, tomatoes had no right being.

My presence was pretty much superfluous – he'd given up trying to pass on his obsessive interest in food and cooking to me long ago. But I was content following him around, half-listening to the in-depth discussions he had with the stall-holders, by the end of which he practically knew the name of the goat whose milk had gone into the cheese (Bunty Farquahar-Smythe, possibly, given the price of the cheese) and the location of the tree on which the apricots had grown.

'Right, all done,' he said at last, hefting the bulging nylon shopping bag onto his shoulder. 'Only the best for your birthday Sunday lunch.'

'Speaking of lunch…'

'Right. God, I'm starving. What shall we get?'

As if pulled by magnets, we both turned and followed the crowd – and our noses – to the row of food carts. There was the familiar burger stall, where two bearded guys were flipping patties, toasting buns and frying eggs on a sizzling hot plate. There was the hot-dog woman, turning a tangle of fragrant, floppy onions with a giant pair of tongs. There was the roast-dinner-in-a-Yorkshire-wrap stall, the rich smell of simmering gravy making my mouth water.

But the longest queue of all seemed to be for a new stall.

'Korean street food,' Joe read. 'Shall we give that a go?'

'Isn't that, like, cabbage and stuff?'

'Kimchi. Fermented cabbage. Like sauerkraut, only Asian.'

I wrinkled my nose. 'I'm not sure you're selling this to me.'

'Come on, Alice! It's good to try new things. And if you don't like it, I'll have yours and you can have a burger.'

I edged closer and read the menu, handwritten in chalk on a blackboard fixed to the side of the trailer that formed the stall.

'Peanut and noodle salad. Pork and kimchi stew. Bleurgh.'

'Fried chicken bao, though. How good does that sound? There'll be spicy sauce on it, too. Give it a go.'

'Fried chicken with spicy sauce. Okay, now you're talking.'

In spite of Joe's foodie adventurousness, he couldn't come close to me when it came to hot sauce. If we went out for a curry, I'd offer him a taste of mine and watch, laughing, as he winced and broke out in a sweat, insisting that it was fine, really delicious, but that he'd stick with his mild chicken korma. On the rare occasions I cooked, it was usually chilli con carne, and he'd hover over my shoulder, watching anxiously as I added spices to the pan, trying not to comment or criticise until he snapped and said, 'Are you sure that's not…?' But he'd always struggle through like it was some test of manhood, bravely having seconds and assuring me that it was the best thing he'd ever tasted, then quenching his burning mouth with a huge glass of cold milk.

As we joined the end of the long queue, Joe took out his phone and started scrolling through messages. Even though it was the weekend, he never switched off. If he wasn't running, he was shopping. If he wasn't working, he'd be in the kitchen, preparing some kind of feast. And when he did take some downtime, it would be to sit on the sofa, Xbox controller in hand, competing furiously with a bunch of strangers online in whatever was the latest game that he was determined to master and win at.

While he scrolled and typed, I watched the couple behind the food cart's makeshift counter. The guy was taking orders, accepting cash and returning change, turning to call over his shoulder at the woman behind him. He was nice-looking, I thought – a dark, stocky bloke with a neatly trimmed beard and a gold ring in one ear. The woman had her back to him, swiftly assembling meals with a pair of chopsticks. But when she turned to say something to him, I was brought up short by how pretty she was.

She was small and lithe, with a cascade of auburn curls held back from her face by a coiled phone-wire hair tie. Her arms were bare in her bright red vest top, and there was a tattoo of a mermaid snaking up one bicep. Her skin was as pale as cream, and as smooth. She moved from one side of the tiny trailer to the other – from the gas burner, to the array of condiments, to the guy at the counter – as if it was a stage and she was a dancer.

When she smiled, it was like a spark of electricity.

'What can I get you?' the guy asked, and I realised I'd been so busy gawping at his colleague that I'd barely noticed us reaching the front of the queue.

'Oh, sorry – one fried chicken bao and one kimchi and cheese arancini please,' I said. 'Joe?'

Joe broke off from his laser focus on his phone. 'Sorry, sorry. One spicy beef bao and one portion of fried dumplings please, mate.'

When he spoke, the girl froze, like the music driving her rhythm had stopped.

Then she turned around, very slowly, and looked at us.

'Oh my God,' she said. 'Joe.'

'Oh my God,' Joe said. 'Zoë.'

I felt suddenly cold, like the sun had passed behind a cloud – and suddenly, definitively, no longer hungry.

I tried to ask Joe about Zoë after that. I mean, obviously I did. She wasn't just an acquaintance he'd bumped into, I was sure. That moment when she'd heard his voice, over the sizzle of her pans and the hubbub of the market, and frozen, right there. The way they'd looked at each other, even when, after those first two identical, breathless exclamations, they'd returned to a more normal 'How random is this?'-type conversation, which had been brief because the queue was building up behind us.

There'd been something there. Something important.

We found a wooden table in the shade to perch at and eat. I took a bite of my bao, which was perfection – crisp-coated, tender chicken in a pillowy steamed bun, piled with some sort of pickly stuff that I assumed was kimchi and slathered with sauce that was pretty damn lethal, even by my standards.

And then I felt my throat close up a bit, and I asked, 'So where do you know her from?'

'Who?'

'Come off it, Joe! You know who. That girl at the food cart.'

'Oh, right. Her. Just from uni. We were mates and then we kind of lost touch once we graduated. You know how it is.'

I kind of did… But I was active on social media – I followed loads of my old friends who I didn't speak to any more on Instagram, as well as those I was close to. I belonged to several dozen different WhatsApp groups where nothing would be said for ages, until there was a flurry of activity when a night out was planned or someone split up with her boyfriend or whatever. Joe wasn't. He'd deleted his Facebook and Insta accounts a couple of years back, when everyone was panicking about data security, and not started up new ones. He posted on Twitter and LinkedIn solely in his professional capacity, and he texted or rang his mates only when they were planning to meet up.

So, when Zoë had said, 'I'll find you online,' I reckoned she had her work cut out for her.

'Were you close, though?' I persisted, taking another bite of my lunch and swallowing it with difficulty.

'Sure.' Joe finished his bao and opened the cardboard carton of dumplings. 'Want one?'

I shook my head, but passed him my rice and cheese ball. There was no way I'd make any headway with that.

'What happened, though? I mean, she seems like a really nice person, and—'

'Hey, Alice.' Joe turned to me, his mouth full of dumpling, then swallowed. 'You're not jealous, are you?'

'God, no. I mean, why would I be? It's not like I care about you, or anything.'

He poked my shoulder with a wooden chopstick, leaving a smear of sauce on my skin. 'She's just someone, right? Someone from way back. We're not close any more. We're not going to get close again. Okay?'

'Okay,' I agreed reluctantly. But for the rest of the weekend, I kept remembering Zoë's sparkling smile, and hearing that unfamiliar note in Joe's voice when he said her name.

Chapter Three

I've never been as terrified as I was on my first day at Billings Pitt Furzedown. Actually, scratch that – the day I came for my interview was even more terrifying. And the one after that was pretty bad, too. But it's that first day that sticks in my mind. I turned up at the twenty-storey glass building in the City fifteen minutes early, wearing the same cheap suit I'd worn to both interviews, my legs so wobbly with nerves that I struggled to walk in my high heels. I waited in the downstairs reception area, watching as several other trainees turned up and waited too. Some of them were in cheap suits like mine; others clearly came from different backgrounds and had the clothes to prove it, too.

There was a bloke wearing a tie from Balliol College, Oxford. One girl had a swishy blow-dry like Kate Middleton's, and another was even carrying a Hermès handbag. I wondered if it had been a graduation gift from her parents, or if she'd just randomly purchased it on a shopping trip, the way I'd pick up a pack of tights in Primark (and, knowing me, ladder them the first time I put them on).

But I didn't have long to speculate and I didn't want my new colleagues to notice my sidelong glances at them as I wondered whether they too felt like they were about to puke up their cornflakes onto the marble floor. It seemed like those twenty minutes passed in a flash, and soon we were all collected by a minion from HR and whooshed up to the sixteenth floor in the lift to begin our first day as trainee solicitors. We were given access cards and a brief tour of the building, issued with passwords for the server and intranet and shown where to find the loos and make coffee, although no one was brave enough to ask how the space-age coffee machine actually worked.

And, at last, I was shown to the desk that would be mine for the next six months.

By lunchtime, I felt like my brain was literally about to freeze and fall over, like my ancient iPhone when I overloaded it with music and had to delete Tinder to free up space. I was also starving, and too shy to ask any of the other trainees if they were planning to head to the canteen – although Hermès girl and Balliol boy had probably brought their own lobster and quails' eggs. So I was filled with relief when Heather, my best mate from law school and also my flatmate, texted me and suggested we meet for a sandwich.

It was her first day as a trainee too, at Borehams, an even more prestigious law firm in a forty-storey glass tower nearby. We bought sandwiches at Pret a Manger – cheese and pickle for me, tuna and cucumber for her – and went and sat in a garden square and ate, not saying much, but taking comfort from the fact that we were both feeling as new, small and bewildered as each other.

And, in the months since then, lunch had become a ritual. On as many Tuesdays as we could (often one of us was in a meeting, or in court, or snowed under with work), we'd escape our separate offices and find each other, at about five past one, in the queue at the sandwich shop. I worked my way through the menu over the months, trying the turkey and cranberry with sage stuffing at Christmas, opting for a salad if I was trying to be healthy, and being regularly reminded throughout the winter that I really didn't like carrot and coriander soup.

But Heather stayed loyal to her tuna and cucumber and, when we met on this Tuesday, almost two years after that first time, with both of us on the brink of qualifying, that was exactly what she chose.

'They'll take it off the menu one day,' I said. 'Then what will you do?'

'Oh my God, don't! Dark days.' She carefully picked up a couple of sandwiches by the corners of their packs, comparing their weight to identify the one with the most filling, while I deliberated between a chicken and avocado baguette and a small box of sushi. 'Tuna and cucumber is the one stable point in my life. They can't take that away from me.'

We paid for our food and wandered out into the sunshine, making our way, as we always did when it was warm enough to eat outside, to our favourite wooden bench under the shade of a chestnut tree in the square. Heather walked slightly ahead of me, her glossy dark ponytail swishing over the shoulders of her tailored grey dress. As always, she was striding comfortably in her ballet flats while I teetered uncomfortably, my pointy high-heeled shoes pinching my toes, wishing I'd changed into my trainers before I left the office.

'Have you moved into your new place?' I asked, once we'd sat down and torn open the packaging of our food. The sushi had won, but I was already thinking longingly of the chicken and avo.

'Last weekend.' Heather took a squelchy bite of her sandwich. 'It's okay. Flatmates seem nice so far, although obviously not as nice as you. And it's pretty convenient, just fifteen minutes on the Tube.'

'That's, what, four house moves in two years? You're hardcore.'

'Well, I can't help it if the landlord wanted the place back. And it's good to have changes in life. I don't want to get stuck in a rut. You and Joe are lucky – you found each other, found your flat and now you're all sorted.'

She sighed and scrunched up her napkin. I supposed that, from her point of view, my life must have looked like the embodiment of stability. In all the years we'd been friends, it wasn't just places to live that Heather had been through. There were things in her fridge that had outlasted more than one boyfriend.

'And what about – what's his name – Kieren?'

'Ah, Kieren.' She sighed again. 'It's been six weeks now, and I don't know if I can do it any more. I mean, he's hot enough to fry an egg on and I swear they were looking at his wang when they designed the aubergine emoji. But all the same…'

I laughed. 'He's not The One?'

'I wouldn't mind that, necessarily. I mean, there's nothing wrong with dating Mr Right for Now. But the thing is, he's seriously boring.'

'Boring how?'

'You know I said he's hot? He works out in the gym for like two hours every day. He's ripped as fuck. But he talks about his workouts all. The. Time. I could legit tell you chapter and verse about how much he bench-presses, what his body fat percentage is, how many grams of protein he eats at each meal.'

I picked up a piece of smoked salmon nigiri with my chopsticks and dipped it carefully in soy sauce. 'So the hotness comes at a price?'

'It does. I mean, he lives on whey shakes and hard-boiled eggs. So we can never go out anywhere nice, not even the pub, because he doesn't drink. And the protein thing – let's say he's not exactly regular.'

'You mean you know…?'

'When he shits. I do. And it gets worse than that. I know because he *tells* me.'

'Oh my God! After six weeks?'

'I know, right? Sorry, I know you're eating. But last Friday, he spent the night at mine, and the next morning he went to the bathroom and shut himself in there for about three-quarters of an hour. I was bursting for a wee and I had to wait for him to finish. And then he came out, with a copy of *Men's Health* that he'd been reading in there, and he said, "Morning, babe. Jeez, talk about constipation."'

I burst out laughing. 'I presume you weren't in the mood for a deep-and-meaningful about constipation?'

'I was not. But that didn't stop him. He told me he hadn't had a poo since Tuesday, and he was going to have to add some soluble fibre to his next protein shake, and he was planning an eight-mile run the next day because, he said, that was the best way to "get things moving".'

'Romance is not dead.'

She rolled her eyes. 'And the sex we'd had the night before was off the scale, but I just knew that next time, I wouldn't be able to look at him without thinking about his impacted bowels. Or go to the bathroom until I'd fumigated the place.'

'Ewww. You mean there's going to be a next time?'

'Not yet. Not for want of trying on his part, though. He said, "I always feel horny after a good clear-out," and then he started groping my tits.'

'Noooo!'

'Exactly. So I said I needed to catch up on some work, and he headed off. To the gym, obviously.'

'So what are you going to do?'

'Well, I mean, most of me is totally grossed out. But then I think, it's just a normal bodily function, after all. Does Joe tell you when he does a poo?'

'God, no. I mean, there was a thing when we first moved in together when he… but he's learned to use a loo brush now, so that's all sorted.'

'Do you know how much he deadlifts in the gym?'

'No idea. I don't even know what he does there. I mean, he goes a couple of times a week – to the gym, I mean, not to the toilet – but for all I know he just sits in the sauna watching YouTube videos. That's what I'd do, if I'm honest. But I just let him crack on.'

'You see. You two are compatible. Kieren and I aren't. It's my own fault really, but when I go on Tinder and I look at all these blokes, I just can't help swiping right on the hot ones. It's like a reflex action – I see a six-pack and whoosh, there goes my finger.'

'Joe's hot,' I said defensively.

'Course he is. But he's other things, too. He's bright, and ambitious, and just a nice bloke into the bargain, and the two of you get on together.'

'And he never talks about his bowels.'

We sat in silence for a few seconds while I finished my sushi, thinking how lucky I was to have a handsome, clever, kind, non-poo-discussing boyfriend.

'It's just not going to work, is it?' Decisively, Heather crumpled up her sandwich wrapper. 'Damn, I wish I'd got a brownie as well. I'm going to have to dump him.'

'It's only been six weeks,' I said. 'Don't people just ghost each other now, if it's not working out? I haven't dated for so long I've forgotten the rules.'

'Some do, I suppose, but I reckon it's moral cowardice. I'm going to do the right thing and tell him it's over.'

'What? You're going to do it now?' I asked in awe.

I looked at her admiringly. Her mouth, the red lipstick unsmeared by her tuna sandwich, was set in a determined line. She reached into her bag for her phone. I remembered the last time I'd dumped someone – ages ago, almost a year before Joe and I got together. Even though it had been clear for ages that Mark was as far as possible from being The One – even though he said 'Ex-squeeze me' when he burped and thought *Ice Road Truckers* was the best thing that had ever been on telly and I'd suspected for a while that he'd been seeing other girls – it had taken me weeks of dithering to end it. And even then I'd delivered the message so tentatively he thought at first I was suggesting we move in together.

'No time like the present.'

Heather pressed a few buttons on her phone and held it up to her ear.

'Voicemail. He'll be wanking around with barbells or something. Hi, Kieren, it's Heather. Listen, I've been thinking. I don't reckon you and I are right for each other, so I'm going to call it a day. You're a nice guy and we've had fun, but it's just not going anywhere for me. I hope you have a good life.'

She paused, glanced at her phone, and then continued, 'And I hate to say this, but the poo thing? It's a massive passion-killer. Word of advice: when you're seeing someone else, keep that shit – literally – to yourself.'

Chapter Four

By seven that evening, dusk was beginning to fall over the City. The setting sun glinted off the prism-shaped glass tower opposite, turning it scarlet and gold like a giant candle flame, and the tall buildings were casting their long shadows over the streets below, so that for the commuters making their way home, it would feel far closer to night time than it did up on the twelfth floor.

But, in the Mergers and Acquisitions department of Billings Pitt Furzedown, no one was going anywhere just yet – perhaps not for a long time. In the glass-walled meeting room, I could see a group of my colleagues hunched forward, heads on one side, leaning in to focus on the speakerphone in the centre of the table. At the desk next to mine, Niamh was typing intently, composing an email to a client for a senior associate to check. Across from me, Rupert had his feet up on his desk, his chair tilted so far back that at any moment I hoped gravity might intervene and send his arrogant, elongated body tumbling to the floor and interrupt his chat with a friend about an upcoming stag party in Prague.

And I was paginating a bundle. Of all the tasks we trainees were lumbered with, making sure that each of the six hundred pages that had been meticulously prepared for a court hearing were laboriously numbered, divided, indexed, separated with appropriately coloured pieces of cardboard, punched and filed was the most thankless, for sure. And that was against stiff competition from other aspects of my job that were pretty downright shitty. Having to look at Rupert's smug, chinless face every morning when I walked into the office, for one. Having to look at it *and smile*.

But paginating bundles wasn't just a rite of passage, it was serious stuff, too. It wasn't just one of those joke things you read about trainees in some other businesses being told to do, like go to the builders' merchant and ask for a can of striped paint or a jar of elbow grease or a long weight. In the first meeting I'd ever had with Gordon, my soon-to-be boss, in my second day at the firm, he'd told me so in no uncertain terms.

'Now, Alice,' he said. 'If you want to succeed in this department – in this firm – in your entire legal career, there are two things you need to remember.'

I'd clutched my notebook so tightly my knuckles turned white, my pen poised over the page, waiting for him to impart his wisdom. He was a figure of awe to me still, sitting there behind his vast, polished desk, in his immaculate charcoal suit, with his heavy cufflinks, his carefully brushed grey hair.

'What are those?' I asked.

'One, pagination might seem like a drag. It *is* a drag. But it's vitally important. If, in court, a judge can't find the document he – or she – is looking for, it pisses him off. Or her.'

'Right,' I said.

'And if the judge is pissed off, the partner is pissed off, the client is pissed off, everyone in the firm is pissed off – except the trainee. They get pissed *on*.'

I managed a nervous laugh.

'And not only that. A properly paginated bundle is a thing of beauty. It represents order, professionalism, methodical thinking and correctness. So don't ever let me hear you complain. Okay?'

'I understand,' I said. 'And what's the second thing?'

'The second what?'

'You said there were two things I needed to know, and remember, if I wanted to succeed.'

'Aha! You were paying attention. Good girl. The second thing is, in the mornings I like to have a double espresso, black, no sugar. At eleven, a cappuccino with one sugar. And in the afternoon, builder's tea with milk, no sugar, at two, four and six o'clock.'

This I hastily noted down on my pad. 'Got that.'

'So…'

I glanced at my watch. 'It's three fifty now. Too soon?'

Gordon laughed. 'Definitely not too soon. Thank you, Alice.'

Relieved, I hurried out to the kitchen. As first impressions went, I reckoned I hadn't done too badly and, a year or so later, he'd told me I could have a job there once I finished my training. And now that was about to happen. Soon, I'd be a newly qualified solicitor, a junior in the Intellectual Property team, dealing with everything from protecting the tiniest detail of a massive corporation's branding to whether a theme park had nicked another theme park's rollercoaster design.

And although I knew how incredibly lucky I was, how privileged to have had the opportunity to make this happen – the good school, the supportive parents, not needing to get a job as soon as I turned sixteen – sometimes the thought of my future terrified me. Sometimes, I imagined coming to this building, or another one so similar it might as well be this one, every day for the next forty years, and felt almost sick with dread. Often, I remembered the day Gordon had told me I had a job in his department once I qualified, and I felt ashamed instead of proud. I felt like I hadn't earned this, not really. It was as if it was an unwanted gift I'd been given that was going to cause me a whole load of hassle and grief, like a tank of tropical fish or a cross-stitching kit or one of those jigsaw puzzles that have a thousand pieces and all of them are plain white.

Wearily, I got up from my desk and crossed the office to the printer. The machine hummed and churned, spitting out page after page after page, until a pile of paper as thick as an old-fashioned telephone directory lay on its tray. I hefted it up and carried it back to my desk, hoping that the paper cut I'd sustained earlier wasn't going to start bleeding again all over the crisp white pages, and wishing I'd had time to run out and buy some plasters.

Wishing, even though it was ridiculous, that the paper cut had been like Sleeping Beauty's spindle in the fairy tale and I could just conk out for a hundred years.

'All right, mate,' Rupert was saying. 'So we'll meet at Gatwick at ten on Friday, yah? Time for a couple of swift ones in the VIP lounge before we board? And you've booked Goldfingers for Saturday night, right? Should be an action-packed night, given what I've heard the girls there let you get away with. Don't worry, I won't breathe a word to Helena. What happens in Prague stays in Prague, haha.'

He stood up, his phone still pressed against his ear, and started shrugging on his jacket. A year ahead of me, already qualified, Rupert was above such menial tasks as preparing bundles, and he never let me forget it. I couldn't be sure, but I had my suspicions that he too had hoped for a place on Gordon's team. I'd got it and he hadn't and – even though he was now happily ensconced in Mergers and Acquisitions, where he specialised in orchestrating hostile takeovers – he was still bitter about it.

But I didn't have the time or the energy to worry about posh, swaggering Rupert, with his designer shirts and his Montblanc pen, which had cost more than Joe's and my monthly rent – not that that seemed to stop him misplacing it all the time and making the entire office hunt for it, leading the other trainees and me to refer to it, mockingly, as 'My precioussss' when Rupert was out of earshot.

I turned back to my print-outs, carefully sorting through the pages, inserting dividers and slotting each section into its place in the row of files. The words on the pages represented months and months of work, the painstaking negotiation of a takeover of one giant construction firm by another, and since I'd been in the department I'd worked on almost nothing else.

I'd be pretty pleased to move on. I'd be absolutely ecstatic when this task was done and I could finally go home.

At last, the final page was filed, the index checked for the last time. I tapped out a one-word text to Joe.

Pub?

Thought you'd never ask. I'm done here too. Meet me in the lobby?

Give me ten.

I resisted the urge to check the files one more time, knowing that if I did, ten minutes could easily turn into two hours. I switched off my computer, put on my jacket and stuffed my things into my bag, joining the small crowd of weary workers heading for the lift. When the doors opened, there was Joe, his tie askew, looking every bit as exhausted as I felt.

Although people knew we were a couple, and we weren't the only people who'd got together during their traineeship, I still felt shy about acknowledging him at work, so we just exchanged small, secret smiles and didn't speak until we'd passed through the security turnstiles and out of the glass door into the street.

Free of our colleagues' watching eyes – not that they'd care – Joe pulled me close and kissed me.

'Good day?'

'Okay. I got a paper cut.'

I showed him my finger and he winced, pulled my hand to his face and kissed that, too.

'Better?'

'Much.'

'So where shall we go?'

We looked around. Although it was gone eight o'clock, the warm evening meant that the City pubs were still heaving with after-work drinkers. We had to dodge crowds spilling out onto the pavements, pint glasses in hand, the volume of conversation and laughter suggesting that they were well into a lengthy session.

'Everywhere round here will be rammed. Let's go home and try the Star and Garter.'

'Wasn't it closed last time we went there?'

'Yeah, but that was like a month ago. They probably just had a gas leak or something.'

'Or something. You're probably right.'

Half an hour later, we emerged from our local station and made our way down the street. Here, the bustle of the City had given way to a more leisurely pace. Groups of teenagers were hanging around outside the fried chicken shop. Couples were seated at pavement tables outside the Italian restaurant. Runners and dog-walkers were still out, enjoying the balmy night.

But something was wrong. There was no light spilling from the windows of the Star and Garter. The windows were covered with metal sheets and there was a sign on the door that said 'Site entrance' with a whole load of stuff underneath about protective headgear and footwear needing to be worn at all times.

'Looks like it's shut,' Joe said unnecessarily. 'See – it's all boarded up.'

'It's a building site. It's not just being renovated, it's being completely converted.'

'It must have been closed since the last time we tried coming here, and we just didn't notice. That's so weird.'

'And annoying. I was dying for a burger – I'm starving.'

'Me too. And thirsty.'

'We could just go home and order a takeaway.'

'But I really fancy a pint,' Joe said. 'I've got… Anyway, let's try the Nag's Head.'

'What? That's crazy talk.'

We paused and looked across the road. It might seem like two pubs situated just yards from each other, on opposite corners in a prime location just steps from the station, would be deathly rivals. But it wasn't so.

The Star and Garter, with its family-friendly ethos, good food and total absence of any bar fights ever, was a different beast altogether from its neighbour. We'd only been into the Nag's Head once, shortly after we moved into our flat. And when I say 'been in', what I mean is we opened the door, stepped inside and immediately regretted it.

On that occasion, the pub, with its deeply ingrained smell of stale beer and an even deeper smell of stale urine, had given off a vibe that was anything but welcoming. In a corner, I remembered, there'd been a bloke with tattoos on his face sitting alone with two fearsome-looking bull mastiffs. Four elderly men were hunched over a game of dominoes in another corner. A group of guys in football shirts were bellowing at the action on a large-screen television.

'We can't go in there,' Joe said, shooting into reverse.

'What? Why not? I mean, I know it's not great, but…'

'They're Millwall fans, and Queens Park Rangers thrashed Millwall three–nil last Saturday.'

'So? They won't know you support QPR.'

'They will. They'll look deep into my soul and just know. Or I'll let it slip somehow and get myself glassed in the face. Come on.'

And he'd practically dragged me across the road to the safety of the Star and Garter.

'I know it looked a bit dodgy before,' Joe said now. 'But you never know. It might have cleaned up its act, and there's no footie on tonight. Let's have a look, anyway, and if it's no good we'll go for a pizza. Okay?'

'Okay,' I agreed, and we crossed the road and pushed open the glass door.

The Nag's Head didn't look like it had cleaned up its act. That smell was still there. The ceilings were stained yellow from decades-old smoke, and clearly hadn't been painted since long before the smoking ban over a decade before. The carpet under our feet was worn and grimy. A battered upright piano against one wall bore countless drink rings like Venn diagrams on its faded lid. The only colour in the place was provided by an enormous portrait hanging over the fireplace of Diana, Princess of Wales, gazing mournfully into the distance beneath her tiara. There were no dogs this time, and no football supporters. I was fairly sure, though, that I recognised the four dominoes players – in fact, it was almost like they hadn't moved from their corner table in months.

But, whereas on our previous, fleeting visit, the pub had been only about half full, now it was packed almost to capacity. There was a group of women at a corner table, who I recognised from the Star and Garter, where they always were on Tuesday evenings with a pile of paperback books on the table in front of them, talking earnestly and drinking Prosecco. They had no Prosecco now – bottles of white wine were clearly the closest the Nag's Head could offer to bubbles. Three bearded guys were squeezed together on a faded green chaise longue beneath the portrait of Princess Diana, balancing pints of beer on their knees as they shared a packet of crisps.

There was a crowd three people deep at the bar, and just one person serving, but the mood was cheerful. Clearly, refugees from the Star and Garter were a resilient lot – or possibly just thirsty.

'There's nowhere to sit,' I said, glancing around the busy room.

'Look – over there. That couple look like they're leaving. Go and nab their table and I'll order drinks. What do you fancy?'

'White wine. No, a gin and tonic.'

Joe nodded, and I threaded my way to the corner table, reaching it just as the couple stood up.

'God, the state of the ladies',' the woman was saying. 'Just as well I had tissues in my bag.'

'And that jar of pickled eggs on the bar,' her companion grimaced. 'How long do you reckon they've been there?'

They brushed past me, and I sat down, feeling the legs of the chair creak and splay alarmingly under me. Over the hum of voices, I could hear the click of dominoes from the next-door table, where the four old men were determinedly carrying on their game as if it was a normal night and there'd been no invasion from across the road.

'It's a proper old-style boozer,' Joe said, arriving with our drinks. 'You don't see many places like this any more, now the area's got so gentrified.'

'Perhaps this place will get gentrified too.' I poured tonic water into my glass.

'I reckon it would be a shame,' Joe said. 'You have to admit, it has character. I got us some peanuts and pork scratchings – there's a kitchen, but I didn't think we should risk it.'

'You weren't tempted by the pickled eggs?'

Joe laughed. 'No, but I got all the local gossip. Apparently the Star and Garter is no more. It's been bought by property developers, and they're going to turn it into luxury apartments.'

'What? That's such a shame. I mean, I know there's a housing shortage in London but it's not like the people who need homes can afford hundreds of thousands of pounds for a luxury flat.'

'I know, right? And Shirley – she's the landlady – reckons she might be retiring soon, because she's been in this game for forty years and her varicose veins are killing her.' He slipped into a convincing south-east London accent.

I glanced over and saw the landlady behind the bar; her brassy blonde, bouffant hair catching the light, as bright as her chandelier earrings and the smiles she bestowed on her customers. She was wearing a low-cut, lime-green satin blouse, the sleeves pushed up to her elbows to reveal a jangling charm bracelet.

'Maybe the people that ran the place over the road will take it over then.'

'Maybe,' Joe agreed. 'But anyway. We're not here to talk about pubs. I've got some news.'

I sipped my gin and tonic and took a pork scratching, checking the best before date on the pack first – not that I cared about potential food poisoning once the crunchy, fatty saltiness filled my mouth.

'Go on.'

'You're not the only one who's got a job after we qualify. Laurel let me know today. As of September, I'll be a newly qualified solicitor in the Public Law department.'

'Oh my God!' I jumped to my feet and hugged him. 'Joe, that's incredible! I'm so proud. You must be over the moon. You loved working on all that human rights stuff.'

He ducked his head in an 'aw, shucks' gesture. 'I'm pretty made up about it.'

'Of course you are! And you know what this means? We'll go from earning peanuts – well, I mean relatively – to both bringing in decent wages. We can book a holiday somewhere where we get bladdered on piña coladas and have all-you-can-eat shellfish buffets and there are sun loungers that you don't have to bagsy with your towel at seven in the morning.'

'We can even think about saving for a deposit on a flat of our own.'

'We can pay off our student loans.'

We looked at each other and laughed. We both knew that, unless we won the lottery or Joe turned out to be Boris Johnson's long-lost son or something equally bonkers, the huge, terrifying debt that had got us through six years of university would still be hanging over our heads when we were doddering around on Zimmer frames and our grandkids had student loans of their own. But this glimpse into our future felt like a ray of light, even in the gloomy surrounds of the Nag's Head.

It felt like things were falling properly into place for Joe and me. Maybe, I thought, in a couple of years, once we were properly settled with a mortgage and everything, and one of us had perhaps even been promoted a rung higher up the long, steep ladder of advancement within the firm, we could get married.

I let myself dream, briefly, of the village church near where my mum and dad lived, sunshine streaming through the stained-glass windows on a perfect summer's day as I, wearing a simple column dress of white satin (or maybe an over-the-top lace meringue), walked up the aisle on Dad's arm to Joe, waiting for me at the altar.

'Alice? You're miles away.'

I felt myself blushing. I knew Joe loved me. I knew we were committed to a future together. But still, after less than two years, I didn't want him to know that I was already daydreaming about our wedding.

And I definitely, totally, wasn't going to tell him that I felt a bit less celebratory about my own job at Billings Pitt Furzedown than he did about his.

'Sorry. I was just thinking… We're really lucky, aren't we? Everything's coming together.'

I didn't know, that night in the seedy pub, that just as quickly as things come together, they can fall apart again.

Chapter Five

I was almost late for work the next day. Joe and I had stayed in the Nag's Head for way longer than we'd intended to, had several more drinks and three more packets of pork scratchings. As we drank and talked about our future, the place had seemed to take on a different feeling altogether – because we were celebrating, the dim lighting felt like a glow of contentment; the foggy atmosphere felt warm and cosy.

And when the landlady finally turned up the lights and said, 'Time, ladies and gents, please,' it felt like waking up from a dream.

So I was sleepy and a bit hungover as I hurried to the station – alone, because Joe had a rare morning off for a dentist appointment. My head was banging, my shoes were pinching my toes as I stood on the packed train with no chance of getting a seat, and the chokingly strong aftershave of the man next to me made me want to sneeze. Again, I had that feeling, that sense of something that was almost dread. Was this it? Every day, for years and years, getting the train and going and sitting at a desk for eleven hours? Seeing the same faces – Rupert's arrogant and sneering, Gordon's benevolence hiding his ruthlessness.

But it was my job. One way or another, I'd earned it, and I had no choice but to make a success of it.

I thought of the trite, cheesy saying, 'Today is the first day of the rest of your life.'

On that sunny morning, it felt profoundly true. I just didn't know how true.

I hurried into the lobby of the Billings Pitt Furzedown building at five to nine, my heels clacking on the marble floor, and squeezed into the lift with a group of people I recognised from my stint in Litigation, who'd apparently already been to a super-early meeting. They were talking amongst themselves, sipping their takeaway coffees, tucking their files under their arms as they checked their phones, casually and normally.

But when I stepped through the doors, just as they were closing, silence fell.

Of course, it was a lift. No one talks in lifts – everyone knows that. It's practically written into the constitution. You face the front, keep your eyes fixed on the digital numbers as they inch upwards, and you say nothing. Need to sneeze? Tough, wait for your floor. Someone farts? Nope, didn't happen. The lift code decrees suspended animation throughout.

But today the silence felt different. It felt loaded and awkward and, facing the door as I was, it was as if those four pairs of eyes were trained so hard on my back that they were practically lasering through my navy polyester shift dress. And when I stepped out on the twelfth floor, I could actually hear a rustle of papers, an exhalation of breath, as they started to move again and – breaking the cardinal rule – to speak.

Weird, I thought. Instead of opening the door to the open-plan area that housed the M&A team, I turned away from the lift and through the door to the ladies' loo. The people in the lift had acted so oddly when they saw me – almost embarrassed. I scrutinised my reflection in the mirror. There was nothing untoward to see: no lipstick on my teeth, no suspicious stains on my dress, no pair of knickers stuck halfway down one leg of my tights. I wasn't wearing mismatched shoes, as I'd done one horrible, hungover morning almost two years before.

Remembering that, my face flamed with shame. It had been Joe who'd noticed, that day, that one of my shoes was black and the other navy; Joe who'd dashed out on an emergency mission to M&S to buy me a new pair so I didn't have to do that walk of shame myself. And then we'd been out for a drink together, and the rest had been history.

Most importantly, the night before the morning with the shoes *was* history. Or, at any rate, it was retreating steadily into the past, one day at a time. If I didn't think about it, it was almost like it hadn't happened at all.

The thought of Joe made me feel better, and forget for a moment the strange reaction of the people in the lift. Maybe they'd just had a difficult meeting, and couldn't discuss it with me there. Maybe they'd been in the middle of a disagreement about something, and had had to suspend hostilities so I couldn't overhear.

I checked my face one last time and hurried to my desk.

Again, there was that subtle feeling that something wasn't right. Niamh glanced up from her computer screen, saw me and glanced away again, not saying a cheerful good morning as she usually did.

Rupert watched me silently from the moment I entered the room, his eyes following me all the way from the doorway to my desk, a strange half-smile on his face like he was in on some private joke.

I put my bag down and switched on my computer. Usually, I'd ask if anyone wanted a coffee, and head off to the kitchen to get one for myself. But the thought of standing up again, crossing the office to the kitchen and returning with a tray of mugs was suddenly an even more daunting prospect than getting through the next hour without my caffeine fix. The room that had become familiar over the past five months, the faces of my co-workers, the photocopy machine and the coat stand suddenly seemed alien, even menacing.

You've got the Fear, Alice, I told myself firmly. *You shouldn't drink on a school night.*

I got my water bottle out of my bag and took a sip, then turned to my computer screen, opening first my email and then my billing timesheet. I wasn't going to make any money for the firm sitting here being unnecessarily paranoid.

But then the phone on my desk trilled urgently, making me jump and sending my stomach lurching. Opposite me, I saw Rupert turn his head ever so slightly, his smile becoming wider. *Something's going on, and he knows what it is.*

I could tell from the ringtone that the call was internal, but I still put on my best professional voice – all that time binge-watching every episode of *Suits* hadn't been entirely wasted – when I answered.

'Mergers and Acquisitions, Alice Carlisle speaking.'

'Hi Alice, it's Fatima from HR, Samantha's PA. Any chance you're free to pop down for a quick chat with her?'

My mouth suddenly went chalk-dry. My water bottle was right next to me, but I didn't dare take a sip – I felt like I wouldn't be able to swallow.

'Do you—' I had to stop and clear my throat. 'Do you mean now?'

'Any time this morning would be great,' Fatima said. 'But, yeah, now would be good. If you're free.'

I glanced at my calendar. I was sitting in on an internal meeting at ten. I had a bunch of changes to input on a contract. But none of it was urgent – there was no way I could pretend I was snowed under and this 'chat' would have to wait. Preferably until never.

'Sure. I'll be down in five minutes.'

The handset clattered as I replaced it in its cradle. Opposite me, Rupert's smirk became positively shark-like and I saw rapidly him type a few words. *She's going downstairs*, or maybe, *They've called her in.*

I stood, gathered a notebook and pen and my phone, and walked back out to the lift, trying to keep my legs steady and my breathing regular.

It's just a chat with HR, Alice. It could mean anything, or nothing.

But everything that morning – the weird reaction of the people in the lift, Niamh's silence, Rupert's grin, that call – *now would be good* – told me that something was up. Something bad.

But I was just a lowly trainee. No one cared about me. Even if I was suspected of having done something terrible – like the guy a few years back who'd gone viral on YouTube boasting that his job was all about 'fucking people over for money' – or made some massive fuck-up, like signing off an email to a client with 'Kind regards' but putting a T in place of the G, it wouldn't have warranted HR's involvement. The head of Mergers and Acquisitions would have given me a massive bollocking herself, or got a senior associate to do it for her.

Maybe something's happened to Joe. But Joe wasn't in the office – he was, probably right this second, in the dentist's chair having his teeth scaled and polished.

My finger trembled as I pushed the button on the lift, and when I got in my stomach lurched far more than it should have done on the gentle descent to the fifth floor.

Most of the Billings Pitt Furzedown offices looked – in spite of the firm's status of being not-quite-but-almost within the elite of magic circle law companies – like any other office, anywhere in the world. Grey desks holding computers and piles of files; used coffee mugs scattered about; people's coats hung over the backs of chairs. But the HR floor was different. This was where prospective new staff members came – where they formed their first impression of what the company would be like to work for. And clearly someone, at some point, had decided to make that first impression count.

The reception area was softly lit, decorated in cool blue tones. A massive abstract painting in sunset colours hung on the wall. My heels sank deep into rug with a swirly, wave-like design as I approached the reception desk.

'Hi, Alice!' Fatima smiled like seeing me was the best thing that had happened to her all morning. Like the room itself, I couldn't help thinking that she'd been carefully selected by an interior design consultant. Her hair was a black, glossy curtain. Her scarlet dress matched the artwork. Her teeth were white and perfect.

'Good morning. I'm here – well, you know why I'm here. Because you just called me.'

In sharp contrast to her friendly, professional poise, I felt shy and clumsy.

'Of course. Sam's ready for you. I'll just take you through to the meeting room.'

I followed her along a corridor lined with more paintings and closed, highly varnished doors at intervals on either side. Fatima opened one and stood aside for me to enter, then softly shut the door behind me. The meeting table was the same shiny, golden wood as the doors, and four chairs stood around it, upholstered in slate-blue fabric. A bottle of water and two glasses were arranged on the table, and Samantha was seated in one of the chairs.

'Hello, Alice.' She got to her feet and extended a cool hand for me to shake. She was tall and slender, her blonde hair cut in an edgy pixie crop. The first time I met her, I'd thought that she looked like Kim Cattrall; now I just thought that she looked absolutely terrifying. Although, let's be honest, Kim's not entirely un-scary either.

'Thanks so much for coming down at short notice,' she said. 'I know how busy you are. Take a seat.'

'That's okay,' I mumbled, relieved to sit before my knees gave way underneath me.

Samantha looked at me for a moment, her expression unreadable. Then she poured water into one of the glasses and pushed it across to me.

'I suppose you're wondering why I asked to see you.'

I nodded mutely.

'I know you were expecting to begin your new role in Intellectual Property at the end of the month. Gordon always spoke very highly of you, and I know he was looking forward to your becoming a real asset to the team.'

Were expecting… *spoke* highly… *was* looking forward. Past tense.

'Has something happened?'

'Unfortunately, there's been – well, let's just say there have been a series of allegations. Serious enough to warrant investigation at the most senior level of the business. While that investigation takes place, Gordon is suspended from the firm.'

'But what…?' I began, and then stopped. I knew what someone in my position should be thinking. What horrible miscarriage of justice had taken place? What could Gordon – my mentor, my future boss, the closest thing I had to a guardian angel – possibly have done?

But the words that were racing through my mind were different. *But what about me?*

I picked up the glass of water and tried to drink, but my hand was trembling so much I splashed the polished surface of the table.

'I see this has come as a shock,' Samantha said gently. 'We like to take care of our people here at Billings Pitt Furzedown. Particularly our younger colleagues, who we try to support unstintingly in the early stages of their careers.'

I said, 'Thank you,' even though I wasn't sure I meant it. I was pretty certain that the next word to come out of Samantha's mouth was going to be 'but'.

'But,' she went on, and I thought absurdly that if I was going to be sacked, at least I could make a living as a psychic medium predicting the future, 'Gordon's departure – at least, suspension – has implications for the IP department. As you know, it's one of the smaller areas of our business. While people are at the centre of everything we do, we do also have to be mindful of the need to keep the business running profitably.'

'Of course.'

'And therefore, a decision has been taken to freeze recruitment into the IP team for the present, at least until such time as this matter is resolved.'

'Does that mean I don't…?'

'It means that the role that was offered to you is also unfortunately on hold. I know this will be disappointing for you, Alice, and please let me reassure you that we're doing all we can to resolve this as soon as possible. In the meantime, you're most welcome to complete your training within M&A. If you feel you'd like to apply for a position in another area of the business, we will support you in any way we can.'

But there are no roles in other areas of the business. They're as rare as hen's teeth. The other trainees have got them all. Joe only found out yesterday he had a job. It's insanely competitive. I thought I was okay, because of Gordon. But now I'm not. The words raced through my head, but I didn't say any of them.

'There's no pressure to make a decision,' Samantha went on. 'I'd suggest you take as much time as you need to think about things. Take the rest of today off, if you like. I can see you're upset.'

I nodded. 'Thank you. I'll do that.'

Because at that moment, I could think of nothing worse than returning to my desk, facing Niamh's anxious scrutiny and Rupert's snide smile. All I wanted was to go home, close the door behind me, and feel – if only temporarily – safe.

I stood up, wondering whether I was going to be sick and hoping that if I was, it wouldn't be all over the plush carpets of the Human Resources floor.

'There's just one more thing,' Samantha said. Up until then, she'd been poised and coolly professional, but now she seemed deeply uncomfortable. 'I'm sorry to ask this. But was Gordon – did Gordon – I mean, was there any inappropriate behaviour you experienced or witnessed? To yourself, or to other female colleagues?'

Inappropriate behaviour. That could mean only one thing – and it wasn't fiddling the books. I understood now what everyone knew about Gordon, and a flood of hot colour washed over my face.

'No. There was nothing. Nothing whatsoever. Not at all.'

Chapter Six

It was almost lunchtime before I made it out of Billings Pitt Furzedown HQ. Pathetic as it seems, I just couldn't face walking back into the office to collect my bag and keys – not with Rupert's malicious gaze on me. Especially not now I knew what he'd be thinking.

Of course she shagged Gordon. That's how she got that job offer. Little tart. I suppose some girls believe in getting to the top on their backs.

The shame was awful. That, and the knowledge that I didn't have a job any more – that the whole future Joe and I had planned together had vanished in front of my eyes, just like that.

So I'd gone into the ladies' and hid. Literally. I'd stayed locked in a cubicle for two hours, with only my phone for company. But I didn't call anyone. I didn't text Joe to tell him what had happened. I told myself that he'd be on the train, he'd be getting to the office, he'd be catching up with the work he'd missed that morning – he wouldn't be in the right frame of mind to hear news like this. Not that there even was a right frame of mind.

So I'd just scrolled blindly through the internet with my feet up on the toilet lid so that no one could see my shoes in the gap under the door and know it was me. I couldn't even cry in case anyone heard me.

It had been like a mixture of the worst game of hide and seek ever and the longest poo stand-off.

At last, twelve o'clock had come and I'd known I was safe. Rupert was a man of habit and at noon every day he left the office to go and play squash with Gerard, one of the senior partners, who – entirely by coincidence of course – had been at Eton with Rupert's father. Afterwards he'd eat the sandwiches his girlfriend made for him every morning at his desk. It was Wednesday so they'd be egg mayonnaise. But I wouldn't be there to see him – or to smell the sandwiches.

I'd darted out of the loo and into the office. Niamh had been on the phone, and she'd waved an anxious hand at me – *What's going on?* But I'd just shaken my head, picked up my things and left. Half an hour later I'd emerged onto our local high street.

By some triumph of self-discipline, I'd managed not to cry on the train either. But the knowledge that I was returning home, and that every step I took was one step closer to having to explain the morning's events to Joe, had been too much for me. I'd thought of our bedroom, the clean sheets I'd put on the bed over the weekend. I'd imagined lying down, finally giving way to tears, safe at last in our little home.

But it might not be able to be home for much longer. Without my salary, could we even afford the rent? What had appeared to be a refuge, a safe haven, now seemed horribly precarious, a little island with waves crashing around it and storm clouds hovering.

And that thought set me off, right there outside Brockley train station. The sunny street was suddenly blurred by a haze of tears. When I saw the Nag's Head pub up ahead and remembered Joe and me planning our future there, just the night before, I heard a huge gulping sob come from my throat. I rummaged in my bag for tissues but found none, so I stumbled on, tears streaming down my face, mascara stinging my eyes.

And then I heard something else: a voice right next to me, saying, 'Excuse me, Miss.'

I stopped and looked around. If this was someone asking for directions, they were asking the wrong person. If it was a charity collector trying to get me to sign up to a monthly direct debit to save the rhino, he'd get a piece of my mind. If it was a local drug dealer, I'd tell him where to shove his bag of weed (even if it would take the edge off).

But it was none of those things. It was an elderly black man, dressed in a cream linen suit and a straw Panama hat.

'Miss?' he said again. 'I'm sorry to bother you, but I just wanted to check you're all right.'

Of course I'm not all right, I could have snapped. Except, of course, faced with his solicitous politeness, I couldn't possibly.

'I've had better days.' It was a feeble attempt at lightness, and it made me give another choking sob.

'Here,' the man said, producing an immaculately ironed handkerchief from his coat pocket. 'Use this.'

I looked at it, imagined smearing my tears and make-up all over it, and hesitated. But my eyes and nose were streaming like a leaking tap, and trying to have a conversation with this kindly gentleman in this state was surely worse than getting snot on his clean hanky. So I wiped my face, realising that my surprise had almost stopped my tears.

'Now,' he said. 'Are you all right? Are you hurt?'

I shook my head.

'Are you safe? Do you need me to call the police?'

I shook my head again. 'I'm okay. I've just had a shock.'

'Well, they say sweet tea is best for that,' he said. 'But personally, I'd recommend a small sherry. I was just on my way in there – would you care to join me?'

He gestured towards the Nag's Head. Of course – I recognised him, I realised. He was one of the group of elderly men I'd seen in there on both occasions I'd crossed the threshold, playing their game of dominoes at the same table.

'I…' I hesitated again. Going into a pub with a complete stranger and being bought a drink was maybe not the smartest idea ever. But he'd been so kind. He'd lent me his hanky. He seemed genuinely concerned. And it was a public place in the middle of the day, after all. 'Thank you, that would be lovely.'

I followed him into the gloom of the pub, and he gestured towards the corner table.

'Take a seat. I'll be with you in just a moment. My name's Maurice, by the way. Maurice Higgins.'

'Alice Carlisle.' I held out my hand and he shook it. His nails were immaculately manicured, I noticed – far tidier than my own.

'It's a pleasure meeting you.' He turned towards the bar, and I sat down, wondering what the hell I was doing here, whether I might soon be embroiled in a game of dominoes and, if so, how the hell you even played dominoes. Ordering pizza from them on my phone when pissed I could do. The actual game? Not so much.

But there was no sign of Maurice's three friends in the pub; there weren't more than a dozen people there. Not bad, I supposed, for a Wednesday lunchtime – but then I remembered the Star and Garter, where Joe and I had been one weekday afternoon after arriving back from a break in Paris starving and wanting to keep the holiday vibe going. The place had been as crowded as ever: a table of pregnant women eating salads in one corner; a few shift workers, still in their high-vis jackets, tucking into burgers and pints before heading home to get some rest; a group of men in suits who looked like they might be estate agents wolfing down sandwiches and animatedly discussing the property pages of the *Evening Standard.*

I didn't have time to muse on the success or failure of the Nag's Head, though. Soon Maurice was back with a half-pint of Guinness and a small crystal glass filled with sticky-looking brown liquid, which he placed carefully in front on me.

'There we are. Now you drink up, and if you like you can tell me what's wrong.'

'Thank you ever so much.' I wondered whether I ought to pay him for the drink, but his old-fashioned courtesy stopped me from asking.

I picked up my glass of sherry and took a sip. It was sickly sweet, lethally alcoholic and oddly comforting – like chugging a medicine spoon of cough syrup when you're feeling poorly.

'Trouble with your young man, is it?' Maurice asked.

To my surprise, I laughed. 'No. I'm all good on the young man front. Only the thing is, I think I've just lost my job.'

His face fell. 'Alice, I'm sorry to hear that. Men – they're two a penny, especially for a pretty lady like you. But a good job, one that keeps food on the table and pays the rent, in this day and age – well, we all like to feel secure, don't we?'

I nodded miserably. 'And the trouble is, now I don't. I suppose I could find something else. I'm not unemployable. But…'

I felt my eyes welling up with tears again.

Maurice said, 'Back in my day, a job was for life. I'm a gentleman of leisure now, since I retired three years ago. But I worked for Lewisham council for forty years. Started off as a bus driver, finished as Transport Supervisor for the whole borough. It's not like that any longer.'

I dabbed my eyes again. 'What's so gutting is I feel like I've let everyone down. My boyfriend, my parents – they were so proud that their daughter was going to be a solicitor. You see, my brother…'

But I didn't have a chance to finish my sentence. The blonde landlady had emerged from behind the bar and was wiping the table next to us, very, very slowly, clearly waiting for a break in our conversation that would allow her to join in.

'All right, Shirl?' Maurice asked.

'Ah, you know what it's like, darling.'

She put down her cloth and spray bottle and leaned her hip against the table. She was wearing purple velvet jeans (which were straining over her ample hips, but showed off her long, slim legs), a black T-shirt scattered with metallic purple stars, and battered black Converse. She smelled of strong, musky perfume and cigarette smoke.

'Rushed off your feet?' Maurice asked.

'All the time. Since that place over the way shut, we've just been packed out, night after bloody night. I've had to order in more wine and the fancy bottled beer all them hipsters drink, and someone was even wanting vegan food the other night. Vegan, I ask you! I told her she could have a packet of salt and vinegar crisps but that wouldn't do, apparently, owing to them being made in a factory that uses whey protein.'

'It's good to be busy, though, right? Bringing in the sheaves, as my mother used to say.'

'We'll need to be ordering in more bloody cheese at this rate,' Shirl carried on. 'Juan's running round like a blue-arsed fly in the kitchen, too, with everyone wanting chips with cheese. Chips with cheese! As if we was a flaming kebab shop. "Poutine", some young fellow said it's called. And then when Juan made it – off-menu, of course; he'll do anything to keep the punters happy – it was the wrong kind of cheese, I was told. The cheek of it!'

Maurice and I both made sympathetic noises.

'He'll tell you himself,' Shirley said, then turned towards a door next to the bar and bellowed, 'Juan!'

A moment later, a man emerged from what I presumed was the kitchen. He was shorter than Shirley and slightly stooped, like he'd spent so much time bent over a cooker he'd forgotten how to stand up straight. He had a droopy moustache and sad brown eyes like a spaniel. He was wearing checked trousers, black rubber clogs and a long stripy apron over a white shirt, which was stained at the cuffs with what looked like tomato soup.

But Shirley looked at him like he was Prince Charming, and he leaned over and kissed her on both cheeks as if they hadn't seen each other for weeks.

'What can I do for you, Princesa?' His accent was a mix of Spanish and south-east London. 'Good to see you, Maurice, how are the tricks?'

'I was just saying to Maurice, how since that place over the way got closed down, we haven't had a moment's peace, with people demanding organic this and vegetarian that and off-menu the other. When you started here, they were grateful for egg and chips, weren't they, sweetheart?'

'Egg and chips.' Juan shook his head morosely. 'Burger and chips, fish and chips, lasagne and chips. All these times, I live and breathe bleedin' chips. And now, when I thought I'd mastered English cuisine, they want cheese and chips. Lady the other day complained about my soup. It wasn't authentic, she said.'

'I'll give her authentic!' Shirley interjected. 'Same bloody soup we've been serving here for years, and never a word of complaint.'

'Not since I started in this place,' said Juan. 'Remember, Princesa? Too much of garlic, they said. We're not in flaming Tenerife now, they said. So I changed the whole menu, and for fifteen years the punters love it. And now…'

'Now it's not bloody good enough.'

'And you can't lead an old horse to new tricks.'

'The sooner we can find someone to take this place over and make our move to the Costa del Sol, the better,' Shirley went on. 'My Spanish is coming on a treat, and Juan's been working on his golf swing, and with a bit of luck by Christmas we'll be over there, starting our new life. And not a minute too soon. I'm cream-crackered.'

Juan nodded in agreement, turned as if the whole weight of the world was on his shoulders, and trudged back into the kitchen.

'You should get some help,' Maurice said. 'This place is too much for one person, as you've always said.'

'That's easier said than done. Back in the day, we'd get locals doing shifts behind the bar, no problem. Then we had a couple of Polish lads, and earlier in the summer there was a Romanian girl, Alina. Lovely young lady and such a hard worker, but she's opened her own beauty salon now. "Come in any time, Shirl," she said to me, "and I'll do your eyelashes on the house." So I took her up on that, and look!'

She fluttered an impressive set of lash extensions.

'Very nice,' Maurice said.

'But never mind that – my manners! I've not introduced myself to your lady friend.'

'I'm Alice,' I said, not wanting to explain that far from being Maurice's lady friend, I'd never even spoken to him until fifteen minutes before.

'Lovely to meet—' Shirley began, but then she broke off, some pub landlady instinct making her wheel around and turn towards the door.

When Maurice and I had arrived, the Nag's Head had been empty apart from one extremely fat man perched on a stool at the bar. While I'd been pouring out my troubles to my new friend, I'd noticed Shirley pouring a pint for him, and then another, and then she'd come over to chat to us. The man's glass was empty now, but that wasn't what Shirley was looking at.

Maurice's friends had arrived, strolling in through the doorway as comfortably as if they were entering their own front room. But behind them was a group of seven or eight women, some with buggies, some with babies strapped to their chests in slings, and about five toddlers in tow.

'This will just have to do, won't it?' one of them was saying to her friends. 'Such a shame about the Star and Garter.'

'Yes, well, if Talitha doesn't get her carrot sticks and ajvar soon she'll have a total m-e-l-t-d-o-w-n,' said another, 'so really, it's any port in a storm.'

I wondered what on earth ajvar was, and why it was so vital for Talitha's ongoing mental health. In my limited experience most toddlers would throw tantrums if they were *given* carrot sticks, not if they were denied them.

'I can't believe the Egg and Soldiers is full. It's always been our fallback option.'

'Frankly, it wouldn't have been mine today. After soft play with these two, cake isn't going to cut it. I need gin, stat.'

While I had been eavesdropping, Shirley had whipped behind the bar with the fierce grace of a tiger preparing to hunt down a gazelle, if that was what tigers ate.

'Gents,' she said, turning first to Maurice's friends. 'A pint of best for you, Ray, a brandy and Coke for Terry and an orange juice for you, Sadiq?'

'Thanks, Shirl, you're an angel,' they all muttered in unison, looking anxiously at the group of women and children who'd colonised three tables in a prime spot by the window.

'And another half of Guinness for me, if it's no trouble, Shirley.' Maurice stood and greeted his friends at the bar. 'And for you, Alice? Another sherry?'

'I'm so sorry to interrupt,' one of the women said, 'but my little boy has sensory issues and when his blood sugar level drops he really does need to replenish nutrients fast. So if you could possibly just give me a fresh orange juice and add it to our tab…'

Shirley looked at her, hard. One hand was on her hip, the other expertly angling a glass below the beer tap. I had a feeling that, pleasing the punters or no, she was about to say exactly what she thought about people dishonouring the sacred system of the pub queue, and probably point out that if bottled J20 was good enough for Sadiq, it was good enough for this woman's little snowflake too.

At the same time, I realised that, now Maurice's crew had shown up, the intimacy that had sprung up between us was well and truly over. I had no desire to be a fifth wheel in a game of dominoes, however the hell you played it.

So I stood, too, moving to the opposite side of the bar to Maurice – to the hatch I'd seen Shirley glide effortlessly through, and where she now stood, looking exasperated.

'You look like you could use an extra pair of hands,' I said.

Chapter Seven

It was late afternoon by the time I left the Nag's Head. Emerging into the bright sunshine from the gloom of the pub made me feel all kinds of weird – or that might just have been all the sherry I'd drunk. I'd refused to let Shirley pay me, so instead she'd plied me with drink after drink, saying, 'Here, love, have another to keep your strength up,' and, because I didn't want to offend Maurice, I hadn't had the heart to say that I'd never tasted the stuff in my life before and would be perfectly happy never to do so again.

My feet were aching, my jaw hurt from smiling, and I realised that it had been hours since I'd given stupid Gordon or stupid Billings Pitt Furzedown a thought. But, as the sunlight hit my eyes, the reality of my situation hit me, too. The past few hours had been a welcome distraction – I'd felt useful, even happy. But now all my troubles descended on me again, if anything heavier than before.

I was going to have to go home, call Joe and tell him what had happened. And then I was going to have to make some kind of plan for my future, whether that was looking for another job, applying for roles in other departments at Billings Pitt Furzedown, or just signing on for jobseeker's allowance – whatever it was, I was going to have to do it fast.

Ideally before next month's rent was due.

I said goodbye to Shirl and Maurice and headed, slightly unsteadily, down the main street towards our road. The sunshine was warm on my shoulders, the sky overhead a radiant, clear blue so deep it was almost violet. But my heart was as gloomy as my brain was foggy.

Those words kept turning themselves over and over in my head: *I've let everyone down.*

No matter how many times I tried to tell myself that it wasn't my fault, that I couldn't be held responsible for Gordon's actions, that no one would blame me and I shouldn't blame myself, it made no difference. I remembered reading somewhere ages ago – in a magazine at the hairdresser – that you should never say anything to yourself that you wouldn't say to a friend, but that didn't help me either. The voice in my head was relentless and harsh.

I felt like a failure. I felt as if all the sacrifices and compromises I'd made had been for nothing. I'd fallen at the final hurdle, and I wasn't sure whether I would be able to pick myself up again. I'd lost my grip on the greasy pole I'd started on at university, which had led me to law school and then my training contract and job offer, and would have led me upwards still further, to a promotion and another and maybe eventually to partnership, if I was very lucky and very good. I'd slid uncontrollably downwards, and I wasn't sure I could face starting to climb again.

The thought of a career that could be filled with failures and disappointments as brutal as today's seemed more daunting than it ever had before – certainly more than when I'd arrived at the firm on my first day, full of apprehension, eagerness and ambition.

All the hard work I'd put in since then hadn't mattered in the end. Without Gordon, there wasn't a place for me at Billings. It felt like I hadn't deserved one there anyway. It felt like there was no place for me anywhere.

I unlocked our front door and stepped into the hallway. The sunny, welcoming flat, which normally felt so inviting and safe, now seemed as precarious as a house of cards. I felt tears stinging my eyes again and almost ran to the bedroom, where I kicked off my shoes, flung myself down onto our bed, and cried and cried.

I must have cried until I fell asleep, because the next thing I was aware of was the sound of a key in the lock and the front door opening. I sat up with a jerk, frightened. It was fully dark, and for a few seconds I had no idea what day it was, or even how I'd made it into our bedroom. My teeth were furry and my mouth tasted like our kitchen waste caddy smelled when we left it too long in summer. My eyes were sore and crusted with cried-off make-up. My throat closed with panic and I squeezed my eyes shut, trying to breathe, trying to make sense of what had happened.

Then I heard Joe's voice. 'Alice? Are you home?'

I looked down at the white duvet cover, my creased work dress, my shoes on the floor next to me. It was all right. I was home. Joe was here.

Then I remembered what had happened earlier. The stuff with work. The news about Gordon. Meeting Maurice outside the Nag's Head.

'Joe?' My voice came out all croaky. 'I'm in here.'

I heard his feet on the floorboards outside and the snap of the light switch, and I blinked as brightness flooded the room.

'Are you okay?' He hurried over and sat on the bed next to me. 'You smell… Alice, have you been drinking? Did you go out after work or something?'

'Fuck. I stink of sherry, don't I?'

'Just a bit.'

'Hold on. I'm bursting for a wee.'

I hurried to the bathroom, peeling off my clothes as I did so. I used the loo, washed my face and cleaned my teeth, then went back to the bedroom and pulled on my pyjamas.

'Alice? What's happened?'

'I think we need a cup of tea.'

'Tea?' Joe sounded like I'd suggested we dance the can-can round our living room. Which, to be fair, we had done once, the first night we moved in.

'Tea,' I said firmly. 'Come on.'

He followed me obediently to the kitchen, and while the kettle boiled I poured out the story of what had happened at work that morning.

'So,' I said at last, relieved that at least I'd managed to get it all out without starting to cry again, 'it looks like it's game over for me. No Gordon equals no job for me. Joe, I'm so sorry.'

'Sorry?' He reached across the table and enfolded both my hands in both of his. 'What have you got to be sorry for? You've done nothing wrong. Gordon has, by the sound of things. God, what a creep.'

'I just can't believe it. I can't believe they sacked him.'

'I can,' Joe said grimly. 'Those are serious allegations. They did the only thing they could. Until – unless – it's proven that whoever accused him was making things up, it has to be assumed he did it.'

'Everyone thinks so. And I think they think I was one of the people who made the allegations.' I remembered the weird atmosphere in the lift that morning – had it been only twelve hours before? My colleagues' silence and stares. 'They were looking at me like I had lipstick on my teeth or something.'

'You probably did have lipstick on your teeth.'

'I did not! And Rupert was smirking at me.'

'Rupert smirks at everyone.'

'That's true, I suppose. But the point is, what am I going to do now?'

'Okay, look, not having a job to walk into when you qualify is a setback. But that's all it is. What you do is simple: you finish your training, you apply for other roles at Billings and if nothing opens up then you look elsewhere. There's lots of vacancies for newly qualified people at other firms.'

I said in a small voice, 'But I'm not sure I want to do that.'

I felt Joe's hands squeeze mine ever so slightly tighter, and I knew he hadn't been expecting that.

'You don't? But it's what you've always wanted.'

'I thought it was. I thought I'd put in the effort, I'd earned that job and it was mine if I wanted it. But now I feel like I've stepped onto a stair that wasn't there. Like I'm all off balance, and falling.'

'Course you feel like that. You've had a shock.'

'The thing is, what happened today… It's made me realise I haven't been sure about Billings for a while now. Like, I know it was this great opportunity and everything, but it wasn't feeling like that. It felt almost like a trap. Like it wasn't a job, it was a prison sentence or something.'

'But you never said anything.'

'I couldn't. We needed me to have that job, especially when you weren't sure you were going to get an offer. I told myself, it's just nerves, it's just not liking my rotation in M&A, it's just Rupert being a dick.'

'Well, Rupert…'

'Is a dick. I know.' We met each other's eyes and smiled, and I felt the warmth deep inside me that Joe always made me feel, like a bowl of hot soup on a cold day. If soup was sex on legs, obviously.

'Okay, Alice. Maybe Billings isn't right for you. There are other firms. You don't have to give up.'

'But other firms will also have Ruperts. And Gordons. And Joe, seriously, when I think I might never have to go back there again – it's just the most massive relief.'

Joe looked at me, his face serious. 'If that's the way you're feeling now, I don't think it's going to change. I think about how full-on the next few months are going to be, the hours I'll be working, the pressure, and sometimes it makes me want to puke with fear. And that's in Public Law, which I love – helping people, really making a difference. People burn out in this profession – we've seen it. I don't want that to happen to you. If you're not sure now, maybe it's just not right for you.'

I felt a flood of relief that he understood – even if he didn't know the whole truth. And I found myself saying in a rush, 'I… I was on my way home, and I bumped into one of the men from the Nag's Head. You know, the old geezers who play dominoes?'

'Mmhmm.' Joe raised his eyebrows.

'He bought me a sherry, in the Nag's Head.'

'Blimey. Sherry with a dominoes player? You're living your best life.'

I laughed. 'He was really kind. We chatted for ages.'

'Okay. So that would be why you smell like a Christmas cake.'

'Or like a pub floor after an eightieth birthday party that got out of hand.'

'Well, now you put it that way…'

I freed one hand and punched him lightly on the shoulder.

'But go on,' he said. 'So what happened?'

'Maurice and I were chatting to Shirl, the landlady. She's desperate for someone to help in the pub. I did this afternoon – I just kind of mucked in. And I'm thinking maybe I could do a few shifts there, just while I figure things out. It wouldn't be much more than minimum wage but at least I wouldn't be bringing in no money at all, right?'

'Shifts behind the bar in the Nag's Head? Are you sure?'

'Look, I know. The place isn't all that. But I don't feel like I'm all that either. And it's something I can do, and hopefully not fuck up too badly. I worked in the local pub back at home in uni holidays, remember? I know how to pull a pint of Guinness properly and everything. It would just be something to do, something to keep me busy until I decide what I really want.'

'Okay,' Joe said again. But this time he kind of drew it out, like 'Okaaaay.'

Like cogs were turning in his mind.

'You think it's a terrible idea, don't you?'

'Not necessarily. Alice, I love you and I want you to be happy. Whatever you want to do with your life, you know I'll support you.'

'Even if I wanted to become a burlesque dancer?' I said, trying to lighten the mood a bit.

'Mmm. Sexy. Especially if you wanted to be a burlesque dancer.'

'Lion tamer?'

Joe laughed. 'You can't even tame the drawer you keep your tights in.'

'Lions are a piece of piss compared to tights. Everyone knows that.' Then, serious again, I added, 'But I do want to do this. I'm almost sure I do, at least for now.'

'You know what, Alice? You're amazing. You only found out about this thing with Gordon a few hours ago, and you've already got a plan. Most people would still be crying into their pints.'

'It won't bring in much money, though,' I said. 'It won't be enough. Not to pay the rent and the bills and stuff.'

'No, but I think there could be another way of doing that.'

I felt a leap of hope inside me, tinged with apprehension. What if he suggested giving up our lovely flat and moving somewhere cheaper, or selling his precious vintage watch that had been his grandfather's? It might be worth quite a bit, but not enough to pay our rent for longer than a few weeks.

'What way?' I asked impatiently.

Joe answered slowly, as if he were thinking out loud. 'So today I stopped off at Sainsbury's on my way home. I bought some of those fresh ravioli you like, by the way. We should eat soon – it's late.'

I realised I was hungry, and sleepy in spite of having slept for a good two hours. But I said, 'Go on.'

'And when I was in there I bumped into Zoë.'

'Zoë? Your… friend, from university? The one with the food cart in the market?'

'Yeah. Except she doesn't have the food cart any more. She's split up with her bloke, Sean, who was working there with her that time we saw them. And he's taken it. Because it was him that paid for it in the first place.'

'Right. Why did they split up?'

I wasn't particularly interested in Zoë's love life, but the idea that it was seeing Joe, just a few days before, that might have brought this on made me feel weirdly cold inside.

'He's moving up to Leeds, where he's from. Apparently the street food scene up there is massive and he reckons it's peaked in London. But Zoë didn't want to move.'

Because now she knows Joe's here in London?

'Right,' I said.

'And she's registered with an agency and she's got a few kitchen jobs lined up, but nowhere to stay. She's crashing on a friend's sofa for the moment, she says.'

'I see.' The cold feeling in my stomach had just got colder.

'So… if she were to move into our spare room, she'd basically cover your share of the rent. It would give us some breathing space for a few months, and with that and whatever you bring in working in the pub, we'd stay afloat, no problem.'

Shit. On the one hand, Joe was offering me a lifeline. A way to mitigate my crisis, whether or not it was my fault. But on the other hand, he was reminding me that it would come at a price.

'Joe…? She wasn't just a friend, was she?'

My boyfriend ducked his head. Then he looked at me, his blue eyes steady.

'No. We slept together. We met when I was in my third year, at a festival. It was one of those drunken things, you know. We hooked up that night.'

Don't be a bunny-boiler, Alice. Everyone has one-night stands at uni.

But there was something in Joe's face, like a shadow of long-ago hurt, that told me this hadn't just been a one-night stand.

'And after that?' I asked. I'd stopped crying hours before, but now I felt like I might be about to start again.

'She kind of didn't leave. She stayed at my flat that night and the night after, and then for the next three months. And then she ended it.'

'And you weren't okay with that?'

Joe sighed. 'No. I wasn't okay with it. I thought I was in love with her. I suppose I *was* in love with her.'

Past the lump in my throat, I couldn't help asking, 'Are you still? In love with her, I mean.'

'Of course not! I'm in love with you now, you noodle. And speaking of noodles, let's cook that pasta.'

He'd been *in love* with her. Properly in love. And now he wanted her to move in, here, with us? Zoë, with her toned arms and her cascade of hair that was like some kind of copper waterfall and her smile that I'd seen stop Joe in his tracks.

Over my dead body, I thought.

But I said, 'Can I think about it a bit? And see whether the thing at the pub even works out?'

And Joe wrapped me in one of his amazing hugs that made me feel like nothing bad could ever, ever happen, and kissed the top of my head and said of course, we didn't need to rush into anything.

But that icy sense of dread was still there, in the pit of my stomach.

Chapter Eight

It had only been two weeks, but already central London felt like a foreign country. Instead of dodging nimbly through the crowds as I used to, I found myself stuck behind a group of tourists, jostled and tutted at by a couple of men in suits, and sworn at by a Deliveroo driver on a bicycle.

Instead of feeling like my natural habitat, the City seemed alien – even hostile. It was very weird and I didn't like it one bit. But it was Tuesday and, after missing our lunch the previous week because she'd been in court, I was desperate to see Heather.

Only two weeks, and so much had changed. I'd had a horribly awkward conversation with Samantha, telling her what I'd decided. She'd made it a million times worse (and I'd had to mute my phone so she couldn't hear me blowing my nose) by being kind and understanding, telling me I didn't have to work any notice, and assuring me that this didn't have to mean the end of my legal career. Joe had brought the few possessions I'd left in the office home. I'd FaceTimed Mum and Dad and Drew to tell them what had happened, and my parents' brave attempt to hide their disappointment and shock had been almost unbearable. And now I was going to see what my best friend's reaction to my news would be.

I was a couple of minutes late, thanks to my inept navigation through the crowds, and Heather was already in the queue when I arrived, her tuna sandwich and Diet Coke in her hands. I grabbed a ham and cheese baguette and an orange juice and hesitated for a few seconds while I considered joining her near the counter. But faced with the prospect of being tutted at yet again – and possibly even passively-aggressively reminded that there was a queue here, *you know* – I humbly waited my turn at the back.

Soon, Heather and I emerged into sunshine so bright it was sending reflections like camera flashes bouncing off the glass towers surrounding us, and heating the pavement so we could feel its warmth through the soles of our shoes. We walked to our usual bench in the square, grateful for the shade of the chestnut tree.

'So,' she said, crossing her legs and tearing open her sandwich, 'you appear to have taken leave of your senses.'

I laughed. 'Yeah, I guess I have. Every morning I wake up and I realise I don't have to get up and stand on the train for twenty minutes with my face in someone's armpit and then spend eleven hours behind a desk worrying I'm going to fuck something up, then repeat the process with the train and get home at nine o'clock too knackered to eat dinner or have sex with my boyfriend, and I'm like, "What the hell have I done?"'

'Fair point. But tell me – this pub malarkey. Is it a permanent career move, or what?'

'Oh, God, no. To be quite honest, it's a bit of a dump. But the woman who runs it is lovely and she's not coping, and she's planning to retire in a few months. So I'm just helping out, earning a bit of cash while I make up my mind what to do. By the time Shirley goes the owner will have brought in a new manager and they won't need me any more, and hopefully by then I'll have figured out what to do with myself.'

'So, basically, you've thrown yourself right out of the frying pan and into the fire, and you're not giving yourself the chance to think about whether you've actually made a really stupid decision. Or why.'

'I… Yeah, I suppose you could say that. But I mean, it's not irreversible. I can still qualify, Samantha says. I can look for a job somewhere else, any time I like.'

Heather looked at me. Her gaze was penetrating and intense, and I felt a bit like I was on the witness stand, about to be exposed for telling a massive porky whilst under oath.

'I don't think you will, though,' she said. 'I mean, come on, Alice. We've known each other a long time. I saw how you got less and less enthusiastic about working at Billings. I totally understand that – you know I do. And you seem totally fired up about this new idea.'

'It's kind of fun, actually. The people are all really nice. It feels like being part of a community, you know, like HR said Billings would be. And then I found out it was only a community in the sense that a tank of sharks is.'

Once again, Heather gave me that look. 'I'll have to come and check it out. See you doing your Tracey the barmaid from *EastEnders* thing.'

'I'm amazed you have time to watch *EastEnders*.'

'Oh my God, I wouldn't miss it for anything. I watch it on my phone on the Tube in the mornings. So what does Joe make of this career change of yours?'

'It's not a career change,' I protested. 'More of a career break.'

'Break, schmeak. What does he think?'

'He's…' I hesitated. 'The thing is, we've both been so busy. Before, when I was at Billings, we didn't get that much time together, obviously. But we kind of had the same timetable, if you see what I mean? We got the same train to the office sometimes, and we had a couple of hours together in the evenings. But now I'm usually still asleep when he leaves for work, and by the time I get in from the pub he's already crashed out. So we haven't had that much time to talk about it – or about anything much, really.'

Or about Zoë, more importantly.

'And there's another thing, Heath. Joe suggested – right on the same day I left Billings – that we could maybe get a flatmate to help pay the rent while I'm not earning much.'

'Sounds sensible.' Heather ate the end of her baguette, wiped her fingers on a paper napkin and glanced at her phone.

'Yeah, but it's not just any flatmate. It's only his bloody ex-girlfriend from years ago. Who he was in love with. Who's properly knock-out gorgeous.'

'Wait, what? His ex? That's, uh, different. I presume you explained that you'd rather eat your own shoes, starting with those Jimmy Choo mules you bought in the Outnet sale?'

'Well, no. I didn't. I said I'd think about it. But obviously what I meant was that it was the most terrible idea ever and we should never speak of it again.'

'So that's okay then. Right?'

'Wrong. You see, I got my credit-card bill this morning, from July. I went a bit crazy that month. It wasn't just the Jimmy Choos – I bought a few new things for work, because I thought I'd be in my shiny new job with a shiny new salary. And I took Joe for dinner at Café Murano and – you know. I went a bit cray.'

'Understandably cray.'

'Yeah, but – well, I got the bill this morning and I kind of panicked. It made me realise that my finances have gone from totally fine to totally not fine. And I had to ask Joe to lend me five hundred quid to pay the bloody thing.'

'Ouch. Was he okay with that?'

'Of course. He was lovely about it. But I felt so guilty, and I was so grateful, I ended up telling him that it does make sense for us to have a bit of extra cash coming in, and I was totally okay about the Zoë thing.'

'Oh no, Alice.'

'Oh yes. Of course as soon as I'd said it I was like, "Nooo, I take that back!" But I couldn't.'

'Maybe she'll change her mind.'

'Maybe she'll meet someone else and move in with him.'

'Maybe she'll realise her life's dream is to move to Outer Mongolia and live in a yurt.'

'Maybe she'll—' But before I could finish, Heather's phone beeped and she glanced anxiously at the screen.

'Shit. The meeting I had at two thirty's been brought forward. The client turned up early and they don't want to keep her waiting. I'm going to have to dash.'

She crumpled up her sandwich wrapper, chugged the last of her Diet Coke and gave me a brief hug.

'WhatsApp me, okay? And we'll do lunch next week as usual?'

'I might have to miss next week.' I stood up and followed her out of the square, hurrying to keep up with her long strides. 'Shirl's got an appointment with her podiatrist.'

'Week after, then. Take care. And don't worry about this Zoë. Joe loves you and I've got your back.'

Watching her swish away, ponytail swinging, her back straight and her shoulders square under her pale blue shift dress, I wasn't sure what to feel. I imagined Heather sitting in her meeting, sipping water, making notes and asking intelligent questions. I imagined her afterwards, at her desk, catching up on her emails, drafting a report for a client, updating her billable hours. And then, later in the evening, maybe managing to steal some time away from her desk to pop to the gym and have something to eat before heading home, much later, to her tidy, serene flat.

Until a couple of weeks before, that had been my life. Minus the tidy and solitary bit. Joe and I did our best but, considering how little time we actually spent there, between us we managed to create a tide of clutter that could only just be contained. But still.

I'd had a career. I'd had clear goals, actionable targets, ambitions. And now I had beer mats to replace, crisp crumbs to hoover up off the carpet, paper towel dispensers to fill in the toilets, and a portrait of the Princess of Wales to dust. Sometimes, as I worked, I imagined those inscrutable blue eyes (slightly wonky; the artist had clearly had more enthusiasm than skill) were following me around the room like the Mona Lisa's are supposed to do, and the late princess was thinking, *Who's this one then? She'll never last.*

Lost in thought, I found myself making my way along the street to the Billings office. Somewhere up there, twelve storeys above my head, Joe would be at his desk, or sitting in a meeting room, or standing by the printer paginating a bundle for court. Just weeks before, that had been my life – now it felt like an alien world in a distant galaxy.

The restaurant next door – not one of the super-swanky ones where the senior partners sometimes entertained clients, but an averagely swanky one where we got to go for our end-of-year lunches or celebrated someone's promotion – was full. The tables were crowded with men in suits eating steak and chips and the occasional woman in a tailored dress eating salad.

In the old world, I'd have been looking forward to a celebration lunch there with my fellow trainees in a couple of weeks, to mark the fact that we weren't trainees any more. We'd abandon the no-drinking-at-lunchtime rule and really give it some, knowing that the firm would pick up the bill. Someone would suggest going on to a club afterwards; someone would end up in bed with someone else; everyone would be too hungover to think straight the next day.

But that lunch would be happening without me.

I paused for a second, looking in through the floor-to-ceiling windows, imagining the roar of conversation and the clink of cutlery, waiting to feel regret or a sense of being shut out. But I didn't. I felt only relief – like it was them who were in prison, behind those windows, with their smart clothes and their classes of carbonated filtered water – and me who was free.

And then I noticed Joe. He was at a table in the middle of the room – a small table, one for two. He hadn't mentioned that he had a lunch booked. He never normally went out in the middle of the day – he was too busy. And the woman sitting opposite him wasn't a colleague or a client – she wasn't wearing a formal white blouse or a tailored dress. She was wearing a baggy checked shirt, and I could see her legs in ripped jeans under the table. They were leaning across it, towards each other, talking animatedly. As I watched, the woman said something, and Joe burst out laughing.

It was Zoë.

Chapter Nine

When I'd been at Billings Pitt Furzedown for about six weeks, an email had pinged into my inbox from Gordon. This was nothing new – he emailed me and his other trainee several times a day, inviting us to sit in on meetings, copying us on notes between him and more senior members of the department, forwarding us links to articles from the *Law Gazette* that he thought we'd find interesting (I found most of them utterly incomprehensible).

But this email was different. It came at almost seven thirty in the evening, just when I was thinking that I might at last be able to leave the office.

And the subject line was just one word: *Drink?*

The body of the email was equally brief.

Any chance you're free, Alice? I like to have the chance to catch up with my trainees outside the office. G.

Well, I was free. My only pressing engagements were with a microwave ready meal in the kitchen of the flat I shared with Heather, a hot bath and *Orange Is the New Black* on Netflix. So

I replied agreeing and thanking him, then dashed to the ladies' loo to freshen up my make-up. Gordon might be old enough to be my father, but that didn't mean I didn't want to create a good impression.

But after that, I wasn't sure what to do. What was the etiquette here? Did I go and stick my head round his office door and say I was ready whenever he was? That was unthinkable – I was far too shy and new to dare. So I sat on at my desk, staring blankly at the screen, waiting for him to send me another email saying he was ready, or asking me to meet him somewhere.

When he appeared next to me, briefcase in hand, I jumped like I'd been caught playing Candy Crush on my phone.

'Come on then,' he said. 'That bottle of champers won't drink itself.'

So I hastily shut down my computer, leaving my timesheet for the day incomplete – a cardinal sin, I'd been warned by HR – quickly tucked my things in my handbag and followed him to the lift. The evening exodus was in full flood, and there were about eight other people making their way down, so Gordon didn't speak to me until we emerged into the street.

And then it was only to say, 'This way.'

I followed him. To my surprise, he didn't turn into any of the packed pubs and wine bars we passed; he kept on walking, and at such a furious pace that I struggled to keep up with him in my close-fitting pencil skirt and high heels, and couldn't even attempt to make conversation. We passed the M&S where I'd bought my lunch, passed the entrance to the Tube station, and turned down a narrow alleyway between two tall glass towers.

To my surprise, at the end of the narrow passage was what looked like a private house: a narrow, five-storey red-brick building with black metal railings across its front and a shiny black door with a brass knocker. But it couldn't be someone's home, could it? As we approached, the door was silently opened by a handsome young guy in a tailcoat. Surely only someone like the Queen would have a literal butler – or a footman, or whatever he was – opening the door to her house.

'Good evening, Georgios,' Gordon said.

'Good evening, Mr Poulton. Would you care to leave your bags in the cloakroom?'

Gordon shrugged off the trench coat he was wearing over his suit and handed it over together with his briefcase. I thought longingly of my phone in my handbag, but I didn't know how to say I'd rather keep it with me, so I surrendered it, muttering a thank you.

'Are you dining with us tonight, sir?'

'Possibly, later on, if there's a table free. But we'll have a drink in the bar first.'

'Certainly, sir.'

With a final, longing glance back at my handbag – what if I needed to brush my hair, or my period started or something? – I followed Gordon across the lobby, my heels sinking deep into a gold and blue patterned carpet. A flight of marble stairs led up into the distance, partly carpeted in the same design. Gold-framed paintings hung on the walls, mostly views of London – or London as it would have looked long before I was born, flatter and more spread out, somehow, with loads of different kinds of vessels crowded on the river – and some portraits of self-important-looking men in suits.

But before I could do more than glance around, we'd turned through a doorway into a smaller room, with a bar at one end and a selection of small tables around the outside. I followed Gordon to one of these, and he gestured for me to sit facing the window, then sat down opposite me. The chairs were upholstered in mustard-coloured suede, and the tabletop was highly polished wood with a complex, wavy grain running through it.

I looked down at it for a second, then made myself look up at Gordon and smile.

'What a lovely place.'

'My club,' he said. 'It's a bit of a bolthole, a home from home. I stay here overnight, sometimes, if I've worked late and have an early start. The food's excellent, and so – more importantly – are the drinks. I usually have a gin gimlet.'

I glanced at the leather-bound menu, standing half-open on the table. It looked like it ran to pages and pages.

'I'll try one of those too, please.'

'Good girl.' He gestured over my shoulder towards the bar, and a few seconds later a waiter appeared carrying two slender-stemmed cocktail glasses on a silver tray. He placed them reverentially in front of us on folded white napkins, then added a tiny bowl of pistachio nuts.

'Now...' Gordon raised his glass and I copied him, but he didn't clink it against mine. 'Cheers. And a very warm welcome to Billings.'

'Thank you. I'm so excited to be working here. I just hope I won't let anyone down.'

I tasted my drink, which was delicious and also, I suspected, way stronger than it tasted. It was kind of like the extra-sour lime sweets I'd been obsessed with as a teenager, only with a fierce kick of alcohol that warmed my throat as I sipped.

'You won't let anyone down,' Gordon said. 'I've seen a lot of trainees come and go over the years, and if there's one thing I've learned, it's that the people who begin their careers without that worry are the ones most likely to flounder. You've got ambition without arrogance; charisma without cockiness. It's a winning combination.'

I felt a glow of warmth inside me that wasn't from the gin. No one had ever called me charismatic before.

'Now, tell me about yourself,' he went on. 'Not all the guff that's on your CV – I've seen that. Alice the person. Where are you living right now? What do you get up to in your spare time?'

I watch Netflix and Snapchat my mates, mostly. Sometimes I go on Tinder. And I look at designer handbags on the Outnet and put them on Pinterest, so hopefully by the time I can afford one I'll have decided which to buy. But I wasn't going to tell him all that.

'I share a flat with my friend Heather, who I met during my law conversion course. We're in Wembley, one of the grotty bits, but it's convenient for work and it's cheap.'

'Of course. I remember those days – living on beans on toast and splashing out on a steak and a decent bottle of red on payday. The partners used to get directors' lunches cooked for them, back when I started out, and we all used to hang around the boardroom like hungry squirrels waiting for them to finish so we could descend on the leftovers.'

I laughed and took another gulp of my drink. It was finished and so was Gordon's; I saw him do that almost invisible gesture to the barman again. His talk of food had made me realise I was hungry, but the little dish of pistachio nuts had no corresponding little dish for their shells, and I was fairly sure that discarding them on the polished tabletop would be a big no-no. Briefly, I considered trying to swallow the shells along with the nuts, but ruled that out, too – choking to death in front of your boss wasn't the best look.

'I know it's daunting, when you first start,' he said casually – but it felt like he'd read my mind.

'It kind of is,' I admitted. 'I know I'm meant to be learning, but it feels like there's just so much to learn – not just the work, but how everything in the firm fits together, if you see what I mean.'

He nodded. 'All the moving parts. All the unfamiliar faces, and the hierarchies, and not wanting to put a foot wrong.'

'Yes, exactly.'

'When I joined the firm, open-plan offices were only just starting to be introduced. Most of us had rooms still, either alone or shared. And the first thing my senior partner said to me was, "Young man, we have an open-door policy here."'

'That sounds nice.'

'That's what I thought. Except he didn't mean that his door was always open – he meant ours were to be, all the time. He didn't want us skiving off – napping under our desks, looking at Page Three, that kind of thing.'

I laughed.

'We used to get to wine and dine clients much more, back then. Now, it's all breakfast meetings and filtered tap water, and salads at one's desk. The work's no easier but things have changed on the hospitality side. I used to get tickets to the cricket at Lord's every year from one client, invited to Royal Ascot by another – now, Compliance would have a fit if we tried to get away with that.'

I laughed again, and said that I supposed it was a good thing we worked a bit more transparently now, then instantly worried that it made me sound judgy and uptight. I was feeling distinctly tipsy after my two cocktails, but I was determined to be on my best behaviour, to make a good impression, to be the girl who could hold her own in a social situation as well as at work.

'But speaking of hospitality,' Gordon said, 'you must be famished, you poor thing. Come on, let's grab a bite to eat.'

He stood and so did I, taking a second to steady my swimming head. Another of Gordon's gestures must have summoned another suited staff member, who was hovering by our side.

'A table for two for dinner, Mr Poulton?'

'That would be wonderful, Danilo.'

'This way then, sir, madam.'

I was fairly sure no one had ever called me madam in my life before. It felt excitingly grown-up, but also slightly absurd. I resisted the urge to giggle and walked obediently through another doorway into the next room. It was more brightly lit than the bar, a huge chandelier suspended from the ceiling illuminating tables with cloths draped in snowy folds like icing on a Christmas cake, and twinkling off crystal glasses and silver cutlery.

Danilo pulled out a chair for me, and when I lowered my bottom down to it he pushed it expertly back in again before draping a napkin over my lap. If I hadn't seen it on *Downton Abbey*, I'd have had no clue what he was doing, and maybe pushed his hand away or something.

'We'll have a bottle of the Taittinger for now, I think,' Gordon said, and I thought, *Oh my God, so that's how you pronounce it!* 'And then seek Gustav's advice on the wine once we've decided what to eat.'

A menu had been placed in front of me, I noticed, and I inspected it blearily. I seemed to have got a bit of mascara on one of my contact lenses, and it was threatening to pop out of my eye. I blinked and tried to focus. All I could see was a list of expensive-sounding ingredients, and no prices anywhere at all.

'You're not a vegetarian, are you?' Gordon asked. 'No allergies, or anything like that?'

'Oh, no. Nothing like that. I eat anything.'

A piping-hot bread roll had been placed on my side plate, and there was a dish of butter in between us, which smelled like some sort of herb had been added to it before it had been whipped into a soft peak like buttercream on a cupcake. I wasn't sure if there was a special way you were supposed to eat bread rolls, but it smelled too good for me to wait and see what Gordon did with his. I cut the roll in half and smeared butter on it before taking a massive bite.

'Oh my God. That's so good.'

'Everything here is. Shall I order for us both?'

I was totally focused on containing the river of butter that threatened to run down my chin, so I could only nod. There was icy cold champagne in my glass, which when I took a gulp I discovered was as toasty and buttery as the bread.

'We'll both start with the scallops,' Gordon told a waiter, who had materialised as if by magic. 'And then the grouse for me and the lamb for the lady.'

I drank more champagne and sipped some water, but only a little – not enough to be sensible, but too much to stop me needing to wee. I was going to have to get up, find the toilet, maybe retrieve my bag and check my face and hair. Did I do it now, or wait until after our starter? Was it rude to go to the bathroom between courses in a place like this? I had no idea, but go I must.

'Excuse me a second,' I said, standing up.

The lights had been dimmed a bit without me noticing, but they still glinted off every surface. The deep carpet under my feet made me feel as if I was wading through water. I made my way back to the door, carefully navigating between tables, but still bumping into the door frame as I passed through.

'I'm sorry, where's the…' I asked yet another suited young man.

'Just through there, madam.'

He leaned forward in a little half-bow and I wondered whether I was meant to do a curtsey in return, but stopped myself just in time.

I found myself in a brilliantly lit, marble room with a vase of fresh flowers on a little table, a squashy pink brocade armchair, vials of expensive liquid soap and hand cream, and a pile of rolled-up fluffy towels. I stared at my reflection in the mirror – my cheeks were flushed and my eyes slightly bloodshot, but my make-up was still mostly in place. I gripped the edge of the washbasin and my reflection swam in and out of focus.

'Alice,' I told myself. 'Please, don't be fucking stupid.'

But I suspect that, at that point in the evening, it was already too late.

Chapter Ten

I didn't have much of a chance to think about seeing Joe and Zoë in the restaurant that lunchtime, because afternoon trade at the Nag's Head was brisk to the point of insanity. I served and cleared and wiped and served again all afternoon, and it was a massive relief when Shirley turned up after spending the afternoon having tea with her elderly aunt and I was able to head home.

I was expecting the flat to be in darkness – it was a weeknight, after all, and Joe was rarely home before eight. But I was wrong. The lights were on, and I could hear music pumping from the flat from a couple of doors away– not unsociably noisy, but loud enough to be heard from the street. It was some kind of nineties grunge – Pearl Jam or Soundgarden or something – one of the bands that Joe liked and I didn't.

Still, if he'd got in early and decided to relax with some tunes, who was I to grumble? He was home, and we could enjoy a rare evening together.

I fitted my key in the lock and opened the door, calling a greeting. But the music was too loud for me to be heard, and I didn't repeat myself. I just stood there in the hallway, looking through to the kitchen. Joe was there, dancing. There was a wooden spoon in his hand and he was holding it like a mic, singing along to the music. And there with him, her wild curls flying, was Zoë. She was wearing a frayed denim mini skirt and a strappy violet top, and I could see the muscles in her arms and shoulders. Her legs were toned and slim, her feet bare. She moved with the same easy grace I'd noticed when she was assembling meals in her food cart: like the whole room – our whole flat – had been especially designed around her.

The track ended, and the two of them whooped and laughed.

I stepped forward, putting down my bag, and said, 'Hello.'

'Alice!' Joe said. 'I didn't hear you come in. Zoë's here.'

I resisted the temptation to say waspishly that I'd noticed.

'Hi, Zoë.'

'Hey, Alice! I'm sorry about the short notice. The friend I've been sofa-surfing with had her new flatmate move in, and he needed the room I was using. So here I am. Thanks so much for letting me stay. We're cooking chilli. It's vegan – I hope that's okay.'

Along with the music, I'd noticed the smell as soon as I opened the door: a rich, spicy aroma. I hadn't eaten since my lunchtime sandwich, but I suddenly didn't feel hungry any more.

I glanced around the flat. The door to what had been our spare bedroom stood open. The desk where Joe and I sometimes worked in the evenings had an unfamiliar laptop on it, surrounded by a tangle of wires and chargers. The bed had been made – badly, presumably by Joe, who, while perfectly house-trained in most ways, was incapable of putting a duvet into a duvet cover without the result looking like a pack of sausages – and was piled with clothes. A half-empty backpack blocked the doorway.

On the kitchen worktop, I could see a set of silver steel knives that definitely weren't ours, several cast-iron pans and a food processor – also not ours. There was a vat of brick-red sauce simmering on the hob, filling the room with its steam.

And on the dining table, on top of a pile of clean washing, was a large, fluffy ginger cat that was definitely, categorically not ours.

When it saw me, it opened its amber eyes, yawned hugely, then twisted around and started to wash its arse.

'This is Frazzle,' Zoë said. 'He's a rescue cat, and an ace mouser. You're not allergic, are you?'

I wasn't – not to cats, anyway. But I couldn't shake the suspicion that Zoë herself might make me come out in an unsightly rash and start wheezing.

Still, she was here now – her and her furry feline friend. I'd agreed to her staying and I had no option but to make the best of it. And, after all, the poor girl had recently split up with her boyfriend. She was probably nursing a broken heart. Although, dancing in my kitchen with my boyfriend with her perfect hair and perfect body, she hadn't looked broken-hearted in the slightest.

I stepped into the kitchen and gave Joe a brief kiss. I wasn't sure whether I should shake Zoë's hand, or kiss her too, or what – but she made the decision for me, folding me into a hug.

'Thank you so much for letting me move in, Alice,' she said. 'You're incredibly kind. Frazzle and I will try not to be any trouble.'

'You're welcome.' I moved out of the embrace of her surprisingly strong arms and tried to smile.

'I hope we won't get in the way,' Zoë burbled on, seemingly oblivious to my discomfort. 'I've got a job in a café in Covent

Garden for the next two weeks, so I'll be out all day. And I can make myself useful here. I'm not great at cleaning but I can cook and stuff. And Frazz just sleeps all day. Once he's settled in we can leave a window open for him and he'll come and go as he pleases.'

I didn't say that, although our area was a lot less rough than it used to be, leaving a window open while the flat was empty was just asking for some opportunistic thief to break in and nick everything of value, starting with Zoë's fancy chef's knives, which would probably turn up a couple of weeks later at a murder scene. And I also didn't say that if anyone seemed in the way right then, it was me.

Instead, I asked about Zoë's job, and she chattered away about the ultra-hip vegan place where she was working, and how more and more people were coming around to the idea of a plant-based diet.

'Of course, I eat meat sometimes, when I have to for work,' she said. 'But veganism isn't seen as this rigid thing any more, you know. It's more about treading lightly on the planet.'

Joe screwed the top off a bottle of wine and poured us all a glass.

'Welcome, I guess. Officially.' I touched my glass to Zoë's.

'I shouldn't really,' she said. 'It's Chilean, and the food miles... But hey, we're celebrating, aren't we?'

'Of course we are,' Joe replied. 'How long until this is ready, do you reckon? And shall I cook some rice? Make a salad? Set the table?'

'We'll need to get Frazz to move,' Zoë said. 'Poor boy, you're so comfy there, aren't you? Are you settling into your new home? I put his litter tray in the bathroom, by the way. I hope that's okay.'

She scooped the cat up, and he draped over her arm like a large, stripy fur coat and began to purr. I put my glass down and picked up the pile of washing, now liberally coated with orange fluff. Oh well – Joe's jeans were on the top of the pile and had borne the brunt of it. Frazzle was Zoë's cat and Zoë was Joe's ex and so, really, he deserved it.

Putting our clothes hastily away in the bedroom, I tried to stifle the feeling of resentment that had crept – or rather rushed – up on me. It wasn't like Zoë had just turned up out of nowhere. Joe and I had discussed her coming to stay. It was the only way we could make up the shortfall caused by me not bringing in a proper wage any more and spaffing money I didn't have on shoes I'd probably never wear. And she'd cooked dinner for us, and that was nice, wasn't it?

But still. She'd been dancing round the kitchen with my boyfriend. In her bloody mini skirt with her auburn hair and her toned shoulders. And Joe, in those few moments before the song ended and he noticed me, had looked so different – so carefree and uninhibited and happy.

And I was going to trip over a cat's toilet whenever I went for a wee myself.

I glanced at my reflection in the mirror over the dressing table. I didn't have time to do anything about my limp hair or lack of make-up or the spot that had erupted out of nowhere on my chin. But I could, at least, do something about the fact that my face looked like the bit of Frazzle's anatomy that he'd just been washing so thoroughly. Having a cat's bum on my clean washing was one thing; having a mouth that looked like one really wasn't on.

'Smile, Alice,' I commanded silently, and my reflection reluctantly obeyed.

'Now go out there and be nice.' In the mirror, my head nodded slowly.

I turned and left the bedroom, closing the door behind me even though we usually left it open. Usually, there was no need to worry about our privacy, but now it felt like there was.

Joe and Zoë were in the kitchen. The table had been set with three places, and Frazzle had settled himself down in the centre of them, looking disapprovingly at the open bottle of wine – a fresh one, I noticed; Joe and Zoë must have torn through the first. I felt a brief flash of empathy for the cat – like me, he'd had his life turned upside down and, like me, he was going to have to make the best of it.

'Smells Like Teen Spirit' was playing on the speaker (that one, even I recognised), but more quietly now. And Zoë and Joe weren't dancing – or not as such. In our tiny kitchen, Zoë was tipping the chilli out of its pan into a serving bowl while Joe placed a sieve full of rice over hot water to steam. Yet the two of them seemed to move around each other easily, naturally, as if there was enough room in there for a whole brigade of chefs.

'So Amanda and Carl got married,' Zoë was saying. 'He proposed to her in New York, in Central Park. There's this thing you can do where you get a company to organise a picnic with fresh oysters and champagne and a violinist serenading you, and you get taken there in a carriage pulled by one of those poor horses. They did that. It cost a fortune. And, like, six months later – over.'

'Carl was always a strange one,' Joe replied. 'Hey, Alice, would you mind popping the salad on the table?'

'Tell Frazzle to get off,' Zoë said. 'He might listen to you – he never does to me.'

'And Ben Denver's in San Francisco,' Joe carried on, as I took the salad bowl to the table and gently nudged Frazzle, who looked at me like I'd just committed a war crime before jumping to the floor with an affronted meow. 'He went out there with some bonkers start-up idea, but as far as I know he's working in a juice bar now.'

Great, I thought. First of many evenings I'm going to have to spend listening to my boyfriend and his ex rehashing their shared history I wasn't part of, their shared friends I've never heard of.

'Loads of people are rejecting conventional employment models now, though.' Zoë whisked past me with the bowl of chilli. 'No one wants a job for life any more. Why would you?'

'Like Alice,' Joe said. They both looked at me, their heads tilted to one side. 'Come on,' their faces said. 'We don't want you to feel left out.'

So, while Zoë spooned chilli into bowls and Joe passed around a bowl of grated cheese (not vegan, but that was apparently okay because it had been in our fridge anyway, and beginning to dry out, and evidently it was more problematic for cows to be exploited if the product of their labour went to waste than if it didn't), I explained about the Nag's Head.

'That's so totally amazing,' Zoë said. 'It sounds so, like, authentic. Do they serve food? I bet they do. I'm thinking cockles and whelks and pie and liquor and stuff.'

I managed to laugh. 'It's not that authentic. Think more oven chips and microwave lasagne.'

'And pickled eggs and pork scratchings,' Joe remembered, and we shared a smile, remembering the evening we'd spent there together.

It wasn't even that long ago, I thought, with a jolt of sadness. So why did it feel like another world?

But Zoë was oblivious to my sudden surge of emotion. 'What's it called?'

'The Nag's Head.'

Zoë shook her head. 'It shouldn't be called that any more. Nag is a pejorative term for a horse that's considered to be of low breeding. It's like being racist, or classist, only about an animal. Totally not okay. Never mind the misogynist connotations of nag when used as a verb.'

'Alice nags me about how crap I am at making beds,' Joe said.

'No she doesn't,' Zoë almost snapped back. 'She points out your strategic incompetence. You can't make a bed properly, what happens? Alice does it for you. Classic man move.'

Zoë met my eyes across the table. I might have smiled, but my mouth was full of blazing hot, unexpectedly delicious chilli. So I had to wait until I'd swallowed, and the moment had passed.

'What would you call it then? Not that I'll have a say in the matter. I'm just a part-time barmaid.'

There was a meow from under the table, and Frazzle leaped up, via Zoë's lap, almost knocking over her wine glass.

'How about the Ginger Cat?' she suggested, pinching up some cheese and feeding it to him.

Chapter Eleven

Over the next few weeks, I found myself spending more and more time at the Nag's Head. I arrived at the pub at around nine most mornings, and cleaned and tidied anything that hadn't been done the previous night. I opened the doors at eleven and welcomed the first regular customers of the day. Maurice was usually the first to arrive. I'd carefully laundered the handkerchief he'd left me and returned it with a little thank-you card, and we'd fallen into the habit of having a five-minute chat, touching on the weather, the cricket score and the ongoing, seemingly endless Brexit negotiations before his friends turned up and settled themselves in their usual corner table, sipped their half-pints of Guinness and bitter (or, in Sadiq's case, orange juice) and started their game of dominoes, which would continue into the early afternoon.

Watching them, I found myself picking up some of the rules of the game. I overheard Ray talking about sharp practices involving rubbing some of the little plastic tablets so they could be identified by touch. I learned that they weren't called tablets, but 'bones'. And crucially, after almost calling 999 because Terry appeared to be having some sort of seizure, I learned that he was just doing the funky chicken dance to celebrate having played all the bones in his hand.

I served behind the bar, I washed glasses, I restocked the packets of crisps, peanuts and pork scratchings that no one ever seemed to actually buy apart from Don, the fat man who appeared to spend all day, every day at the Nag's Head and worked his way steadily through pack after pack during his long hours perched at the bar. Shirl even showed me how to clean the beer lines to stop sinister-sounding things called 'beer stones' crudding up the pipes and spoiling the punters' pints.

The rhythm of the pub and the street outside was becoming familiar. I found myself anticipating the sound of the police horses' hooves as they clattered down the road on their morning exercise. I recognised the voices of the group of mums who passed by outside after doing the school run on the way to their yoga class. When I arrived in the morning, the florist next door would be setting out her display outside, and I grew used to the scent of flowers as I unlocked the cloudy glass door to the Nag's Head.

But it wasn't just that the pub seemed to have a particular power to lure me in – or that the meagre wage Shirley was paying me was a particularly powerful motivator. Home – the home that had been Joe's and mine – was feeling increasingly alien, even hostile, with Zoë there.

She was always perfectly friendly to me. She didn't put salt in my coffee or stick my cashmere jumper on a boil wash or replace my conditioner with hair-removal cream or anything like that. Not that I was tempted to do those things to her either – honest.

But she was *there*. And, more specifically, she was where Joe was. One Sunday, when he settled on the sofa for a nice long session playing *Resident Evil*, she joined him and turned out to be ace at it, and I couldn't even muscle in and be a third wheel because I'd told Joe many, many times that computer games bored me witless. She offered, ever so helpfully, to cook dinner some evenings, and made all Joe's favourite things – mac and cheese, jacket potatoes with beans, carrot cake – and although they were all vegan versions, he tucked in and had second helpings of everything. She wandered into the bathroom when he was in the bath, and although I heard her say, 'Oh my God, I'm so sorry, I didn't realise you were in there,' it took a good ten seconds for her to re-emerge. Long enough for her to have had a good old stare at my boyfriend's naked body.

And, one Saturday morning in early October, I woke up later than usual and rolled over in bed, reaching out for Joe. But there was no warm body next to me under the duvet – not even the warm indentation his body would have left if he'd just got up. The other side of the bed was empty and, I realised, the flat was silent. I sat up, pushing my tangled hair off my face and rubbing a lump of sleep out of my eye. It was raining; the sky outside was leaden and the light coming through the window was grey and gloomy.

That must have been why I'd overslept. I didn't need to be at the Nag's Head until eleven; Joe and I could have enjoyed a long lie-in together, a leisurely brunch, maybe even a sneaky shag, if Zoë had taken herself off somewhere.

Which she clearly had; angling my head, I could just see more dim light filtering through her open door. She was out, and so was Joe. Out together? Surely not.

Fully awake now, I picked up my phone, but I had no new messages from either of them, just a note from Heather saying she had the most brutal hangover in human history and were we still up for lunch on Tuesday.

Then I heard an unfamiliar, clicking sound on the floor, like the world's tiniest pair of stiletto shoes cautiously entering the room. Not a pair though – four. I looked down and saw Frazzle next to the bed, looking up at me with an expression that was half-wary, half-hopeful.

'What is it, cat? I bet you've had your breakfast.'

Frazzle meowed, then opened his jaws in an enormous yawn. I couldn't help it – I found myself yawning back at him. He looked at me steadily for a second, then jumped up onto the bed.

'Hello there. Have you decided you want to be friends?'

He butted his fluffy ginger head against my hand, angling it just so, so that my fingers reached the space behind his ears. The fur there was bright orange and softer than the softest thing. I started to scratch and, seconds later, was rewarded with thunderous purring.

'Awww. You're a good cat, aren't you? You just wanted a cuddle.'

I talked nonsense to him for a bit, and he graciously accepted my fuss, but soon he made it clear that he'd come here for more than ear scritches. He walked over me to Joe's side of the bed and pushed at the duvet with a fluffy paw.

'What? You want to get in?'

Clearly, the answer to that was yes. Frazzle's head joined his paw, burrowing determinedly under the duvet. I lifted it up, curious to see what he'd do, and within seconds, like a ginger guided missile, he was under the covers, thumped onto his side, kneading away at my bare stomach with his paws, purring like a maniac.

I turned over, pulling the covers up over us both, and lay still. I had the feeling that I'd been awarded some kind of rare privilege, and I wasn't going to blow it. By some form of cat willpower, Frazzle was making it quite clear what he expected of me: I was to be warm and still for as long as he required it.

The sound of his purring was soothing, and the pressure of his claws against my skin oddly comforting, and I found myself drifting back into sleep, and into a strange half-dream in which it wasn't Zoë's cat in bed with me, but someone else – a different body that certainly shouldn't have been there. In my dream, I tried to move away – and I must have done so in real life too, because Frazzle squirmed away from me, snaked his head out from underneath the duvet and wriggled out, walking back over me and jumping to the floor with an affronted meow, just as I heard the front door opening and voices in the hallway.

'Oh my God, I'm absolutely soaked through! That was mental.'

'We'd better take our shoes off here – they're covered in mud.'

'We're basically wearing half your local park.'

Joe. Joe and Zoë. Laughing together like they were having the best fun two people can have.

Wide awake now, feeling a hollow coldness in my stomach, I pulled on my dressing gown and left the bedroom.

Zoë and Joe were in the kitchen, dressed in running kit, both covered in mud from their ankles up to their thighs. Joe even had a smear of it on his cheekbone.

They must not have heard me approaching in my bare feet, because they carried on talking as if I wasn't there.

'You're bloody quick, though,' Joe said. 'Your first Parkrun and you totally killed it. What do you reckon your time was?'

'Twenty-two thirty, maybe?' Zoë said. 'I'm not normally a runner but I guess the stuff I do in the gym helps.'

She turned round, and the smile faded from her face when she saw me. But still, even with her hair scraped back from her face, not a trace of make-up and a grass stain on her white top, which had gone see-through from the rain so I could see the turquoise sports bra she had on underneath, she looked bloody gorgeous.

'Morning, Alice. Did you enjoy your lie-in?'

'I did try to wake you,' Joe said. 'But you weren't having any of it. I know you hate running in the rain anyway, so I left you to sleep.'

'Hello, Frazz,' Zoë said, bending over to fuss her cat. 'Where have you been?'

Standing there, looking at the two of them, contrasting Zoë's lithe vitality with my own frumpy sleepiness, the sound of her and my boyfriend's laughter echoing in my ears, imagining the admiring glances all the men would have given her as she raced past them, I didn't think I'd ever felt more inadequate.

I had only one weapon, and it was a pretty feeble one. But I used it anyway.

'Frazzle came into bed with me,' I said. 'He slept under the duvet for, like, ages.'

Zoë's face registered surprise, then outrage, and I felt a small twinge of triumph.

'Well,' she said. 'I'd better get out of these wet things and into the shower.'

'And I'd better get myself off to the pub,' I said, wondering with a sick-making blend of fear and resentment what the two of them might get up to together while I was at work.

But when I opened the door of the Nag's Head, all thoughts of Zoë vanished from my mind. The pub was never the most fragrant of places – decades of stale beer and an even older ghost of cigarette smoke permeated the atmosphere. But this time, there was a stronger, more pronounced smell – so strong it made my eyes water. I switched on the lights and stood there for a moment, breathing shallowly.

'What the hell…?' I said aloud, my voice sounding small in the silence.

But there was no mystery – not really. There was no mistaking that smell. It was like the Portaloos at the end of a festival, or a nightclub toilet at three in the morning. I followed it easily to its source: the men's toilet.

When I opened the door, I was smacked in the face by a wave of it. The floor was soaking wet, and I could see a creeping tide of liquid flowing slowly over the edge of the metal urinal at the end of the room.

I slammed the door shut and hurried outside, taking deep gulps of fresh air.

I'd come, over the past weeks, to feel like I was beginning to understand the pub: the way that it worked and the things that didn't; the routine of its days; the people who came and why those that didn't stayed away. I'd begun to become quite fond of it, as if it had a personality, like a cantankerous old car that ran more or less okay so long as you checked its tyre pressure once a week and topped up the oil and water, even if you'd just done so the day before.

But now, it had revealed a side of itself that I hadn't known was there: a rebellious streak that I was going to have to tame – and on my own, too, because Shirley was out at a funeral all morning, and had said that if the wake was anything like the last one she'd been to, she'd be in no fit state to work for the rest of the day either.

Only there was no way I was opening the door to that men's toilet again without some serious backup.

I took my phone out of my bag and googled emergency plumbers.

Ten minutes later, I was still standing outside the door. But now, I was staring at my phone with growing bewilderment and frustration. I'd called no fewer than six different plumbing firms, trotting out a speech that had become second nature after the third call.

'Hi, I'm calling from the Nag's Head pub on the high street in Brockley. We seem to have a blocked urinal.'

The responses had all been slightly different, but they might as well have been the same.

'We're booked solid right now, love. We might be able to make it out to take a look in a few days.'

'That's a big job, darling. We can come out this afternoon but you won't get much change out of a thousand pounds for the work.'

'My guv'nor's out on another job. I'll ask him to ring you back, but don't hold your breath.'

As if, considering the stench I could imagine spreading out from the gents through the rest of the pub, I had any option other than to hold my breath.

Finally, on the last call, I got an answer that might not have been what I wanted to hear but was at least honest.

'I'm not coming out for that, love. Not for all the tea in China.'

'But it's your job!' I said desperately, but it was too late. The line had already gone dead.

I had no idea what to do. The dominoes players would arrive in just a couple of hours, followed shortly by the other regulars. Most of them were men – men of a certain age. Which meant they went to the loo often. If I didn't sort something out, the whole place would be awash.

I was staring at my phone in frustration, as if a solution might appear by magic on the screen, when a van pulled up outside the empty unit next door to the Nag's Head. The driver reversed expertly into a parking space, just inches from the kerb, and seconds later he appeared around the back of the van.

Rattling a set of keys, he hurried over, rolled up the shutters that covered the unit next door's bare windows, then turned and began to walk the few steps back to his van. Then he saw me and turned around again.

'Hello! Are you working at the pub?'

'That's right. My name's Alice.'

'Archie.' He held out a hand and I shook it. 'I guess we're neighbours, then. I've taken over the shop next door. Craft Fever, it's going to be called. We're selling artisan beer and locally made wine, and gin I distil myself. Oh, and honey. My sister has beehives on the roof of her house.'

He was a guy about my age, wearing camouflage shorts and a white T-shirt worn almost transparent with age and washing. His hair was somewhere between blond and brown, and his teeth were very white against his tanned skin when he smiled. He must have been on holiday recently, somewhere hot.

'We should have a coffee sometime,' he said. 'Catch up on the local gossip.'

'That sounds great,' I agreed. 'Only not right now. I'm a bit snowed under. Or rather, pissed under. I've got a plumbing problem and no bugger will come out and look at it.'

'Let me guess. It's a blocked urinal, right?'

'Yes! How did you know?'

'My uncle's a plumber. He used to tell me and my brother stories – you know when you're, like, twelve and you love hearing about gross stuff?'

I didn't; when I was twelve I'd been into ballet and *Cosmo Girl* magazine. But his smile was so warm and infectious that I felt myself smiling too.

'Go on,' I said.

'Yeah, so we used to get Uncle Ray to tell us all about rats climbing up drainpipes and being found swimming around in people's toilets, and fatbergs and all those good things.'

'Fatbergs? What the hell are those?' As soon as I asked, I wished I hadn't.

'They build up in sewers. They're solid lumps formed from congealed cooking fat and wet wipes and… uh—'

'Stop! I've heard enough!'

'Sorry.' Archie grinned. 'But anyway, Uncle Ray reckons the grossest thing he ever had to deal with was blocked urinals in pub toilets.'

'I can kind of see where he's coming from. The smell in there is… Well, it's quite something.'

'Ray told us what happens is – tell me if you want me to stop – the urine forms crystals in the pipes that build up over time. And that, together with the urinal cakes and cleaning products and stuff, gradually builds up into a kind of slime and clogs up the whole pipe. And loads of pubes get stuck in the blockage too, and—'

'Stop! Too much information!'

Archie laughed. 'Sorry. Anyway, it's basically every plumber's worst nightmare. So lots of them won't touch it, and those that will charge an absolute fortune.'

'That's exactly it! I called five different ones and none of them would come out for less than a grand. So what the hell am I going to do?'

'You don't have to do anything,' Archie said. 'I'm going to ring Uncle Ray. He's semi-retired now and he was always kind of old-school, so he never had a website, which I guess is why you didn't find him online. But he's based just down the road. He's got this secret formula he uses to deal with it. Involving Fairy Liquid, apparently.'

'What? You mean ordinary washing-up liquid?'

'I'm pretty sure that's what he said. Or was it fairies? Anyway, I'll call him and then we can go and get a coffee. Okay?'

'Okay,' I said, bemused. 'I mean, if you're sure…'

But Archie was already on the phone.

'He'll be here in half an hour,' he said, after he hung up. 'So we've just got time for a coffee. And possibly a bacon roll. Shall we head to the greasy spoon?'

So I locked the front door of the pub – relieved to leave the stench behind – and Archie and I walked the few steps to the Express Café, one of the high-street businesses that had so far escaped the creeping tendrils of gentrification and redevelopment.

Over coffee and breakfast, he told me how he'd taken out the lease on the shop that was to become Craft Fever four months ago, and was refitting it with the help of some mates in the building trade.

'Craft beer hasn't peaked yet,' he said. 'The market's still growing, and artisan spirits are even stronger – so to speak. I used to work in sales for a brewery, but I've always wanted to run my own business, so I saved up and borrowed from everywhere I could, and here I am. How about you?'

I regaled him with the story of how I'd accidentally found myself helping Shirley out behind the bar and decided to work some shifts in the pub, but left out the bit about losing my job and being found in tears in the street by Maurice.

'It's kind of sucked me in,' I said. 'I never thought this was what I'd do with my life, but – for now, anyway – it looks like it is.'

'So what were you doing before?' Archie asked, biting into his bacon roll like he hadn't eaten for months.

'I was about to qualify as a lawyer. My boyfriend Joe still works at the firm where I was. I sometimes think he worries I've gone completely bonkers.'

Not to mention that he's moved his ex-girlfriend into our spare room. But I didn't say that either.

'My girlfriend Nat thinks the same sometimes. She's a physiotherapist. Works at the hospital just there.' Archie gestured, a spatter of butter falling from his hand onto the table, as if the local hospital was right outside the door, even though we both knew it was more than a mile away.

But that wasn't what we'd been saying, really. By acknowledging the presence in our lives of Joe and Nat, we were making this breakfast okay. We were opening the door to a friendship that wouldn't go any further. Even though he'd been kind and helpful and we were sitting smiling at each other across the laminate tabletop, our mouths full of bacon, our relationship would develop in one direction only.

I relaxed, taking a big gulp of milky coffee and a bite of my own roll, feeling melting butter and shards of crisp bacon fill my mouth.

A few minutes later, we were done. I paid the bill as a thank you for Archie roping his uncle in, and we headed back towards the Nag's Head, just as an anonymous dark blue van pulled up outside.

'Here he is!' Archie said. 'Come the moment, come the man. Hello, Raymond.'

'When I heard there was a problem with the bogs here at the Nag, I had to come straight over,' said Uncle Ray. 'My prostate not being what it used to be. Got to make sure we get to play our bones in comfort, don't we?'

After he levered himself out of the driving seat, I recognised him straight away. He was the fourth member of the dominoes group that included Maurice, Sadiq and Terry.

'We'll have this sorted for you in two shakes, love,' he said to me.

'That's so kind,' I gushed. 'Thank you. Thank you ever so much. But before you start, do you mind me asking how much this… I mean, could you possibly give me a quote for the work?'

He rubbed his moustache and looked at me thoughtfully for a few moments.

'How about a round on the house for me and the lads? I know money's tight right now.'

I didn't need to do the maths. I knew perfectly well that thirty days of one or two halves of Guinness, three or four of bitter and a few litres of orange juice would come nowhere close to what Ray could have charged, let alone a single round.

I found myself leaning in and hugging him, and then I turned to hug Archie too, but at the last moment we both kind of side-stepped, and he just grinned and said he'd see me around.

Chapter Twelve

In the end I didn't get to tell Shirley about my urinal-based adventures. Although I hadn't been expecting her to make it to the pub that morning, I was surprised when she and Juan didn't arrive for evening service either – surprised, but too busy to give their absence much thought, and also slightly flattered that she thought I could cope fine without her. I explained to the couple of customers who asked for food that the kitchen was closed, assuming that my boss and her other half were having a high old time at their post-funeral knees-up.

Somehow, I survived the evening trade alone. There were a couple of sticky moments, like when Fat Don tried to sit back down on his bar stool and missed, ending up in a heap on the floor, but fortunately the local five-a-side football team were able to help him to his feet. It was after midnight when I got home, aching in every part of my body, my arm so sore from pulling pints that I could barely lift my toothbrush, and I slid as quietly as I could into bed next to Joe's sleeping form and instantly fell asleep.

The furious buzzing of my phone woke me from a dream in which the beer taps at the Nag's Head had malfunctioned and a steady tide of best bitter was threatening to engulf the place. I forced my eyes open and rolled over. Joe's side of the bed was empty. My phone – which I reached for just in time to miss the call – told me it was eight o'clock.

The call had been from Shirley. While I waited to see if she'd leave me a voice message – whenever she had before, they'd been rambling minutes-long affairs full of general chit-chat before she got around to the actual reason for her call – I showered and dressed.

Zoë's bedroom door was closed – presumably she too had had a late night and was enjoying a lie-in – but Frazzle was up and about, twining around my legs and crying piteously. There was a scrawled note on the kitchen worktop from Joe:

> Gone to the office to catch up with some stuff. Don't listen to Frazzle – he's had his breakfast xxx

I laughed, feeling a rush of affection for him, and then realised that Frazzle was Zoë's cat and the note – and therefore the kisses – were meant more for her than for me. I imagined Joe adding those three Xs to the page torn from his work notepad. I wondered whether he'd hesitated before writing them, or put one down and then impulsively added the other two. I imagined Zoë finding the note and seeing them, and smiling a little secret, satisfied smile – *He gave me kisses!*

I told myself that it was just a note, just a casual, friendly sign-off, no reason at all to worry. But I couldn't help it – I was worried.

The washing machine was full, I noticed – a tangle of wet clothes bunched up against the door. If I took them out and hung them up, they'd be dry by the evening. I hauled the bunch of wet fabric out and started to drape it, rather haphazardly, over the airer. Just a few weeks ago, there would have been loads of my work clothes in there – tights and blouses and dresses. Now, the only garments of mine were jeans, jersey tops and underwear. There were a few things that must have been Zoë's, and some of Joe's work shirts, too.

And then I came across another unfamiliar garment, and stopped, looking at it bemusement.

It was a pair of silk boxer shorts, printed with Bart Simpson's face.

Joe had silk boxer shorts, but they had Rudolph the Red-Nosed Reindeer printed on them. I'd given them to him for Christmas, a kind of joke gift, and he'd been delighted.

'Cool, thanks, Alice!' I remembered him laughing. 'I had a pair of these ages ago, only they were *Simpsons* ones. I've no idea what happened to them – they just kind of disappeared.'

Surely this must be some random coincidence. Surely if Zoë had a pair of men's boxers that she wore in bed, or to watch telly in, or whatever – which was slightly weird, maybe, but not alarming in itself – they couldn't be ones that had belonged to Joe years before, when they were together, that she'd borrowed or stolen and kept all this time?

Because that would be *seriously* weird.

Then I remembered Shirley's call and hurried back to the bedroom to retrieve my phone. There was a message, as I'd expected, but it was a surprisingly brief one.

'*Hello, my love. Could you meet me at the pub early today please? There's been a crisis.*'

Oh God, another one? If it was the men's toilets again I was handing in my notice – not that I had an employment contract or anything.

But it couldn't be, I realised. Shirley only got to work at around nine, and from the sound of her message she'd had a late night; her voice was even hoarser than usual. Well, there was only one way to find out.

I pulled on some clothes, not bothering with any make-up, and hustled out of the door, ignoring Frazzle's entreaties for second breakfast but giving him a scratch behind the ear, to which he responded with a look that said quite clearly, 'That's not what I wanted and you know it.'

I reached the Nag's Head just as Shirley was getting out of her car. She used to live in the flat above the pub, she'd told me, but her relationship with Juan had put paid to that. 'He wanted us to have a proper love nest,' she'd said, 'so we do. A semi in Bromley.'

'Morning, Shirl. How are you? What's up?'

'Oh my days, love. I feel awful. I don't know what they put in that Bacardi and Coke but my head's proper banging and my stomach… I should have avoided those egg and cress sandwiches, that's all I'm saying.'

Her face was immaculately made-up as usual, but she wasn't wearing her normal skintight jeans and draped top, but instead a velour Juicy Couture tracksuit and trainers.

'I'm so sorry you're feeling rough,' I said. 'What can I get you? Coffee? Paracetamol?'

She shook her head. 'Don't mind me, love. I can't stop here anyway. That's why I asked you to come in.'

'What's happened? Are you all right?'

'I'm all right. Well, I will be, once time and Mother Nature have done their work. It's Juan.'

'Juan? Is he ill?'

'If he wasn't, he would have been by the time I'd finished telling him what I thought of him. A grown man, making a spectacle of himself like that, in front of everyone. Doing himself an injury. Bloody men, they just can't be trusted to look after themselves.'

'What happened?'

'Well, this wake last night, you know how it is. You want to give people a decent send-off, and Len wouldn't have wanted his funeral to be a gloomy affair. So a good time was had by all, shall we say, including yours truly. But Juan – well, he's never been much of a drinker, but he let his hair down good and proper.'

'So he's hungover, too?'

'Hungover? If that was all he was, don't you think I'd have told him to drag his sorry arse out of bed and get down here, same as I have?'

I had no doubt that was true.

'It was "Come on Eileen" that did it,' she said. 'I don't know about you, but I've always disliked that tune. Juan, though, got on the dance floor and started carrying on like a fifteen-year-old, doing all the moves and everything.'

I tried to imagine lugubrious, silent Juan tearing up a dance floor to Dexy's Midnight Runners and failed.

'And then what happened?'

'And then,' Shirley paused, 'the dozy bugger only went and stepped on a miniature Scotch egg someone had dropped and went flying. Bloody thing must've been hard as a bullet; if he'd tried to eat it he'd likely have broken a tooth. I know I complain day and night about all them health and safety regulations, but I have to admit they have a place, and the management at the Spotted Dog in Plaistow will be hearing from the local council once I have a moment to get on the blower to them. But I can't do that, because I need to get his highness off to the minor injuries unit ASAP. I'm no expert, but I think he's done his knee in. Can barely hobble, never mind work in the kitchen. He went arse over tit, right in front of all my friends. There's no fool like an old fool. And now I'll have to stop at home with him, waiting on him hand and foot, helping him to the bathroom and listening to him moan on about how much pain he's in. Pain indeed! It's *him* that's the pain.'

In spite of her ranting, I could tell she was concerned.

'That's okay,' I said. 'You do whatever you need to. I'll be absolutely fine here on my own.'

'But what about the kitchen?' she wailed. 'The punters will be expecting their home-cooked food, same as usual.'

Describing the microwave cheese omelettes and powdered tomato soup Juan prepared at the Nag's Head as home cooking was a stretch at best, but I wasn't going to diss him.

'They can order from Deliveroo on their phones,' I said. 'I'll print off some notices and put them out instead of menus, saying the chef's indisposed. And I'll get extra crisps and stuff in. It'll be fine.'

'You're a treasure, you know that? A real treasure.'

'It's nothing, honestly, Shirl. You get back to Juan. I've got this.'

She reached over and gave me an Obsession-scented hug, then swung back into her car and drove away on her errand of mercy.

I paused for a moment before fitting the key into the lock. I'd opened up on my own before, but this time felt different. Turning the key, stepping into the familiar-smelling interior of the pub, seeing the dust motes drifting in the morning sun, thinking of the long list of tasks that needed to be completed before eleven o'clock – all those things, which I'd done numerous times, now felt laden with a new significance.

It took me a moment to realise what it was like. It reminded me of the first time Joe and I had walked into our flat after collecting the keys from the estate agent.

'This is ours now, Alice,' he'd said, and pulled me into his arms and danced me around every room before we collapsed on the bedroom carpet and had a hasty celebratory shag, not caring that the bed we'd ordered wasn't going to arrive until the next day.

The Nag's Head wasn't mine. It never would be – it was owned by the absentee landlady who lived abroad and, from what Shirley had said, never gave a thought to the place. But I was in charge, as least for the time being.

To celebrate, I opened the lid of the ancient piano and plinked out the first few bars of 'Ode to Joy'. It had been fifteen years since I'd given up music lessons but somehow my fingers remembered what to do – although I could hear that the poor old thing was hopelessly out of tune.

Sitting down on the faded velvet chaise longue, I put my feet up, allowing myself a 'queen of all she surveys' moment, channelling Daenerys from *Game of Thrones* and wondering if I should pour myself a glass of Prosecco – or possibly a flagon of the blood of my enemies. Except I didn't have any of Zoë's blood and it was too early for Prosecco. Then, with extra vigour, I hoovered the threadbare carpet, checked the stock in the cellar and wiped the tables, which, even though they were cleaned after closing time, always seemed to have acquired a new film of dust by the morning.

I looked around my domain. It was just the same as it had been the first time I saw it – a small, dingy, shabby pub that had seen better days. But now I could see its potential. I imagined stripping off the faded flock wallpaper and seeing what was underneath it – more wallpaper, I guessed. But eventually, there'd be a wall. A wall made of honest bricks that could be revealed and celebrated. And the floor – between the islands of ugly red carpet, there were bare boards, dented with age and coated with layers of varnish. I imagined how they'd look if the carpet was taken away and they were sanded and polished, back to the natural gloss they must have had when they were new, which was probably around the same time Queen Victoria got a crown on her head for the first time.

And, speaking of crowns, there was Diana, Princess of Wales, regarding me steadily from her portrait over the mantelpiece. Was it just me, or was there a new wariness in her gaze?

'Don't you worry, Di,' I told her. 'I'm just keeping the place warm. Shirley will be back in no time. If it was down to me, you'd be straight off to the charity shop. But it's not, so you can relax.'

I forced myself out of my daydream and took some money from the till, which I invested in stocks of crisps, peanuts and pretzels at Tesco, pausing for just a second before throwing in some tubs of the poshest olives they had for good measure.

If today was the first day of the rest of the Nag's Head's life, I might as well start as I intended to carry on.

Over the next couple of weeks, I worked harder than I ever had in my life. Shirley informed me that Juan had torn an anterior cruciate ligament, and that they'd both be off until he was – literally – back on his feet again and able to walk without crutches.

'You're in charge, my love,' she said. 'Do what needs doing. Do your Deliveroo thing. Hire in some extra pairs of hands, if you can get them. We'll find the money somehow. And give me a ring any time you need advice.'

So I did. I got a local deli to deliver platters of sandwiches at lunchtime, and charged a few pounds a head for them, which made a small profit and went down brilliantly with the local mums as well as with Fat Don, who was at least getting some vitamins down him for a change. They went from turning up their noses at Juan's food menu and saying how they did wish there was somewhere decent and family-friendly to come to after baby yoga, to remarking how fortunate they were to have found this place – a real hidden gem.

I rented an industrial coffee machine and installed it in the corner of the bar, and started opening earlier in the mornings to attract local home workers, who came for coffee with their laptops, stayed the morning, and often wanted lunch, too. I met the rep from the brewery and asked him to recommend some decent but affordable wine to add to our order. I popped next door and asked Archie to advise me on what craft beer we should stock. I put an ad in the local job centre and recruited two part-time staff members, Kelly and Freddie, who between them could cover a few shifts a week and give me an occasional break or an evening off.

When business was slow, I spent some time sorting through the accumulated junk in the rooms upstairs. There were empty plastic crates stacked three-deep along one wall, almost up to the ceiling. There were framed prints, their paper speckled with mould and their glass cracked. There were tea chests full of old beer mats, branded pump handle clips from beers that had gone out of production years ago, chipped glasses and bottleneck sleeves. There were more chairs and stools, most of them with missing legs or cracked seats. I barely made a dent in it all, but it was something.

One morning, Maurice arrived earlier than usual. His friends weren't with him, but he wasn't alone – he was accompanied by another, slightly younger man. In sharp contrast to Maurice's dapper style, the newcomer was dressed casually, in jeans and a white linen shirt, a leather jacket slung over his shoulders. A gold cross hung from a chain round his neck.

'Good morning, gents.' The cheery greeting had become second nature to me now. 'What can I get you?'

'I'll have my usual, thank you, Alice,' Maurice said. 'But just a glass of water for my brother. It's all I could do to persuade him to set foot in this den of iniquity, isn't that right, Wesley?'

Wesley laughed. 'Don't take no notice of him. The church teaches that we should be filled with the holy spirit instead of being drunk on wine, but I don't judge those who enjoy an occasional drink. I'm not here for carousing, though.'

'I hope you don't think I'm taking a liberty, Alice,' Maurice went on. 'But I mentioned to my brother that you've been making a few changes and improvements here, and I asked him if he'd be kind enough to come along and have a look at that.'

He gestured towards the piano.

'The horn's my instrument,' Wesley said. 'I play in a jazz band, in clubs in Soho – dens of iniquity, as he likes to point out – but I know my way around strings and percussion too. Maurice said this old lady could do with some attention, and I had a free morning, so I came along to see if I could help at all.'

'That would be amazing! I mean, I don't know if it's even salvageable, the poor thing, but if we could get it vaguely in tune, that would be so cool. You could even play a gig here sometime.'

Wesley opened the piano and ran a clean handkerchief – folded and ironed just as crisply as Maurice's – over its keys.

'Oh my days, the poor old thing,' he said. 'The wood needs polishing, the springs on that stool are all gone. It's a job for a professional, really.'

'Don't worry if you think it's beyond repair,' I said. 'It's really kind of you to come and take a look.'

'Nothing's beyond repair. "I will restore you to health and heal your wounds, declares the Lord." Jeremiah chapter thirty, verse seventeen.'

'I doubt the prophet Jeremiah ever saw a Joanna in such bad nick as this one,' countered Maurice.

Wesley shook his head. 'I very much doubt he ever did. Well, I'll see what I can do.'

He shifted the stool out of the way and knelt down in front of the piano, carefully levering off its lower front board. A spider scuttled out across the carpet and Wesley jumped.

'Don't go having a heart attack before you even get started,' teased Maurice, grabbing a glass from the bar and carefully capturing the spider before tipping it out of the front door.

'I'll leave you to get on, shall I?' I said. 'Are you sure you wouldn't like anything else? A hot drink? Something to eat?'

But Wesley was engrossed in the innards of the piano, occasionally sucking his teeth and tutting just like the IT guy at Billings Pitt

Furzedown used to do when he was called out for a software crash. Any minute, I expected him to suggest switching the piano off and on again.

Soon Maurice's friends arrived and they began their game of dominoes, and the group of mums soon showed up too, with a few of their older kids with them because it was half-term. I served drinks, called the deli to increase the day's sandwich order and took delivery of a load of soft drinks, all to the accompaniment of regular bongs and plinks from the piano, becoming increasingly less discordant.

Soon, Wesley was surrounded by a group of kids, all watching in fascination and asking questions about what he was doing, and how, and why, which he answered patiently.

After more than an hour, he replaced the top board of the piano and wiped his dusty hands on his hanky.

'I've done all I can,' he said, this time sounding like a surgeon on *Casualty* who'd just stitched up a patient, leaving something lethal inside. 'Shall we see how she sounds?'

'Yes!' chorused the children, crowding eagerly around. Their mums stopped chatting. The click of dominoes fell silent.

Wesley sat down, wiped his hands again and caressed the yellowing keys. A stream of notes poured from the piano, slowly at first and then more confidently, as he began to play.

'Amazing grace,' he sang softly, and his rich baritone was joined almost immediately by the kids' higher-pitched, clear voices and Fat Don's booming bass, 'how sweet the sound…'

As the pub filled with music, hearing the words, 'I once was lost, but now am found,' I felt tears sting my eyes. Then I looked up at the portrait of Princess Diana, and I could have sworn her previously solemn lips were now smiling slightly in approval.

Chapter Thirteen

While I'd been spending more and more time at the Nag's Head, Joe had also been working punishingly long hours. Often, he'd send me a text at seven – or eight, or even nine – to say that he still had a couple of hours' work to do, and there was no point my waiting up for him. And, because I didn't particularly want to spend time alone in the flat with Zoë – or rather, with Zoë and Frazzle, who followed her around like a furry shadow, when she wasn't cradling him in her arms or draping him over her shoulders like a scarf – I found myself staying at the pub late into the evening, then heading home and going straight to bed.

It was beginning to feel like the only time Joe and I got to spend alone together was when we were in bed – and that wasn't exactly quality time, because all we did there was sleep. I bet there were pensioners with more active sex lives than ours. Hell, I bet there were *plants* with more active sex lives.

One Tuesday morning, I woke up early. Joe was still asleep next to me; I hadn't even been aware of him coming in, so it must have been after midnight. Carefully, so as not to disturb him, I turned over and looked at him. He was lying on his back, one arm thrown up over his head, his face slack in sleep. Even peaceful and relaxed as he was, I could see the exhaustion in his face. He'd lost weight, there were dark circles under his eyes and a scab on his jaw where he'd cut himself shaving, still half-asleep, before he left for work the day before.

But it was almost seven. Exhausted or not, soon he'd have to wake up and get ready for work.

I wriggled closer to him under the duvet, rested my head on his shoulder and put my arm round his waist. I could feel his ribcage jutting through his skin, more sharply than it used to. But he sensed my body next to him and turned towards me, the arm that had been above his head pulling me closer to him.

I could feel the hardness of his cock pressing against my stomach – whether because of my closeness, or because of something in a dream (*not Zoë. Please not Zoë*), I wasn't sure. But my body reacted to his nearness; I pulled him even closer, my face pressed to his chest, breathing in the smell of him, running my hand down his smooth back, over the tight curve of his buttocks, down to the hard muscle of his thigh.

He thrust against me, giving a sleepy sound of desire, his hand caressing my own body.

'Hey, you,' I whispered.

'Hey, Alice.'

He bent his head and kissed me, his eyes still closed, but his hand moving more surely now, reaching for my breasts.

'What time is it?' he asked.

'Not too late. Not if we're quick.'

He lifted himself up on one elbow, smiling down at me, his hand moving between my legs and stroking me delicately, instantly finding the right spot so I heard myself gasp with pleasure. I reached for his dick and held it, feeling the hot, pulsing hardness. He edged himself further over me, and I wrapped my legs around his hips, pulling him closer as our lips met. I guided his penis to where his hand had been, waiting for that first gentle push that would take him deep inside me.

Then we heard footsteps on the landing outside, and Zoë's voice.

'Come on, munchkin. Who's a hungry cat? Is it time for your breakfast? Did your lazy mother oversleep?'

Alongside her footsteps and her voice, I could hear the lighter thud of Frazzle's paws on the floorboards, and his eager meows. In my hand, I felt Joe's erection become… well, not an erection.

'Shit,' he whispered. 'Sorry.'

'Do you want me to…?'

'Nah. I should get up.'

He turned away from me, swinging his feet onto the floor and standing, stretching and yawning before pulling on boxer shorts and a T-shirt. Before, he always used to walk to the bathroom naked – we both did. But that obviously wasn't possible any more. I heard him swear under his breath as he tripped over Frazzle's litter tray on the way to the basin. I pushed myself up against the pillows and swiped my phone to life, checking my email and WhatsApp while I waited for Joe to shower. From the kitchen, I could hear Zoë chattering away to her cat.

'Now, I've got a busy day, Frazz. I've got to go into town in an hour, and I won't be back until five. So you're going to be left in charge, aren't you? And you're going to be a good, responsible cat. No scratching the sofa. I know you want to go outside but you're not allowed yet. You need to learn to be patient. Don't you?'

Frazzle didn't reply. Not that he could have got a word in edgeways, even if he'd wanted to.

The flat was small – it had always been. But now it felt claustrophobic. And our bedroom, which had been a haven and a refuge, felt almost smothering these days, like a prison – even though I knew I could leave any time I wanted. This was my home, after all.

So why did it feel like it had been taken over?

Joe reappeared from the bathroom, wrapped in a towel, and dressed hastily.

'I've just about got time for a coffee and a piece of toast. Want anything?'

'Coffee would be amazing.'

I pulled on jeans and an old T-shirt. My own shower could wait – once Zoë had left for work, I'd have the place to myself for a few short minutes before I too needed to leave for the day. Having to wait for the bathroom, having to leave space for Zoë's stuff in the fridge, not being able to watch what I wanted on telly in the evenings because she was glued to endless repeats of *The Big Bang Theory* – all this was new. It hadn't been so long ago that I'd had flatmates, of course – but it had been long enough for me to get used to the luxury, the privacy, the intimacy of having a home that was just mine and Joe's.

Now, I was being forced to share it. And not just the flat, but Joe, too.

I followed the sound of their voices to the kitchen. Zoë was frothing milk and Joe was standing at the counter, spooning some weird bruise-coloured sludge from a bowl. She was wearing pyjamas – but they were nothing like the shabby cotton sets I owned. They consisted of a skimpy black satin camisole top with lace straps and a pair of even skimpier satin shorts that showed off the smooth muscles of her thighs. Even though she hadn't combed her hair, she looked totally beautiful. She and Joe were both laughing, but they stopped when I came in.

Great. Not only was there a Jessica Rabbit lookalike in my kitchen chatting up my boyfriend, but there was no sign of my coffee.

'I'm making chai latte,' Zoë said. 'With oat milk. It's not as good as the almond milk I used to get, but it's locally produced and it's really hard to find organic nut milk so I've switched. Want one?'

'I'm good, thanks. What's that?'

Normally, Joe had toast for breakfast. Usually with peanut butter, sometimes with cream cheese. But never weird purplish mush.

'It's porridge with chia seeds and blueberries. Zoë made it. It's good – try some.'

He held out his spoon, but I shook my head, waiting for Zoë to finish with the coffee machine. There was a bowl in the sink that looked like it had had cat food in it, and a banana peel on the counter. No big deal, no drama – just minor mess. But it had been created by someone who wasn't Joe or me.

I put a coffee pod into the machine and found a mug in the cupboard – not my favourite one, the one with gold spots that had been my Secret Santa gift in my first year at Billings Pitt Furzedown. Zoë was using that. Of course she was. Not that I minded that anything like as much as I minded the glance I'd seen Joe give her legs.

'You can get reusable coffee pods now, you know,' she remarked. 'Those plastic ones just go straight into landfill, which isn't great.'

'I'll bear that in mind.'

She was right, of course – it wasn't great. I mean, I'm not trying to give the impression that Joe and I didn't care about the destruction of virgin Amazon rainforest or that we were in favour of fracking or anything like that. We weren't. Joe cycled to work most days. We separated out our recyclable waste, even if we sometimes got confused about whether things like those plastic collars that go round cans of beer were recyclable or not.

But the point is, we probably shouldn't have been buying cans of beer with plastic collars around them in the first place. Or forgetting our reusable bags for life half the time and having to pay for plastic ones when we went to Sainsbury's. Or drinking bottled water, or buying coffee in takeout cups.

We just shouldn't. But we were so busy, sometimes we didn't have the headspace for thinking about how lightly we trod on the planet, as I remembered Zoë putting it.

So I knew that Zoë was right and I was wrong. But I couldn't help myself resenting her not just for pointing out that I was wrong, but for being right herself.

And when Joe finished his weird purple porridge, announced that he'd better get a move on or he'd be late for work, and kissed not just me but Zoë too – even if it was just a peck on the cheek – I resented her even more.

And when Frazzle hopped up onto the kitchen counter and Joe leaned down to fuss him and got a bonk on the nose from the cat that was, for all intents and purposes, a kiss too, I practically exploded with the chemical reaction that my annoyance at her and my love for him created inside me.

But Zoë was utterly oblivious to my turmoil.

'So this pub where you're working, Alice. The Ging— I mean, the Nag's Head. You mentioned that it's got a kitchen, right?'

'It does, yes. Well, if you can call the place where Juan deep-fries stuff and microwaves other stuff a kitchen. He's a great guy but he's not much of a chef, to be honest. He only got the gig because Shirl fancied him, and now they're a couple. But he's off work right now with a knee injury, so there's no one in the kitchen.'

'So there's, like, a vacancy? For someone temporary?'

No. Well, yes, but that isn't going to be you. Not over my dead body.

'I suppose so…'

Zoë was looking at me steadily, her hazel eyes almost exactly the same colour as Frazzle's. He was gazing at me too. Suddenly, I felt like I'd walked into a trap.

'Well, a cook,' I said hastily. 'I mean, I don't know much about that side of things – I'm totally learning as I go along – but I think it'll be all ready-made stuff, same as it is now. It's not like we're aiming for a Michelin star or anything.'

'But don't you see how much potential there could be?'

Zoë's eyes were wide and eager. So were Frazzle's, but when he saw me looking at him he did a slow, languid blink. I found myself blinking back, and the cat jumped down off the kitchen table and came over and rubbed himself against my legs, purring.

Stop with the charm offensive, I thought. But I bent down and fussed him anyway.

'Potential for what?'

'To really become representative of the community. Like, championing local producers. Showcasing the cuisine of the people in the area – West Indian nights, Eastern European nights, stuff like that. Being carbon-neutral and sustainable. It could be really zeitgeisty. And tasty too.'

I thought of the meals Joe and I had eaten in the Star and Garter before it had closed to be turned into trendy studio flats. The fish pies, the burgers, the lasagnes. All perfectly nice, of course, but thinking about it now, we could have been in any pub anywhere in the world. Reluctantly, I admitted to myself that Zoë had a point.

That didn't mean I was going to admit it to her, though.

'Okay, yeah, I hear what you're saying. But it all sounds complicated – and expensive.'

'But it wouldn't have to be!' She did that thing with her eyes again that made her look like a cross between Bambi and a rabble-rousing pastor. 'The idea that ethical sourcing costs more has been proved wrong again and again. If you cut waste right down, use economical cuts of meat – or, better still, little or no meat – plan your energy use sensibly and – well, all that stuff, it doesn't have to be at all. I worked at a primary school up in Glasgow for a while where we had a budget of less than a fiver per child per day, and we managed it. Including breakfast and snacks. And there wasn't a chicken nugget in sight. Isn't that right, Frazzle?'

The cat glanced round at her, then carried on giving himself a back massage against my calves. I knew where Zoë was going with this, and now I was going to have to let her know that I did.

'So you're saying that someone like you could run the kitchen at the Nag's Head?'

'Not someone like me. Me! My job finishes in November when the chef gets back from maternity leave. My horoscope today said there's a new challenge in my future, and this could be it! Don't you see how brilliantly it could work?'

I thought, *You've muscled into my home and I think you're still in love with my boyfriend and I can't even have sex without you ruining the moment nattering away to your cat, and now you want to come and work in the pub because Mystic bloody Meg thinks it's a good idea?*

And then you'd be around all. The. Time.

But then I thought, *If you were with me, then you wouldn't be with Joe. I could keep an eye on you.*

And I felt my face flame with embarrassment, remembering what I'd done just two days before.

I hadn't meant to snoop on Zoë. Honestly, I hadn't. It was a horrible, shameful thing to do and I've only been less proud of one thing in all my life. But anyway, against my better judgement – almost by accident, honestly – it happened.

I blame Frazzle.

Okay, fine. I had only myself to blame. But Frazzle started it. What happened was, Joe had left for work and, an hour or so later, so had Zoë. It was Freddie's day to open up so I was taking it a bit easy, having a long shower with the door open, blow-drying my hair with no clothes on, making my favourite breakfast (eggy bread, only made with crumpets instead of bread, slathered with butter and strawberry jam) – all the little things I'd missed doing since Zoë had moved in.

I was sitting at the kitchen table in my dressing gown, just finishing off the last bite of my breakfast, when I heard a noise coming from our spare room – or Zoë's room, as it was now. It was a kind of scratching sound, and for a second I panicked and thought, *Fuck, do we have mice?* And then I remembered what Zoë had said about Frazzle being a next-level mouser, and told myself I must be imagining things.

Then I heard the noise again, and another noise too. A pitiful kind of moan. I got up and walked the few steps from the kitchen to the short passage that our room and Zoë's led off, and listened. The scratching came again, and the moan. And they were coming from behind Zoë's closed bedroom door.

I realised straight away what had happened. She'd only gone and shut her cat in by mistake, the dozy cow. And I was just as bad, freaking out over a cat scratching and meowing. I turned the handle and pushed open the door and Frazzle emerged, complained noisily about false imprisonment without trial, wound himself around my legs a bit, then stalked off to his favourite spot on the back of the sofa, where he'd already left a dent and a mat of ginger fur on the cushion.

I didn't follow him, though. I stood there in the doorway and looked into the room. It was gloomy, because the blind was pulled down all the way down, and it had a smell I couldn't immediately identify but recognised straight away – something herbal and clean, almost grassy. It was Zoë's smell – whatever natural, organic toiletries she used, whatever phosphate-free oil kept her hair permanently glossy and frizz-free, it had seeped into the very air of what used to be our spare room slash study.

I thought, *I should open a window*. And at the same time, I thought, *I've got no right to be in here*. But the second thought came too late, because I was already in there. I'd stepped over the threshold. I'd broken the snoop barrier. And once I did that, it didn't seem unreasonable to have just a little look around.

It was our flat, after all. Zoë was just visiting, really.

The small double bed was unmade, the sheets Joe and I had chosen as being tasteful and guest-appropriate (white cotton with a smudgy pale blue paisley print) scrunched up at its foot, surrounded by more swathes of cat hair and a few coils of longer, brighter hair that must have come from Zoë's head. The small cabinet we'd thought was more than big enough for anyone staying a couple of nights to fit their stuff in was full to bursting, its drawers spilling out clothes like it had tried to eat too many of them and stopped mid-chew. I was sure I recognised the red top she'd been wearing the first time I saw her, lolling out like a tongue.

Well, if Zoë wanted a messy room, that was her lookout. It wasn't like she was leaving dirty plates lying around or smoking weed or doing anything else I could legitimately object to. And it certainly wasn't my business to clean up after her.

But I took another step into the room, anyway. It was like my feet were moving of their own accord. On top of the chest of drawers were a scented candle (a fire risk, maybe, but its wick was white and pristine so I knew it had never been lit); a couple of vegan cookbooks, their pages crinkled with use, a greasy orange stain on the cover of one; and a tablet with headphones plugged into it.

I picked up the tablet and switched it on, then was immediately confronted with a screen asking for a passcode. I don't know why, but that brought home to me what I was doing: walking into a room in my own home, even if it was occupied by someone else, was one thing. Being caught trying to snoop by a piece of tech was quite another. I put the tablet back where I'd found it – quickly, as if it was too hot to hold – and turned to leave.

Then I caught sight of something else. Peeping out from under the pillow was a bundle of envelopes, wrapped loosely but not tied by a shiny red ribbon. Its ends had once been curled, the way florists and gift-wrapping services in department stores do them, but the curls were squashed now into folds and wrinkles.

Whatever was in that bundle had been moved many times, squeezed into Zoë's backpack as she shuttled from one temporary home to another.

I'd have left the room right then, I'm quite sure of it, except for one thing. I recognised the handwriting on the top envelope, and it was Joe's. Even though it was only one word – Zoë's name – I'd have known it anywhere. Joe had terrible handwriting – a messy scrawl, the ends of the *o* not meeting as they should, the *Z* so wonky it could almost have been a *2*, the *E* an awkward capital letter. The first time I'd noticed and teased him about it, he'd been defensive and embarrassed, explaining that he was not only left-handed but also mildly dyslexic, and had struggled to learn to write at school until he'd had additional help, and I'd felt terrible for taking the piss.

I felt terrible now, because I knew that there was no way I *wasn't* going to open that envelope. I knew I'd regret it, knew I'd hate myself, knew I'd struggle to meet Zoë or Joe's eyes – but I was going to do it anyway. A horrible, self-destructive urge had overtaken me, and there was only one way to make it release its hold.

I picked up the top envelope. Its flap had been torn open at an angle, like Zoë had been impatient to see inside. Either that, or she hadn't cared about damaging it or its contents, hadn't realised that this was something she was going to treasure, keep and look at even after six years.

Inside was a card. It was a shiny square of white with a big red heart on it, and it said, ***For our first anniversary.***

Wait, what? Joe had told me that he and Zoë had only been together a few weeks. Had he lied? Had he wanted to make their relationship seem shorter and less significant than it really was, because he could tell I was insecure? Or for some other, more sinister reason?

My heart hammering, I opened the card.

Seems anniversary cards for one week aren't a thing – they should be. Happy first week-iversary, my gorgeous Zoë. Love Joe.

I closed the card and put it back in its envelope, feeling sick with remorse and fear.

I wasn't going to open any more of them – I didn't need to. I counted the envelopes and there were twelve of them: one for each week of the three months Joe had told me their relationship had lasted, before Zoë ended it.

She'd ended it – but she'd kept his cards, all this time. And now, in our home, with Joe and me sleeping next door, she'd taken them out from wherever she kept them, and looked through them again, reading over all the words of love he'd written to her. She'd kept them under her pillow.

Maybe she'd held on to them out of sentimentality. Maybe she was the kind of person who couldn't bear to throw things away. But I knew that wasn't the case – this was a woman whose entire life fitted into a backpack, whose entire wardrobe could just about be squeezed into four Ikea drawers.

She still loved Joe. Whatever her reasons for finishing with him, she regretted it. And now she was here – a clear and present danger, right in our home.

And – and I know this makes me sound like the worst kind of psycho bunny-boiler ever – a phrase I'd heard Gordon use once, when he was on his way out to lunch with a barrister who was representing the other side in a case we were on, popped into my head.

Keep your friends close and your enemies closer.

'You know what?' I said to Zoë now. 'Actually, I think that's a great idea.'

Chapter Fourteen

So, the next morning, instead of walking to the Nag's Head alone, I had company. Although the journey only took ten minutes, it felt like an eternity. Zoë chattered away non-stop about places where she'd worked, trends in restaurant food and her 'vision' for the pub, which she insisted on referring to as the Ginger Cat, before hastily correcting herself. But I could barely hear her; I couldn't tear my mind away from that stack of glossy cards, each one carrying a message of love to her from Joe.

'It's not much, you know,' I warned her. 'Don't go expecting a snazzy kitchen with all the latest gadgets, because you'll only be disappointed.'

Still, when I unlocked the door and we stepped inside, I found myself feeling strangely nervous and protective, like if she sneered and criticised I wouldn't be able to help taking it personally.

'Right then,' she said. 'Show me where the magic happens!'

I guided her round the back of the bar to the door marked 'Staff only' and pushed it open, standing aside to let Zoë through.

'Oh.' She stood in silence for a moment, looking at the microwave, the deep-fat fryer, the large freezer.

The kitchen was Juan's turf; even though I'd checked with Shirley that it was okay to get a temporary person to hold the fort, I'd barely been inside there myself and certainly not had a proper look around. But Zoë didn't hesitate. She pulled open the door of the freezer and rifled through the foil trays of pre-prepared meals inside. She picked up one of Juan's knives and tested its edge against her thumb, shaking her head. She looked in the fridge and pulled out a box of tomatoes and a bag of wilting salad leaves.

'There's a local homeless shelter, right?'

'I don't know. I suppose so.'

'Well, I'll find out. We can donate some of this stuff, and we'll put the fresh things – well, the things that used to be fresh – out for the food waste collection. Now, how about a coffee?'

Without asking, she whisked over to the new coffee machine – my pride and joy – and fired it up, expertly producing two perfect espressos.

'Thank you.' I took a mug and sat down – there was work to do, but I might as well enjoy my hot drink first.

Zoë joined me, taking a notepad and pen from her bag.

'I'm thinking quite a small, simple menu to start off with, until I get the sense of what the market wants. Maybe five or six small plates that'll do for starters or sharing, and three mains. Lots of plant-based stuff – that'll help keep costs down, apart from anything else.'

She chewed her pen for a second before starting to scribble rapidly. I inhaled the fragrant steam coming off my coffee, then took that first sip – always the best one – and waited, thinking again with a pang of envy how pretty Zoë was, with her perfect white teeth biting into her full bottom lip as she thought. Even sitting there, writing in a notebook, she fizzed with vitality.

'How about this?' She turned the notebook around and passed it to me. I hoped she couldn't sense the waves of resentment I could feel radiating towards her.

'Seitan fried "chicken",' I read. 'What's that?'

Zoë's eyebrows rose ever so slightly. 'Seitan's a meat substitute. It's made from wheat gluten. It replicates the texture of animal protein far better than soy or tofu. It's become incredibly popular recently.'

Not with me, it hasn't, I thought. 'Shepherdless pie?'

'It's kind of a joke. Lentils and veg with a potato topping. Proper pub grub, only meat-free.'

'Okay,' I said. 'I mean, will people order this stuff? The menu before was all meat, apart from the cheese omelette.'

'And did people order that?'

'I guess,' I said, then added honestly, 'But if they did, I doubt they ever did again. Juan ordered them in frozen and nuked them.'

Zoë grimaced, then laughed. 'Fair play. But you say the clientele here's changing – you're getting loads of younger people, mums with kids – just look at this area, Alice. It's hipster central. When Sean and I had the food cart we sold loads of plant-based stuff. It's the future.'

'Well, I suppose you know what you're doing. Do you miss him? Sean, I mean?' *As opposed to Joe. I* know *you miss him.*

Zoë twisted her hair up and secured the knot of copper curls with her pen.

'Yeah, a bit. We were only together for a few months, but we were mates first, so it's that I miss, more than him as a boyfriend. You know what I mean? But it had kind of run its course. He's a decent guy, but we weren't in love or anything like that.'

Not like you were with Joe.

'You're really passionate about this whole food thing, aren't you?' *Focus on the job. Never mind the other stuff she's passionate about, like your boyfriend.*

'It wasn't what I thought I'd end up doing with my life. I studied sociology at uni, but I realised even before I graduated that it wasn't for me. And I had a holiday job in a restaurant, started off washing pans and then they got me chopping veg and it sort of went from there. I like the freedom of working in new places. I even like the unsociable hours.'

'Well, you'll get those here,' I said.

'How about you?'

'How about me what?'

'It's quite the jump, isn't it? To go from being a lawyer to doing this.'

'It wasn't even a conscious decision,' I admitted. 'And I have no idea how long I'll do it for. It's like, I was so sure I had my future all mapped out, and then the job I was sure I had in the bag wasn't there any more, and I had to do something, so I ended up doing this. And now, with Shirley off, I've found myself in charge. I don't actually have a clue what I'm doing. Just making it up as I go along.'

Zoë laughed. 'Isn't most of life like that, though? What's your star sign, Alice?'

The one that maintains – rightly – that astrology's a load of bollocks, I thought. But I answered pleasantly, 'Leo, I think. My birthday's the seventeenth of August.'

'Ah, so you thrive on challenges and have big ideas. You're made for this. Who wants to work in a law firm, anyway?'

'Joe does.'

We sat in silence for a moment, like Joe's name was a barrier that had suddenly sprung up between us, interrupting the first proper conversation we'd had. I'd wanted to see how she reacted to his name, when I said it, to see if there was an echo of pain, or longing, or regret in her face. But she was carefully impassive.

'But doing human rights stuff, not high finance, right? He was always idealistic like that, wanting to change the world. Typical Sagittarius. He's a good person, Alice. You're good together. You're lucky.'

With a cold shock of realisation, I thought, *We were good together. And if I'm not careful, my luck could change.*

'It's been difficult for him. This… change. And now we're both working so hard, and in different places. I feel like we hardly see each other any more.'

It was a weird feeling: saying that to Zoë, of all people, made me admit it to myself. Over the past weeks, I'd been conscious of a distance opening between Joe and me – one that hadn't been there before. I'd blamed it on Zoë herself – her presence in our lives and our home. But maybe there was more to it than that. Maybe the new direction my life had taken was moving me out of the orbit Joe and I had been in. And if I moved too far away from him, would I ever be able to return?

And what about Joe? He hadn't said anything to suggest that he was unhappy, or even that he was aware of a change in our relationship. But then, he hadn't had the chance to say anything at all, really. The few minutes we had alone together each day were barely enough for me to tell him that things at the pub were okay, and him to tell me things at Billings Pitt Furzedown were likewise okay, but frantically busy, and to fill me in on fragments of gossip about my old colleagues, who now seemed like creatures from another planet.

Had he been spending time with Zoë when I was out at work? It didn't seem possible – his working day was longer even than mine. After that first night, when I'd seen them dancing together in our kitchen, they'd barely been alone together, either. Or had they?

'What happened with you and Joe?' I heard myself blurt out.

Zoë pulled the pen out of her hair and it cascaded down over her shoulders.

'I ended it,' she said. 'You know what it's like, at uni. There's so much going on. I didn't want to be tied to one person.'

'Was he okay? How did he take it?'

Zoë stood up. The energy that had radiated from her before had faded; she looked tired and a bit sad. 'I don't know. It was a long time ago. You should ask him.'

I had asked him. I had, and he'd gone all weird.

But there was no time to press her further; the tasks I'd managed to set aside for those few minutes were crowding in on me; soon the first of the morning coffee crowd would be arriving.

'I could make some muffins,' Zoë suggested. 'Get a bit of a breakfast menu going. What do you reckon?'

'Sounds good,' I said, and went to open the door for our first customers.

All that morning, I found my mind returning to Zoë – Zoë and Joe, those sweet cards, the same kind of romantic gesture he made towards me. Back then, he'd been a student, and skint, so cards had been the best he could do. There'd been no hot tub in the garden for Zoë. No garden at all, in a grotty hall of residence. But he'd marked each one of their twelve weeks together, counting them off as if they were precious objects – links in a chain, maybe, forged one by one to hold the two of them together.

And then Zoë had ended it. Maybe she hadn't loved him like he'd loved her. Maybe the cards had been too much for her. Maybe it had put her off him as definitively as Kieren's poo talk had put Heather off. But then why keep them? Why tie the ribbon carefully around them time after time, to make sure none of them went astray? Why look at them in bed, knowing that the man who'd written them was just a couple of metres away, in bed himself, with his girlfriend?

From the kitchen, I could hear Zoë's voice. She must have been singing along to whatever was playing through her headphones, because her voice sounded oddly tuneless, the way people's do when they can hear the music and you can't.

I listened for a moment, wondering if I could recognise the tune, and I could.

It was 'Nothing Breaks Like a Heart'. But when Zoë got to the bit about the world cutting you deep and leaving a scar, she switched on the electric mixer and its roar drowned out her voice.

Chapter Fifteen

Over the next few weeks, Zoë did at the Nag's Head what I guess would have been called 'bedding in' in a corporate environment. But the pub was as far from corporate as it was possible to get, so her version of settling in didn't involve online form-filling or PowerPoint presentations by the managing partner.

Instead, she gradually made her mark on the kitchen, emptying out the boxes of ready meals from the freezer, bringing in her own razor-sharp knives, and finding suppliers of everything from goji berries to organic lamb and vegan cheese. She also became a bit of a hit with the regulars – which I tried unsuccessfully not to mind a bit.

The first time she walked up to Maurice, Sadiq, Ray and Terry's table with a plate of home-made beetroot brownies, they eyed them with extreme suspicion.

'What's this then?' Terry asked. 'Looks like it came out of the wrong end of a cow.'

Zoë smiled sweetly. 'It's on the house.'

The prospect of free food made the dominoes players overcome their reservations in record time, and they were soon tucking in. After that, they became her official tasters – or perhaps guinea pigs would describe it better. Every time she experimented with a new dish, she'd send a plate out for them to try and await their verdict with deadly seriousness, standing with her head on one side and her hands twisting the ties of her apron like a *MasterChef* contestant waiting to be told whether their chocolate fondant was oozy enough.

'This dhal's not as good as what my missus makes,' Sadiq said one time.

'Really?' Zoë's face fell.

'Really. It's miles better.'

'Oh my God! Are you serious?'

'Unfortunately,' Ray cut in, 'everyone knows Sadiq's old lady is the worst cook in Lewisham.'

And they all fell about laughing, even Zoë. However much I resented her presence, though, I couldn't help noticing the effect it was having on the bottom line. Whether it was the new menu, or just the presence of more customers who weren't determined daytime drinkers, trade at the Nag's Head was up. The pub was busy from ten in the morning until midnight. I was run off my feet and, as often as not, I found myself needing to ask Kelly or Freddie to come in for a shift even though I was working myself.

And Zoë carried on working her magic in the kitchen. Another time, she brought Maurice and his friends a plate of puffed-up little pastries, like eclairs only savoury, which she was planning to add to the menu by way of a bar snack.

'Cheese gougères, gents. What do you reckon?'

'This is delicious,' Maurice said. 'That pastry! It's feather-light. Ethereal. How do you do it? I need the recipe for Wesley. He's the cook in our house.'

'I'll show you,' Zoë said. 'If you teach me to play dominoes in return.'

'You've got yourself a deal, young lady,' Maurice said, and Zoë took a seat.

'You want to get to a hundred and fifty points, see,' Ray began. 'That's the magic number. Now, first we put the bones on the table, face down, like this.'

'And we mix them all up,' Sadiq said.

'And then we each choose five,' Maurice said.

'Don't let any of us see them, mind,' Terry said.

I drifted away, leaving them to it. Once again, I had to suppress a bubble of resentment inside me. This was my pub. Maurice was my friend first. And then I reminded myself that not only was I being childish and petty, but that if Zoë turned around and pointed out that Joe had been her boyfriend first, where would that leave me, exactly?

A little while later I looked around. No one was waiting at the bar; I'd served the last couple of customers on autopilot, my face smiling but my mind miles away. Freddie was clearing tables, Kelly was shuffling bottles of wine around in the fridge, making sure the coldest were at the front, and Zoë had retreated to the kitchen. Maurice and his mates had left and I knew we wouldn't see them until the next day.

'I'm popping out,' I said. 'Might go for a walk, or maybe go home for a nap.'

'We've got your back,' said Kelly. 'If things get mad this evening, I'll give you a shout.'

Relieved, I collected my things and walked out into the chilly evening. It was five o'clock but dusk already. The sky was an intense deep blue and I could see the edges of ragged, sunset-hued clouds over the tops of the neighbouring buildings. Back in the day – in my old life – I'd still have had hours of work to get through before I could even think of making my way home. I'd be coming out of a meeting, possibly, or painstakingly trying to make sense of a contract one of the senior associates had drafted, or sitting across the desk from Gordon while he patiently explained some arcane point of copyright law.

Gordon. There on the pavement in front of me was a man in a suit, tall and confident, with coarse, wavy grey hair receding from his forehead in a widow's peak. He was walking fast towards me, his legs scissoring underneath him, his shoulders slightly hunched as if he was walking into a cold wind, his phone clamped to his ear. Although he was several yards away, I was sure I could smell the spicy rosewood aftershave he wore.

I froze. Gordon lived miles away. There was no reason for him to be here. But he was, and there was nowhere for me to hide.

He strode towards me, but it was like he hadn't seen me or recognised me at all. And as he grew closer, I realised I'd been wrong. It wasn't Gordon at all – just another middle-aged man in a suit with a weirdly uncoordinated gait, like he was on stilts. Just a stranger.

As he passed me, I realised the smell hadn't been real either – only my imagination. But instead of relief washing over me, the strangest thing happened. I felt as if a tight band was pressing around my chest – like when you wear a new bra for the first time, and when you put it on in the morning you're all good, but by lunchtime you start to feel the underwires digging into your ribs, and once you've noticed you can't stop noticing it, however many times you try to adjust it, and by the time you get home you're in agony and rip the horrible thing off without even taking off your top.

Except this had happened all of a sudden, and the constriction I felt was way, way tighter than any bra. It was so tight I wasn't sure I'd be able to get the next breath into my lungs. My heart was pounding and my head was spinning. Black spots were swimming in front of my eyes. I wanted to run, to get home as fast as I possibly could, but somehow my legs wouldn't do that – and anyway, the blood was thumping in my head so hard I worried I'd pass out from lack of oxygen if I tried to hurry.

I veered to the side of the pavement and leaned against the nearest shop window, trying to steady my breathing, to slow down my heart, to shake off the awful sense of dread that was hovering over me like a thundercloud, even though the sky above was clear and blue. My knees felt like they might buckle under the weight of my body, but I was sure that if I let them I'd fall down and never be able to get up again.

I felt a hand on my shoulder and heard a voice call my name, and the urge to run kicked in again, even stronger, But I couldn't move – I was frozen into a solid lump like a bag of peas left in the freezer for too long.

'Alice!' the voice came again, as if from a long, long way away. 'Are you okay?'

Somehow, I managed to turn my head, and saw a man's worried face, leaning in close to me. The black dots cleared for long enough for me to recognise Archie.

'I'm fine,' I managed to gasp, although I didn't believe it myself and I didn't expect him to either.

'Here.' He put a hand under my elbow and gently steered me in through the door. It was his shop, I realised – I'd barely made it ten yards down the street before this – thing – had happened. 'Do you need a doctor?'

I shook my head, and the black specks danced wildly before retreating to the edges of my vision.

'Glass of water?' He passed me a tumbler dripping with condensation, and I took a grateful gulp, then held it in my mouth, waiting until I was sure my throat would let the liquid through.

'Thank you,' I said, once it was safely swallowed.

The constriction round my chest seemed to have loosened a bit; I felt limp with tiredness and relief, the way you do when something you've been dreading is over, or hasn't happened at all. Like when you run across a road away from a safe crossing, thinking you can make it just before the approaching double-decker bus reaches you, but then a cyclist appears in your path and there are a few terrifying seconds when one or both of them could mow you down – but somehow, with a blare of the bus's horn and a furious shout from the cyclist, you're there, on the opposite pavement, in one piece.

Archie had let go of my arm, but his hand still hovered under my elbow as he guided me towards a wooden bench that looked like it must have started life as a church pew.

'I did a first-aid course years ago,' Archie was saying. 'But I can hardly remember any of it. You're not having a seizure, are you?'

I shook my head. The swarm of specks had retreated.

'No chest pain?'

The clamp that had gripped so tightly below my breasts had released, so I could breathe normally again.

'I don't think so.'

'You're not diabetic?'

'Nope.'

'Had a shock?'

'I'm not sure. Not that, but it kind of felt that way. Like, just a normal day, then I was freaking out.'

'Have you eaten anything today?'

I opened my mouth to say I wasn't sure, then remembered the half a brie and tomato baguette I'd had at lunchtime and nodded.

'In that case, although I know sweet tea is usually considered more appropriate, I think I can risk giving you a drink. Gin?'

I looked at the rack of bottles behind the marble bar top. They were all colours and shapes: some like bells, some square, some so tall they towered like supermodels over their companions.

'Yes, please.'

'Any particular kind?'

I shook my head. 'You choose. I've got no idea.'

He looked at the bottles for a second, then poured some bright pink liquid into a cut-glass tumbler and added an ice cube.

'Rhubarb,' he said. 'It's made by the wife of the guy who grows it up in Yorkshire. There's quite a bit of sugar in it, so that's belt and braces, I reckon.'

I took a sip, a burst of sweet-and-sour liquid filling my mouth, the alcohol warming my throat and making me feel immediately better. I was reminded of Maurice buying me a sherry, back when the Nag's Head was still just a run-down neighbourhood pub to me. It had been just a few weeks ago, but it felt like a lifetime ago.

'Better?' Archie asked.

'Much. I'm really sorry, I don't know what came over me there. It was horrible.'

I glanced around the shop, admiring the fridges full of bottles of beer with colourful, quirky labels; the rack of bottles behind the counter; the polished parquet floor, glowing where the street lamp outside shone through the glass front of the shop; the framed posters of local landmarks, painted or maybe Photoshopped into pop-art style, hanging on the walls.

It was all gorgeous, and looking around meant I didn't have to look at Archie himself, which was a relief. For no reason at all, I felt like if I met his eyes I might start to blush.

'Wow. You've made the place look amazing. And you got it all done so quickly.'

'It was pretty easy really. I started with a blank canvas – the landlord had already ripped everything out. He had to – it was a carpet shop before and totally infested with moths, so he had to get fumigators in. A mate of mine laid the floor and I did the plastering. It's not that hard; I watched a couple of videos on YouTube, fucked up the first few bits and then I got the hang of it.'

I ran my hand over the wall closest to me. It was unpainted, the raw plaster a kind of pale ochre, and satiny to the touch. Archie reached out and stroked it too, and for a second our hands were right there next to each other, resting on a surface as warm and smooth as skin.

'I love this,' he said. 'It's my favourite bit.'

Again, I felt that weird shift inside me. *If it wasn't for Joe, I could really fancy him.*

'Wow,' I said again, trying to bring my mind back to safer territory. 'I wish I knew how to do stuff like that. The Nag's Head desperately needs a facelift, but I've got no idea where to begin.'

'Anything I can do to help, just shout. I'm right next door, after all. And Uncle Ray's got mates who know all kinds of trades. All the businesses along here look out for one another – the barber next door cuts my hair in exchange for a few beers, and these are from the florist on the corner.'

He gestured to the vase of fleshy, cream-coloured lilies on the counter. He had nice hands, I noticed, with long fingers and neatly clipped nails. There was a watch on his left wrist that looked vintage, but he wasn't wearing any rings.

'Thanks,' I said. 'For the drink, and for rescuing me – again. You mustn't make a habit of it.'

'I think it's you who's making a habit of needing to be rescued.'

I laughed. 'Sorry about that. I'm not normally the damsel in distress type.'

'I don't know.' He looked at me for a long moment, his head tilted to one side. 'Aren't damsels meant to be blonde and blue-eyed and beautiful? I'd say you're the exact type.'

Shit. Shit, he's flirting with me. But instead of shutting him down, I heard myself say, 'I'm not sure knights in shining armour normally come to the rescue with artisan gin. But maybe they should.'

'Exactly. Watch and learn, Sir Galahad.'

Our eyes met and he smiled that beguiling, cheeky smile. I opened my mouth to make some quip about how he ought to have a white horse, not a white van – but then common sense prevailed. I had a boyfriend. I had no business flirting with Archie, beguiling or not.

'I should get home. Thanks, Archie.'

'Take care, Alice. I'll see you around soon, I'm sure.'

I was sure too. But we said goodbye without so much as a handshake. So that made it totally okay, didn't it?

I pulled my phone out of my bag as I hurried down the street towards home. Joe wouldn't be back yet, but he might have been trying to get hold of me to let me know when to expect him, and worried when he hadn't been able to. But instead of the single missed call and brief text I expected – *Hey you! Hope you're ok. Home nineish xx* – I had a whole slew of messages and six missed calls.

Well, I was just a few doors away from the flat; there was no point checking them now. I'd sit down on the sofa and pour myself a cup of tea, or maybe have a bath – even though the evening wasn't especially cold, I was still feeling out of sorts and a bit shivery – and read and reply to them then.

I let myself wonder what had actually happened to me, back there outside the pub. But already I could barely remember the feeling I'd had – the constriction around my chest, the dizzy feeling of fear that had made my head lurch and the soles of my feet tingle like I was standing on a high diving board, waiting for the courage to jump – and the memory was already fading. I'd thought of something, remembered something, and it had made me feel ill. But not a normal kind of ill – a strange, frightening sensation I'd never experienced before.

Now, though, I felt almost normal again. Probably Archie, with the benefit of his long-ago first-aid training, had been right and I'd just needed a nip of gin to sort me out after a hard day of physical work and not enough food. So I wasn't going to worry. The last thing my overstretched GP's surgery needed was for me to turn up, in two weeks or whenever I could get an appointment, and say I'd had a funny turn for no reason I could recall, with symptoms I'd struggle to describe, which had lasted just a few minutes.

Fitting my key into the lock, I resolved to put it out of my mind and hope nothing like it ever happened to me again.

As I'd expected, the flat was empty and silent. I put down my keys and bag and walked through to the kitchen. But before I got there, I realised that the door to the garden was open, and I could see the glow of a fire and hear voices and a burst of laughter.

Zoë. She must have finished her dominoes lesson and come back here with someone. A guy? She was single, as far as I knew. So maybe she'd met someone new and brought him back for a drink. The idea of Zoë with a boyfriend – a boyfriend, crucially, who wasn't Joe – suddenly struck me as quite a good thing.

Then I heard another burst of laughter and realised that the man's voice was familiar.

My glass of water forgotten, I stepped out into the garden.

When Joe and I had first moved into the flat, we'd been giddy with excited plans. We had a new home! We were living together! Him and me, like a proper grown-up couple! We'd have dinner parties, and drinks parties (whatever those were – surely every party worth having involved drinks?), brunches and barbecues. We'd get to know the neighbours and have street parties. We'd buy chic little pieces of art at markets and upcycle furniture from charity shops. We'd plant pots of herbs and geraniums and climbing roses in the little square of garden.

Which was all very well, except we'd realised quite quickly that come the weekends we were generally both too knackered to even think about any of that stuff, and the few things we'd planted in our initial bursts of enthusiasm had died, gone to seed, or – in the case of one particularly determined green-and-yellow-leafed shrub – taken on a life of their own and flourished in spite of our neglect.

So the garden, in the middle of autumn, was anything but a shady bower of bliss. The patch of lawn was mostly bare earth, carpeted with leaves that had fallen from the neighbour's huge birch tree. The wooden picnic table we'd bought at Argos, assembled hastily and never got around to varnishing, was bleached grey by the sun and jagged with splinters.

And now, at that table, saucepan of mulled wine and two glasses between them, were Zoë and my brother Drew. Oh, and Frazzle, who was lazing in the centre of the table, paws in the air, his belly stretched out towards the glowing heat of the fire they'd lit in our barbecue.

'Alice!' Drew swung his long legs out from under the table, stood up, stretched and came over to hug me. 'Sorry to barge in. I tried calling you, and when you didn't answer I rang Joe, but that went to voicemail too, so I dropped in at the Nag's Head and Zoë took pity on me and brought me back here.'

He turned and gave Zoë the benefit of his megawatt smile.

'We were thinking we might roast some potatoes in the coals,' she said. 'Or maybe just order in a curry.'

'Let me get you a glass,' Drew said. 'Oh, wait, you've got one already.'

I realised I was still holding the tumbler I'd picked up from the rack by the sink and not got around to filling with water. Hesitantly, feeling almost as if I was intruding, I took a seat on the side of the table where Drew had been, and Zoë filled my glass with ruby-coloured liquid, fragrant with orange and cinnamon.

'I'll stick it back on the stove to warm up a bit,' she said, reaching for the pan. 'Drew brought a couple of bottles of red and I had some cider brandy hanging around so we added some of that too. I'm two glasses down and I'm already shitfaced.'

She headed, slightly unsteadily, back inside.

'So what…?' I began.

'What the hell am I doing here?' Drew grinned, lighting a cigarette. 'I thought I'd drop in, since it was so successful when I did that on your birthday. And since we're going to be neighbours for a while, you're going to have to get used it.'

'Neighbours?'

'Didn't Mum and Dad tell you?'

It was typical of my brother that, rather than communicating his news to me himself or sharing it on social media like everyone else, he expected our parents to provide me with regular bulletins about his life.

I shook my head.

'So my mate Lauren – you know, I met her in Vietnam a couple of years back – just got offered a part in a movie, and she flew out to LA yesterday. It's not a starring role or anything like that but she's pretty excited, and it's not like she needs the money;

her family's minted. Anyway, her parents just bought her a flat in that new development up the road – you know, the one with the studio apartments and the communal living space that's run by that start-up guy?'

'That used to be our local pub.'

'Did it? It's a bit of a shithole if I'm honest. It's been thrown up in a massive hurry. The heating's dodgy as fuck, the walls are so thin I swear I can hear when the neighbour's on Pornhub – which I guess could be a selling point, if you were skint enough for an audio-only wank – and there's not enough space to swing this dude.' He stroked Frazzle's tummy and the cat writhed with pleasure. 'Anyway, Lauren's seriously into bonsai and she's got all these trees that needed looking after. So that's where I came in.'

If I was seriously into bonsai, I thought, *Drew would be the last person I'd entrust with my precious plants.* By the time Lauren got back from California, I was willing to bet all her trees would either be dead or have taken over the tiny apartment, like some kind of urban rainforest.

'And to be honest,' Drew carried on, 'I needed a place to live, because I've been driving Mum and Dad spare. I was going to ask if I could stay with you guys for a bit, but now I won't have to, which is just as well because it looks like there'd be no room at the inn.'

He gave a sidelong glance at Zoë, who'd reappeared with the full pan of mulled wine. There was no chance to explain to him how she'd come to be living with us – or confide in him about my deep misgivings about the situation.

'I was just telling Drew about the pub,' Zoë said. 'And how you're basically running it at the moment, while Shirley's off.'

'It sounds dead cool,' Drew was saying, taking a deep draught of wine; although when I tasted mine it was so strong I almost choked. 'Place like that, there's so much potential. You could have games nights and live music and life drawing and bingo and all sorts.'

'Bingo? Have we entered a time warp and ended up in Blackpool in the 1960s?'

'On the contrary,' Drew said. 'Bingo's enjoying a massive resurgence among young people. It's one of the most popular online games, and now it's become massively on trend in bricks and mortar venues too.'

'I should be taking notes,' I replied, hoping I didn't sound as dull as I suspected. It occurred to me – not for the first time – that there could hardly be a person in the entire world with their finger less on the pulse of what was on trend than me. Hell, up until a few weeks ago my idea of a happening night out had been a few glasses of rosé with a group of my suited and high-heeled colleagues in a City bar.

'You don't need notes,' Drew said. 'You need me. Haven't I worked in bars all over the world? Haven't I slung out drunk sheep farmers at closing time in the Outback? Didn't I persuade a bunch of Hells Angels in Stockholm that three in the morning was about time for them to go home to their wives for a nice cup of tea?'

'Obviously you're the Gandhi of the pub world,' I said. 'But we don't need big ideas like that right now. We just need to keep the place ticking over and hope the rats in the cellar don't take over.'

'Frazzle would sort them right out, wouldn't you, my little furry psychopath?' Zoë scratched her cat behind the ears and he purred thunderously, looking about as unlike a cold-blooded killer as you could possibly get.

'But I can help with that, too,' Drew insisted. 'Not the rats, obviously, but keeping it ticking over. Go on, admit it – you could do with some extra help. I can build a website for the place, promote it a bit, work behind the bar and carry heavy things. I've worked in a lot of bars, and there hasn't been a single one that couldn't do with extra help. And I'll do it for free – I'm between gigs at the moment. I've got a place to live – I don't need anything else. Just a project. It'll be fun.'

I looked at my big brother, leaning back on the shabby wooden bench, his hands behind his head. The fading light cast his perfect bone structure into sharp relief, and I could see the muscles of his chest and abs beneath his grey sweatshirt. He was infuriating, and I loved him to pieces. I often worried whether he felt bored and frustrated by his aimless life – even though he seemed to have acquired so many useful skills during it.

But then another thought struck me. Drew was Drew. Drew was irresistible to women. Zoë was single. If the two of them spent some time together – and it would be loads of time, if they were both working in the pub – wouldn't Drew be the perfect person to help Zoë get over Joe?

'You know, you might be on to something there,' I said.

Chapter Sixteen

Drew was as good as his word. Next morning, shortly after I opened the doors of the Nag's Head, I saw him strolling across the road from the former Star and Garter, which had now been snazzily rebranded Garter Apartments. He spent the whole morning in a whirlwind of activity: taking out the heavy bags of bottles to the recycling bin, hoovering the carpet, mopping the floors in the bathrooms, even helping Zoë change the grease filter in the kitchen extractor.

But I knew my brother, and I knew he'd get bored with the heavy lifting before long and move on to bigger ideas. Sure enough, by lunchtime, he was sitting at a table with his laptop, beginning the design of a new website for the Nag's Head. Then he created a slew of social-media accounts for the pub. Then he went out for a fag. Then he suggested that he and Zoë head off on a fact-finding mission to Borough Market, to check out street-food ideas for the new menu.

And the next day, he came to work bearing an armful of brightly coloured boxes.

'Board games. I picked them up at a charity shop – twenty quid for the lot. And they're almost new. Bang on trend right now – you watch, the punters will love them.'

He spread them out on a table for us to admire. There were some I recognised, like Monopoly, Cluedo and Risk, but loads of others I'd never heard of – Cosmic Encounter, Photosynthesis and, in a box so old it was practically falling apart, a pirate-themed game called Buccaneer. And then Drew spent the rest of the morning huddled over them trying to figure out the rules.

'If I'm going to compère the Nag's Head's inaugural games marathon, I have to know my stuff,' he said.

'Games marathon? It's the first I've heard of it.'

'You should follow your own pub on Instagram then, Alice. It's two weeks this Saturday.'

'Hey, is that Dungeons & Dragons you've got there?' Zoë asked, hovering over his shoulder. 'I've been wanting to play ever since I watched *Stranger Things*, but I can't find anyone who's interested.'

'It almost needs a separate event of its own, I reckon,' Drew said. 'It's well complicated. Look at all the cool dice.'

'Wow.' Zoë picked up a multi-sided translucent blue shape and examined it. 'What does this do then?'

'You use them for combat situations, I think. And to figure out your character's attributes. But we really need someone who knows what they're doing to be our Dungeon Master.'

'Project for another day, maybe?' I said from behind the bar, where I was serving a group of guys who were gasping for refreshment and sandwiches between their morning workout and going home to get some sleep before their night shift.

'What? Oh, yeah, maybe.' Taking the hint, my brother came over to help me behind the bar, where he managed to remain for most of the rest of the day, only occasionally drifting over to his laptop or to look longingly at the shelf of board games.

There was no doubt he was an asset, when he could manage to avoid distraction. Having someone I could chat to and confide in was a massive relief. And the customers absolutely adored him. The group of mums and babies had swelled to around a dozen; the mothers became positively skittish when Drew brought over their cappuccinos and smoothies, even the babies going into fits of gurgles and giggles when he blew raspberries at them.

And, crucially, the next Friday, his presence meant that I could take a much-needed evening off, leaving him and Kelly in charge. Not that I'd planned to. I was out of sight behind the bar, kneeling to check the stock of cold drinks in the fridges, when I heard him call out, 'Gentleman here to see you, Alice.'

I stood up, wondering who on earth could have rocked up here to see me at six on a Friday evening. Then I saw Joe and felt my face break into an enormous grin. It had been at least three days, I realised, since we'd actually seen each other properly. Sure, we'd slept together – but only slept, since most nights I'd already been in bed when he'd got in from the office at gone ten – and we'd dodged around each other and Zoë in the mornings while he got ready for work. We hadn't had a chance to talk properly, to connect.

And now here he was. And he'd brought me shoes.

Now, let me explain. I'm not some Paris-Hilton-style diva with a pair of Manolos for every day of the year (although don't get me wrong, a girl can dream). But it had become a thing with Joe and me. Kind of an ironic, joke thing, but lovely too. It started on that awful morning two years ago, six weeks into my training contract at Billings Pitt Furzedown, when I'd come into the office so broken by my hangover and the Fear that I'd put on shoes that didn't match. In the lift on the way up to our respective floors, I saw Joe look at me, give a half-smile, then look down at my feet. When I got out at my floor, he got out too and pulled me aside.

'Hey, Joe.' I'd been able to remember his name, but only just. That morning, I could barely remember my own.

'It's Alice, isn't it?'

'That's me.'

'Sorry to bother you, but I couldn't help noticing... It might be a fashion thing, or something, but do you know you're wearing odd shoes?'

'What's odd about them?' I asked crossly. Normally, of course, I wouldn't have snapped at a colleague, especially one I hardly knew, especially only weeks into a new job. But that morning, I wasn't exactly myself.

'Nothing. I mean, not on their own. But...' Joe looked pointedly down at my feet, and I looked too.

'Oh fuck.'

'I thought it might just have been the light in the elevator, but it's not, is it?'

'No. Shit. One's black and one's navy and the toes aren't even the same shape. I wondered why I was walking with a limp, but I thought it was just...'

'One of those mornings?'

'Something like that. I had a bit of a heavy night.' I felt a huge rush of blood to my face and a corresponding rush of sickness in my stomach, and I wished, not for the first time that morning, that I could run away from Billings Pitt Furzedown and never come back.

He winced sympathetically. 'Ouch. Have you got a busy morning?'

I shook my head. It was only the knowledge that Gordon would be out until almost lunchtime, and my earliest meeting was at eleven, that had stopped me chucking a career-limiting sickie.

'Okay. Go to your desk and lie low. If anyone asks you to make coffee, say you're about to go into a conference call. I've got this.'

He turned back towards the lift, then glanced back at me over his shoulder.

'Size?'

'Five. Thank you!'

Having clear instructions made me feel a whole lot better. I pushed open the door to the IP office and strolled as naturally as I could towards my place, which, fortunately, was in the first bank of desks. Getting my feet under my desk and out of sight was the best thing that had happened to me that morning.

I switched on my computer and turned my burning eyes to the document I'd been reading the previous evening, trying to make sense of the words, wishing my head would stop throbbing. Would Joe call my extension, forcing me to go all the way back to the lobby, or – worse still – up to the floor where he worked, before doing another humiliating walk of shame back to somewhere I could do my shoe-swap discreetly?

But I needn't have worried.

Less than half an hour later, Joe strolled in, as relaxed as if he was walking from his kitchen to his sofa with a cup of tea. He was carrying a photocopier-paper box with a lever-arch file perched precariously on top.

'Reception asked me to bring these up,' he said. 'They're for Gordon, apparently. Do you mind looking after them?'

It was such a normal, innocuous request that even Rupert barely glanced up from his screen.

'Sure,' I said, trying to sound normal too.

'I'll just…' Joe squatted down, and I inched my chair aside while he slipped the box under my desk.

'Thank you,' I said.

'Any time.'

Once I was sure my colleagues had lost whatever interest they'd had in this temporary diversion, I pushed my chair back again and investigated the box. The file was empty. Beneath it was a pair of beige suede court shoes, their tags still attached, a sausage and egg McMuffin, a can of Coke and a box of paracetamol.

I reached for the tablets first, and noticed that there was writing on the box – a hasty Biro scrawl. *If you ever want to drink again, any chance of a sneaky pint with me? Joe x*

That was how it all started, him and me.

Since then, on any occasion when another boyfriend might buy flowers – our anniversary, my birthday, the day I got the job offer from Gordon – Joe bought me shoes. Not fancy ones; after the first time we slept together, for instance, he'd given me a pair of fluffy slippers with little sheep's faces on them, which I'd worn until they literally fell apart. But it was our thing.

And now, here he was, holding a Nike box out to me like it was a bunch of roses.

'I've come to take you out for dinner,' he said. 'I knocked off work early.'

I flung my arms around him, pulling him into a hug so tight the hard corners of the box dug painfully into my breasts.

'Oh my God, this is just the best surprise.'

'You haven't even looked at them yet.'

'Not the trainers, doofus! You. I just wish I was…'

I looked down at my navy and white Breton top and faded jeans. I wasn't exactly scruffy – the pub was a workplace, after all – but I wasn't date-ready, either.

'I've booked that new place down the road for seven thirty,' Joe said, as if he'd read my mind. 'What's it called? Fire and Knives. So there's time for you to go home and shower and change, if you like.'

I dithered for a second. 'I don't know… I really ought to…'

'Alice!' Drew called over from behind the bar. 'Get out of here! Enjoy your night off! Kelly and I have everything under control.'

'Are you sure?'

'Course I'm sure. Now get your skates on, before we change our minds.'

I didn't need telling again. Ten minutes later, Joe and I were back in the flat, alone together for the first time in what felt like ages – probably because it *was* the first time in ages.

Even Joe's birthday, two weeks before, which I'd prepared for by putting on my best lacy underwear, cooking a beef Wellington for the first (and probably only) time in my life, and laying the table with champagne and candles, had been interrupted by Zoë. Just as we'd been sitting down to eat, she'd turned up with a cake she'd baked in the pub kitchen, complete with twenty-seven candles, and a gift for

Joe of *Red Dead Redemption 2*, and I'd had to pretend that I didn't mind at all if she joined our dinner, although she fed all her beef to Frazzle. And then afterwards Joe had said he'd just check out the game quickly, Zoë had joined him on the sofa and I'd gone to bed alone in my sexy underwear, falling asleep long before Joe joined me.

But there was no point feeling resentful about that now.

'Right, let me jump in the shower quickly,' I said.

'No need to be quick – there's masses of time. Want me to come in and wash your back?'

'That's an offer I can't refuse.'

We smiled at each other for a second, and I felt a lovely surge of desire inside me – a switch being turned on that had been off for far too long. And, to my relief, it was untainted by any thought of Zoë.

So we squeezed into the too-small shower cubicle together and took it in turns standing under the too-weak trickle of water, and I got shampoo in my eyes and hoped Joe hadn't noticed that it had been several days since I'd last shaved my legs, and I wasn't going to be able to now, obviously, with him there. But if he did, he didn't say anything; he just ran his strong, soapy hands all over me, his slippery caresses making me gasp with pleasure.

Half-wrapped in towels, we pulled each other to the bedroom and fell onto the bed, our hard, urgent kisses turning into hard, urgent sex that lasted only a few minutes – not that I was timing it, or could have cared less about anything except the bliss of him close to me, inside me, there with me.

'Oh my God,' I gasped, when we were lying together afterwards, the last of the water from the shower drying on my skin with our sweat. 'You're the best.'

'I'm out of practice. I've had ready meals that took longer than I did back there.'

'That was better than any ready meal I've ever had.'

'You're only saying that because it's been so long you're forgotten our normal high standards.'

'Possibly.' I squeezed his hand. 'Right. Let me get ready. How long have we got?'

'About twenty minutes.'

'Shit!'

There was no time to dry my hair, so I bundled it up with a clip. I did my make-up as quickly as I could, then stood in front of the wardrobe feeling something like panic. I had, I realised, almost forgotten what to wear on a date, what would make Joe look at me and go, 'Phwoar.'

I pulled on a pair of coated black skinny jeans that I hadn't worn for ages because they were too tight, only to find that they were now slightly baggy around the waist and hips. Being on my feet all day wasn't just going to mean I'd end up with the varicose veins and arthritic knees Shirley complained about – it had apparently made my curves vanish. I added a draped silk cowl-neck top, which was a bit OTT for a casual dinner, but seemed like my only option, and earrings with black tassels, and then turned to Joe.

'Phwoar,' he said. 'Aren't you going to check out your new shoes?'

'Of course! You distracted me from the most important thing.'

I retrieved the box from the hallway and opened it. The trainers were metallic gold, with a chunky sole, a limited edition I'd been coveting for ages. They were pure, fabulous bling, and I knew Joe didn't get them at all. He'd bought them purely because they were comfortable and they'd make me happy.

'I thought they'd do for work,' Joe said.

'They're perfect. Just totally gorgeous. I love them, and I love you.'

'Come on then, get your coat or they'll give our table away. Fire and Knives is seriously happening right now, I'm told – almost as much as the Nag's Head.'

I laughed and we hurried out into the street, holding hands, full of giddy expectation of a rare and precious evening on our own together.

The restaurant was lit by bare filament bulbs in sconces on its face-brick wall, and the banquette our waitress showed us to was squashy teal leather. Bright paintings hung on the walls, each with a little plaque saying which local artist's work it was and listing a price. We were brought menus printed on stiff card with the date at the top, water and fresh brown bread with what the waitress said was chicken-skin butter.

'Wow,' I said. 'This place is seriously posh.'

'Seriously,' Joe agreed, grinning with pleasure. 'Maria and I took a client out for lunch yesterday, to Brigadiers, which is pretty snazzy. But I'd much rather be here with you.'

I studied the menu. 'What do you suppose ticklemore is?'

'I reckon it's a cheese. Although I could tickle you more, if you want.'

'And delicata?'

'Some sort of pumpkin, I think.'

'Posh squash,' I said. 'You should bring Zoë here – she'd know what all the things are.'

I looked at Joe across the table, but there was no flicker of emotion in his face when I said her name; nothing to fan the spark of insecurity that Zoë's arrival had ignited in me, which the passing weeks had almost, but not quite, managed to extinguish.

We ordered two glasses of champagne and – unable to decide from a menu on which everything sounded delicious – a whole bunch of starters and side dishes to share, so we could try as many things as possible.

'Small plates,' I said. 'Zoë says they're a massive thing in restaurants right now.'

There it was again – Zoë. It was as if she was sitting next to me on the leather banquette, her copper-coloured ringlets tickling my bare arm, reaching over to drink from my glass. Possibly even playing footsie under the table with my boyfriend.

Don't be paranoid, Alice! I chastised myself. *Come on! You're having a lovely romantic evening – enjoy it for heaven's sake!*

'Don't know so much about small,' Joe said, as a bowl of steaming, golden risotto, heady with the fragrance of truffles, appeared on the table in front of us. 'This looks amazing, and there's loads.'

We both dived in with our spoons and gave identical sighs of appreciation – it was buttery and light, exotic and comforting, all at once.

'So, what made you decide to take me out tonight?' I asked. 'I mean, it's amazing and everything, but it's not like it's a special occasion. Is it?'

Joe shrugged, smiling. 'Not exactly. The case I was working on finished early today – our side won – and I was in the office until midnight last night, so I figured I could get away with skiving off and spending some time with my favourite person.'

'I'm glad you did,' I said. 'I've missed you.'

'Me too. It's been hard, hasn't it? I mean, it would be hard anyway, if we were both still at Billings, but at least we'd see each other in the lift sometimes. Have a sneaky shag in an empty meeting room.'

'Joe! Oh my God, just thinking about that makes me cringe. How would you not get caught?'

Joe grimaced. 'Rupert's having a thing with one of the associates in the property department. They've never actually been caught, but everyone knows about it anyway.'

Intrigued, I begged him for more details, and Joe, being Joe, provided them, exaggerating to make me laugh.

'Imagine shagging Rupert, though. He's so fucking superior. He'd literally be looking down his nose at you the whole time.'

More food arrived, and Joe ordered a bottle of Malbec. We clinked our glasses and I sipped the rich, velvety red wine, beginning to feel pleasantly floaty from food, alcohol and the comfortable familiarity of being with him.

'Anyway, so I was wondering,' he said, 'when you're going to make a decision about what to do next.'

'What do you mean?'

'The pub thing. It was only meant to be for a bit, right? Just so we could keep things together financially.'

'Yes, and we are, aren't we? With Shirley off, I'm working so many hours and she's paying me a manager's rate instead of just minimum wage. I'll be bringing in loads this month.'

I told him just how much.

'Alice, that's great. You know I said I'd support you, whatever you decided you wanted to do. But I'm just wondering how sustainable this really is, long term.'

'You mean you want me to stop? Get a "proper job"?'

'No, I don't mean that!'

'What do you mean, then?'

Joe paused. It felt like our evening was at a tipping point – it could either go back to being right, or segue into horribly, horribly wrong. I knew neither of us wanted it to go in that direction – but still, wrong was there, hovering right above the table, over the dish of mussels in an aromatic Thai-style broth, waiting to descend and turn everything sour.

'It's just...' he said. 'Just that, remember, when we talked back in August, it was like our future was all sorted. We knew where we were going. And now everything feels so uncertain, so temporary and kind of – flimsy.'

I did remember. I remembered all too well that night in the Nag's Head, with my gin and tonic and our pork scratchings, how safe and secure and certain I'd felt. And then all that had been torn away from us.

My guilt made me defensive.

'So exactly what am I supposed to have done differently?'

'Alice, it's not for me to tell you what you ought to have done. We're a team, remember? I said I was on your side, I'd support you in whatever choices you made. But this choice – well, it just doesn't seem to be going anywhere. You're working in a pub. I mean, it's great, I'm proud you're doing it and everything. But isn't it kind of... studenty?'

'So you *are* saying I need to grow up and get proper job? Like you. Like being a lawyer.'

'You could, you know. You could walk into a job next week, if you wanted to.'

'And what if I don't want to? What if I've actually – for the first time in ages – found something I actually enjoy doing?'

Joe's face softened. 'I love that you're passionate about it. Really, I do. I love that you're having fun. But it's crazy, working all those hours, for… You know.'

'For about a quarter of what you're earning working "all those hours".'

'It's not about the money, Alice.'

'Really? Then what is it about?'

The mussels were growing cold in their bowl, ignored by both of us, and I took another big gulp of red wine.

'It's about our future,' Joe said, with an intensity that was almost despairing. 'I thought we'd be buying a place of our own in a couple of years. I thought maybe we could – you know – settle down. I know I sound like the most boring person in the world, but I thought we'd maybe get married. Have kids.'

Those words, three months ago, would have made me feel like I was looking at a winning lottery ticket. Now, all I felt was a horrible surge of guilt, and it made me leap straight into defensive mode.

'Well, I've let you down, haven't I? Sorry about that. I guess you'd rather I spent the whole rest of my life in a job I hated, so we could have a *future*.'

And that was that. Wrong had entered the building. To be fair to Joe, he did try to make it right again.

'I didn't realise you hated it.'

Neither did I. Not at first. 'Well, I did. I hated it so much even having your ex-bloody-girlfriend move in with us was worth it, so I could get out. Okay?'

'Don't make this about Zoë, Alice.'

'Why not? I have to see her every damn day. You two were in love. For all I know you still are.' The words were out of my mouth before I could stop them.

Joe's face went all kind of still, like steel shutters had been pulled down in front of his eyes – or behind them.

'What the hell do you mean?'

'I think she wants to get back together with you. I don't think she cares about me – about us. I think she moved in with us so she could be close to you. Playing video games with you, prancing around the flat in her underwear – or your underwear. I found a pair of boxer shorts in her washing that I think used to be yours, and I—'

'You what? You've been going through her stuff?'

'No! Of course I haven't!' *Except when I did.* 'They were in the washing machine.'

'Jesus, Alice. Do you know what you sound like?'

'If you mean I sound like someone whose boyfriend's ex has been hanging around him like a lovesick teenager, then yes, I guess I do.'

'You sound crazy, Alice. Crazy and jealous and… and obsessed. This isn't the person I thought you were.'

It's not the person I thought I was, either, I realised miserably. I'd been secure in my relationship with Joe, happy and contented and sure that everything was all right, until Zoë turned up. And now he was looking at me as if I was a stranger – someone he barely knew and didn't particularly like.

Desperately, I said, 'I just don't trust her, Joe. And this whole situation – sometimes it makes me wonder if I can trust you.'

'If you're wondering that, then there's no point having this conversation, is there? Or any conversation, about anything, ever again. If you don't trust me, then we don't have a relationship at all. Do we?'

There was a pause, and we both looked at each other, aghast. I knew Joe was thinking the same thing I was: *What the fuck just happened?* Within the space of little more than an hour, we'd gone from having gorgeous, joyful sex to being locked in one of the worst rows we'd ever had. *The* worst, because before, all we'd really done was bicker about things like whose turn it was to take the bins out. And the horrible thing was, neither of us knew how to get out of it.

I stood up and made my way to the loo, where I stood in front of the mirror, washing my hands with patchouli-scented gel, staring at my wide, panicky eyes in the mirror and wondering what the hell to do. I was furious but also frightened. I wanted to make peace, but at the same time I wanted to say my piece. And, most of all, I wanted to understand what was actually going on.

If Joe resented my working at the Nag's Head, why hadn't he said so before? Why had he turned up with a gift of trainers that had cost north of a hundred pounds and taken me out for this extravagant meal?

And suddenly, in my wired brain, it seemed to click into place.

He wanted to finish with me, so that he could be with Zoë. But he wanted me to be the one who ended it, not him, so he could have a clear conscience, tell himself it had been my decision, nothing at all to do with him or with her.

But I wasn't going to play that way.

Returning to the table, I picked up my bag from the banquette and shrugged on my coat. I fished three twenty-pound notes from my purse and put them on the table.

'Joe, I can't discuss this right now. We're both upset. I'm going to leave now,' I said.

I walked out into the night, alone, regretting it even as I was doing it. But once I'd started, there was no way of turning back, sitting down again, trying to make things right.

And, as the cold air hit my face, I realised that I'd been remembering another night – one when leaving *would* have been the right thing to do.

'All right, darling?' Gordon asked when I returned to our table. 'I've ordered a bottle of Châteauneuf-du-Pape, and our scallops should be on their way any second.'

My napkin had been neatly folded again, I noticed, and the breadcrumbs I'd scattered on the tablecloth swept away. The greasy smear my butter knife had left was still there, though – I moved my wine glass to hide it, then took another gulp of champagne.

While we ate our starter – delicious, melting seafood on dollops of cauliflower puree so rich it was almost like a pudding and drizzled with an unfamiliar, pungent oil that I realised later on must have been truffle – Gordon asked me about my family.

'Dad's an estate agent – he has his own business – and Mum's a maths teacher, although she hasn't worked full-time since I was little. They live in Reading, and I've got a big brother, Drew, who's travelling at the moment. Well, he's been travelling for the past few years, on and off. He's Mum and Dad's favourite.'

'Really? With a beautiful, gifted daughter like you?'

I sipped my champagne, and as soon as I put the glass down it was filled again, with the last of the bottle.

'That's sweet of you to say. But Drew's the gifted one. He writes poetry and paints and stuff, and he's properly gorgeous. Girls love him.'

'And boys love you, surely? You must be fighting off admirers all the time.'

I shook my head. 'I'm single. I haven't had a proper boyfriend since uni. I mean, I'm on Tinder and I've been on a few dates and stuff. But I figure I should get my career sorted first and then worry about having a relationship. Heather – my flatmate – goes on dates all the time and she tells me all her horror stories.'

'Oh, do go on! I've been married for thirty years; when it comes to that sort of thing I couldn't be more behind the curve if I tried.'

So, reassured by Gordon's mention of his wife and emboldened by my first glass of red wine, which was in a totally different league from anything I'd ever tasted before, after several glasses of other alcoholic stuff, I regaled him with as many of Heather's favourite dating anecdotes as I could remember. I told him about Crisp Boy, whose idea of a romantic evening was sitting on a park bench with a bottle of Frosty Jack's and a bag of Cheetos, 'Like he was practising to be homeless,' as Heather had said. I described Triple-Denim Tim, who my friend had said she took one look at and wrote off as someone who must have got dressed in the dark, but then went through the ordeal of a two-hour date with just to be polite. I even told him about her horrific almost-shag with Knob-Cheese Nick, whose personal hygiene was not his strongest point. Gordon roared with laughter and, flattered, I carried on, even exaggerating Heather's stories for effect, basking in his attention, the wine and the tender, pink-centred lamb cutlets. He offered me some of his grouse to taste, passing the fork across the table for me to eat from.

'It's an acquired taste,' he warned.

'You know what, I actually think I might have just acquired it.'

'A sophisticated palate, to add to your talents,' he said.

'But come on, I've given you all the dating stories I've got. Tell me all the gossip about the people at work.'

Obligingly, he did – although with hindsight I realised that he left out anything that could actually incriminate anyone. He didn't name the woman who'd been fired when it was discovered that the healthful glass of tomato juice she drank at her desk every morning was actually a Bloody Mary. The senior partner who he said used to entertain colleagues and clients in strip clubs ('So there I was, with a stunning Russian girl's tits in my face, and all I wanted was to get home to my wife') had been retired for a decade. He claimed to have forgotten the name of the admin assistant who'd embezzled thousands of pounds to fund her scratch-card habit.

Still, I was agog and listened as attentively as he had to me, barely noticing that our food was finished and so was the red wine.

'Now, I think something light for pudding, and perhaps a splash of cognac, don't you?' he said.

I excused myself and went to the loo again, by which point I'd lost count of how many drinks I'd sunk, but this time when I looked in the mirror I thought I actually looked pretty damn hot, and I was sure no one noticed that I'd wandered into the men's by mistake. And when I got lost trying to find my way back to the dining room and one of the smiling staff had to show me the way, I was positive I styled it out just fine.

And Gordon – why had I ever been nervous about him inviting me out for a drink? Why had I been intimidated? He was lovely. So kind, so funny, so interested in what I had to say. So full of compliments about my work so far, my telephone manner, my looks. And there was surely nothing inappropriate about that – after all, he was a professional, a partner in the firm, and – of course – old enough to be my dad. Older than my dad, probably.

'This has just been such an amazing evening,' I said, sipping my cognac and taking a spoonful of crème brûlée. The cognac wasn't as nice as the wine had been, I thought – it was almost too alcoholic, burning my throat as I swallowed. But Gordon had been so generous, treating me to this amazing meal, which must have cost hundreds and hundreds of pounds and was easily the poshest I'd ever had. There was no way I was going to let on that I was completely full and beginning to feel dangerously drunk.

'It's my absolute pleasure.' He did another of those discreet signals and a waiter appeared at his side. 'Are you sure you wouldn't like anything else? Another brandy? Coffee?'

'Honestly, I couldn't possibly. It's all been delicious, thank you so much.'

'Just the bill then, please. And would you get a car for us?'

Us?

'I can quite easily get the Tube,' I protested.

'We can't have that,' Gordon said. 'It's late, and it's raining. I'd be failing in my duty of care if I left you to make your way home alone. I can easily drop you off in – Wembley, was it? – and go on home from there.'

'Well, if you're sure…' I was far from sure, but I also had a feeling that the homing instinct that got pissed people safely from clubs and pubs up and down the country back to their own beds might let me down on this occasion. I wasn't even sure I'd be able to find my way to the Tube.

Gordon paid the bill with a gold credit card, I thanked him yet again, and we stood up. I felt my knees buckle slightly, and he guided me out of the room with a firm hand on my elbow. One of the doormen produced his coat and briefcase and my bag, but I resisted the urge to check my phone.

The waiting car was black and sleek – a Mercedes, not a standard Uber or a black London taxi. One of the doormen opened the door for me – another first; no one had ever done that before – and I slid onto the cream-coloured seat, feeling like I was some kind of celeb and any second a bunch of paparazzi might jump out and try to upskirt me. The interior was warm and smelled comfortingly of new leather. It was raining, as Gordon had said – quite hard. How lucky I was, I thought, to be making the journey home in luxury rather than getting onto a crowded Tube with my face in someone's armpit or waiting for a night bus and ending up sat next to someone stuffing a lamb doner kebab into their face.

'What's your address, darling?'

'Twenty-five B Tunley Road.' Obedient as a child, I recited the postcode, and the driver entered it into the satnav.

As the car inched through the City traffic, busy even at this time of night, I leaned my head back and let my eyes close, lulled by the swishing of the windscreen wipers.

I must have fallen asleep – okay, passed out – almost straight away. For what felt like hours, I was aware of the pull of consciousness bringing me almost back to the surface, but not quite. I was so tired. Very, very tired. Also, I was starting to feel quite powerfully sick. It was better – safer – to drift in oblivion, to stay in the warm, still darkness for as long as I could.

At least, I suppose that's what must have been going on in my mind, if indeed anything was. I don't remember much about that journey at all. Only the thrum of the car's engine, the sweeping windscreen wipers and a phrase that I became aware of, repeating itself over and over in my head to their rhythm. It was like a dream, only I wasn't dreaming.

It was something I'd seen in the newspapers, in reports about some scandal involving politicians. A quaint phrase, one I'd never used or heard anyone say until I read it.

Handsy in taxis. Handsy in taxis. Handsy in taxis.

It meant something. It meant something to do with me – to do with what was happening.

My brain was still almost shut down, but I became aware of a new sensation. I was warm – too warm. I could feel hot breath on my neck, a body pressed up against mine. But my legs were cold. Cold, and somehow constricted. My skirt wasn't where it should be, nor my tights. And there was a hand touching me, caressing me through my knickers.

I froze – not that it mattered. I hadn't been moving anyway. I was as limp and unresponsive as a piece of warm meat. My befuddled, drunken brain managed to make sense of the situation.

He's groping me. More than groping. So much more.

I don't know why, but it seemed like the most important thing in the world not to open my eyes. If I did that, all this would be real – would actually be happening to me, and I'd have to do something about it. If I stayed very, very still, perhaps it would stop, or turn out to be only a dream. If I stayed silent, perhaps I'd be safe.

So I did. I kept my eyes closed, I breathed, I waited. I did nothing to stop him while his hand carried on.

And when the cab finally slowed, and the driver said, 'Number twenty-five B, was it?' Gordon stopped.

That was it. I felt him rearranging my clothing as best he could – pulling my pants back over where his hands had been, twanging my tights back over my waist, rucking down my skirt.

'Number twenty-five, yes, that's correct,' he said. 'Alice? We're here.'

And then, at last, I allowed myself to open my eyes. He'd moved across to the other side of the seat, but I could still feel the warm place on the leather where he'd been.

'Don't worry,' he said. 'I'll look after you.'

Chapter Seventeen

I'd never seen the Nag's Head so busy. We'd brought in extra tables and chairs, and all of them were full. The platters of sliders, sandos, sweet potato wedges and fake fried chicken were disappearing as fast as Zoë could turn them out of the kitchen. The four of us behind the bar were faced with a crowd three-people deep.

Drew was working the room, chatting and laughing, enjoying his moment of glory.

Not only had the games afternoon been his idea, but he'd taken to social media and promoted the hell out of it, Instagramming every new board game he purchased, running ads targeted to local users of Facebook, posting on Nextdoor and blogging furiously on the Nag's Head's own website.

It helped that it was a miserable November Saturday, heavy drizzle falling outside and the light almost gone, even though it was only mid-afternoon. I imagined the families and groups of twenty-somethings stepping out of their front door, thinking they might go for a walk or do the weekly shop or take their kids to play in the park, then passing the inviting, brightly lit windows of the pub and thinking, *Sod that, let's have a drink and a sit-down in the warm.*

There was mulled wine, mulled apple juice and hot chocolate with marshmallows floating on top for the children. There were regular Scotch eggs and a vegan version Zoë had come up with, as well as chopped-up raw veggies with hummus, which health-conscious parents were foisting on their children. There were strings of fairy lights festooned over the bar. Princess Diana was looking down on it all from her spot above the fireplace with an expression I thought was slightly bemused but not disapproving.

The pub was buzzing with conversation as people approached the shelves of board games, selecting their favourites, saying, 'Oh my God, remember this? We used to play this at Christmas when we were kids!' Around the tables, there was fierce concentration, bursts of laughter and occasional groans of despair. There was a table of poker players that included Fat Don, stacks of coloured chips in front of them, their faces impassive. There was a little crowd standing around Maurice and his friends as Ray patiently explained the rules of dominoes – which, no matter how often I watched their games, were still a total closed book to me.

And, most importantly of all, the tills were practically smoking with a level of activity I was fairly sure they hadn't seen in years. I hadn't sat down or taken a break for what felt like hours, but I didn't care – I'd never felt prouder of the pub, of the little team that had worked so hard, or of myself.

I turned to serve a waiting customer and stopped in my tracks. There was Shirley, wearing a leather mini skirt and a fluffy angora jumper, her fuchsia lipstick freshly applied and outsize gold hoops swinging from her ears.

'I was going to ask for a Bacardi and Coke, love,' she said. 'But it looks like you could use an extra body behind the bar.'

'That would be amazing! It's so good to see you. How's Juan?'

'He's back on his feet, and he'll be rid of the crutches soon,' she said. 'But I don't know when – or whether – he's going to want to come back to work. But since I'm here, I may as well see if I've forgotten how to pull a decent pint.'

I opened the hatch and Shirley stepped in, immediately swinging into action. I watched her gratefully for a couple of seconds, in awe of how she seemed to know by instinct which of the crowd waiting to be served had been there the longest, admiring the way she could recall even the most complicated order without having to ask whether that was regular or slimline tonic and a pint of London Pride or a half, amazed that she remembered the names of all the old regulars.

Over the past months, I thought I'd gone from totally incompetent to more or less knowing what I was doing, but Shirley was still in a league of her own.

While we worked, she quizzed me about the new website, the new chef, the new programme of events Drew had planned.

'This is the first games afternoon, obviously,' I explained. 'But we're planning to make it a regular thing. It brings in a more diverse group of people than just having the football on. But of course if you'd prefer to go back to doing that…'

'That bloody Sky Sports subscription costs a fortune,' she said. 'And nowadays most people have got it at home, so why would they come here? I reckon you're on to a good thing here, love.'

'I didn't want to take over…' I began.

'But I *asked* you to take over! If it hadn't been for you, I don't know what would have become of the place, with me off for so long waiting hand and foot on his nibs. And you've kept the kitchen going, and there's even a cocktail menu now, if I'm not mistaken.'

'Yes, well, we thought people would want that, you know. It's pretty basic but they do sell well.'

Shirley picked up a food menu from the bar and perused it. 'Brussels sprouts with nduja. Veggie haggis toastie. Spaghetti aglio e olio. Quinoa with sprouted grains. I don't know what half this stuff is when it's at home. If Juan put scampi in a basket on the menu we'd think we were practically The Ritz.'

'No, well,' I mixed a Manhattan and stirred it vigorously, 'I didn't either, if I'm honest. Zoë offered to help out in the kitchen and she seems to know what people like.'

'Personally, I'd rather have fish and chips,' Shirl said. 'But what can I say? It looks like I'm behind the times.'

She turned to take a food order.

'There are still some classic things on the menu,' I said.

'Like a burger,' Shirl sniffed. 'A burger served with lactic-fermented pickles. That sounds like something they'd have called the environmental health on you for, back in my day.'

I didn't mention that, when I'd seen the jars of pickles fermenting away on a shelf in the kitchen, I'd almost called the food safety inspectors myself, before Zoë explained what they were. I felt torn between loyalty to Shirley and a conviction that what I was doing was the right thing to make the pub thrive.

And there was another thing. Shirley was still, officially, in charge. If she didn't like what had happened on my watch, I'd be out on my ear. And that would leave me jobless and incomeless once more. And possibly boyfriendless. I pushed the horrible sense of impending crisis to the back of my mind and turned to Shirley again.

'Of course, now you're back, we can go back to the old menu,' I suggested. 'Juan could supervise, even if he's not up to working in the kitchen full-time. It's your pub, Shirl. I was just keeping it warm for you.'

'It's not either of ours. It's Cathy, the landlady's, and who knows what she'd make of all this.'

From what Shirley had told me about the Nag's Head's absentee landlady, I was fairly sure she wouldn't have cared one way or the other, as long as the rent was paid. But I sensed that Shirley was hovering between being impressed – with the packed pub, the efficient bar staff, the delicious smells wafting past every time a plate of food made its way from kitchen to table, the constant opening and closing of the tills – and a quite natural feeling that she'd been usurped and her old ways overturned.

I badly wanted her to come down on the side of impressed and forget about the growing resentment I was sure I'd be feeling if I were her. I wondered, desperately, what would be the right thing to say. But there was no time or space to think – orders were flooding in, Kelly had had to abandon the bar to bus glasses and as soon as one table got up to leave, it was filled again.

'Oh my God, you must be Shirley!' Drew appeared at my side, aiming the lighthouse beam of his smile at her. 'I've heard so much about you. I'm Alice's brother Drew, I've been helping out here a bit. Would it be possible to ask a huge favour? There's a table over there about to start a game of Trivial Pursuit, and there's just one space. I've made you a Baileys espresso martini as a bribe. I can help Alice at the bar, because I'm semi-competent at that, but I can't answer any general knowledge questions apart from about geography. Do you mind joining them? Someone will bring you a burger, too. Don't be put off by the bone marrow thing – you won't actually notice it and, if you do, it's really delicious.'

Shirley had never been brought face to face with a full Drew charm offensive before, and she didn't stand a chance. For a second it looked like she might be about to object, but then Drew put his head on one side, smiled again and said, 'Please?'

The next thing I knew Shirley was sitting with a group of strangers, sipping her drink, her eyes narrowing as she remembered how long the River Nile was, which Shakespeare play featured the character Robin Goodfellow, and the names of the original members of NSYNC. I mean, I was a massive fan back in the day, but my crush on Justin Timberlake was so overwhelming the others might as well not have existed. But Shirl clearly had a memory like a 256GB iPhone, and she wasn't afraid to use it. Soon, the little coloured segments were taking their places in her plastic token as it moved around the board, and she was clearly having a brilliant time. Occasionally, I could hear her voice rising above the general chatter, triumphantly answering 'Sheffield United!', 'George Bush Senior!' or 'The lesser spotted dogfish!' and seriously, I couldn't even.

'Well done,' I said to Drew. 'How did you know that was her thing?'

'Ray mentioned that she always used to set the Tuesday night quiz herself,' he answered. 'And apparently she went on *Mastermind* once, back in the day. Specialist subject, the Kray brothers. Who'd have thunk it?'

'Really?' I'd known for some time that Shirl had hidden depths, but I'd never have guessed that London's most notorious gangsters would be her forte. 'Well, you certainly calmed her down. I was worried she was really pissed off with me there, for a bit.'

'When you want people to do what you want, you've just got to offer them something they want more than not doing it,' Drew said. 'Basic psychology, innit?'

'Well, whatever it is, it worked. I'll have a chat to her later and check that she's okay, because I really don't want her to be hurt, or feel like I thought she wasn't doing a great job before. Because she was. Her and Juan.'

'But they weren't moving with the times,' Drew said. 'Go big or go home, right?'

'But I don't want Shirl to leave! She *is* the Nag's Head.'

'Maybe the Nag's Head isn't her any more, though.'

'But…'

Drew shrugged and turned to pick up an order from the kitchen, whisking it away to a table, saying a few words to the group there and making them all laugh. I soon lost sight of him again, though, as a round of cocktails were ordered and then another table wanted food, and then someone dropped a full glass of wine and I had to dash over with a roll of paper towel and a dustpan and brush.

But by about seven, the pub was beginning to quieten down. The normal Saturday evening crowd was arriving, of course, but the families were taking their children home to baths and bed, the raucous groups of twenty-somethings heading off to more exciting entertainment than Risk and Racing Demon, and the hardcore poker players had decided to call it a day, one woman having smugly collected all the chips.

Sadiq, Terry and Ray were putting on their coats, their impromptu dominoes coaching session having evidently wound up. There was no sign of Maurice – I recalled seeing him with the group earlier, but he must have left early. Perhaps he hadn't enjoyed being the centre of attention as much as Ray had seemed to.

'You look like you need a sit-down and something to eat,' Drew said, and as soon as he said it I realised my feet hurt like crazy, my mouth was bone-dry from having barely had time to sip my pint glass of water and I felt light-headed with hunger.

'Yes, you take your break, Alice,' Shirley said, her good humour restored by her triumph in the general knowledge game. 'I'll mind the bar. Go on!'

I hesitated for a second, then checked my phone. I'd texted Joe earlier, a conciliatory but not grovelling message saying how sorry I was that we'd had a row the previous night. I'd already been in bed by the time he got home, and, to my shame, I'd pretended to be asleep until eventually I actually did fall asleep; and when I'd woken up that morning he'd either been asleep or more likely pretending to be. He'd read my message several hours ago, and now there was a reply: *Okay, I'm sorry too. But we need to talk. I love you.*

Should I go home? I could be there in ten minutes, talk to Joe and try and make things right, and be back in a couple of hours to see the rest of the evening service through and close up.

But then Drew handed me a bottle of Peroni, its sides beaded with condensation, and said he'd get Zoë to shove a shepherdless pie in the oven for me. As if pulled by a magnet, I moved towards one of the free tables, the one by the shelves of games, and collapsed into a chair like a puppet with its strings cut. Taking a deep swallow of my cold, almost bitter beer, I ran my fingers over the piles of brightly coloured boxes, thinking how weird it was that this old-fashioned entertainment should have proved such a hit.

'Mind if I join you? I brought this over.' Archie was standing next to me, holding my plate of food and a glass of red wine. 'Looks like you've had quite a day.'

'It's been insane.' I gestured to the seat opposite and he passed me my dinner and sat down, resting his elbows on the table. 'I don't think I've ever been so knackered.'

I picked up my fork and dug into my food. It was delicious, the lentil filling laced with red wine, the mashed potato smooth and rich with a crisp golden top. I couldn't help it – even though she might be my rival, even though I'd brought her to work in the pub for reasons that weren't entirely about the profitability of the business, I had to admit to myself that a large part of the success of the night had been down to Zoë's cooking and her relentless hard work.

'Fancy a game of Scrabble?' Archie asked.

'Scrabble?' Even though I'd been surrounded by board games all afternoon, his suggestion took me by surprise.

'One of the most popular games of all time. More than half of British families own a set.'

'Do they?'

'I'm sure I read that somewhere. Anyway – shall we?'

I should go home. Go home and talk to Joe. But my legs were so tired and the beer was so refreshing and I still had almost half my dinner left.

'Go on then.'

I reached behind me for the set and Archie arranged the board between us while I finished my food. Drew brought over another beer for me and another red wine for Archie and introduced himself. I felt a fleeting sense of weirdness as they shook hands, but then told myself that there was nothing weird about it at all – they were just business neighbours, after all.

I scrutinised my Scrabble tiles, my tired brain seeming to change into a different gear as I looked at the letters. Across the table, Archie was frowning, too, his fingers shuffling the tiles around. Suddenly, the letters in front of me jumped into place, without me even having to order them. I tried to keep my face calm, then remembered it wasn't poker I was playing.

CHINTZY, I spelled out on the board.

'What? Way to start the game! Jeez, and you get a bonus for using all your letters, too.'

'I know, right? How lucky was that?'

Then I saw a similar spark of excitement in Archie's face, just like the one I'd felt. Across my Z, he spelled out JEZEBEL.

'What the… That's amazing.'

'Yup. Without your Z I'd have been screwed.'

We looked at each other, and suddenly we were both laughing helplessly.

'Your go,' he said, when I'd managed to catch my breath. There were no more epic scores – Archie turned out to be a two-letter-word ninja, wringing the maximum score out of each turn by spelling EM, ID and YO, but I got lucky with a blank and managed to get QUEASY.

'What?' I asked when he'd taken his next turn. 'Qi? That's never a word.'

'It certainly is. It's a concept in Chinese philosophy and medicine. Means life energy. Here, I'll show you.'

He tapped on his phone and passed it over.

'Sheesh! Okay, genius, I was wrong.'

'And you lose a turn.'

'What? No way. That wasn't an official challenge. I was just checking.'

And we both cracked up again.

Fifteen minutes later, Archie had played his last letters and I was left with an unusable K and a D.

'So that's three hundred and forty-three to me, and three hundred and…' He paused.

'Go on! Come on, spill! I won, didn't I?'

'Three hundred and fifteen to you.'

'Bollocks! I'll have to get revenge sometime.'

Archie grinned. 'You can try.'

We both laughed again, and then, abruptly, I stopped. I could feel a cold draught on the back on my neck, like someone had left the door of the pub open. I got up to go and close it and saw Joe standing in the doorway, watching us. There was no way of knowing how long he'd been there for.

Chapter Eighteen

'How's the crayfish and rocket?' Heather asked.

We were eating our lunch in the upstairs seating area overlooking the garden where we sat in summer; it was a cold, blustery day and I'd been battered by gusts of rain on my walk from the station.

I looked morosely at my sandwich. 'Disappointing. I knew it would be, before I even bought it, but by then I'd committed. You know how it is.'

'Pret regret. If it's not a thing, it ought to be. That's why I always have the same. You know where you are with tuna and cucumber.'

'I thought you always had it because it's your fave? Like, your death-row meal?'

'Death row? Oh my God, no, that would be… I don't know. The set menu from Hawksmoor, maybe. The Yorkshire pudding thing, then a steak with triple-cooked chips, then the salted caramel sticky toffee pudding. Or my mum's lasagne, with garlic bread and a bucket of red wine. Or cheese. Like, a whole cheese board all to myself. I only order this every time because I know exactly what I'm getting. It's perfectly nice, under five hundred calories – bosh. I've got enough to think about in my life without having to waste valuable decision-making energy on lunch.'

I laughed. We'd missed our lunches together for a few weeks – Heather had been in New York with work, then on annual leave before her sister's wedding, then in court. And I'd been busy, relentlessly busy at the pub. But recent events had made me long to catch up with my friend, and I'd sent her a WhatsApp that – I'd realised as soon as I'd pressed the blue arrow – sounded like I was having some sort of crisis.

'Anyway, so,' Heather said, 'you were just playing Scrabble. What's the drama?'

'I know.' I nodded miserably. 'Just bloody Scrabble. But it's like it's set off the Cold War between Joe and me. I mean, I can kind of see it from his point of view. We barely see each other, we had a horrible row over Zoë when he tried to take me out for a romantic dinner, and then he turns up at the pub and there I am sitting on my arse drinking beer with a hot man.'

'So he's hot, is he? This Archie?'

'He's all right.'

Heather raised an eyebrow.

'Okay, okay. Yes, he's hot. He's hot, and he's nice, and he's funny. But that's almost not the point. What's winding Joe up is that he's *there*, the same way Zoë being there winds me up. He runs the shop next door to the pub. We see each other a few times a week. He comes in for lunch, I go round there to ask for craft beer recommendations.'

'Craft beer recommendations? Is that what they're calling it now?'

'Heather! Don't be daft. I was about to say, more to the point, he's got a girlfriend. Both of us are, like, totally not interested in each other that way. At all.'

With a twinge of guilt I thought of the online Scrabble app Archie had sent me an invite to download, the long-running games we'd been playing over the past ten days, the thrill of pleasure it gave me every time I came up with a killer word. Oh, and the way, when I checked my phone in bed in the mornings, I angled the screen ever so slightly away from Joe when I went on to that particular app.

But it was just a game! Scrabble, for fuck's sake. Since when has getting a Z on a triple-letter square counted as cheating? Okay, maybe if you played an American spelling in the British English version it might, but still.

'Well, then surely you just said to Joe, "Yeah, I was having a break from work and a chat with an acquaintance, what's your problem?"'

'I would have done. But things are so weird between us right now, I couldn't even do that. If he'd been like, "Are you shagging that man with the beard and the mad two-letter word skills, bitch?" then I could have told him to cop on and stop being so ridiculous. But he didn't. He came over and said hi and he and Archie had a chat about the declining bee population – Archie's sister's into bees, it's seriously cool; he gave me some of their honey to take home – and then I had to get back to work and they carried on sitting together, all civilised.'

'That's okay, though, right? I mean, civilised is good.'

'Yeah, it would be. But Joe and I'd had a massive row and we still hadn't sorted it. We still haven't now, not really. I mean, we're talking and stuff, but things between us have been so off for a while now, and now they're even more off.'

'Off how?'

'He's being distant. Almost polite. In the mornings, if we're up at the same time, which we aren't always, he'll say, "Can I make you a coffee, Alice?" When before we used to argue about whose turn it was. And with Zoë living with us, I suppose I notice it more. The only time I see him acting like his old self, having a laugh and stuff, is when he's with her. With me he's all kind of formal. And I can't properly talk to him, because whenever we're both there, she's there too. It's all kinds of weird.'

'You all living together? Slightly like a later episode of *Friends*, yeah, it is.'

'The one where Joe realises he ended up with the wrong girl?'

'Pfft, he didn't. You two are great together. I'm sure this is just a blip. But you and Zoë, working together – how's that working out?'

'Better than I thought it would. She's okay, actually. Like, I wouldn't want to be her friend or anything, necessarily, but she's okay. She's an incredible cook. And her cat's cute, now I've got to know him. But she's just so… I dunno. All the things I'm not.'

'Thick? Incompetent? A bitch? Looks like the back end of the number thirty-three bus?'

I laughed. 'Thanks. No, none of that. She's really pretty, and she works out at one of those fucking terrifying gyms where all the weightlifters go, so she's got this amazing figure. But it's not that. She's just kind of… sparkling. Dynamic. Like, she goes after what she wants and she gets it.'

'And you don't? Cos it kind of looks to me like you wanted to be a lawyer, and you worked your nuts off for that, and you could still have it if you wanted it, but you decided you wanted this pub thing instead, and now you've got that. And you wanted your perfect relationship with Joe and you've got that too. It's just you're maybe going through a rough patch right now.'

'What if it's not a rough patch? What if it's terminal? What if Joe's still in love with Zoë?'

'What makes you think he might be?'

'I… I don't know. Just the way she is, and the way he and I are. And he was in love with her, when they were together. I asked him. And with things so off between him and me, if she did decide to make a massive play for him, then now would be the time, wouldn't it?'

I thought again of that little bundle of cards in Zoë's bed and cringed inwardly. There was no way I was going to admit to Heather that I'd been through Zoë's private stuff.

'She stole some of his underwear,' I said.

'She *what*? Okay, now we're going full *Fatal Attraction*. Lock up your bunnies. This is not a drill.'

'Not now,' I admitted. 'But years ago, when they were together. Joe told me he had a pair of silk boxers with Bart Simpson on them, and they'd mysteriously vanished, and what did I find in Zoë's washing?'

'Oh, give over, Miss Marple. One, zillions of people have Bart Simpson kecks. You've no way of knowing they're the same ones. Two, even if she did end up taking them when she and Joe were together, and kept them, that's only, like, two out of ten on my weirdness scale.'

'Maybe,' I agreed reluctantly. 'But honestly, Heath, you should see her legs. And more importantly, you should see Joe looking at them sometimes.'

'Alice. Come on. Seriously, you need to stop doing this to yourself. If things aren't great with you and Joe, talk to him. Stop projecting stupid stuff onto this Zoë girl. Everyone thinks they're in love at some point, when they're young and daft. Well, everyone except me.'

I looked at her, surprised. She was looking at me almost confrontationally, as if she'd said something shocking. Which she kind of had, in the sense that it was news to me.

'What?' she demanded.

'You mean you've never been in love? Never even *thought* you were? Not even with whatsisname, who you said was the hottest man you've ever banged, only you couldn't stand the way he ate toast?'

Heather smiled, which I was grateful for. 'Rufus. Oh my God, he was lovely actually. We went out for about six weeks, and if only he'd been gluten-intolerant or a low-carber or something, we might still be together. But then I made the fatal error of offering him breakfast one morning at my flat.'

'Go on,' I urged, although I'd heard the story before.

'I mean, for the love of God. Toast. Doesn't everyone learn how to eat toast when they're, like, two? Not Rufus. I swear, it was like he suddenly turned into a Visigoth. Chomping, tearing at it with his teeth like it might run away, spraying crumbs everywhere – it was grotesque.'

'And once you'd seen it, you couldn't unsee it?'

'Exactly. After that, I had the Ick.'

I nodded. This was also ground we'd covered before.

'Every time he kissed me, I wanted to wipe my mouth afterwards in case he'd left toast crumbs on it. Even if it was first thing in the morning, he hadn't eaten anything for twelve hours and he'd just cleaned his teeth. That's how the Ick works.'

'I got that with one of my very first boyfriends, back when I was uni,' I said. 'It was pretty short-lived. The relationship, not the Ick.'

'Because once the Ick's there, it's there to stay.'

'Correct. With this bloke – Stephen – it was… Oh my God, I can hardly bear to think about it.'

'Go on, Alice! What did he do?'

'He…' I covered my face with my hands. 'He had a name for his penis.'

'No!'

'Yep. Nigel. I mean really, fucking Nigel. Although in hindsight, it did look a bit like Nigel Farage.'

'Nigel Farage looks like lots of people's penises.'

'This is true. But anyway, he talked about it all the time, like, "Come and give Nigel a kiss, Alice."'

'Eeeuuuw!'

'Exactly. The Ick set in right there. But I thought I was in love, and I tried to pretend it was all cute and quirky.'

'My God, woman! Have some self-respect! Okay, I guess it was a long time ago and you were young and naïve. But what happened to make you see how wrong it was?'

I looked around. Lunch hour in the City was almost over; the tables around us were empty. Heather would have to go soon, too, as would I. I lowered my voice a bit and carried on.

'He gave my fanny a name, too.'

'He gave your… No way. Are you going to tell me what it was, or shall I guess?'

'You'd never get there. It was Belinda.'

Heather doubled over, her hair almost brushing the tabletop. 'Belinda? Did you ever find out why? His childhood nanny? A *Playboy* centrefold?'

'I honestly have no idea. I never asked, but every time he said, "Is Belinda feeling frisky?" I just about died from the Ick.'

'You were still shagging him? Jesus. What happened to make you realise what a terrible mistake that was?'

I put my hands up to my face. My cheeks were burning, just remembering it.

'So he must've given all his girlfriends' minges names. And one time, he called mine the wrong one.'

'Oh for fuck's… He didn't.'

'He did. He was like, "Nigel's grown, look. Nigel wants to get intimate with Veronica – I mean Belinda."'

'Veronica! I'm dying.'

'Mmhmm. So that became a terminal case of the Ick, right there.'

'Alice, you poor thing. No wonder you're worried about this Zoë. Basically, you've got deep-seated ex-related trauma thanks to Nigel and Veronica.' Heather looked at her watch. 'Shit, it's almost two. I've got a meeting in fifteen minutes, so I'm going to have to leg it. Thanks so much for this – you've cheered me right up. And talk to Joe, okay?'

'Okay. I will,' I said, although I wasn't sure whether – or how, or when – I was going to be able to keep my promise.

Heather threw her coat over her shoulders – it was new, I noticed, a glorious calf-length swishy slate-blue trench that gave me a pang of regret that my finances might prevent me owning anything that gorgeous, ever – gave me a brief hug and ran lightly down the stairs.

As I walked through the rain to the station, I found myself pondering my friend's revelation that she'd never been in love. Never felt that sickening rollercoaster lurch of excitement when a text arrived, nor the thud of disappointment when it wasn't from the right person. Never gazed into someone's eyes, blurry with closeness, and thought, *I could do this forever*. Never spent far too much time composing WhatsApp messages that encapsulated all the feels, then waited longingly for a response that was just as heartfelt.

I felt, with a pang of fear for her, that when she did eventually fall for someone, she'd fall hard. I only hoped that when it happened, it would be with someone who felt the same and was a totally Ick-free zone.

And I thought about me and Joe. I remembered how I'd felt when we met – that heady, soaring sense of possibility and rightness, coupled with a feeling of security that was quite new to me. I remembered the first time we slept together. He'd made me dinner at his flat – smoked salmon and fillet steak and chocolate mousse, which I'd thought was the most perfect, sophisticated menu ever – and served it at a table set with a white sheet instead of a cloth, candles and a rosebud in an empty Amstel bottle, because he didn't have a vase.

Afterwards, we'd moved from the table to the sofa to his bed as if it was the most natural thing in the world – which, of course, I suppose it was – and there was no awkwardness, no self-consciousness about my body, just straight-up delight in how we could make each other feel.

And then the next day at work, at around eleven o'clock, when he hadn't texted and the first niggling doubt had begun to send its toxic tentacles into my head suggesting that maybe he wasn't going to, a parcel had arrived for me in the internal mail, and it had been those silly slippers with their smiling sheep's faces.

I'd been so sure, then, that everything would be all right, that I'd found a person who'd always keep me safe. And he had. We'd kept each other safe. Until now: now I felt that everything we'd built up together was in danger of being swept away like a sandcastle by a high tide.

Chapter Nineteen

'Would you like a coffee, Joe?'

'What?' Joe glanced up from his phone. 'Oh, yeah, thanks Alice.'

Relieved, I switched on the machine, its hum filling the awkward silence that had been there between us. Things must be pretty grim, I thought sadly, if my boyfriend agreeing to be made a hot drink felt like some kind of breakthrough. But the weirdness I'd told Heather about had shown no signs of resolving itself. Although Joe was perfectly polite and pleasant to me, and texted me as usual to tell me when he was going to be home (generally late at night), and although he still kissed me goodbye in the mornings, I couldn't shake the feeling that things between us weren't right. Any more than I could shake the little thrill of happiness I got whenever a message from Archie popped up on the Scrabble app on my phone.

Although I wasn't actually doing anything wrong, I knew that what I was *feeling* was wrong. But Joe's... I couldn't even think of it as coldness, because he wasn't cold. He still wrapped his arms around me in bed at night, although by the time we were in bed we were both so tired that was all that happened. I sometimes sneaked a glance at his dick when he got up in the morning, just to check it was still there. It was, but for all the action I was getting he might as well have left it at the office by mistake.

It was more a sense of distance; a feeling of a chasm opening between us, growing gradually wider and wider. I longed to bridge it, but I wasn't sure how.

'I've got the evening off tonight,' I said. 'I could come into town and meet you. We could go for some food, or whatever.'

'That would be great,' Joe replied. 'But I'm not sure what time I'll finish tonight. I'm in court tomorrow.'

'Oh.' I felt hurt, and rebuffed, even though he was being perfectly reasonable. 'Why don't you text me when you know what time you're finishing, and we can see if we're both up for meeting?'

'Sure,' Joe said. 'Let's play it by ear.'

Wounded and frustrated, I chalked that one up as not going to happen.

'Joe,' I said. 'Listen, I've been thinking – I've been feeling – are you okay? Are we okay?'

'What do you mean? As far as I know, we are. How about you?'

'It's just…' But then Zoë came into the kitchen, Frazzle following on her heels, and Joe finished his coffee, gave me one of those kisses that felt more like a 'yours sincerely' on an email than a gesture of affection, and left for work.

At first, it seemed like that morning would be like any other at the Nag's Head. We opened the doors at nine thirty. Soon after, the first of the laptop-carrying coffee-drinkers arrived, shortly followed by the mums with their toddlers, eager for babyccinos and Zoë's linseed and goji berry muffins.

At eleven on the dot, Ray arrived, ordered his pint of bitter and sat down at the usual table in the corner. I already had Sadiq's orange juice open, waiting on the bar for him, when he walked in two minutes later and, as usual, Terry arrived just before ten past and I poured him his brandy and Coke.

'Maurice running late?' I asked.

Terry frowned. 'Didn't turn up yesterday, did he?'

'Didn't he? I wasn't here.'

'Nope. Sadiq tried ringing, but he didn't pick up.'

I realised I knew absolutely nothing about Maurice's life, apart from the few hours of every day he spent at that table, sipping his Guinness, playing his bones and chatting to his mates. He'd always seemed in pretty good health to me, but what would I know? He wasn't young. All sorts of health emergencies could befall an elderly man.

'Is he okay, do you think?'

He'd never mentioned a wife, but perhaps there was a Mrs Maurice, even now bustling round her husband's bedside bringing him hot lemon and honey for a heavy cold. It was that time of year; maybe he had flu. The last time I'd visited my GP for a smear test, there'd been posters up all over the surgery reminding over-sixties that they were eligible for a free vaccination on the NHS.

'I expect he'd let someone know if he wasn't. Or Wesley would.'

I hesitated for a second. Should I ask if Terry knew Maurice's address and pop round to check on him? But they were his friends; they weren't worried. I was just the woman who served his half of Guinness every day. I had no right to interfere.

'Right. Well… let me know if you need anything else.'

I pushed Terry's drink across the bar to him, and he ambled off to join the group – a group of only three now, though. I watched them set up their game, sipping their drinks, talking sporadically as usual. I wondered what it was like for these men to share one another's company each day yet know relatively little about each other's lives.

And I knew even less. Sadiq and Ray were married; I remembered Sadiq's joke about his wife's cooking, and Archie had mentioned an Auntie Hilary, who used to help Ray run his plumbing business but was retired now, too. As for Terry? I hadn't a clue. They were just there, every day, as much a part of the pub as the faded carpet or the stains on the ceiling or Princess Diana, watching aloofly from her frame above the fireplace. But, somehow, it was Maurice I felt was the most important of the four. It was he who'd looked after me when I was in desperate need of kindness, who'd given me his hanky to mop up my tears and bought me a sherry that had made me feel far better than it had tasted.

If it hadn't been for Maurice, I wouldn't even be here, part of this new community I'd discovered through the Nag's Head.

As if summoned by the power of my thoughts, Maurice pushed open the door and walked in. He was dressed immaculately, as always, in his suit and tie, a handkerchief folded neatly in his breast pocket and a trilby hat perched on his greying hair. But he wasn't smiling as usual. He looked tired, older – somehow smaller.

He walked over to the corner table and greeted his friends, clapping each of them briefly on the shoulder. But he didn't sit down, even though I would have brought his usual half of Guinness to him without him needing to order it. Instead, he came straight over to the bar.

'Morning, Maurice. Same as usual?'

'Not right now, thank you, Alice. As a matter of fact I was hoping for a word with you.'

'With me? Sure.'

I waited expectantly, wondering what on earth he could want. Some complaint about the service, or the state of the pub? But it was the same as it had always been, barring the new menu and the shelf of games.

'In private, if you don't mind, Alice.'

'Of course.'

I felt the same lurch of anxiety I'd felt when I was summoned to the HR department at Billings Pitt Furzedown all those months ago, even though I was as sure as I could be that I'd done nothing wrong. I ducked out through the hinged hatch on the bar and gestured towards the little room next to the kitchen that Shirley used as her office. It contained a rickety computer table, a filing cabinet so full of old brewery catalogues, order books and magazines that the drawers were impossible to open, and an upright wooden chair that had clearly been borrowed from the bar years before and never returned.

There was nowhere else to sit, so I pulled the door closed behind us, and we stood.

'Is everything all right?'

He took the handkerchief out of his pocket and twisted it, looking down at his hands. I reached out and touched his shoulder.

'Maurice?'

'I need your help, Alice.'

'Of course. Anything I can do, I'll try.'

My head spun. I hadn't the faintest idea what he could need from me – or whether I'd be able to provide it. It couldn't be money, surely? Anyone who'd spent more than a few minutes with me knew I was skint. Something to do with the pub? But then he'd have approached Shirley, not me.

'Your help as a lawyer,' he said.

Shit. I looked at his grave, worried face and knew that now wasn't the time to remind him I wasn't *actually* a lawyer – I hadn't formally qualified, I'd fallen at the last fence. And anyway, what kind of advice might he want? Maurice had always struck me as a total pillar of the community, about as likely to commit a crime as Frazzle the cat. Actually, given Frazzle's propensity for murdering rodents in cold blood, considerably less likely.

'Okay,' I said. 'Would you like to tell me what's happened?'

'It's Wesley. He's been… detained.'

'Your brother?'

Maurice nodded.

I said, 'Maurice, I'm so very sorry this has happened. Once you've explained it all to me I'll help if I possibly can. But honestly, I don't know how much use I'll be. I've never worked in criminal law – I haven't had anything to do with it since university. I'm almost certainly not the right person to be talking to about this. I'm no more of an expert than any other barmaid.'

'It's not criminal. Wesley's a law-abiding man.'

'I'm so sorry, I didn't mean to offend you.'

He shook his head. 'I'm not offended. I'm just not thinking straight; I'm not explaining things right. He's being held in a detention centre. They're going to deport him, back to the West

Indies. Even though he's lived here for forty-five years. Even though his whole life's here – his friends, the church. Me. Even though he's paid his taxes and never even had so much as a parking ticket.'

'Maurice,' I said. 'If it's an immigration matter, it's highly, highly specialised. I can support you as a friend but I can't offer you any advice at all. I know someone who can, though.'

The rest of that lunchtime service felt like just another day at the Nag's Head – except it didn't. Although the usual smattering of regulars came in for their first pint of the day and the usual Tuesday delivery arrived from the brewery and I pulled pints and wiped tables the same as always, I couldn't shake off my worry about Maurice.

I'd given him all the reassurance I could, but my words had felt hollow and, ultimately, all I'd been able to provide was a phone number. He'd left his friends to their dominoes and headed off into the gloomy afternoon, his head bowed as if someone had replaced his felt trilby hat with one made of lead.

Even Archie's admiring annoyance when I got FLAPJACK on a triple word score could only make me smile briefly.

Drew arrived to start his shift, and I was about to head off for a much-needed break when my brother nudged me and said, 'See that bloke over there?'

I glanced over to the corner of the room, where Terry, Sadiq and Ray's vacated table had been taken by a young guy with a laptop. He looked perfectly ordinary at first – just a bloke, with thick-rimmed glasses and longish dark hair curling over the neckline of his faded red sweatshirt.

Then I looked again, and he didn't seem quite so ordinary. The shoulders under his jumper were broad and heavily muscled. His face looked strangely immobile, the way Heather's had gone the one time she had Botox done on a Groupon offer and couldn't raise her eyebrows for six months. His eyebrows were plucked and trimmed into perfect arches, and the hands on his keyboard looked like they'd been manicured, the nails smooth and glossy.

'What about him?'

'That's Fabian Flatley, my landlord. Well, Lauren's landlord.'

'Oh, right? So?'

'So, he's trouble.'

'What, you mean like one of those property tycoons from the 1950s? Like Peter Rachman or someone? Does he menace you for protection money and run a brothel from your apartment block?'

Drew smiled. 'Nothing like that. But he's dodgy AF.'

'Dodgy how?'

'He's…' Drew began, but then a group of junior doctors came in, knackered and starving after their shift in A&E, started inhaling pints of Coke and devouring baguettes, and we didn't have the chance to discuss the troublesome Fabian Flatley further.

I watched him, though, sitting there focusing intently on his computer screen, pausing occasionally to take a sip of the slimline tonic with lime, no ice, that I'd served him when he came in. Dodgy or not, the man could certainly make a drink last.

The weird thing was, he didn't actually appear to be working. Over the weeks, I'd got used to those customers who, for whatever reason, had decided that the Nag's Head made the ideal base from which to run their eBay store or write their screenplay or code their website, or whatever they were doing, and they were all the same. All of them alternated quite long periods of frantic activity – up to an hour, for some of the more diligent or deadline-driven ones – with short breaks, when they'd get up, stretch, go for a wee, order another coffee or mess about on their phones.

Fabian Flatley wasn't doing that. It wasn't like he was working at all – it was like he was waiting.

And as I watched, I eventually saw what he'd been waiting for – or rather, who.

Shirley had let me know that she'd be in late after taking Juan to a physiotherapy appointment, so it wasn't a surprise when she came hurrying through the door just after three. But I was taken aback when, instead of taking her place behind the bar so I could have a late and much-needed break, she went straight over to Fabian Flatley's table.

I saw her greet him, head on one side, not quite sure whether he was the right person but pretty confident. Like they'd never met before but she'd looked him up on LinkedIn. Or – given Shirley was about as likely to use LinkedIn as order a bowl of seitan chicken wings – had known she was looking for a dark-haired bloke in a red jumper with a laptop.

But clearly Fabian knew exactly who she was. As soon as she walked in, he snapped his MacBook closed and the expression on his face changed from neutral, almost bored, to alert and brightly smiling. His teeth were just as I expected – blinding-white and dead even.

I saw him say something to Shirley and she gave a pleased little laugh, stroking her faux-leopard skin coat as she shrugged it off and hung it on the back of a chair, and although I couldn't hear their conversation, I could imagine it just as if I'd been standing right there.

You must be Shirley. What a fabulous jacket!

Oh, thanks, love. It's only TK Maxx.

She sat down.

Irresistibly curious, I moved to duck out from behind the bar and go over to offer her a drink and him a refill, but Drew was too quick for me. He was there already, hovering solicitously, notepad in hand. Seconds later he was back.

'Flatley wants another slimline tonic. Slice, no ice.'

'Gotcha. And for Shirl?'

'The same.'

We looked at each other, wordlessly understanding. Before lunchtime, Shirley drank strong tea with milk and two sugars. In the afternoons, it was lemonade, and after six o'clock she'd have a Bacardi and Coke, but never more than one. Her routine never varied – you could literally tell what time of day it was by what was in her glass. And it was never, ever slimline tonic water.

'She's trying to impress him,' I observed.

'Yep.' Drew flipped the caps off two bottles and I tonged lime slices into two glasses. 'God only knows what they're up to, but it's bad news.'

Chapter Twenty

Reluctantly, I put on my coat and left the pub. I was eager to try and overhear what Shirley and Fabian were saying, but it would be impossible from my position behind the bar and loitering around them pretending to clear tables and put out food menus for the evening would be too obvious. And anyway, the way the two of them had been leaning in towards each other, close as lovers, I'd have had to practically stick my head in between them in order to earwig on their conversation.

So, my coat wrapped tightly around me and my woolly scarf tied high under my chin, I made my way out into the street. Evening was falling already; the trees poked their bare branches up against a slate-grey sky and the pavement was slick with drizzle. I could go home for a bit, I thought, put a load of washing on and do some much-needed hoovering, getting rid of the specks of cat litter that Frazzle somehow managed to spread throughout the house. Or I could go and sit in a coffee shop somewhere and catch up on my social media. But neither idea appealed.

I had a horrible sense of foreboding – a feeling that, again, my life was about to change – and it made me restless. Worry about Maurice, about Joe, about what Shirley and Fabian might be discussing, niggled at my brain. Head down, I strode down the high street towards the park. I'd go for a walk, get some fresh air, and when I returned for the last couple of hours of my shift Drew might have gleaned some useful gossip.

I was so deep in thought that I heard the sound of footsteps hurrying towards me only when they were right at my back, and then I jumped and actually let out a little shriek of alarm.

'Sorry, Alice! Oh my God, I didn't mean to scare you. Did you think I was a mugger?'

Archie was wrapped up against the cold too, in a dark green down jacket, a blue knitted beanie pulled down low over his forehead. It matched his eyes.

'No, not exactly. I was just miles away. Having a bit of a shocker of a day and I guess I was thinking about stuff.'

'Like whether you can play a Z on that double letter square?'

I laughed. 'Not even that. Are you taking a break too?'

'Yeah. No bugger ever seems to want to buy craft beer and artisan gin at four in the afternoon. I can't think why. So I normally close the shop for an hour or so in the afternoons, have a break, and then get back for the evening rush.'

'I was going to walk round the park a bit. It's bloody miserable but I needed to get out.'

'Mind if I join you?'

I shook my head, and he fell into step next to me, our shoulders almost touching. Joe's height and long legs meant I always had to hurry to keep pace with him, but Archie's strides matched mine like we'd been choreographed.

We turned into the park and, not speaking, took the path that led to the top of the hill – the same hill I used to labour up, far behind Joe, when we were still able to go to Parkrun together every Saturday, before my weekends became consumed by the demands of the Nag's Head.

That felt like a lifetime ago, but the hill clearly hadn't got the memo – it was as steep as ever. Our steps slowed and I heard Archie's breath coming faster next to me, just as I knew mine was.

'God, I'm so unfit,' he said. 'You'd think lugging crates of bottles around all day would be enough exercise to keep you going, but…'

'It's not, is it? Nor's dashing around with trays full of glasses, apparently.'

Still, we made it to the top and stopped there, chests heaving, huddled into our coats against the biting wind. Up here, we could see a gap in the clouds, where the relentless dull grey gave way, like a blanket that had worn to pieces, letting bright slashes of crimson and gold show through.

Normally, we'd have been sharing the space with dog-walkers, joggers, mothers hurrying their kids home from the playground, groups of youths chatting or listening to music or smoking weed. But now, on this miserable winter evening, the park was deserted.

Below us, the distant lights of central London gleamed almost as brightly as the setting sun.

Archie took out his phone and tapped the screen a few times, then tilted it to show me. He'd taken a panorama photo of the view.

'No filter needed, right?'

'Is that going to go on your Insta? Hashtag no filter?'

He laughed. 'Probably. I try and keep the account active for the business, you know, building engagement and all that. Talking about how amazing the local area is. Because it is, isn't it?'

I nodded in agreement. But the truth was, when Joe and I had first moved to south-east London, we'd literally just gone online, searched for two-bedroom flats we could afford, ruled out anywhere that was too far out of town and too obviously dubious, and ended up here. And in the intervening months, we'd found a couple of restaurants we liked, decided Sainsbury's was a better bet than Tesco, discovered the farmers' market and the now-closed Star and Garter, and not given much more thought to the place we'd made our home.

Then, it had just been a place to live, with our real lives taking place among those tall, sparkling towers in the City.

It was only since I'd been working in the pub that I'd started to understand the area, to get to grips with its character, the layers of wealth and poverty, the fabric of people that somehow held it all together.

'I wanted to be a photographer,' Archie was saying. 'I did a course at college and everything. But you've got to basically work for nothing while you build up a portfolio, and contacts and stuff, and it all just felt too uncertain. I wanted to be earning a proper living.'

'And you are, now?'

He laughed. 'God, no. Now I've got a grant from the council and some investment from Uncle Ray and a massive bank loan and I'll be lucky if Craft Fever breaks even next year. But I feel like I'm finally following a dream, even if it's a different one from what I used to have. Know what I mean?'

'I never had a dream,' I admitted. 'I did a law course because it felt so kind of responsible and sensible. Like, that's what ambitious people do. People who want to live proper lives that end up with a mortgage and two kids and holidays abroad and good shoes. I guess I assumed that was where I'd end up. But I never yearned for it, if you know what I mean.'

'And the Nag's Head? Running a pub? Is that your dream come true?'

'Not really. But it makes me feel… connected, somehow. To all this.' I gestured around us to the park, the quietly glowing streets beyond, the deserted children's playground and outdoor exercise equipment. 'Working in the City felt remote from everything. At least it seemed that way to me. Like what I was doing had nothing to do with people's real lives. Not even mine.'

My stomach lurched as I remembered Maurice, and I realised that emails and files and precedents, long hours of conferences and, eventually, which side of the bed a judge had got out of in the morning would have a huge, make-or-break impact on his brother's life.

'Maybe I just ended up in the wrong specialism,' I finished lamely.

'Come on,' Archie said. 'View like this, we need a selfie, right? Before the light goes completely.'

We turned around, so the view was behind us and we were looking down into darkness. He put his arm around my shoulder and, after a moment's hesitation, I put mine around his waist. The warmth of his body, so close to mine, made me realise how cold I'd got, standing there talking.

He tapped his phone's screen a few times and I saw our faces come into focus, lit from the front but also silhouetted against the last streaks of brilliant colour in the sky behind us. He even managed to get the twinkling lights on the horizon below.

'Ready?'

I smiled. 'You're good at this.'

Archie pressed the shutter button a few times, and I tried not to mind that my mascara had smudged and my nose was all red and shiny from the cold.

'All done,' he said. 'Back to work now, right?'

'Back to work.'

And then, to my surprise, we were suddenly enfolded in a hug that might only have lasted a few seconds but seemed to go on for the longest time.

Chapter Twenty-One

Before I got out of the taxi, I said, 'Thank you,' to Gordon.

As soon as the words left my mouth, I hated myself for them. But there was no taking them back. Mum and Dad's dutiful, compliant daughter, the girl who'd been brought up to be polite and respectful always, the trainee lawyer who wanted her senior colleagues to like her, said that. The drunk, frightened woman, the person who had just had something happen to her that she didn't fully understand, was silent.

I grabbed my bag and stumbled out of the cab. I stood for a few moments by the front door, fumbling with my keys. Perhaps Gordon didn't want the car to leave until he could see I was safely back inside – but there was no way I was opening that door until I was sure he'd gone.

He must have given up before I did, and I must have got myself inside somehow, because the next thing I remember about that night was waking up, still in the middle of it. My phone – which, thanks to that instinct for self-preservation that had deserted me entirely earlier, I'd remembered to plug in to charge – told me it was quarter to five in the morning. Before I could sort through my memories of the previous night – which were only just beginning to come back to me – I realised with a rush of horrible urgency that I was going to be sick.

I was still dressed, even still wearing one of my shoes, and I just made it to the bathroom. I flung myself down on the floor and spewed and spewed, wishing I could die and end my misery but knowing I couldn't. Knowing that, somehow, I was not only going to have to survive that night but also get dressed, go to work, see Gordon.

When the worst of the nausea had passed, the horror descended on me. There was no relief from having been sick – it was like I'd moved from one circle of hell to another.

What had I done? How had I allowed that to happen? What had even happened?

I clutched the toilet bowl and moaned out loud. Then I heard a tap on the door and, without waiting for a reply, Heather came in.

'Jesus Christ, Alice. Are you okay? I heard you crashing around everywhere when you came in. It sounded like you were totally spangled.'

'I was. I think I still am. I legit want to die. Could you ring the local vet or something and have me put out of my misery?'

She laughed. 'Come on, let's get you sorted out. Have you finished vomming, do you reckon?'

'Not sure.' But I answered my own question when I felt a fresh rush of sickness and threw myself over the loo again. I felt Heather's warm, gentle hands holding my hair back from my face.

'Fucking hell,' she said once I was done, passing me a glass of water from the tap, 'you must've given it some, for a school night. Who were you out with?'

I sipped and spat, flushed the toilet and wiped my face. Then I stood unsteadily, realised it was a bad idea and sank back down onto the blissfully cool tiles.

'Gordon.'

'Your head of department?'

I nodded miserably.

'God, Alice. So you not only went out and got bladdered, you went out and got bladdered with a senior partner? Who else was there?'

She wrung out a washcloth in cold water and passed it to me and I pressed it to my face.

'No one,' I said, the flannel muffling my voice. 'Just me and him.'

'Just you and… Are you sure that was a good idea? I mean, clearly it wasn't, but…'

I started to cry.

'Alice!' Heather squatted down next to me and put her arms round me. 'Come on. It'll be okay. Did you make a tit of yourself?'

I pressed my face, damp flannel and all, into Heather's shoulder, and sobbed. I cried for a long time, while she stroked my hair and patted my back and shushed me, kindly ignoring the fact that I must have absolutely stunk of booze and worse. At last, I moved away from her, blew my nose and looked at her.

The expression on my friend's face had changed. Before, she'd been amused, even a bit annoyed with me for being an idiot, as well as concerned. Now, there was something else in her face – a hardness, almost anger.

'Alice? What did he do? What happened?'

'Nothing. He took me to his club for dinner and we drank all the booze and I got shitfaced. It was stupid of me – and unprofessional. And now I have to face him at work later, and for the next six months until I can move to another department.'

She met my eyes, and I could see the lawyer she'd become one day – a woman with an unerring ability to detect bullshit.

'What happened afterwards? After you left his club?'

'We – I got a taxi home.'

'Just you? Or you and him together?'

'I don't want to talk about it. Seriously.'

'Seriously,' she said, 'something's happened to you. This isn't just beer fear. Come on, you can talk to me.'

'I don't want to talk about it,' I insisted.

'About what? About what happened on the way home?'

'Yes. No. Nothing happened.'

'Alice. Come on. Something did.'

'Heather, please. Just leave me alone, okay?'

Reluctantly, she stood up. 'There's no point going back to bed now. We may as well get ready for work. Why don't you have a shower and I'll put some coffee on, and we'll see if you can drink it without puking again. And take a couple of paracetamol.'

'If I can without puking?'

'Yeah.' She hugged me again, and I felt fresh tears threaten to fall.

In the shower, it was hard to tell what was hot water running down my face and what was tears. I could taste them in my throat, along with the acrid sourness of vomit, which even cleaning my teeth over and over hadn't managed to dispel. I scrubbed my body from top to bottom, over and over again, like Gordon had somehow marked me, with fingerprints or the faint smell of dry-cleaning chemicals I'd noticed clinging to his suit when he'd been close to me in the taxi – so, so close; so much bigger than me and stronger and more powerful in ways that had nothing to do with his physical size.

I felt like nothing – no amount of lime shower gel or deodorant or the Flowerbomb perfume I sprayed on – could make me feel clean. I felt like the heavy mask of foundation and concealer I applied couldn't hide the shame in my face. I felt like even through my drab charcoal suit and slightly crumpled white blouse (I'd been going to catch up on my ironing the previous night, I remembered, but that hadn't happened; the Alice who'd planned a quiet evening and early bed was like a girl from another world) everyone would be able to see the parts of me that Gordon had touched.

I put my slippers on over my nude tights and went through to the kitchen, soaked in misery.

Heather was leaning against the counter, drinking coffee and picking at a plate of sliced ham and avocado. Low-carbing was her thing at the time; she'd read somewhere that it helped keep her energy levels up.

'Coffee? Orange juice? Tea?' she offered.

I shook my head, a fresh surge of nausea threatening to overwhelm me. She poured water from the tap into a glass and handed it to me, wrapping my cold hand around the glass with her warm, dry one.

'He hit on you, didn't he?'

I shook my head. Then, deep inside my mind, an idea surfaced. Maybe that was all that happened. A bit of minor flirtation with a senior colleague over dinner, with drink taken. A tiny bit beyond what was appropriate, but no more than that. Nothing to be ashamed of; nothing to end a career over.

I said, 'Yeah, kind of. A bit. I encouraged it, I suppose. He was nice to me.'

'*Nice*? People don't come home spewing and crying after an evening with a senior partner who's being *nice*. Cop on, Alice.'

Her words might have been harsh, but her voice was gentle and her face full of concern.

I forced myself to meet her eyes and I said, 'Okay. In the taxi on the way home, he groped me. Worse than groped.'

'Oh shit,' Heather whispered. 'He didn't – he didn't rape you? Did he?'

I shook my head. There it was – less than rape but more than groping. And now someone else knew. Even though it was Heather, my best friend, who I loved and trusted implicitly, I felt a fresh tide of shame and panic rising in my throat.

'Alice,' she said. 'You should go to the police. You know that.'

'Heath, there's no fucking way I am going to do that. No way on earth.'

We stood there silently for a minute in the warm, quiet kitchen, the first rays of the morning sun spilling through the window. I knew what Heather was thinking, because it was the same thing I was thinking. If I reported this, it would go nowhere. Gordon was powerful. He was rich. He was well respected. Maybe a police officer would interview him, and he'd say it was just a drunken fumble between two contenting adults. I'd led him on, he'd say. And all I'd have to counter that would be my increasingly shattered memory of the night, and the phrase that still ran tauntingly through my brain: *handsy in taxis*. And in the vanishingly unlikely event that the police did decide to prosecute and it went to trial, what then?

There'd be witnesses: the staff at Gordon's club, who he'd tipped lavishly over the years, who'd seen me happy, laughing, eating and drinking with him.

His word against mine. That was all there was. That and the central principle of criminal justice: innocent until proven guilty.

'HR, then,' Heather said. 'Go and see them today. You could take a union rep with you.'

I shook my head. 'Heather, I've been a trainee at that firm for less than two months. He's a senior partner. Whose career is going to end over this?'

'His. His fucking should. That filthy bastard.'

'I'm not going to, Heath. I'm just not. I can't.'

I wrapped my arms tightly around myself. I could feel my shoulders shaking, even though it wasn't cold.

'I understand, Alice. I do, honest. But just think about it. It doesn't have to be today. You've done nothing wrong. People will support you. You know it won't be just you, right? There'll have been other women he's done this to, in the past. And…'

She stopped, but I knew what she'd been going to say. And in the future. Other women who I'd be putting at risk through my silence. I said, 'It's almost seven. We should get to work.'

I turned away, blinded by tears again, and hurried to my bedroom to finish getting ready. It wasn't until I arrived in the office and one of my fellow trainees, a tall, lanky man with a kind face, took me aside and told me, that I realised I'd put on one black and one navy shoe by mistake.

Chapter Twenty-Two

Later that week, for the first time in ages, I had a day off. I had big plans: I was going to sleep and sleep for as long as I could, then have a long bath with the bathroom all to myself, put a treatment on my hair, sort out my nails, and then spend as much time as I wanted on the sofa, mainlining tea, biscuits and Netflix. I'd already had a word with Frazzle and told him he was welcome to join me.

I was as excited by the prospect as I would have been, in my old life, by a night out at a fancy restaurant or a weekend in Paris.

But I'd reckoned without the workings of my body clock. When Joe got up to get ready for work, I found myself awake too, lying sleepless in the darkness while I listened to him try to get ready super-quietly so as not to wake me.

I heard his toothbrush buzzing and the shower running, Frazzle's grumpy morning food order, Zoë's voice chatting to him, Joe saying, 'Ssssh, Alice is having a lie-in,' and Zoë whispering back, 'Oh my God, I forgot! Sorry!'

Then their voices dropped to nothing more than whispers, and I felt the last wisps of sleep vanish as I wondered what they were talking about.

I heard Joe come back into the bedroom and the not-so-quiet rattle of hangers as he rifled through his wardrobe, trying to select a shirt by touch alone. And then I heard an almighty crash as he dropped a shoe on the floor, and a muttered, 'Oh for fuck's sake!'

'It's okay. I'm awake. You can turn the light on.'

'Sure?' The room blazed with light. Joe stood there, shirt and tie undone, his trousers not yet on, his hair sticking up at odd angles because he hadn't put gel or whatever he used on it yet, and I felt a sudden, equally brilliant surge of love for him.

I stretched and sat up in bed, holding out my arms for him, and he leaned over, giving me a tantalisingly brief hug, his warm, freshly showered body pressed against mine, smelling of toothpaste and shampoo and his citrussy aftershave.

'I should be home early tonight,' he said. 'I'm going to see a client in Harmondsworth and they won't be expecting me back in the office.'

'Is it W—'

'Let's talk later. We could go for a drink, if you like?'

'Sounds good. Although maybe just one day without seeing the inside of a pub…'

He laughed. 'Fair point. Text me and tell me what you fancy. I should be back at sixish.'

He kissed me and turned the light out again. I heard him pick up his bag and keys and open and close the front door. Then I heard Zoë pottering about, the hum of the coffee machine, the ping of the microwave, her telling Frazzle off for jumping on the kitchen counter, and her own tooth-brushing and shower routine.

At last, she too opened and closed the front door, and the flat was in silence.

I realised I could barely remember the last time I'd been there, at home, alone, and it seemed like too precious an opportunity to waste sleeping. I could have a sneaky nana nap on the sofa later, I told myself, swinging my feet out of bed and pulling on my dressing gown.

The wooden floor chilly under my bare feet, I wandered through to the kitchen. Zoë had left her and Frazzle's breakfast bowls in the sink, along with Joe's coffee mug. There was a buttery knife on the counter, and I could feel grains of cat litter under my feet. The washing basket in the bathroom was overflowing, I'd noticed when I passed the open door – almost tripping on a damp towel that someone had left there.

How long had our flat been in this state? Months, probably. Every now and then someone would stack the dishwasher and switch it on, or do a load of laundry, or run the Hoover round – but the tide of mess and dirt had been creeping steadily higher and higher, and we were all too busy to do anything about it, and not home enough to care.

My idea of collapsing on the sofa was forgotten.

'Right, Frazzle. I'm going full fifties housewife,' I said aloud.

The cat didn't respond; he was up on the counter, diligently licking the butter off the knife.

'Oh, you're helping, are you? All right then, you crack on while I get dressed.'

Two hours later, I'd begun to fight back. I'd sprayed and wiped the kitchen surfaces, hoovered and mopped the floors, changed the sheets on Joe's and my bed, and was drinking coffee while I waited for the first load of washing to finish.

By lunchtime, all the washing was done and draped over the airer and radiators to dry, and the bathroom scrubbed cleaner than it had been in months. Frazzle's litter tray was the one thing I didn't touch – but I didn't need to, because Zoë's carelessness didn't extend to her cat's welfare; it was scooped out and refilled every day.

'Lucky you, having someone to take care of you,' I told the cat, but he'd fallen asleep on the sofa and barely opened an eye when I chatted to him.

I opened the fridge and saw a half-full bottle of milk, the oat milk Zoë put on her porridge, an unwrapped pack of butter that was full of crumbs, an open pack of cheese slices that had gone dry and curly round the edges, and a bag of salad leaves so wilted they'd practically turned to compost.

'Bloody hell, Frazz, it's all gone to shit, hasn't it?'

Seeing me in the kitchen, the cat hopped off the sofa and came over to wind himself round my legs, making hopeful suggestions about lunch.

'I'm bloody starving myself, actually,' I told him. 'Time for a supermarket run, I think.'

I made my way to the high street, resisting the urge to just pop into the Nag's Head and check everything was okay. But then I saw the sun glinting off the glass door of Craft Fever and remembered that Archie had played BROWSER almost twenty-four hours before and I still hadn't worked out what to do with my jumble of vowels and single N, and found myself crossing the road. I hesitated outside the door for only a second, then pushed it open. Archie was behind the counter as usual, his back to me as he rearranged the display of bottles on their glass shelves, but when he heard the ping of the bell he turned around, his expression changing from polite anticipation to surprise – shock, almost.

'Morning! How's your day going? I'm off – I stayed in bed until nine and I feel like a new woman.'

He smiled, but his smile looked slightly forced. 'Lucky you. Kind of busy here – run-up to Christmas, I guess. Everyone's planning out-of-control alcohol consumption.'

'Sounds like that's good for business.'

'Yeah, it's—' Then he looked around, and a woman emerged from the door behind the counter. She was tall – almost Archie's height – with long legs clad in Lycra leggings printed with Christmas baubles. Her glossy dark bob was almost hidden by a red hat with a grey pompom, and her clear, pale skin was free of any trace of make-up I could see.

'Er, Nat, this is Alice, who runs the Nag's Head next door,' Archie said. 'Alice, my girlfriend Nat.'

'Hello.' Nat reached out a hand and I stretched across the counter to shake it. Her skin was cool and soft, and her nails unpainted.

'I just popped in,' I said, wishing I hadn't and wondering how soon I could pop right back out again.

'So did I,' said Nat. 'Archie left his laptop at home, and I'm on my way to the gym so I dropped it off.'

She paused for a second, looking curiously at me as if to say, 'And what's your excuse?'

'I wondered whether that ginger and cinnamon ale you were telling me about has come in yet,' I said, although I knew it wasn't due for another week.

'Not yet,' Archie said. 'I'll drop you a line when it arrives.'

'Okay, great, thanks.'

Shit. Why the hell would I go there, on my day off, for any reason other than wanting to see Archie? That was my reason – my excuse was tissue-paper flimsy. But we weren't doing anything wrong. We were friends, that was all. And then I thought, *I wonder whether Archie hides his phone from Nat when he's playing Scrabble, like I hide mine from Joe?*

'Right then,' I added. 'I'd better head off. Got to get some grocery shopping done, haha.'

'And I've got to get my workout done,' Nat said.

'Bye, Archie,' we both said together. Together, we headed for the door, and there was an excruciating 'after you', 'no, after you' moment that ended with us both squeezing through together.

Nat hesitated, her face serious, like she might be about to ask me something. But I said, 'Great to meet you. See you around,' and headed off down the high street as fast as I could.

There was nothing between me and Archie, I insisted to myself. Nothing to feel guilty about. No reason for Nat to look at me in that curious, doubtful way. Nothing.

Forcing the image of her face out of my mind, I joined the throngs of shoppers in Sainsbury's. Somehow, almost without my noticing, Christmas had landed. There were stacks of mince pies and selection boxes in the aisles, wreaths and tinsel strung everywhere, plastic-wrapped turkeys and gammons in the chiller cabinets, and cheesy Christmas music playing.

And then I thought: *decorations!* It was like a string of coloured lights going off in my brain.

When I got back to the flat, I was carrying not only a carton of soup for my lunch, the ingredients for roast lamb and all the trimmings for dinner, but also the world's tiniest Christmas tree and a whole load of baubles, tinsel and lights. If I was going to spend the day being a domestic goddess, I told myself, I might as well do it properly.

I pulled the now dry washing off the radiators, put it all away – I wasn't going to iron anything; I wasn't that far gone – and arranged the tree in a corner of the living room, festooning it with sparkly things until hardly any of its green needles were visible. I peeled potatoes and chopped carrots and stuck cloves of garlic into the lamb and left it in the fridge.

Then, finally, I showered, dried and straightened my hair, painted my nails, put on some make-up, and I was sitting on the sofa with a glass of wine when Joe arrived home just after six thirty, early like he'd said he would be.

He walked in and looked around the flat, smiling, then put his arms round me and held me tight.

'The place looks amazing. I thought you were just going to chill.'

'I was, but then I got started and I couldn't stop. You know how it is.'

'I don't, actually.'

I laughed and punched him playfully on the shoulder. But his face was serious again.

'God, I need a shower and a massive fuck-off drink.'

He pulled off his jacket and tie and dropped them on the floor, then looked at them, looked at me again, picked them up and went to hang them up in the wardrobe. I switched the oven on and put some water on to boil for the potatoes.

Once I heard the shower running, I went and stood in the bathroom doorway, so he could hear me.

'How was it? Did you see Wesley? Was Maurice there?'

Joe looked at me, shampoo lather dripping down his face.

'I saw Wesley,' he said carefully.

'And? What's going to happen? They can't deport him, after he's lived here all these years. Can they?'

'Hold on.' He moved back under the shower head, soap suds and water streaming down the angles and planes of his body. 'That feels so good. The smell of that place – it feels like it's in my clothes, my hair, everywhere.'

'Why, is it dirty? Surely they can't detain people somewhere that's not…'

Joe switched off the shower, wrapped a towel and scrubbed his face and hair.

'It's not dirty. Not the bit where I was, anyway. But it smells institutional, you know. Of disinfectant and shit food. Like a hospital. And of fear, too. Frightened people smell. Especially when they're cooped up in a cell thirteen hours a day.'

I moved out of his way as he hurried through to the bedroom, dragging on a pair of ancient jogging bottoms and a T-shirt worn almost transparent with washing.

'But they can't keep Wesley there for long, can they? I mean, it must be a mistake, surely, them threatening to deport him?'

I followed Joe back to the living room. He rummaged in his bag for his phone, put it down on the sofa, then went through to the kitchen, pouring a glass of wine for himself and filling up mine. He bent down to fuss Frazzle, peered into the oven and tipped the potatoes into the pan of water, which I hadn't realised was boiling.

Then he walked back to the living room, looked at the little Christmas tree, touched the star on its top and came back to join me in the kitchen.

It was strange. It was like those horrible videos you see of animals in zoos, pacing and pacing and going nowhere because they can't. I wondered whether Joe was imagining what that would be like, or just enjoying being able to walk around his own home, knowing he could leave it any time he liked.

'Joe? It's a mistake, right?'

'Alice.' He stopped, right next to me, and wrapped his arms round me. My face was level with his chest and I could see the tiny bobbles on the fabric of his T-shirt, from it having been washed over and over again. 'I can't talk to you about this. Not about Wesley specifically. I know he came to us through you, and I know you care about Maurice, but I can't. It's a client confidentiality thing. Because Wesley's my client now, I can't discuss this matter with you.'

'But you can, surely? I mean, it's just me. I'd never tell Maurice about anything you said.'

'Alice… Fuck.' Finally he sat down, flopping on the sofa, his long legs extended in front of him. 'I wish I could. Because this whole thing is totally weird and I can't make it make sense.'

I said carefully, 'They're the Windrush generation, right? They came to the UK when places like Grenada were still colonies – that's where Maurice was born, he said – and then there was that whole thing about clamping down on immigration and the hostile environment and loads of people got deported unfairly. It's been a huge news story recently. Everyone knows the deportations are unfair and wrong. Maurice is a British citizen – he must be; he worked for local government for years and he owns a flat and claims a pension and everything. So surely his brother is here legally too?'

Joe said, 'Look, Alice. I want to get my head around this. I wish I could talk to you about it. There's no one I'd rather talk to. But you know about legal professional privilege – come on, it's basic, first-year stuff. I'd be breaking my client's trust if I disclosed any details to you. I don't want to lose my job over this and I don't want to act unethically. So please stop asking me about it. Okay?'

I don't want to lose my job. I felt blood rushing to my face – a mixture of shame and anger. Joe didn't want to lose his job like I'd lost mine.

'Alice? Come here.'

Reluctantly, I sat next to him on the sofa and he took me in his arms again.

'I love you,' he said.

'I love you too.'

And, in that moment, I remembered how much I did, and why. He'd tried to let me sleep in that morning, even though he was knackered himself. He bought me random presents for no reason. He'd chosen to work in an area of law that was all about helping people, not about making money for them. About helping people like Wesley. He was a kind man. He cared about things that mattered.

He kissed me and I kissed him back and suddenly the closeness of him – his strong back under my hands, his soft hair tickling my face – and his need for me made me frantic with longing to restore the closeness I worried we were losing. We didn't even undress properly – we had fast, hard sex right there on the sofa, and when it was over we ate the meal I'd cooked in stilted near-silence, the lights on the Christmas tree twinkling behind us.

Chapter Twenty-Three

I arrived early at the Nag's Head for my shift the next day. I'd slept badly, Joe's head beside mine on the pillow, his body next to me in bed reminding me that there was a new distance between us that was nothing to do with his arm around me. I'd had weird dreams all night, jerking awake, Joe's closeness making me feel afraid instead of secure, as if it wasn't him in bed next to me but a stranger who ought not to be there. And I started that day with a horrible, overshadowing feeling of dread that not even the twinkling Christmas lights on the high street, the Salvation Army band playing carols outside the station and the posters advertising the annual Festive Fair could shift.

But still, I tried to greet Shirley cheerfully when we arrived at the pub to open up.

'I was thinking, we need to get our Christmas decorations up, don't we? It's the third of December already. All the shops on the high street have theirs out.'

Shirley sighed. 'We've had the same tree for years. A silver one, with blue lights. I love that frosty look, don't you? And back in the day, we always used to have a lock-in on Christmas Eve, people still in here drinking until three or four in the morning. Those were wild times!'

'I can imagine.'

'I remember one time, John Sutcliffe – he passed away a couple of years back – his missus came down in the small hours, banging on the door and shouting that she'd already got up to put the turkey on, and what the hell was he playing at, still down the boozer.'

She laughed, and I joined in, although if I was honest my sympathies were entirely with John's missus.

'Joe and I normally go to my mum and dad's,' I said. 'Mum does the whole shebang – turkey, beef, Yorkshire puddings and bread sauce – and my granny and aunt and cousins will be there too. But obviously that might be different this year, if you need me here.'

Shirley pushed back her hair. She looked tired, I realised – just as knackered as I felt.

'Shirl? Are you okay?'

'Make me a cuppa, would you, love? You know how I like it.'

I obliged, piling three sugars into Shirl's tea after brewing it until it was the colour of a *Love Island* contestant's tan, and made a coffee for myself, and we sat down together at one of the tables. I normally loved the pub at this time of the morning, quiet and sleepy still, as if it was taking a deep breath in readiness for the rush to come, calm in contrast to the bustle of the street outside.

But this morning it felt different. It felt as if it might not rouse from its slumber as it usually did. It was just me, I told myself, that weird, almost hungover feeling I'd had all morning, the vague, unspecified unease I'd felt around Joe, as if we'd had a row. Except we hadn't. Not really.

'Did you see that young fellow I was talking to the other day?'

'Fabian Flatley?'

'Oh, so you know him?'

'I've never met him. But his company owns the place across the road, that used to be the Star and Garter. It's studio apartments now. Drew lives in one of them.'

'He's an astute businessman. Ambitious.'

I couldn't help wondering whether Shirley had formed her own impression of Fabian as an astute businessman, or whether he'd told her he was one.

'What about him? What was he doing here? You two were talking for ages.'

Shirley nodded. 'What he said to me, love, was… Well, he said things have moved on. He said young people now don't want to drink in pubs like they used to. They want to sit at home with their herbal tea and stream things, don't they?'

'Sometimes they do,' I replied defensively. 'But they go out too. I mean, come on. Look how many people came to our games night. Look at all the people that come here every morning, and drink coffee and work.'

'Coffee's all very well,' Shirley said. 'But it don't butter no parsnips. This place is still running at a loss. It has been for a while. And all the time, the value of the property's going up and up.'

'We could turn it around,' I insisted. 'We are already. I mean, I know I don't get to see the accounts or anything. But the takings have been up, haven't they? We're full most days.'

'And run off our feet. And if you hire more staff, that means more costs. It's not sustainable, that's what Fabian said.'

Fabian again, I thought. *Like he's some big cheese who's just connected with you on LinkedIn.*

‘He wants to buy the place, doesn’t he? And turn it into flats, like across the road?’

Shirley nodded. ‘He’s spoken to Cathy, the landlord, already. He’s made an offer, and it’s been accepted.’

Although I’d been expecting her words, they still felt like a punch in the stomach. ’So does that mean the pub will close?’

‘Well, to be fair, love, that’s been on the cards for a while. Juan and I want to move to Spain, start our new life there. And let’s be frank, no one’s going to take on a place like this, not when it needs so much work.’

‘But I—’

‘Oh, Alice, I know you think you would. I know you’ve fallen in love with the old place. And I know how much time and work you’ve spent on it. But it’s a money pit. Last time Cathy was out here she got some workmen to quote on upgrading it, giving it a spot of TLC, and – well. Let’s just say that idea got shelved, right there. So we’ve just been limping on, waiting for the time when it would finally need to close. And now that’s happening.’

‘But we’ve done so much! The new menu, the new website, the games afternoon, even the coffee machine – it’s really made a difference. We’re getting far more customers in than before. Almost all the people that used to go to the Star and Garter come here now.’

Shirley’s face softened. ‘I know, love; you’ve done a great job. It’s been wonderful to see the old place getting some love. But a few coffees in the morning, them fancy vegan things on the menu, even a load of punters sat around playing cribbage on a Saturday afternoon – it’s a drop in the ocean, compared to what the place needs spending on it.’

I took a sip of my coffee, but it had gone cold and tasted horribly bitter all of a sudden. I felt queasy, the feeling of unease I'd woken up with now crystallised into cold fear that seemed to have closed itself around my throat so I couldn't swallow.

The Nag's Head was going to close. There'd be no more early mornings wiping the tables and pushing the Hoover around. My plans to clear out the rooms upstairs would never be realised – or at least, they would, but only when the builders turned up to divide them up into tiny studio rooms like the one where Drew was staying. The open mic poetry nights we'd been talking about would never happen. The chestnut wellington Zoë had talked about putting on the Christmas menu would never be cooked.

And I wouldn't have a job. I could get one, of course – there were far more bars desperate for staff than there were people wanting to work in them, as I'd discovered when hiring help for the Nag's Head. *But*, my brain said, petulant as a child, *I don't want to work in just any bar.*

I wanted to work *here*. I wanted to be in charge. I wanted it to be mine.

But even as my mind articulated the thought, I realised how far-fetched and downright stupid the idea was. Not only would refurbishing the pub cost a fortune, but the land on which it stood and the structure of the building itself was a valuable asset – and would be more valuable divided into residential units than it could ever be as a pub.

'I know you're fond of the place,' Shirley said. 'Heaven only knows I am, too. But it's no more my pub than it is yours. And really, this was only ever a bit of fun for you, wasn't it? Something to do while you got your head back in the right place and then went back to being a lawyer.'

I shook my head. 'I'm not going to go back to being a lawyer.'

'Well, you were never going to spend your whole life working here, were you? You're too good for this place. That's what I saw on your face, clear as day, first time you walked in with your other half. You were thinking, "Look at us, in a place where common people drink. Isn't it bizarre?"'

My face flamed with embarrassment. The Alice who'd walked into the Nag's Head all those months before and looked around in fascination at the stained ceiling, the worn carpet and the jar of pickled eggs had thought she was too good for it. She'd felt like she'd arrived on another planet. And now, it seemed to me like that girl, so confident of her future, so secure in the life laid out for her, was the one who was an alien.

'But you should have seen some of the places I drank in when I was a student. Absolute dives. This place – sure, like you say, it could do with a bit of a facelift, but deep down it's all right. It's more than all right. And it's the people that make a place, anyway.'

Shirley shook her head. 'Whatever you say. It's neither here nor there, anyway. Cathy's accepted Fabian's offer and that's that. End of an era, but it's a relief in a way.'

'When's it going to happen?' I asked, desperate for at least a small stay of execution.

'Cathy reckons we may as well stay open over the festive season,' Shirley said. 'No point missing out on what profit there is to be made over Christmas and New Year. She thinks they'll be ready to complete on the sale by mid-January, although of course

Fabian'll need planning permission for the change of use. He'll get it though, you mark my words. He's the type who's got every bent local councillor on speed dial.'

So that was it – weeks, just a matter of six or eight – before the deal was done and the Nag's Head closed its doors forever.

We sat there in silence for a moment. Then Shirley said she had a pile of admin to get through that was enough to give a person a nosebleed and she'd better crack on. Heart sinking, I said I'd finish off the cleaning before the doors opened. And we both stood up and took our cups to be washed and got on with our work as if it was just another normal day.

At half past ten, Zoë arrived, breezing through the door and calling out, 'Hello, hello! You'll never guess what, I managed to persuade the guy from Ready Steady Bread to part with some of his sourdough starter. So it won't be long before we're baking the Ging— I mean, the Nag's Head's very own artisan bread. How cool is th— What's the matter, Alice?'

I shook my head and pointed to the office, where Shirley was sitting staring silently at her computer. She wasn't typing anything and her hand wasn't even on the mouse, and I'd have bet anything that if you'd asked her what was on the screen, she wouldn't have been able to tell you.

'Kitchen?' Zoë whispered.

I nodded and we went through to the space that used to be Juan's and was Zoë's now. So much had changed since the days of the catering-sized bags of frozen chips and the ready-meal lasagnes. Now, fresh vegetables were stacked on shelves, kimchi and dill pickles were fermenting away in their jars, and the freezer was home to several chicken carcasses waiting to be turned into stock and later soup.

Zoë dumped a shopping bag on the counter and pulled out a jar of beige-coloured sludge that was presumably her precious sourdough starter. Giving the glass a little pat, she put it on the shelf next to the pickles.

'What's going on?' she asked.

Leaning my hip against the counter, I told her. I didn't make any more of an attempt to soften the blow than Shirley had when she'd told me – but, whereas my reaction had been to want to cry, Zoë was made of sterner stuff.

'But we can't let that happen, Alice. We just can't. It's bullshit. They can't close this place down and turn it into shitty, poky little studios that wankers pay a fortune to live in because there's some ridiculous communal living space with a water cooler and a pot plant. Not Drew, obviously – he's not a wanker. But that Flatley man is.'

'What? How do you know him?'

'He goes to my gym. Never puts his weights away, sits on the bench talking on his phone when you're waiting to use it, doesn't clean his sweat off the equipment. Pillock.'

I sighed. 'Pillock or not, he's buying the Nag's Head.'

'Not if I have anything to do with it.'

'But there's nothing we can do.'

'Of course there fucking is!'

I felt, for the first time that morning, a brief flare of hope, mixed with a completely unfamiliar emotion: a new respect and liking for Zoë. It had never occurred to me before that whatever her feelings for Joe and me, she genuinely loved the pub.

'What? What can we do?'

'I don't know! I haven't figured it out yet. But we can bloody well fight for this place, and I'm going to. Aren't you?'

Chapter Twenty-Four

It wasn't Tuesday, and Heather and I weren't in Pret a Manger. Rather than waiting another five days, I'd asked her if she was free to meet that evening, and she'd suggested a cocktail bar near her work. I'd arrived first, a few minutes early, and been escorted to the table Heather had booked, where I ordered a pisco sour and took a look around.

Heather might have valued reliability, consistency and convenience when it came to lunch, but clearly she took a different approach to her evening entertainment. I'd entered the bar through a fridge in the back of a greasy spoon café in Hoxton. The room was so dark I could only just see that it was decorated with Barbie and Ken dolls in various sex positions (and yes, gay, lesbian and polyamorous relationships were represented). When the waitress brought my drink, she put a little bowl of popcorn flavoured with Aleppo pepper down on the table too.

I realised that this was the kind of place Heather came with her Tinder dates. It was so off-the-scale hip; the people around me were so self-consciously having fun, the waitress's multiple piercings were so clearly what she'd describe as a 'curated ear'. It had been so long since I'd been anywhere even vaguely fashionable, and part of me felt giddy with excitement to be somewhere fabulous again. But a bigger part felt flooded with sadness for the Nag's Head, which was now never going to have the chance to become a favourite hangout of beautiful people.

'Hello!' Heather came dashing through the not-a-fridge door. She was wearing a cocoon dress in a pale lilacy grey that would have made me look as if I'd been dug up after being dead for several weeks but was subtle and interesting on her. Her hair was scooped back in an elaborate half-French plait, which managed to look casual and undone even though I knew it would have taken her ages to get it that way. Unusually, she was wearing heels: charcoal suede peep-toe shoe boots with a sculptural, bulbous heel.

I stood up and returned her hug, wishing I'd worn something more fashion-forward than my jeans and Bardot jumper. And then I thought, *I bet that girl with the earrings doesn't know how to clean beer lines, and I do.*

Heather ordered something called a cereal martini – or it may have been serial, I had no idea; it seemed equally implausible that someone should order a drink that tasted of cornflakes as one that kept repeating on you – and took a handful of popcorn.

'Christ, that's hot! Practically took the roof of my mouth off. But I'm going to eat all of it anyway, I just know it. I had the most depressing salad for lunch, all cold and damp like this pissy weather. How are you?'

'Awful. Everything's gone to shit.'

'Oh no. It's not you and Joe, is it?'

'Not that. We're okay.' Hanging on to okay by our fingernails, but still just about okay enough that the word could be used about us.

'So what…?'

Briefly, in between large gulps of my cocktail that left an alcoholic egg-white moustache on my top lip, I told her.

'The pub's being sold. Shirley's retiring to Spain. I'm going to have to get another job.'

Heather sipped her own drink and listened, her head on one side, as I explained about the Nag's Head being sold to be converted into flats and Juan wanting to play golf in the sunshine and eat paella that hadn't come in a box from Iceland. I could almost hear the thoughts forming in Heather's mind: *Well, the sensible thing to do is to get a job at a law firm. Wasn't it only ever meant to be a temporary thing, to make ends meet? There are other bars you could work in, if you really think it's the right thing for you, although it seems a bit – you know…*

But to her credit, she didn't say any of those things. She said, 'That must be gutting.'

I nodded miserably.

'After all the work you put in,' Heather went on. 'And the worst thing is I never actually got around to coming and seeing it, visiting you there. I'm sorry. I'm a rubbish friend.'

'You're not. You're busy, and you weren't to know the plug was going to get pulled on the whole thing.'

'Is it definite, though? A done deal? I mean, property stuff usually takes ages to get through.'

'Zoë says we should fight for it. But it just seems impossible, and I don't know how much fight there is in me right now, to be honest.'

'What?' Heather shovelled more popcorn into her mouth. 'Ouch, that bloody burns. Of course you must fight for it, if that's what you want to do. And I can totally see why you would. This city – this world – needs places where people can get together and have a laugh more than it needs luxury bloody apartments.'

'There is a housing shortage, though. You read all the time about the escalating homelessness crisis for young people in British cities today.'

Heather gestured the waitress over. 'Same again, Alice? Another pisco sour, please, and I'd like a vodka saketini, and could we have another bowl of this napalm popcorn?'

She turned back to me as the waitress sloped off. 'Of course there's a housing crisis – everyone knows that. But you're not going to solve it by charging millennials north of fifteen hundred quid a month to live in twenty-five square metres. I mean, come on! If he's supporting rough sleepers to find sustainable, safe roofs over their heads or addressing the problems experienced by families living in insecure private rentals, then whoever this dude is who wants to buy the place can be all smug on his website. Until then he can shut the fuck up.'

I laughed. 'I agree. But, worthy cause or no worthy cause, people do want to live in those places. Drew says the one where he's staying – which is just across the road – has a massive waiting list.'

'Hmmm. Well, the first question is, will he get planning permission? I bet he won't.'

'He did across the road,' I pointed out. 'Shirley reckons he's bribing a planning officer.'

'Well, if he is, that's a criminal offence. Can you find out if it's true?'

'I don't know. I don't know how I'd even begin to look into it.'

'Bribe one yourself?'

I laughed. 'If only. I've got no money, for one thing. And anyway, that wouldn't be right. Would it?'

'Guess not. Not exactly a good look on your CV, if you ever do decide you want to get back into law.'

'Heath, you know I don't. Not ever.'

'Okay, okay, fair enough. Well then there's only one solution I can think of.'

'Which is?'

'They go low, you go high.'

'Yeah, sure, Michelle Obama. That's easy to say. But what would I actually do?'

'Buy the place yourself.'

'Oh, right. With my amazing assets totalling thirty pairs of worn shoes, a laptop that's on its last legs and a fluffy ginger cat that isn't even mine.'

'Okay, so maybe not just you on your own. But aren't community-owned pubs a thing now?'

'I don't know. Are they?'

'I'm pretty sure they are. There's a place in the village where my dad lives that was closed for ages, and everyone moaned about how the heart had been ripped out of the community, and eventually they stopped moaning and did something about it. Hold on.'

She pulled her phone out of her bag and tapped at the screen impatiently for a bit.

'Honestly, I like this place and everything but the reception's dire. Last time I met a Tinder guy here we literally sat on opposite sides of the room for half an hour because we couldn't message each other and it's so frigging dark I couldn't recognise the bloke. Which may also have been because he was completely different from his photo. Looked like the love child of Adam Driver and an alpaca.'

I laughed. 'Poor alpaca. Or poor Adam. I'm not sure who gets the shitty end of that stick.'

'Yes, well, anyway. Here it is. The Gladstone Arms. "Serving the community of Winterborne Newton since the seventeenth century, the Gladstone Arms fell into disrepair..." blah blah. Says it got closed down ten years ago – that's about right, I remember sneaking in there after I got my A Level results and getting completely wankered on snakebite and black – "Members of the local community decided something needed to be done. Establishing a co-operative shareholding, they invited residents to become part of the solution, and together turned the Gladstone Arms into an asset of real community value."'

'How did they do that?'

'Probably started by picking a load of used hypodermic needles out of the carpet. The place has loads of social problems. But they don't say that here.'

'What *do* they say?'

'Hold on, there's a link here, "Our story". It's taking ages to load – no, got it. They say they started out by forming a committee and appointed a chair, secretary and treasurer. Then they held their first public meeting. They invited loads of people from the community: local councillors (hopefully not bent planning officers), someone from a charity that works with elderly people, the local vicar – all the worthies, basically.'

'Surely local vicars are massively down on pubs?'

'You'd think so. Anyway, then they embarked on a massive fundraising exercise. It explains how the co-operative model works, but you'll remember that from when you studied corporate law, right?'

'Wrong. It was ages ago and I was probably hungover.'

'Okay, so essentially everyone buys a shareholding, and however much money they put in, their shares are of equal value. So if you get someone with deep pockets who bungs you a grand, they get the same voting rights as an old dear who puts in a fiver.'

'Makes sense.'

'And then – here's the good bit – they contacted a charity that exists purely to bring derelict pubs into community ownership and reopen them, and they applied for funding through them.'

'Is that really a thing?'

'Looks like it. They're called Heart of the Community. I'll send you over the link.'

I imagined sitting at one of the tables in the Nag's Head with my laptop, composing an email that might be a final lifeline for the pub. I imagined pressing send, then waiting and waiting for a reply. I imagined trying to persuade people to donate money – people who were struggling anyway, barely getting by month to month – and the first donations trickling in, like a few grains of sand when what was needed was a mountain. I tried to guess what Shirley would say when I mentioned the idea to her, but my imagination completely failed me on that one.

It seemed like the most fruitless, thankless task ever. It felt doomed to failure.

'Heather? This is a totally daft idea, isn't it? I should just accept that it's been a fun few months, let the place be sold and move on with my life. Shouldn't I?'

'You know what, if you'd asked me that a couple of months ago, I'd have said yes. But now I've seen what you've put into that place. You love it. And I reckon you're good at it. So maybe this won't work. Maybe it's a stupid idea. But if you give it your best shot, at least you'll know you tried, right? It's like when I go to court. There's always a chance I'll lose. The judge could be in a foul mood, the other side could have stronger arguments, something could come to light at the last minute – anything could happen. So all I can do is work my hardest, go in there and fight for it.'

'Fight? Funny, that's what Zoë said.'

'I reckon Zoë's right,' she said. 'How about another cocktail?'

On the way to the Nag's Head the next day, I filled Zoë in on what Heather and I had discussed – although it had all got a bit blurry after the fourth pisco sour.

'Obviously I was a bit drunk by the end,' I said. 'But it felt like there's hope, you know. Like, other people have done this and maybe so can we. Now, though, in the cold light of day…'

'Cold is right.' Zoë dug her hands deep into the pockets of her coat. It was a long, military-style grey number, slightly too big for her, which she said she'd bought from a charity shop after resolving to buy no new clothes for at least a year. It was eight o'clock and the morning was a deep, depressing grey. 'Light, not so much. It's funny how everything seems so positive when you've had a couple of drinks and you're with a mate and you're having a laugh, and then the next morning the Fear gets you.'

'Too right. I mean, it's so much money and we've only got as long as it takes Fabian to get his planning permission in principle, and then he'll rush the deal through as quick as he can.'

'Then we've got to be quick, too,' Zoë said. 'Agile, right? First thing is to get as many people through the doors as we can before Christmas. Let's talk to Drew. He's the social-media marketing guru – he'll have good ideas. And I'll get cracking on that Christmas menu.'

For a second, the optimism I'd felt the previous night with Heather resurfaced, but then, as we approached the pub, the scale of the challenge facing us descended again. In my head, I mostly only saw the good bits of the Nag's Head: the way the lights above the bar made its wooden top glow when it was freshly polished; the smell of Zoë's cooking when plates were carried through from the kitchen; the buzz of chatter and laughter when the place was full of people having a good time.

But now, on this overcast, freezing morning, I saw all the things I'd noticed when Joe and I had walked through the door that first time: the ugly, threadbare carpet; the dingy walls hung with old-fashioned prints of nothing in particular, like they'd been ordered as a job lot years ago by someone who didn't really care; the musty smell that never quite went away, which I was sure was due to rising damp or some other dread condition that would cost a fortune to fix. Not to mention the ever-present pong from the men's toilets – evidence, surely, that every pipe in the place would need replacing sooner rather than later.

'The first thing we need to do,' Zoë said, 'is get those bloody Christmas decorations up. Let's crack on before Shirley gets in. Once they're done she can't make us take them down again.'

'She might,' I said.

'She won't.'

So, as soon as Drew arrived, we sent him up to the attic room on a treasure hunt that I was sure was just as likely to turn up spiders as spangles.

But, although there were cobwebs in his hair when he emerged from the warren of upstairs rooms after twenty minutes or so, and he was covered in dust, he was grinning cheerfully.

'Check this out!' He dumped an armful of black bin liners and boxes on the floor. 'It's a tack fest straight out of the eighties. Fabulous.'

One long box contained the white and silver tree Shirley had described; another was full of red and green baubles. There were swathes of slightly moth-eaten tinsel and a huge tangle of fairy lights.

'God only knows if these still work,' he said.

'We'll probably switch them on and trip all the electrics.' Zoë eyed the plug dubiously.

'Or there'll be some fault that creates a spark and we'll burn the whole place down,' I predicted.

'Well, then Cathy can collect the insurance money and all our problems will be over,' Zoë said.

'If we go down, we'll go down in flames.' Drew eased the tree's branches open, and a shower of glittery fake needles rained down onto the carpet.

'Jesus, the plastic in that thing,' Zoë said. 'It's basically a bio-hazard in Christmas tree form.'

'Never mind that. Help me get it up.'

'Do you normally need help getting it up?'

Drew and Zoë shook with laughter, and I couldn't help joining in. Any spark of attraction I'd hoped might develop between them hadn't materialised, and I was fairly sure it wasn't going to; the banter that passed between them seemed purely friendly. But what that meant about Zoë's feelings for Joe, if anything, wasn't a problem I could dwell on right now.

I heaved one of the corner tables aside, and Drew lifted the tree onto its rickety stand. After wrestling with the knots and kinks in their wire, together we wound the lights round and round its trunk and hung what seemed like hundreds of baubles on its balding branches, hiding the worst bits with swathes of tarnished tinsel.

'Ready for the big reveal?' Drew knelt and reached for the plug socket. 'God, this carpet still reeks of fags.'

'Go on then. Hope you've got the fire services on speed dial, Alice.'

I knew Zoë was joking, but I kept my phone in my hand, just in case. Drew pressed the switch. For a second nothing happened, then, one by one, the lights glimmered to life. Blue, violet, silver and white, they blinked steadily among the sparkly branches, reflecting off the multicoloured balls and stars.

Suddenly, the dingy interior of the pub felt cosy and welcoming. The glow of the tree made the gloomy room look like a picture on an old-fashioned Christmas card; it only needed a couple of stockings hung up over the fireplace and a ginger cat snoozing beneath them – and a fire in the grate would have helped, of course. The grey, rainy street outside seemed a world away, and I knew that if I was there, I'd want to walk through the door straight away, into the warm, and stay as long as I could.

'It certainly hides a multitude of sins,' Drew remarked.

'Be amazing to see it scrubbed up properly,' Zoë mused.

'Shit,' I said, hearing the familiar rattling car engine outside, 'Shirley's coming.'

We looked at each other like three kids caught snaffling mince pies out of the tin.

'I'd better get cracking on some muffins.' Zoë fled to the kitchen.

'I'll just get everything back to how it was upstairs.' Drew legged it through the 'Staff only' door.

I glanced around, but there was nowhere for me to hide. Own it, I told myself.

But one look at Shirley's face when she walked in the door told me it was going to be okay. She gazed around, her hands clasped to her chest, and then she reached up to wipe away a tear.

'Oh, my poor old pub,' she sighed. 'It looks just like the old days. I suppose the place deserves one last hurrah.'

'Shirl,' I said. 'Listen to me. This doesn't have to be the end, not necessarily. I mean, I know you and Juan are looking forward to starting your retirement in Spain, and that's great. But the Nag's Head doesn't have to close, you know. There's a way to save it. It's an outside chance, but it might just work.'

She shook her head. 'I've backed plenty of outside chances in my time and the buggers always pull up lame around the third fence.'

'Maybe they do. Maybe this will. But I think we should try. Let me explain.'

I made her a cup of tea and sat with her while I explained all about community ownerships and co-operative shareholdings – all the stuff that had seemed so logical and possible when Heather and I discussed it. But I could see from Shirley's face that I was on a hiding to nothing.

'You don't know what it's like,' she said. 'Taking on someone like Fabian Flatley. That man's a shark and we're minnows. People like him always get their own way, with their money and their sharp suits and their laptops and their gift of the gab. We'll be eaten alive.'

I looked at her careworn face, the dark roots growing out of her peach-blonde hair, the cerise lipstick settling into the lines around her mouth. I felt sorry for her, and I recognised that she was almost certainly right. But at the same time, I felt a surge of frustration. She might not want to take on Fabian Flatley, but I did. She might not know how to fight this kind of fight, but I did. Or at least I hoped I did.

'Shirley,' I said. 'You're forgetting something. I got a training contract at one of London's top ten law firms. I own sharp suits, and a laptop. I've been told I have the gift of the gab. I'm not just a barmaid; I'm a solicitor. Or I almost am. And you know what they call lawyers? Sharks. So why don't you leave this with me and let me see what I can do?'

She looked at me like I was a greying sheepskin rug that had lain in front of the dead hearth for decades then suddenly jumped up and started gambolling around the pub bleating away.

'All right, Alice. You do what you think best. I think you're daft as a brush but I won't stand in your way. Now I've the stocktake to do, if you'll excuse me.'

Chapter Twenty-Five

I looked at Shirley's departing back for a moment as she headed towards the cellar stairs. She'd known and loved the Nag's Head for far longer than I had; it was her pub far more than it was mine. And although she seemed resigned to it being sold, even complicit in it, I knew it must hurt her at least as much as it did me – more, even.

But she had her own life to lead, her longed-for retirement in the sun with Juan. I, on the other hand, had a mission. If the Nag's Head was to be saved, it was for me – and Zoë, and Drew, and whatever ragtag army of volunteers and donors we could marshal – to do it.

And the frightening thing was, I had no idea where even to begin.

Wearily, I began setting up for the day, but before I'd finished arranging the menus on the tables, the door opened. It wasn't one of our early regulars with a laptop, eager for coffee. It wasn't the mums with their buggies.

It was Maurice.

'Good morning, Alice.'

'Hello! I didn't expect to see you here so early. What can I get you? Tea? Coffee? Half of Guinness?'

Surely not at this time of the morning, not even in the midst of the horror Maurice was still enduring with Wesley.

'Actually, Alice, I came to talk to you.'

'To me? Of course.'

I led him over to a table at the back of the room where we would have more privacy, rather than his usual one in the corner by the window. We sat down, and Maurice removed his hat, placing it carefully on his lap, but I could see that his hands were twisting the fabric, restless and anxious.

'How are you bearing up?' I asked. 'How's Wesley?'

Maurice took the carefully ironed handkerchief out of his pocket and looked at it, but his eyes were dry.

'I went to see him yesterday. In that place.'

'The detention centre?'

He nodded. 'It's horrible, Alice. It's like a prison. Not that I've ever been to a prison. We're law-abiding people.'

'I know you are. Of course you are.'

'He says the room where he sleeps is tiny – and cold. He has to share with another man, a refugee from Syria. There's no privacy, no door to the toilet even. And Abdul – he's not a violent man, Wesley tells me. But I was worried, wondering if he should ask to be moved. Because Abdul is traumatised. He screams in his dreams at night, and Wesley can't sleep.'

'I'm so sorry. It must be awful.'

Maurice nodded. 'The food is horrible, he says. He's got so thin. They eat off plastic plates so they can't use them as missiles, or break them and turn them into weapons.'

I nodded. He must know, I thought, that I could be of little or no help to him. Perhaps he just wanted me to listen, so I would.

'The worst thing, he says, is that all the people there are so sad. It's like limbo, you know, in the Bible. Purgatory, they call it. No one wants to be there, but they dread leaving more.'

'Because leaving would mean being deported?'

'We can't say "deported". Wesley says your young man explained it to him. Deportation's only for criminals. For people like him, it's called removal.'

Removal. As if they were talking about an inconvenience, like a piece of unwanted furniture or a load of rubbish, not people at all.

'And Wesley's not a criminal. Of course he isn't.' I was reassuring myself as much as Maurice.

'He's no criminal. Not here. But back in Jamaica, he would be.'

My mind whirled with confusion. Different scenarios rushed through my head – had Wesley killed someone, back in Jamaica, and fled justice to join his brother? But it couldn't be – not that gentle, church-going man. And surely Maurice wouldn't have harboured a fugitive from justice for all these years, even if he was his own brother?

'I don't understand.'

'The problem is…' Maurice folded the handkerchief and tucked it carefully back in his breast pocket, and his hands returned to twisting the brim of his hat. 'The problem is that he isn't telling the truth.'

I waited.

'Your young man, Joe, says he can appeal the decision to remove him. But Wesley doesn't want to. He says he must live with the consequences of what he's done. And that means I must too.'

I said, 'But if there's a reason why he should be allowed to stay here, surely you should use that? I don't know anything much about immigration law, although I know how harsh and unfair it is, but people do get offered asylum, all the time. Joe will help him, I'm sure. He'll do everything he can for Wesley.'

'He's a good man.'

I wasn't sure whether Maurice meant his brother, or my boyfriend, but either way I was sure it was true. I nodded again.

'But he can only help if Wesley tells him the truth. And Wesley doesn't want to do that. He's too ashamed. He's afraid of the consequences.'

'Maurice,' I said, 'whatever Wesley's done, surely it can't be that bad?'

'I don't believe it is. So last night, I made up my mind. I decided to speak out. To tell you, so you can tell Joe, and he can help Wesley.'

I felt a heavy weight of responsibility. Part of me wanted to bundle Maurice into a taxi and take him to the Billings Pitt Furzedown office, shut him in a meeting room with Joe and leave them to it. But I couldn't. He'd chosen to confide in me, and so I had to hear him out.

I listened, there in the Nag's Head in the flickering light of the Christmas tree, the glimmer of the tinsel, while Maurice told his story. And the strange thing was, once he'd told me the truth, it was like I'd known all along.

I sent Joe a message as soon as Maurice had left and stared at my screen for a few seconds, waiting for the little blue ticks to appear alongside it, but they didn't. This wasn't unusual – he could have been in a meeting, or in court, or even, for all I knew, at the detention centre speaking to Wesley. It was still frustrating – I needed to speak to him, to pass on the information Maurice had entrusted to me. But there was nothing I could do; I could only wait.

The pub was quiet: a few people were working; the mums with their babies were enjoying their lattes and date and banana muffins. There was no dominoes game. I suspected there wouldn't be – not today. Shirley had finished her stocktake and left to take Juan to a physiotherapy appointment. Zoë was in the kitchen, plugged into headphones as she cooked. Drew was hunched over his laptop at a corner table, so I fetched myself a glass of water and joined him.

'I've set up a crowdfunder,' he said. 'That Heart of the Community charity your mate recommended says that kind of thing – small donations from individuals, people running marathons with sponsorship, cake sales and shit – won't raise much. Not nearly as much as we need. But it's a start, right?'

'It's a start,' I agreed.

He pushed the computer over to me and I looked at the page. 'Save our local pub' he'd written, and he'd included a load of information about the Nag's Head that made it sound far more of an asset of community value than it really was. Already, someone had donated twenty pounds.

'That was me, to be fair,' Drew said. 'I had to check it was working, didn't I?'

I felt a surge of affection for my brother, whose only income came from working in the pub. But then, so did mine – I supposed

I'd find myself donating twenty pounds too, another tiny grain of sand on the mountain we were going to have to build.

'And check this out,' Drew went on, opening the Nag's Head website.

'"Upcoming events",' I read. '"The Nag's Head inaugural open mic poetry night. Five pounds entry on the door or book your ticket online – this one's sure to sell out fast. One hundred pounds in prize money for the winning poet." Poetry? Really? Doesn't sound like much of a crowd-puller to me.'

'That's what you said about the games night. Poetry's having a moment right now. It's edgy as fuck. That online magazine I write for sometimes has tripled its mailing list in the past year.'

'What, to two hundred?'

'Three and a half thousand, as it happens. Don't knock it.'

'Twenty-second of December. That's two weeks away. Reckon you'll be able to get your masterpiece written in time?'

'Done it already. Loads of them, in fact. It's just a question of deciding which one's most likely to bring the house down and win me the hundred quid first prize.'

I laughed. It was typical of my brother to be so casually self-assured, totally undaunted by the prospect of standing up in front of what would surely be a tough audience and reciting poetry he'd written – and to assume that there'd be more than about three other people prepared to do the same.

I wished I felt even a fraction of his confidence.

'Well, clearly you've got it all under control.' Feeling the buzz of an incoming message from my phone, I added, 'I'm going to take a break. Grab something to eat. Okay?'

But Drew wasn't listening. He'd already turned back to his screen, where he was promoting the hell out of the poetry night on social media.

I pushed open the door and stepped out into the cold. It was brighter now, but still overcast, and a cutting wind was sending empty crisp packets and crushed Coke cans scudding and rattling along the pavement.

I glanced at my phone, hoping for a reply from Joe, but the alert had been from my Scrabble app. Archie had made his move: QUOTIENT, on a double word score. Instinctively, I glanced through the window of Craft Fever and saw him behind the counter.

I pointed at the screen and gave him a thumbs-up, and he laughed, gesturing to the door for me to come in. There were no customers in the shop – and no Nat either – and I guessed he could do with some company. And, I realised, I could do with some advice. Archie had started his business from scratch; he'd understand the horrible sense of impending failure I was feeling about the pub.

I pushed open the door and stepped into the bright, warm interior, with its smell of malt and honey.

'Morning!' Archie stepped around the counter and hugged me. He smelled amazing, too, of whatever aftershave or hair pomade he used – something dry and woody. 'How's the day been so far?'

'A bit rubbish,' I said. 'We got the Christmas tree up, at least.'

'I saw when I opened up this morning. Festive. What can I get you? Coffee? Water? Is it too early for gin?'

'That's a tempting offer, but it definitely is. Water would be great.'

He handed me a glass and opened a packet of crisps.

'Try these. They're a new thing – black truffle flavour. I guess they might be a bit Marmite, but I love them.'

I took one. 'Oh my God, that's amazing. Black truffle crisps – who knew?'

'What a time to be alive, right? They do a caviar flavour too, but I reckon that might be a bit much. You should get them for the pub – I'll give you the guy's card.'

'Thanks. Only I'm not sure there's going to be a pub for much longer.'

'Huh?'

I took another crisp and a gulp of water, and then I poured out the whole story. It was strange – when I'd regaled Heather, Zoë and Drew with the threat of closure from Fabian Flatley and Shirley's apparent indifference to it all, I'd been factual, even positive, focusing purely on what could be done to keep the business alive. But now, sitting there on the polished church pew next to Archie, I felt only despair.

'I mean, we're doing what we can. A crowdfunder, and we're going to try and launch a community shareholding scheme. But it just seems hopeless. I don't know if it's worth even trying.'

Without warning, I felt a massive lump in my throat, and tears stinging my eyes.

'Shit, Alice.' Archie leaned over and put his arm around me. 'Hey, don't cry.'

I don't know what it is about those words, but they have the same effect on me, every single time. If I'm in danger of collapsing into a sobbing heap and someone says, 'Don't cry,' and is kind, it sets me off, every time. And it did then.

I found myself burying my face in his soft corduroy shirt, weeping like I'd never stop.

'Ssssh,' he murmured. 'It's okay. Come on.'

Gently, he helped me to my feet and led me behind the counter and through a door. Through my tears, I saw a small desk with a laptop on it, and something halfway between a biggish armchair and a tiny sofa. A love seat, I guess you'd call it.

'Can't have people crying right in my shop front,' Archie said, his arm still around my shoulders. 'Bad for business. People would think I'd sold you off beer and refused to refund you.'

I managed a laugh, then sobbed even harder, and Archie sat me down on the love seat and held me close, not seeming to care that I was soaking the front of his rust-coloured shirt with my tears.

'It's all going to be okay,' he said. 'Whatever happens, it'll be all right. It seems like the worst thing in the world right now, but it's not. You'll get through this, Alice. You're amazing and strong and brilliant. You've got this. I promise.'

His words didn't mean a whole lot – not really, not as words. They were empty things, the only comfort he was able to give. Because what else was he going to do, PayPal me half a million pounds? But that wasn't the point. He was there: warm and safe and comforting. And I let myself be comforted, realising even while I cried how much I'd needed this release, this outpouring of all the tension and tiredness that had been building up inside me over the past months and had been brought to a head by worry about Maurice, Wesley and the very survival of the Nag's Head.

I cried until I couldn't cry any more, and then Archie tore off several squares from the roll of kitchen towel on his desk and handed them to me, waiting silently while I blew my nose and mopped my eyes. It was just my luck, I thought, that whenever I saw Archie I was windblown, tear-stained or swooning like a heroine in a Victorian novel – and then I wondered why on earth I cared about that.

'Shit,' I said. 'I'm so sorry. I've got no idea what that was all about.'

'Quotient was a pretty awesome word, especially on a double. But I never had you as such a sore loser.'

I laughed again, and this time I found I couldn't stop, any more than I'd been able to stop crying a few minutes before. My laughter set Archie off, and soon the two of us were helpless with giggles, squeezed hip to hip on his comfortable chair. Every now and then one of us would gasp out a silly, random comment and set the other off again.

'Imagine if you'd got MUZJIKS.'

'Oh shit, that would have been terrible.'

'My life wouldn't have been worth living.'

'Or ZA. With the Z on a triple.'

'ZA? What the fuck is ZA?'

'Slang for pizza. Ninja two-letter word right there.'

'Oh my God. I'd have had to ring the Samaritans. Who the fuck calls pizza za anyway?'

'People who win at Scrabble.'

We both doubled over again. Then, just as I was about to point out that he was still twenty points adrift in the game, thanks to my killer play of JESTER in the previous round, and that the best he'd been able to come up with so far in that game was LAGER, we heard the ping of his shop doorbell.

'Bollocks. Let me get that. Stay here, Alice, I'll be right back.'

I shook my head. 'I should go. I'm only on a break.'

We stood up, and as we did I realised again how very close together we'd been.

'Will you be okay?' he asked softly.

'I guess. Yes, of course I will. Thank you for being here.'

He pulled me close again and dropped a kiss on my forehead, so feather-light it was hardly a kiss at all.

'I'm always here.'

As we emerged back into the shop, I heard myself saying, 'Cheers, Archie. Appreciate your advice.'

And, after only a second's hesitation, he replied, 'My pleasure, Alice. That gin's the real deal, everyone loves it.'

As I left, wondering uncomfortably why we'd both felt the need to dissemble, I heard him greeting his customer and asking what he could do for her. I hurried back to the Nag's Head, feeling limp and almost elated, the way you often do after a good cry. But I suspected that it wasn't just the crying that made me feel that way. It was something else: something dizzyingly exciting and also terrifying, like being at the top of a ski slope waiting to let go and allow gravity to take you to the bottom.

Chapter Twenty-Six

It felt really weird to be approaching the Billings Pitt Furzedown office again. I remembered all the other times I'd walked through those doors: gibbering with nerves when I came to be interviewed for the trainee position; thrilled and daunted on my first day; punishingly hungover and wearing odd shoes on the day that Joe had come to my rescue, wrestling with emotions too complicated to face the day after Gordon had made me a job offer. And, of course, any number of other days, too ordinary to remember at all, once it had ceased to be a mysterious glass tower and become just the place where I worked.

Thinking of Gordon, I felt my footsteps slowing and I looked around me, apprehensive, as if he might suddenly appear through the glass doors, his briefcase swinging from his hand, his phone clamped to his ear. But there was no sign of him, and I hurried past the building unnoticed by any of my former colleagues.

I wasn't going into the office today – or any other day. I was meeting Joe for a drink at the wine bar down the road, which used to be the favoured watering hole of all the trainee solicitors, mostly because if you ordered two large glasses of wine, they'd throw the rest of the bottle in for free. Looking at the groups of young men and women in their smart-but-cheap suits, bulging laptop bags slung over the backs of their chairs, knocking back their drinks at speed while gossiping loudly about their colleagues and less loudly about their clients, I judged it was still the place to go for post-work drinks on a Thursday.

And Thursday, it seemed, was still the new Friday.

Pushing open the heavy glass door, I was met by a roar of conversation, voices bouncing off the bare walls, glasses rattling on the steel tabletops, phones trilling everywhere. Perhaps, I thought with a shiver of dread, I'd end up back working in the City in a few months. If my plan to save the Nag's Head failed – and it felt as if it was doomed to – what else could I do?

I'd find myself employed as a newly qualified solicitor in a different firm, probably a less prestigious one than Billings. I'd have a desk and a company email account, and my life would go back to being chopped up into six-minute chunks, my value calculated by how many of them could be billed to clients.

I'd spend my Thursday nights in a place like this, getting drunk with people I worked with but didn't necessarily like very much, because Fridays were for real friends.

I looked around the crowded bar, but I couldn't see Joe. I wasn't expecting to – I was ten minutes early and he'd warned me that his five-thirty meeting was likely to overrun. So I bought myself a glass of wine and, with ninja skills I thought I'd lost, narrowly beat a blond-haired guy in a suit to the last remaining spare table.

He glared at me for a second, then grinned and said, 'Fair dos. Let me buy you your next drink.'

'Thanks, but I'm meeting someone.'

'It was worth a try. Have a fun evening.'

He grinned and slouched off to stand at the bar, and I was left trying not to laugh. It was so long since I'd been approached by a stranger in a bar, I'd completely forgotten what it felt like. That moment of disbelief – *what, he fancies me?*

I didn't want to go back there, either.

'Hey,' I heard Joe's voice behind me, 'was that guy hitting on you?'

'I guess. Kind of. He just offered to buy me a drink.'

'And you said no?'

'Course I said no.'

'Rookie error. You could have saved yourself eight quid.'

I laughed and he leaned in to kiss me. He looked tired, I thought, which wasn't surprising given his day had started twelve hours before. Although everything about him was familiar – his dark blue suit, his slightly askew pink tie, the tiny marks the glasses he wore in the office had left on his face, even the smell of the shower gel he used after his lunchtime workout in the gym – in that moment, he felt like a stranger, too.

It was just the weirdness of being back here, I told myself. The sense of dislocation – almost of having travelled back in time to my old life.

It was definitely nothing to do with what had happened between Archie and me. Because nothing had, my brain insisted. I'd been upset and he'd comforted me, like any friend would. That was all.

So why did I feel like the place on my brow where Archie had placed that brief, barely there kiss was marked permanently, for all to see? Especially for Joe to see?

'I'm just going to grab a drink. I'll be two seconds.'

'You'll be lucky,' I said, eyeing the crowd around the bar.

'If I'm not back in half an hour, send help. I'll get you another while I'm there.'

I sat down at my hard-won table and sipped my wine, ordering my thoughts while I waited. Maurice's story, while it had made perfect sense when he'd told me, was complicated, and I wanted to make sure I didn't get it wrong, or leave anything out. I wished I'd made notes, like I used to do in meetings with clients. But that would have felt too cold and impersonal – like I was Maurice's solicitor and not his friend.

I tried to remember the dates he'd given me, but they'd all got jumbled up in my mind, because so much of what he'd described had happened so long ago – long before I was even born. But that didn't matter. I hoped it didn't, at least. What mattered was whether Wesley would be willing to admit the truth to Joe, to a judge, to the whole world.

'Christ.' Joe put his glass of red wine and my fresh one of white down on the table between us and pulled a packet of crisps out of his suit pocket. 'They only had cheese and onion. It's mayhem in here.'

'Thursday, right?'

He nodded. 'And payday. Thanks for coming all the way into town.'

'That's okay. I wanted to see you as soon as you were free.'

He took a gulp of wine and ripped open the crisp packet. I took one, thinking of the posh truffle-flavoured crisps I'd tasted earlier, with Archie. How could the memory of a snack feel like a betrayal?

'Yeah, so,' I said in a rush. 'Maurice came into the pub earlier. He wanted to talk to me about Wesley. He said he went there yesterday, to visit, and it was horrible.'

Joe nodded. 'It's a horrible place. God knows I've been there enough times to get used to it, but I never have.'

I reached over and squeezed his hand. 'He's lucky to have you representing him. I know you can't discuss his case with me, but can you at least listen if I discuss it with you?'

Joe sipped his wine. 'I don't know. I mean, I guess so.'

'Because Maurice told me something that might help Wesley appeal against the removal order. If he instructs you to, obviously. I know based on the information you've got right now, there's not much chance that an appeal would succeed. It seems clear-cut. He's got no papers, nothing to prove when he arrived here. No naturalisation's taken place, there's no indefinite leave to remain, he's got no birth certificate and no passport.'

Joe nodded. I wasn't telling him anything he didn't already know.

'Didn't you think it was weird that Maurice has got all those things and his brother doesn't?' I asked.

I saw Joe hesitate, thinking again of the rules of client confidentiality he was bound by. But he said, 'Of course. But I put it down to his having worked mostly casual jobs as a self-employed musician, all the time he's been here, whereas Maurice had a stable job in local government. They'd have made sure all his papers were in order.'

'But didn't you wonder why Maurice didn't make sure his brother got his nationalisation sorted and all his papers straight? I mean, he would have done, surely?'

'Alice, people do all kinds of unlikely things. It's not for me to question why Maurice didn't tell Wesley to get hold of a copy of his birth certificate, or proof of when he arrived here, or any of that stuff. Maurice isn't my client, anyway.'

'Yes, I know that…'

'And anyway, I couldn't have done. Their parents split up forty years ago. Their dad went up to live in Scotland with another woman, and he's almost certainly dead now. And their mum went back to Grenada and she passed away some time in the 1990s. There's no record of anything. It's not like I haven't tried.'

'I'm not saying you did anything wrong.'

'Good, because I didn't. I've worked hours on this case, not just in the firm's time but in my own. And we're going to fucking lose without some kind of miracle.'

We looked at each other across the table, then Joe squeezed my hand.

'I'm sorry. It's just getting to me. I think Wesley's not being honest with me, and I don't know why. Why would a respectable, church-going bloke like him lie? Especially when I'm the only thing right now between him and flight out of here to Grenada?'

Because there's something he's even more afraid of.

Even though Maurice had asked me to talk to Joe, it felt like I was about to share a secret that should have been kept, as it had for so many years.

I took a deep breath. 'Not Grenada. Jamaica.'

'What? No, it's Grenada they're from.'

'Maurice is. Wesley's not.'

'So the two brothers have different places of birth? Wesley never said. But I doubt it changes anything much.'

'No, but something else does. They're not brothers.'

Joe opened his mouth to speak, then closed it again. I could see his mind working furiously – the mind he'd once told me proudly that his uni tutor had described as 'a fine legal brain'. And now, that fine legal brain wasn't allowing him to jump to any conclusions that might be wrong.

'Okay, Alice. I think you need to explain before my head literally explodes.'

'Hold on, I think first we need another drink. And more crisps.'

I hurried to the bar, trying to get the facts straight in my head again. While I waited, I looked again at the people around me – their suits, their handbags, their confident voices and swishy hair. They were all just embarking on their careers in banks and law firms and insurance companies, like Joe was and I had been. I remembered how proud I'd been to become part of this world – like I'd achieved something amazing.

But now I realised that I hadn't really. I'd started life with all the opportunities anyone could possibly have, never really wanted for anything. Of course I'd worked hard, but would hard work have got me here if I hadn't grown up in a nice area with good schools? If I hadn't had loving, comfortably off parents who would have sacrificed anything for me to succeed? It was impossible to know; they hadn't had to, because succeeding had been so easy. How different my life had been, I thought, from Maurice's. Coming here with nothing but a battered cardboard suitcase and his parents' dream of a better future, carving out a life for himself, becoming by any measure successful – only to have it all torn apart because of an accident of birth.

I carried our drinks back to Joe and sat down, and then I told him everything that Maurice had told me. How he'd come to Britain with his parents, alone, as a child of eleven. How, after his parents had split up and his mother returned to Grenada, he'd decided to stay because now he had a good job and London felt like home.

How, on 14 May 1983 – he remembered the exact date; of course he did – he'd been out with friends to a jazz club in Soho and seen a man a bit younger than him playing the saxophone.

'You know what they say, Alice,' he'd told me, leaning across the table in the Nag's Head, his hat on his lap, 'about love at first sight? Like you've found someone you've always been looking for without knowing it. That's what it was for me. And I was fortunate, wasn't I, that it was the same for Wesley?'

'But it wasn't a happy-ever-after ending,' I said to Joe. 'It was the eighties, after all. People were starting to panic about AIDS. And religion was really important to Wesley, and the church he goes to – I think they're Pentecostal or something – believes homosexuality is a sin.'

Joe was listening intently, his wine and crisps forgotten.

'But they moved in together anyway. Maurice says he didn't know it was possible to be so happy. But they couldn't come out. They decided that the only way for them to be together was to pretend that Wesley was Maurice's younger brother, who'd recently come out from Grenada to join him. So that's what they did. And they lived like that almost forty years.'

'Didn't it occur to them that they might get found out?'

'Why would it? There were loads of people who'd come out here from the West Indies, and most of them were undocumented.'

Joe nodded. 'The Windrush generation.'

'That's right. And besides, the longer they carried on living that lie, the harder it became to tell anyone. I think they hoped that they could just carry on forever. A few years back, when there was all that hostile environment stuff and illegal immigration was being cracked down on, Maurice said they were both worried – of course they were – but they didn't feel there was anything they could do. They just hoped it would all be okay somehow.'

'And then Wesley's father passed away, and he tried to apply for a passport so he could go home for the funeral and was detained as an illegal immigrant.'

'And here we are.'

Joe took a big swallow of wine. To my surprise, he was smiling.

'You know what? This is great.'

'What? Why? Wesley's going to be sent back to Jamaica.'

'Maybe he is. But I think, once we tell that story to an appeal judge, he might not be. Homosexuality's a crime in Jamaica. There's a strong human rights case for allowing him to stay, and good cultural and religious reasons for them having… dissembled.'

'You really think so?'

'There are no guarantees, Alice. You know that. But I've got something to work with now. I really think there's hope for them.'

Chapter Twenty-Seven

I didn't forget about what had happened that night with Gordon. Of course I didn't; no one could have. But I managed to force the memory down into a place where it was safe, locked away, so that I could see Gordon every day in the office and smile, and ask intelligent questions, and perform my work competently.

It helped that now – since that very first wretched, horrible morning – I had Joe. There was our first date, when we went to a cocktail bar near work and discovered that we both loved chocolate oranges and the Avengers and cheesy 'knock knock' jokes. And the date after that, when we went to Pizza Express and quite honestly I can't remember a single thing we ate or drank because when we said goodbye outside the Tube station he kissed me and it was everything. And then the third date, which was at his flat and we both knew it would end up in his bed, and it did.

So I was happy. Seriously, giddily happy. And I was working flat out and seeing Heather and my other friends for nights out, and enjoying having a bit of money for the first time in my adult life, so I could get my highlights done in a flash salon in Shoreditch (spoiler: my hair looked just the same as when my mum's hairdresser in Reading did them) and buy a couple of sets of sexy matching underwear to wear when I went out with Joe.

It was my happiness, more than anything, that allowed me to compartmentalise what had happened that night. That and the fact that Gordon never gave any hint that anything had happened at all. He was cordial and professional. He gave me advice and praised my work. He never so much as shook my hand. And although I couldn't help noticing that he gave me more challenging and interesting tasks to do than Rupert, when it should really have been the other way around because Rupert was in the second year of his training contract and I was only in my first, I put that down to the fact that I was working harder, and anyway Rupert was rumoured to be almost certain to be offered a job in Mergers and Acquisitions once he qualified.

So, like I say, I compartmentalised the events of that night. I tidied them away in a place in my mind where I hardly ever needed to look, and I hoped that, one day, I'd be able to remember what Gordon had done without that sick-making rush of panic and shame and just see a thing that had happened to me, long ago, when I was drunk – a thing that wasn't so bad really, given how much worse it could have been.

But I knew that the memories were there. I knew when I woke up in Joe's bed sometimes sweating and gasping out muffled screams from a nightmare. I knew when a tall man with a briefcase brushed against me on the Tube and I felt my heart racing so hard with shock and fear I could hardly catch my breath. I knew because I made sure I was never, ever alone with Gordon in the office at night.

Heather never tried to pressure me into saying anything, and as the weeks and months went by she stopped asking me quite so often if I was okay. She only asked me the once if I'd told Joe what had happened, and I guess my horrified reaction put her off ever asking again.

And soon, my six months in Intellectual Property were over and I moved on to my next seat, in Litigation, and then on to Tax. And I moved home too, all the way to South London with Joe. I started to feel like my life was following its pre-ordained course, like everything was going to be all right, like that night would never impinge on my life again.

And then, when I'd been at Billings Pitt Furzedown for just over a year and living with Joe for three months, something happened to rip that compartment in my mind wide open again.

It was a Sunday in October. Joe and I had had friends over the previous night, and we'd sat around in our living room drinking Merlot, eating nachos and watching *Luther* on Netflix until almost four in the morning, and I woke up feeling scratchy-eyed and fuzzy-headed. But that didn't matter. It was Sunday, Joe was next to me. Soon he'd wake up too, and we'd have our usual minor argument about whose turn it was to get up and make coffee, which would be resolved by the other one agreeing to make breakfast. We'd spend what was left of the morning slobbing around in our pyjamas and eventually get dressed and go out for a walk, possibly ending with a pint in the Star and Garter. In the evening, Joe might make his famous special fried rice, and we'd eat in front of the TV, then go to bed early and have lazy, comfortable sex.

Not the most exciting day in the world, but every bit of it felt perfect, because I'd be spending it with Joe.

I sat up in bed, swiped my phone to life and tapped through to my social media. And straight away, it was like a cloud had passed over the sun. There was a hashtag trending. Trending everywhere: on Facebook, on Twitter, on Insta, on Buzzfeed, even on the front page of the *Guardian*.

Women were talking. All over the world, they were sharing stories that were different, but also the same.

'He pinned me against a wall.'

'He said I was asking for it.'

'I felt like it was my fault.'

And, over and over again, 'I'm speaking out.'

I tapped through to WhatsApp and tapped a message to Heather.

Have you seen that thing that's trending?

#MeToo? Yup, on account of not living under a rock. You okay?

Ish. I feel kind of weird. Like everyone's looking at me and waiting.

They're not. Have you changed your mind though? About talking to HR?

Don't know. But I think so.

She sent me a fist-bump emoji.

I'm here if you want to talk, K? Love you.

Then Joe woke up, turned over and reached for me. I lay with my head on his shoulder for a bit, thinking. Then I said I'd get up and make coffee.

The rest of that day went just like I'd thought, only I didn't enjoy it as much as I'd expected. I was silent and edgy, and Joe kept asking if I was okay, but I said I was just hungover. But I wasn't. I was rehearsing in my head what I was going to do the next day. Should I ask for a meeting with Samantha, the head of HR? Should I send her an email? Should I talk to Gordon first? Should I talk to Joe first?

I couldn't decide. Each option seemed worse – more frightening, more exposing – than the last. And by the time I arrived at my desk the next morning, I still hadn't decided. On social media and in the mainstream press, #MeToo was growing and growing. More and more women were talking about what had happened to them – celebrities, politicians, ordinary people like me.

It should have emboldened me, but it didn't; it only made me more apprehensive, more unsure. What if Samantha thought I was just jumping on a bandwagon, attention-seeking, making #MeToo all about me?

I imagined what Heather would say: 'You can do it. You're strong. You've got this.'

You've got this, I told myself, reaching out an unsteady hand for my desk phone. But just as I touched it, it rang. My hand sprang back like I'd been stung, and I could feel cold sweat breaking out on my palm.

My voice was unsteady when I said, 'Tax department, Alice Carlisle speaking.'

'Good morning, Alice.' It was Gordon. 'I'm sure you're having a busy morning, but are you able to spare a minute?'

'I… Yes, of course I can.'

'My office?'

'Of course.'

I couldn't feel my legs as I stood up. It was like I was having an out-of-body experience, watching myself walk past the ranks of desks to the lobby, seeing my hand press the button on the lift, looking down at the top of my head as it inched up towards the tenth floor, stepping through the doors and making my way to Gordon's office, my head held carefully high and my back straight.

Gordon was behind his desk as usual, surrounded by files, a half-drunk cup of coffee next to him. I could smell it on his breath when he spoke.

'Thank you for coming down, my dear. Take a seat.'

I did, and felt myself return to my body in a rush. My heart was beating like I'd sprinted up the stairs instead of taking the lift. My calves were trembling, sending my knees bumping against each other.

'I know this is somewhat irregular,' Gordon went on. 'But I wanted to speak to you in person.'

If he apologised, what would I say? If he asked me not to tell anyone, would I agree? If he terminated my contract, how could I possibly manage not to cry?

'I hear you're doing well up there.' Gordon smiled. 'Max speaks highly of your work.'

'Thank you.' My voice sounded croaky. 'It's challenging work, but I'm finding it fascinating.'

'And showing an acute grasp of it. That doesn't surprise me – I always knew you had talent. And that's why I've asked you here today, Alice. To get my offer in early, so to speak.'

'Offer?'

'A job. Here, in Intellectual Property. As soon as you qualify next year. I've been in touch with HR about it and they're drawing up the necessary paperwork.'

I felt dizzy with shock and confusion. If he was offering me a job, it must mean that my memories of that night were wrong – that what had happened hadn't been so bad after all. That I was exaggerating, being overdramatic and stupid. He'd already spoken to HR. If I were to go to Samantha with my sordid little story, there was no way at all I'd be believed. I'd look like a fantasist, making up lies about a senior partner who'd been generous enough to offer me a chance most people would do anything for.

And if I said no, people would find out. I'd be known as the girl who'd turned down an opportunity for a career in the firm, who'd snubbed a senior partner. My career at Billings Pitt Furzedown would be finished before it had even begun.

It was, literally, an offer I couldn't refuse.

It was also blackmail; a conspiracy of silence. It was thirty pieces of silver, like in the Bible – except it wasn't someone else I was betraying; it was myself. But I didn't see that then; I felt only shock and shame.

'Thank you,' I heard myself gasp.

'You'll carry on with your planned rotation to Mergers and Acquisitions, of course, but I'll let the other partners know you'll be joining us here. Congratulations, Alice.'

I thanked him again.

'I told you I'd look after you,' he said.

Chapter Twenty-Eight

Over the next ten days, I felt like I didn't have time to think. Every moment that I didn't spend going about my normal duties in the pub, I spent trying to save it. I drafted a letter to the local planning department setting out in exhaustive detail all the benefits the Nag's Head brought to the community, and chivvied people in the pub, in the street and on social media to sign a petition. I put together a business plan and met with Heart of the Community, the charity that supported community pubs, to see if there was any chance of securing some funding from them. I chaired the first meeting of the steering group, but then happily handed over the chairman's role to Maurice, who said that he'd been on more committees when he'd worked in local government than I'd had hot dinners.

I found myself hunched over my laptop at our kitchen table at six in the morning, and still hunched over it at midnight most nights, having put in a full day's work in between. My eyes were permanently sore from lack of sleep and my shoulders burned with tension, but when I tried to rest I found myself jerking awake with worry about all the things that I still needed to do.

Occasionally, a notification from my Scrabble app would distract me and bring a smile to my face. EMBRACE, Archie spelled, even though he could have got a higher score with CAMBER, putting the R on a triple letter square. The word sent a little shiver down my spine as I remembered his arms around me, the feather-light brush of his lips against my skin. I sorted through my own letters in my head. LUST, TUSH, HURL, HURTS, CURST. But I played CRUSH, thinking as I tapped my screen to confirm the word, *This is a terrible idea. Isn't it?*

But Archie replied with a smiling emoji, and on his next turn he played EROS. Blushing like I'd been caught doing something shameful, I tucked my phone away in my bag.

Meanwhile, Zoë was rushed off her feet with a hectic schedule of Christmas parties. Joe was working punishingly long hours preparing Wesley's appeal as well as dealing with his normal caseload, and Shirley kept saying she had no idea why we thought any of this was a good idea; her lumbago was killing her and anyone could see that running a pub was a mug's game.

The only one of us who seemed to be living his best life was Drew, who was consumed with planning the poetry evening. Every day he'd chirpily update me on the numbers who'd booked.

'That's forty-five who've confirmed and bought tickets, Alice! Two hundred and twenty-five pounds of free money! And they'll buy food and drink on the night, too. It's turning into a nice little earner. If we make it a monthly thing it'll grow, too – you watch.'

I didn't want to piss on his chips by pointing out that two hundred and twenty-five quid, while obviously a whole lot better than nothing, would go precisely nowhere to solving the Nag's Head's ongoing financial woes. Nor that in a month or so's time we wouldn't actually have a pub in which to hold poetry nights, however successful the first one turned out to be.

I managed to sneak into town to meet Heather for lunch, but it was even more rushed than usual, because she was working sixteen-hour days on the initial public offering of shares in a tech start-up.

'It sounds dodgy as all fuck, if I'm honest,' she said, devouring her tuna sandwich as if it was the first square meal she'd had in days, which it might well have been. 'You know what these companies are like – all smoke and mirrors, crazy money valuations, and then it all goes tits up.'

'Do you reckon this one will?'

'Who knows. But for now it's all set to go ahead, and while that's the status I'm basically chained to my desk. I can't think straight; when I close my eyes at night all I see is clauses and sub-clauses. I even deleted Tinder because if I went on a date with anyone I'd end up falling asleep in my beer.'

'But you'll be able to come on Saturday, right? To the poetry night?'

'Of course. I wouldn't miss it for anything. This should be mostly wrapped up by then, anyway. Three more days of craziness and then I can sleep for fourteen hours straight and then I'll be back to normal. Don't worry, Alice, I'll be there.'

We hugged each other goodbye and she hurried off back to her office. I couldn't help noticing the weary slump of her shoulders and the red rims round her eyes, and I worried about her. But she'd cope – she always did. I had to believe that, so I went back to worrying about all the other things that were jostling for position on my brain.

The way much-anticipated events do – whether it's Christmas when you're a little kid or an exam you haven't prepared for properly when you're a student – the poetry night seemed like ages away, until suddenly it wasn't.

The day began like a normal Saturday, except Drew was fussing about in a way that was entirely different to his usual casualness. He counted chairs, he replaced the posters in the windows that said, 'Poetry night this Saturday' with ones that said, 'Poetry night tonight'. He fielded questions on social media and found a website that would draw the poets' names out of a digital hat to decide the running order. He looked over and over again at Princess Diana hanging over the fireplace, but clearly thought better of asking if it could be removed.

'They'll think it's ironic. Of course they will,' I heard him mutter to himself.

I imagined her replying, with a glint in her eye, 'I'll show you who's ironic, young man.'

He asked Zoë so many times whether there'd be enough vegan bean burgers – the overlap between poets and plant-based eaters being a massive thing, apparently – until she came storming out of the kitchen and said, only half-jokingly, that if I didn't get that bloody brother of mine out of her hair she'd hand in her notice and leave, thanks.

At last it was five o'clock, the pub was relatively quiet and the event wasn't due to kick off for another hour and a half, so I said, 'I thought I might pop home and shower and change, if that's okay?'

'What?' Drew said. 'But I was going to pop home and shower and change.'

'Both of you go, right now,' Shirley said. 'Honestly, you've been wearing me down to my last nerve all day with your mithering.

I could do with a bit of peace and quiet before all this nonsense gets started. Go!'

So Drew crossed the road to the old Star and Garter, and I went the other way, passing Archie's shop on my way to our road. He was behind the counter; I gave him a quick wave and gestured to my watch, and he replied with a thumbs-up. Great – that was one more person who could be relied upon to turn up.

At home, I quickly washed and dried my hair, did my make-up and changed into a black velvet maxi dress that I'd bought for a Halloween party a couple of years back and not worn since. Joe was slumped on the sofa, simultaneously reading case law on his laptop and watching the football.

I waited for him to look up when I came in and say 'Phwoar!' like he usually did when I'd got ready to go out, but he didn't.

'Does this look okay?' I asked. 'I thought it was kind of bohemian but I think it might be too much.'

He looked up. 'You look like an arty witch.'

'Is that good?'

He shrugged.

'You are coming, aren't you? Tonight?'

'Not sure. I've got work to do, and Azerbaijan are playing Cyprus later.'

'But…' But there was no point arguing with him, or begging him to come. I just blew him a kiss and hurried out.

The pub was already filling up when I got back. Shirley and Kelly were working so quickly behind the bar that their hands were almost a blur. Freddie was hurrying from table to serving hatch and back again with laden trays. Drew was working the room, introducing himself to people, handing out flyers, establishing who wanted to have a go at the mic and checking that their names were in the digital draw. Judging by the smells coming from the kitchen and plates of food being delivered to tables, Zoë was being kept busy too.

At six thirty exactly, Drew switched on the mic and spoke into the roar of voices.

'Good evening, everyone.' The noise abated slightly. 'Good evening. I'm Drew Carlisle and I'm delighted to welcome you all to the Nag's Head's inaugural open-mic poetry evening. First of all, a few house rules…'

He explained about the four-minute time limit, the need to be respectful to the poets, the prize for the winner, and all the rest.

Then he said, 'As you know, we're doing a draw for the order. When your name is called, please come straight up and I'll start the timer for you. Now, kicking off an occasion like this is not for the faint-hearted, so we're fortunate to have a volunteer to be first at the mic. Please give a very warm welcome to our lovely landlady, Shirley Pearce.'

There was a burst of applause. As it ended, Shirley stepped up and took the mic. Taking her special guest appearance seriously, she'd deserted her post at the bar earlier to get a voluminous blow-dry, have her eyelash extensions topped up and change into a sequinned scarlet dress. It was like Oprah had taken the stage. I saw Heather push open the door and hesitate there for a second. I waved, and she looked relieved and came over to join me at the bar.

'Blimey, what a crowd,' she whispered.

'Good, isn't it?'

I looked around at the people packed around tables, standing against the walls, even perched on the stairs, contravening all the health and safety regulations. There was rather a lot of blue hair, beards and hats in evidence – not exactly the Nag's Head's regular clientele. I was pretty sure the last time someone turned up at the pub in a flat cap, they hadn't been wearing it ironically.

Shirley cleared her throat and the room fell silent.

'This is called "People's Princess",' she said, and cleared her throat again:

'England's rose, our Queen of Hearts
Remembering you makes my eyes smart.
Taken from us so young and true
Closed forever, your eyes so blue.'

Heather and I caught each other's eyes and I could see she was trying not to laugh. I didn't know much about poetry, to be fair, but even I could tell that Shirley would do better to stick to her day job. Mawkish and sentimental, her tribute to Princess Diana carried on for another four verses, sometimes rhyming, sometimes not. I couldn't even look at Heather.

But the respectful attention Drew had requested was provided, and when Shirley eventually finished, there was a warm round of applause and even a few whoops of appreciation.

'Not such a tough crowd as I'd have expected,' Heather said.

'She's the landlady, and she went first. They're being kind, I reckon.'

'Thank you, Shirl, for that moving and heartfelt work,' Drew said, without the faintest hint of sarcasm.

Next to me, I heard a little gasp from Heather. 'Who the actual fuck is that?'

'The landlady, Shirley, like I said.'

'Not her! That man. He's off the scale.'

'That's my big brother, Drew.'

'Your what? Seriously, Alice, you've had the most drop-dead gorgeous man on the planet sharing your DNA for twenty-seven years and you never told me?'

'I've had twenty-seven years to get used to him,' I said.

'You've got to introduce me. Promise you will?'

'Promise.' Drew and Heather, I thought. I've never been much of a matchmaker, but they didn't strike me as obvious couple material. But what did I know? Opposites attract, apparently.

'And now for the first name out of the draw,' Drew was saying, tapping his phone. Heather watched him, wide-eyed and admiring. 'Leila Jones. Leila, please come up and take the mic.'

A girl with dyed silver hair, wearing ripped jeans and an embroidered linen blouse, came up and took the mic. Drew smiled at her, and next to me I felt Heather tense, like a precious prize might be about to be snatched from her.

'Should I write a poem quickly?' she hissed. 'Try and impress him?'

'Who are you and what have you done with my friend? That's crazy talk.'

'I guess.'

Leila Jones took the mic and launched into a piece of what she said was performance poetry. Bits of it were recited, bits were sung and at one point she lay on the floor and writhed around a bit. As far as I could tell, it was all to do with the live export of animals for meat, but it all went a bit over my head and it rhymed even less than Shirley's effort had done. Still, she also received a warm round of applause.

Then a heavily tattooed bloke came up and recited a poem called 'Hurting Time', which seemed to be all about how he was still bitter five years after being dumped by a girlfriend ('I've moved on to a better sitch, but you are still a mardy bitch/Now that I'm getting all the sex, I bet you're sorry I'm your ex'). A girl with a shaved head was next and did something about a bird in a cage, which I figured was a metaphor for her brilliant artistic soul withering while she worked in admin for an insurance company.

Then Drew said, 'Last to go before we take a ten-minute break, and it's…' He tapped his phone. 'Oh my God, it's me.'

There was a ripple of laughter around the room and a smattering of applause.

'What if he's shit?' Heather whispered.

'Then you can uncrush on him just as quickly as you started crushing.'

But Drew wasn't shit. His poem was about populism, about the alt-right and Brexit and the forces that drew people to political causes, and it was furious, sad and also hilarious. His comic timing was on point; he waited just long enough for each burst of laughter to die down before carrying on, throwing in bits of impersonation and even mime.

When he finished, the room erupted with applause, and I could see that Heather, next to me, was lost. As soon as he put the mic down she hurried over with two drinks, joining the throng of people around him, and soon they were talking and laughing together.

I flung myself into work, serving drinks and clearing tables during the break, then watched the next set of poetry alone. As far as I could tell, some were good, some were awful, and most were somewhere in between. But the atmosphere stayed cordial and supportive, and even the most dire poems were greeted with applause.

Drew was in his element, keeping up a strong stream of patter, making the audience laugh, smiling his radiant smile, the blue laser beam of his gaze raking the room, and Heather couldn't take her eyes off him. I could see Maurice and his friends at their usual table, but there was no dominoes game; they were entirely focused on the action at the mic. In another corner, Archie was chatting to a few people I didn't know – regular customers from his shop, maybe – but Nat wasn't in their group.

Two more sets of poetry followed, and at last Drew said, 'Right, we're down to our last name, everyone.'

There was a chorus of 'awwws' from the audience.

'Maurice Higgins,' Drew read from his phone.

There was a pause. I saw Sadiq give Maurice's shoulder a squeeze, and he stood up, his expression serious but not betraying any nervousness. Slowly, he made his way through the crowds towards the mic. I could see a little line of perspiration snaking down his jaw.

When he took the mic from Drew, the page of lined paper in his hand was trembling slightly, and I realised he was absolutely terrified.

'This is…' He cleared his throat and tried again. 'This is called "Words for Wesley".'

The silence in the room seemed to grow deeper, as if everyone was just as afraid that Maurice was going to mess it up as he was. This elderly man in his suit and hat, so different from everyone else who'd come up to the mic, the last to go – if he was terrible, it would be a real buzz-killer, I sensed them thinking.

'We loved in darkness,' Maurice began. 'In the arms of the friendly night.'

His poem wasn't long, but it was beautiful. It was about desire and loss, secrecy and shame. It was a love poem and a coming-out poem. I felt tears pricking my eyes as he read, and I could see lots of other people in the pub were crying too, or trying not to. When he finished, the applause was rapturous.

To my surprise, no one seemed to want to leave. More and more drinks and food were ordered, groups formed and re-formed. Everyone wanted to talk to Maurice, so I didn't get a chance to do much more than give him a hug and tell him he'd been amazing.

There was no time for me to take a break or mingle until almost ten, when the crowd at last started to thin. Zoë closed the kitchen and headed for home, knackered but triumphant. Heather came over to say goodbye, pulling me into a huge hug and saying she'd call me very soon. I couldn't help noticing that she and Drew left together, and I was fairly sure that they were going to go across the road to Drew's flat together.

And at last, I felt able to take a break, go for the wee I desperately needed and find a glass of wine. But Archie found me first.

'Hey, Alice. What an incredible evening. You must be pretty pleased with yourself.'

'I am. But not as pleased as I'll be when I've finished this drink. I'm roasting hot as well.'

It was true; I realised that my velvet dress was sticking to my back and my face felt like it was on fire.

'Want to come outside for a second?'

Suddenly, the idea of the cold, damp night air seemed like the best thing ever. I grabbed my bag and pushed open the door and we walked out into the street, quickly and purposefully, away from the groups of smokers outside the pub, the people chatting as they left the Italian restaurant, the little huddle in the bus shelter.

Archie turned down a side street and I followed him, my heart starting to beat harder in my chest.

'Alice, I… I need to talk to you.'

Abruptly, he stopped and turned to face me. The cold had been welcome at first, but now I was starting to shiver.

'Of course,' I said. 'I'm listening.'

'This is awkward as fuck, so I'm just going to come out and say it. You know that photo I took of us in the park that day?'

I nodded.

'Nat found it on my phone.'

'Your girlfriend? Shit. I'm sorry about that. Is she okay?'

It was just a photo. Just a photo of two friends out for a walk together. But it was also more than that. The cold seemed to seep from the night to a place deep inside me.

'She freaked out a bit. She remembered you coming to the shop that day, when she was there, and she said you'd seemed weird with her. I told her nothing had happened and she didn't need to worry.'

'Okay.'

'But then I realised, actually, she does need to worry. I need to worry. This – it's more than just a bit of Scrabble and banter between mates. Isn't it?'

I wrapped my arms around myself, looking down at my feet. Then I made myself look up at him.

'I don't know.'

'Alice, this feels dangerous. I don't know what's going on with you and your bloke, but I love Nat. We're good together. I don't want to do anything to jeopardise that, and I think I – we – have been.'

I thought of that kiss, light as a snowflake. I thought of the words we'd exchanged – EMBRACE, CRUSH, EROS. I thought of the way I felt when I got a notification from the Scrabble app – that spark of excitement and happiness. And I felt a horrible, choking tentacle of shame and guilt unfurling inside me.

I wondered if, in a part of me that wouldn't even allow myself to see, I'd expected – hoped, desired – that Archie had brought me here to do or say something entirely different from these awkward words that basically meant, 'I'm ending it', even though neither of us could acknowledge what 'it' even was.

And I wondered what, in the parallel universe where he'd said or done something quite different, my reaction would have been.

'I'm sorry, Alice,' he was saying.

'Don't be sorry. You've done nothing wrong. We haven't done anything wrong.'

'But we could have done. I was starting to want to. And I feel appalling about it.'

So do I.

But there was no way I was going to let this become a mutual 'aren't we noble, acknowledging our feelings and deciding together not to act on them' session. 'An emotional wank-fest', I could imagine Heather calling it.

I said, 'Archie, this isn't church and I'm not your confessor. If you want to talk about stuff that almost happened, or could have happened, I think you need to talk to Nat or a friend, not me. Because that's more of the same, don't you see? More creating a closeness that you say you don't want. And I don't, either. We're friends – kind of. Our businesses are next door to each other – at least they are for now. I think it's best we park it there, don't you?'

He nodded. I'd kept my face composed, I hoped, but he looked every bit as miserable as I felt.

'Thanks, Alice. Thanks for understanding, and for being you.'

This was dangerous ground. I felt the urge to cry welling up inside me, along with cold fury at myself and at him – and, overwhelming them both, that sick sense of guilt and panic over what I'd almost thrown away.

'It's not such a massive achievement, you know,' I said lightly, 'being me. I'm glad we spoke. Let's leave it there. No more Scrabble, right?'

'No more Scrabble,' he agreed. 'Although, you know, next round I was about to play NUBILE.'

'Well, maybe it's time you started playing Scrabble with Nat then. Night, Archie.'

I turned and walked back up the narrow street as fast as I could. I was trembling all over with cold and something else – shock, horror, relief? I wasn't sure. I was sure of only one thing: I needed to get home – fast. I needed to get home to Joe and tell him what I'd been in danger of forgetting: how important he was, the most important thing in my life, someone I'd almost unconsciously let become eclipsed by other things, other people.

I didn't go back to the Nag's Head. I fired off a text to Shirley telling her I was done in and would see her in the morning. My coat could stay there overnight too. The longing for Joe and safety was so strong I almost ran the last couple of hundred yards down our road, and I was all out of breath when I fitted my key in the lock and flung open the door.

I nearly sent Joe flying. Joe and Zoë. I almost didn't see her at first, because the two of them were locked so tightly together in each other's arms, like Lego pieces that were made to fit together.

Chapter Twenty-Nine

'So it looks like I won't have to go into work today after all.' Heather put her phone down on the table and took a sip of her coffee. We were in the communal area downstairs from Drew's borrowed flat, at a table in the café next to the yoga studio. I'd never been in there before, and I could see why Drew hadn't ever invited me. The tables were small and crowded together, the coffee was okay at best, and the carrot and date muffins Drew had bought us tasted like sawdust.

Although very possibly that was just me. That morning, nothing would have tasted good. My whole life, I reflected, tasted like sawdust.

But I still felt a rush of gratitude towards my brother. When I'd turned up, unannounced, and knocked on his door at half past midnight, he'd just asked if I was okay, accepted that I didn't want to talk about it and given me his double bed to share with Heather while he slept on the floor next to us.

There couldn't be many things worse, I knew, than having a tearful sister or friend turn up when you're about to have amazing first-time sex. But neither Heather nor Drew had done anything to make me feel like the third wheel I knew I was. I'd have to go home, of course, sooner rather than later. I'd have to confront Joe and Zoë, find out what was going on, retrieve what scattered fragments I could of my life.

But for now, my phone was turned off and I was grateful to be with these two people who wouldn't judge, wouldn't ask questions and, most importantly, wouldn't offer the kind of gushing comfort that would only make me cry.

'How so?' Drew asked. Heather looked at him and I saw again what I'd seen in her face the previous night – the look of disbelieving wonder that someone as perfect as my brother was there, next to her, breathing the same air as her, his hand resting lightly on her denim-clad thigh. And there was a similar look on Drew's face. Whatever had happened last night, whatever lightning-bolt of chemistry had struck my friend, it clearly hadn't missed my brother.

In one way it was amazing to be with two people so newly smitten with each other. In another, it was bloody horrible.

'The IPO's gone pear-shaped,' Heather said. 'It seems the CEO of the company that was going to float on the stock exchange has been up to some seriously dodgy stuff. He was selling the freeholds to his properties on to a company he owns in the Cayman Islands to evade tax, and he's probably going to be disqualified from being a company director. Obviously all the investors have got the jitters and are pulling out, and we've sacked him as a client. He owes us almost fifty grand, which I reckon there's no chance we'll ever see. The company was massively overvalued anyway – they reckoned the initial share offering would fetch more than a billion pounds, but that's been downgraded to ten million. There was a story in the *Financial Times* today, and now my boss has emailed me to say it's all off.'

'Wow,' I said. 'Do you think someone leaked the tax-dodging thing to an *FT* journalist, then?'

'Looks that way.'

'So you get to have your Sunday off?' Drew asked.

Heather looked at him and they both smiled – a smile that was so full of pleasure and promise it made me want to cry.

'I do indeed,' she said.

'What would you like to do? Proper Sunday roast somewhere? These muffins aren't cutting it, are they? Or a walk? We could watch a movie? Join us, obviously, Alice, if you want.'

Once again, I felt that stab of bittersweet happiness for them, along with sadness for myself.

'So tell me more about this dodgy CEO, Heath,' I said, desperate for distraction. 'It sounds like a totally bonkers situation.'

'Bonkers is right,' Heather said. 'The guy's built up a whole portfolio of companies and property, and it's had a crazy value put on it when it's all built on debt. The journalist who broke the story in the *FT* just tweeted that he was seen boarding a flight to San Francisco so I guess he's decided to call it a day in London and go back to Silicon Valley.'

'Blimey,' Drew said. 'What's the bloke's name?'

'Fabian Flatley,' Heather said.

Drew choked on his coffee and I almost spat out a bite of muffin, which would probably have been a better idea than swallowing it.

'What?' Heather said. 'You know him?'

'Technically, we're his guests right now. Or customers, rather. He owns this place, and the freehold of the building – at least his offshore shell company does. Lauren bought her flat from him when he developed the property.'

'And he wants to buy the Nag's Head,' I added, 'and turn it into a co-living place as well. But I guess that's not going to happen any more.'

'It seems unlikely,' Heather said. 'I mean, once the bank did their anti-money-laundering checks on him, who knows what they'd come up with.'

'He was a cash buyer, though, Shirley said.'

'I doubt he would be any more. All his creditors are calling in their loans now the company's not this amazing unicorn any more, so he'll be lucky if he's got the cash to buy a pack of fags, never mind a London property.'

'So the Nag's Head might be safe after all?' Drew said.

'I don't know. I'll have to talk to Shirley, and she'll have to talk to the landlady, I guess. But there's a much better chance that we could buy it as a co-operative, now there's not an amazing cash offer on the table.'

'I suppose I should tell Lauren.' Drew took out his phone. 'I mean, I doubt it'll make much difference to her, because she owns her place, but she was talking about how the freehold was going to be sold on and their service charges would go through the roof. She's quite worried about it, but she said she'd try and sort it out when she gets back. Which is tomorrow, by the way, so I guess I'll be moving back in with Mum and Dad.'

'In Reading?' Heather looked alarmed.

Drew smiled. 'In Reading. But don't worry, it's only half an hour from Paddington. It's not the International Space Station.'

From the look on Heather's face, I could tell she didn't want to let Drew out of her sight for two minutes, never mind endure the yawning chasm of a half-hour train journey between them.

I said, 'Look, I'd better go and tell Shirley what's going on. Hopefully she'll give me Cathy's email address and I can fill her in on it, too. I guess her solicitor or the estate agent will be in touch with her and let her know her buyer's absconded, but not on a Sunday.'

We stood up, and I put on the leather jacket Drew had lent me over my black dress. I was going to have to go home and change at some point, but not now. I wondered if Joe and Zoë were there together – together in our bed? If whatever was going on between them had been going on for a while, or if last night had been the first time. If, having come so close to losing Joe over my own stupidity with Archie, I was now going to lose him over Zoë.

I wondered if I should switch my phone on and see if there was a message from either of them, but I wasn't brave enough to do that yet. As long as I didn't know the truth, I could pretend there was a different reality – one where everything was okay between Joe and me.

Welcome to denial. Population: me.

'I guess I'll catch up with you guys later,' I said.

'Do you want us to come with you?' Heather asked. 'I could explain to Shirley what's happened.'

'We will if you want,' Drew said. 'And you know you can crash here again tonight, if… you know.'

If whatever's gone so badly wrong with you and Joe is still wrong.

I looked at them standing there, holding hands as naturally as if they'd been doing it for years, identical worried expressions on their faces.

'I'll be fine,' I said. 'Promise. And if I need you, I'll call. Okay?'

'Okay.' We pulled one another into an awkward group hug and, as I left, I saw Drew and Heather heading towards the stairs, back up to Drew's tiny studio flat where there was space for little more than a double bed.

I paused for a moment before crossing the road. I could see the Nag's Head, all lit up ready for Sunday lunch, the Christmas tree sparkling bravely in the window. I wondered whether any of the people who'd been at the poetry event would come again; whether there'd even be another one. I wondered whether Maurice had told Wesley about his plans and shown him the poem. I hoped he had, and that that public, written declaration of Maurice's love for him gave him hope.

I knew that if anyone would put in the hard yards to get a compelling case for Wesley's appeal together, Joe would. Thinking of him was like being punched in the stomach. I'd let myself lose sight of what a good person he was – of how good we were together. I remembered how patient and understanding he'd been when I'd told him I was leaving law to work in a pub. He must have thought I'd gone crazy, but he'd supported me as best he could.

And in return? I'd embarked on a stupid flirtation with Archie, neglecting our relationship, using lack of time together to excuse the fact that we weren't communicating, weren't connecting, weren't having fun or dates or sex or any of the things that should have kept us close.

And because of that, he'd turned back to Zoë. His first love. He'd been honest with me about that – of course he had; Joe wasn't a man who lied or hid things. So if he still had feelings for Zoë, or if – having faded years ago – they'd returned stronger than ever, why hadn't he told me? It made no sense. It wasn't like him at all.

I was the one who'd kept a horrible secret from him, all through our relationship.

If I was able to get a second chance, an opportunity to make things right between us, there'd be no more secrets. Not even that huge one. If not? If things had passed the point of no return with Joe and Zoë, which I'd stopped clear of with Archie? I'd be wounded and furious – of course I would. But I'd blame myself as much as them.

And if I couldn't save my relationship, at least there was a small chance I could save my pub.

I hurried across the road and pushed open the door. As I did so, Zoë came out of the kitchen, wearing her chef's white jacket. There was no way I could avoid her.

'Alice! My God, I've been so worried about you! Where were you?'

The cheek of the woman. She hadn't looked so worried when she was wrapped round my boyfriend like a flaming Band-Aid.

'I stayed over at Drew's.'

'You turned your phone off.'

What did she expect me to have done? Bundled in for a group hug? Suggested cracking open a bottle of champagne?

'I didn't want—'

'You didn't want to talk to me. Or Joe. We've been calling and calling you.'

We? Were she and Joe a *we* again?

'No,' I said. 'I didn't. I'm here to talk to Shirley. And to work my shift, obviously.'

'Shirl's not here. We ran out of milk for the Yorkshire pudding batter, so she popped out to Tesco.'

'Well, I'll wait until she gets back.'

'Alice, please. Come in the kitchen and let me talk to you.'

She sounded a bit like she might be about to cry and, looking at her, I realised she looked like she *had* been crying. Her eyes were red-rimmed and there were dark hollows under them. Her hair, normally a cascade of ringlets, was frizzy and dull, and there was an angry-looking spot next to her mouth.

She certainly didn't look like a woman who'd reconnected with her first love. She looked knackered and sad.

'Okay,' I said.

Zoë pushed open the fire door to the kitchen and I followed her in. There was a smell of roasting meat in the air, richly savoury – pork today, I guessed. But instead of making my stomach rumble like it usually would, it made me want to throw up. On the stovetop, a pan of apple sauce was keeping warm, an occasional bubble breaking its surface with a soft blip. Two massive trays of potatoes, peeled and par-boiled, were waiting to go in the oven.

Eat your heart out, Aunt Bessie, I thought, *your frozen roast accompaniments are about as welcome in this kitchen as I felt in my flat last night.*

'Last night,' Zoë began. 'Me and Joe. I'm really sorry you had to see that, but it wasn't what you think. Joe didn't do anything wrong.'

She looked up at me, then down at her hands. Her nails were bitten to the quick, and there was a blue plaster on one finger where she must have cut herself on one of her lethally sharp chef's knives.

'Joe told me that when you were together, it was really intense,' I said. 'He was in love with you, and you broke his heart when you ended it.'

'I'm sorry. That can't have been easy to hear.'

'No. It wasn't.'

But at the time, things had been different between Joe and me. There'd still been that closeness, that sense that everything was good between us – good enough even to withstand the return into his life of someone he'd cared about so deeply. That had changed, and changed because of me.

'But it was stupid of me to mind so much. I mean, everyone has a past, don't they? Everyone's had their heart broken at some point.'

Except Heather, I remembered. I felt a pang of protective affection for my friend, remembering how happy – and how amazed by the experience of being in love – she'd looked that morning.

'I guess,' Zoë said. 'The thing is…'

I waited.

'I feel awful saying this, Alice. I've been a really shitty person, and I owe you an apology.'

'So you and Joe, last night. Something did happen.' The cold knot of dread was back in my stomach.

'No! Honestly, not last night, and not ever. Well, not since we were together seven years ago.'

'Then why are you apologising?'

'Because I meant it to. I wanted it to.'

'But you split up with him! You dumped him!'

'Alice, I… I've behaved horribly, I know. But I didn't set out to be shitty. Well, I kind of did. Please let me explain.'

'I think you'd better.'

'Joe and I. You know what it's like when you're that age. It was all really intense. We met at a gig and we went home together that same night and I never really left. I told him I loved him after, like, a week. And it was true. I did love him. It wasn't just a daft infatuation.'

My mouth felt dry, and tasted sour from the coffee I'd drunk earlier. I poured a glass of water from the tap then, after a second's hesitation, poured one for Zoë too.

'So what happened? What went wrong?' I sounded bitter. Bitter and angry, and I didn't like myself one bit for it.

'For a few months,' Zoë continued as if I hadn't spoken, 'everything was wonderful. Perfect. We were in that smitten, loved-up stage where you just shag and shag all the time, and in between you lie on the bed together and gaze at each other like loons. You know.'

I did know. Joe and I had had that, too. I could feel my heart beating so hard in my chest I could hardly breathe, and I felt like I might be sick.

'And then I fucked it all up. It was stupid. It was like I woke up one morning and I was like, *Shit. I'm twenty-one. I'm not ready for this.* I thought, *I can't have found The One yet. I don't even know who I am.*'

I tried to swallow, but my mouth was too dry. 'Go on.'

'It was so sudden. As sudden as falling for him had been. I changed from feeling all happy and secure to being in this blind panic because I'd got myself into a relationship that felt like it was going to be forever, and suddenly forever seemed like the longest, longest time. I felt like all the things I wanted to do with my life weren't going to happen. Like I'd given away my independence, my autonomy. Like I couldn't be me any more, because I'd become half of two people. Does that even make sense? I know how silly it sounds now.'

I nodded slowly. What she was saying kind of did make sense – I thought how relieved I'd been as I'd gradually drifted into becoming half of Alice-and-Joe – like we were two sides of the same coin, or two different-coloured threads, gradually weaving together into something better than we could have been alone. But would I have felt the same if I'd met Joe when I was twenty-one? I couldn't be sure.

Zoë carried on, just as if I wasn't there. 'The funny thing is, I knew that if I'd talked to him about it, he'd have understood. He'd have said we could take things slowly, have some time apart, whatever. He wouldn't have been a dick about it. And I knew that if that happened, I'd just have let myself fall right back into it – this massively intense relationship that I wasn't ready for, that could have been forever. I knew I had to do something to make sure that never happened.'

'What did you do?'

'That same day – well, that night – I was out with some mates. Just a girls' thing – most of us were single and the ones that weren't didn't bring their blokes. We went to a few bars and then a club. I was drunk, but I still knew what I was doing. I hooked up with someone else, that night. Some random bloke. We had sex in a back alley outside the club. It was sordid and grim and I never even knew his name. But I knew once I'd done that to Joe, I'd have to break up with him. And that's what I did.'

'I see,' I said. And I did see – that kind of answered the question of why, out of the blue, after just a few weeks, when their relationship was in its earliest, headiest stage, Zoë had told Joe it was over. But it didn't answer another question: why had she kept his notes to her? Why was she even here?

'The thing is, Alice, I regretted it straight away. It was like I'd had something precious that I'd deliberately smashed, because I was too scared to cherish it. And once it was broken, I could never fix it or even replace it. I carried on regretting it for years and years, and I never felt the same about anyone else, ever. But it kind of stopped mattering quite so much. I mean, I wasn't pining away like some princess in an ivory tower. And then I saw him, that day in August, with you. And it all came back. I thought I could get him back.'

'Even though he was with me?'

She nodded miserably. 'Even though he was with you. I'm sorry, Alice. I told you I did a shitty thing. When Sean said he wanted to move up to Leeds, I was like, off you go then. We weren't serious, but I treated him badly, too. I hurt him, because he could tell I didn't really care. I only cared about Joe.'

'So what happened last night?'

'It was Maurice. Maurice and his bloody poem. Him talking about hiding love, and how it could eat you up inside. And after living in the same flat for four bloody months, Joe never gave any sign at all that he still had feelings for me. I tried, you know. I tried to give him the chance to say he still loved me.'

I thought of her lacy camisole, the meals she'd cooked for Joe, the hours she'd spent next to him on the sofa playing computer games.

'Yeah,' I said. 'Don't think I didn't notice. I did.'

Zoë winced, like I'd raised a hand to slap her. 'So last night, I decided to tell him how I felt about him. I left the pub as soon as I could and went back to the flat to see him. But I needn't have, actually, because I met him just outside. I told him you'd already left, and we walked back together. And I told him I still loved him.'

I waited, my heart feeling like it was about to jump right out of my chest.

'He was so kind. So fucking kind and decent. He even said sorry, because he'd made me cry, and hugged me. That was when you came in the door. But also, he couldn't have been clearer. The feelings he'd had for me were history. Long gone. Since round about the time he met you.'

My heart was working overtime. Now, it seemed to have sent a massive rush of blood to my head, so I felt like I might faint. Part of me wanted to burst out with something like, 'But he's my boyfriend! You came into my home and tried to steal my man!'

But I knew that no one could be stolen unless they wanted to be. And Joe didn't. He'd chosen me, because he loved me and valued what we had. And, really, that was all that mattered.

'I'm a horrible person,' she said. 'I'm sorry, Alice. I really am.'

I shook my head, not quite ready to say I forgave her.

'There's another thing,' she went on. 'I had it all planned. I thought, if I got back together with Joe, you'd be okay so long as you had the pub.'

'Hold on,' I said, the pieces slowly falling into place in my mind. 'Was it you who told the press all that stuff about Fabian Flatley's business being dodgy?'

She nodded. 'I told you he talks on his phone all the time in the gym. I didn't even understand half of what he was saying, but it sounded off to me. So I recorded him on my phone, and then I bought a copy of the *FT* – and oh my God, that's something I'm never going to do again. Who reads that stuff? Insomniacs? – and I found a journalist who writes about companies floating on the stock exchange, and I emailed her.'

I stared at her. My mouth must have been gaping open like a goldfish's. Zoë had made a massive play for Joe, my boyfriend. But at the same time, she'd done this crazy thing to save the pub we both loved. She'd promised to fight for it, and she had. She'd fought and won, just as surely as she'd lost Joe.

'Thank you,' I managed to say. 'That's actually fucking amazing. And you're not a horrible person. You really aren't.'

Zoë turned her face up to mine. Her freckled cheeks were wet with tears.

'Fuck off. You're too kind, too, Alice. You and Joe. Damn it, you're so bloody right for each other. I can see it now. I could see it all along.'

Suddenly, in spite of everything, I could see it too. And more than ever, I felt horrified by what I'd almost lost.

'Go on,' Zoë said. 'Get out of here. Go home and talk to him.'

'Are you sure? Are you okay?'

'Of course. But that fucking apple sauce isn't – it's catching on the heat.'

Zoë turned away from me, reaching hastily for the pan, and I knew that she'd reached the limit of how much she could bear to relive all her heartache. So I opened the kitchen door, slowly, in case there was anything else she wanted to say.

But neither of us had a chance to say anything more, because Shirley was right there, four litres of milk in her hands.

'You need to get a wiggle on with those Yorkies, love. The queue in Tesco! I thought I'd end my days in the place. And before you ask, no it's not bloody organic.'

Chapter Thirty

The previous night, before I opened the door to find him and Zoë together, I'd hurried – almost fled – home in my eagerness to see Joe and make things right between us. Now, I walked more slowly. I knew that what I needed to say to him went far beyond 'I love you – please say you love me too and everything will be all right', which had pretty much been the extent of my plan before.

I realised that I needed more than just reassurance from Joe – and I owed him more, too. The past few months had revealed fault lines in our relationship that I hadn't ever suspected were there: fears and insecurities and untold truths that might not have mattered so much in the beginning, but made for a fragile foundation on which to build a life together.

I needed to give him more than just declarations of love: I owed him honesty, an unvarnished version of me.

And unvarnished was certainly what he was going to get, I thought ruefully, looking down at my creased black dress and realising I hadn't had a chance to take off my make-up from the previous night or do more than run a finger and some of Drew's toothpaste round my mouth.

Joe was in the living room when I got home, the iron plugged in and a row of shirts on wire hangers waiting to be pressed. But he hadn't been able to make a start on them, because Frazzle had stretched himself out on the ironing board and was fast asleep. So Joe was slumped on the sofa, flicking through his phone, presumably there for the long haul until the cat decided to wake up and move.

When he saw me he sat upright and put his phone aside. His face was full of doubt.

'Where have you been?'

'At Drew's.'

'Drew's? Are you sure about that?'

'Of course I'm sure! Where else would I have been?'

He looked at me for a long moment, and I felt blood rush to my cheeks.

'I saw you with Archie last night.'

'We just went for a walk.' I could hear the defensiveness in my voice.

'A walk. Right.'

I took a deep breath. I'd resolved that there would be no more secrets between us, and here I was, tempted to renege on my own promise already, because telling the truth was too hard.

'It honestly was just a walk. But there's been more than that, in the past couple of months. We've been playing Scrabble together online.'

'Scrabble?' Joe spat the word out with an angry half-laugh.

'Yes, Scrabble. And we got kind of close and kind of flirty. But that's over now. I promise. Nothing happened – nothing physical, nothing even close to cheating – and nothing is going to. Because

I've realised I was almost the world's most massive dick, and I almost lost you.'

Joe shook his head. 'I almost let you get away. I should have realised how hard it would be for you, Zoë moving in. I did realise, if I'm honest. But in a way I guess I wanted to make you see you'd made a mistake, leaving law to work in a pub. I thought you'd change your mind, come to your senses.'

'But I didn't. And Zoë—'

'I didn't realise she still had feelings for me,' Joe said. 'Not at first. We went for lunch together before she moved in and it was cool – it was like we could be mates after all this time, all this water under the bridge. But then I started to realise…'

'That she wanted you back?'

He nodded. 'And I should have had it out with her, but I didn't. I'd seen you with whatsisname, in the pub on the games night, and I wanted you to feel a bit of how that made me feel.'

'I'm sorry,' I said. 'I did feel that way, for ages. It's shit.'

'Shit. And stupid, because I've hurt Zoë and I've hurt you, and for all I knew you could have gone off and shagged that other bloke and quite honestly I wouldn't have blamed you, after what you saw here last night.'

'I didn't,' I said. 'I never want to shag anyone except you.'

'Not even Kit Harington?'

'I believe he's taken.'

'And I guess you're taken, too.'

Our eyes met and we both started to smile. Then Joe stood up, slowly, hesitantly, and gave me a kiss on the cheek that felt almost tentative. I put my arms around his waist, not hugging him but just holding his body against mine, almost cautious, same as he had been.

'I could really do with a bath,' I said.

'Want me to run you one? With that poncy bergamot stuff you got for your birthday?'

'Perfect.'

And so, twenty minutes later, I was lying in fragrant hot water, bubbles up to my chin, and Joe was perched less comfortably on the edge of the bath, his feet next to Frazzle's litter tray. I'd got so used to it being there, I realised; it was ages since I'd last kicked it on my way to the loo in the morning. The fear and jealousy I'd felt over Zoë was gone. The attraction I'd felt for Archie was gone too, and I realised it had never been real – just a way of making myself feel desirable when I hadn't for the longest time.

But still, there was a knot of tension deep inside me. I thought about the other thing I hadn't told Joe, which I'd resolved to be truthful about now. I would. I'd decided. It was the right thing to do. But did I really have to do it now?

'Could you pass me my shampoo please?'

I ducked under the water, then lathered my hair, rinsed it, lathered it again and combed coconut and honey conditioner through it.

'God, the state of my hair. The ends are split to fuck and my highlights need doing.'

Joe smiled. 'You have beautiful hair. Beautiful everything.'

But an ugly secret that I've never been able to admit to you, because I'm too ashamed.

I cleansed my face, rubbing it twice with a flannel the way I'd seen some woman on YouTube say you should do. I needed to shave my legs, but I wasn't doing that with Joe there. Two years wasn't enough time together for that. I wondered how long it would take before all those tiny barriers between us were broken down, eroded by time and familiarity. Maybe they never would be.

I said, 'Joe,' and then I stopped.

'Alice.' He reached under the water and gave my foot a squeeze. He was looking at me, not smiling, his face still and expectant. I looked at my flannel and wondered if I could put it over my face, like the screen in a confessional, literally hiding my feelings.

But that would be ridiculous, and I'd get soapy water in my mouth.

'There's something I need to tell you.'

'I'm listening.'

'I know you think it's crazy that I was okay about leaving Billings, just like that. I know you think it's really weird I didn't fight to get another job offer there, when I could have done. Or try other firms, or whatever.'

'I did think it was kind of strange.'

'The thing is, when Gordon lost his job, I… It made me realise that my whole career there had been a sham.'

'What do you mean? Of course it wasn't a sham. You did brilliantly in the other departments you worked in. It was just him that got a job offer in first. You could have ended up in Litigation, or in Public Law with me, or on the commercial side like Heather, or… anywhere you wanted, really.'

'I don't think so, Joe. Because Gordon had a reason for offering me that job. For favouring me over the other trainees.'

Joe slid a bit along the edge of the bath, close enough that he could hold my hand. I saw drops of water from my skin darkening the sleeve of his sweatshirt.

'You see,' I said, feeling like I might choke on the words, 'what happened was, one night when I was quite new there, he took me out for dinner. And afterwards, in the taxi home…'

I stopped. I couldn't say it. This time, I did put my flannel over my face. I wished I had a full-body-sized one. At least the bubbles on the water hid most of the rest of me.

'He… he sexually assaulted you,' Joe said. His voice sounded kind of croaky, like getting the words out hurt his throat.

'No! It wasn't like that.' I'd been right – I was getting soapy water in my mouth. I moved the flannel and sat up, hugging my knees to my chest. 'I let him. I fell asleep in the taxi and when I woke up he was touching me. I wasn't sure what was happening at first. I was really, really drunk. But I didn't try and stop him. I let him carry on. He didn't hurt me or anything.'

I put my head down to my knees, my wet, slippery hair trailing over my shoulders. Joe reached out and touched my shoulder.

'Alice, you know that's what happens, don't you? In cases of assault… People don't struggle. They don't scream, or try to fight off their attacker. It's shock – and self-preservation. Most of the time, people just wait. Disassociate. It's normal.'

'But I… It felt okay. He didn't hurt me. And I never said anything, not that night or afterwards, to anyone. And whenever I saw him, there was this thing between us, like he knew I'd keep quiet. And then he favoured me over the other trainees. I got the interesting work to do. I got the job offer. And I took it. I let it all happen to me. I was going to tell Samantha about it, but I bottled it. I was too scared of what would happen to me.'

'My poor Alice. That's normal, too. You kept your head down. That's what survivors do.'

I lifted my head to look at him. I could feel tears streaming down my face, my eyes stinging from the conditioner.

'Other women didn't. Other people he did that to were brave enough to tell. Even though it could've damaged their careers. They spoke out. And once they'd done that, I knew everyone would know I hadn't said anything. I'd let him do what he wanted to me and shut the fuck up because I felt so ashamed, Joe. I knew I could never, ever work there again after that. And not just there – anywhere I went, it would be on my CV. People would know. They'd think I wasn't bright, or talented, or hard-working. I was just easy. Easy and complicit.'

'No one would think that of you. No one does.'

'And I never even told you.' I carried on like he hadn't spoken, the words coming in an unstoppable flood. 'That first day, when you bought me those shoes. That was the morning after it had happened. And I went on a date with you, just the same, and I realised how much I liked you and I knew if you found out you wouldn't like me back.'

Joe pushed up the sleeves of his jumper and turned on the shower head. He checked the temperature of the water and then gently and carefully started to rinse my hair. One hand supported my head, the other guided the water carefully along my hairline so that none of it got in my eyes. He didn't say anything until he'd finished; I wouldn't have been able to hear him, anyway, over the sound of running water.

'How could I not like you?' he said, once he'd switched off the tap. 'This incredible, strong, brilliant, beautiful woman? I'd have been mad. You could have told me practically anything and I'd still have fallen for you.'

'But I didn't tell you.'

'You've told me now. That's all that matters.'

I stood up, pulling the plug out of the bath. Joe handed me a towel for my hair and wrapped another around my body, holding me close like it would stop me from shivering.

I pressed myself against him, relief wrapping around me like the warm towel. Joe didn't seem to think there was anything to forgive me for. I'd expected him to react with horror and disgust, and he hadn't. For the first time, I truly understood that what had happened that night wasn't my fault. That I hadn't asked for it, or covered up for it. That I wasn't to blame. And for the first time, the weight of guilt I'd been carrying for so long lifted. I'd got so used to it being there, I hadn't realised how heavy it was, but now it was gone I felt light as a balloon, as if I might float all the way up to the bathroom ceiling, if it weren't for Joe's arms holding me safe.

Chapter Thirty-One

Three months later

Joe and I walked through the unfamiliar park together, hand in hand. The morning was chilly still, but the sun was shining in a radiant blue sky. A flock of green parakeets wheeled, shrieking, overhead. On the grassy slope, daffodils shone acid-yellow against the green, clashing with the purple crocuses that had sprung into bloom alongside them.

'Sorry to drag you all the way to north London on a Saturday morning,' I said. 'But I didn't have a free minute last week, and the people from Heart of the Community said this pub's really worth checking out. It was going to be bought by developers, too, and a few of the regulars managed to save it.'

'Yeah,' Joe said. 'Because going for a walk in the sunshine with my girlfriend, finishing at a pub, is a really shit way to spend a Saturday morning.'

'Especially when you've got a party to go to in the afternoon.'

'Right. My life basically sucks right now.'

'And that massive win you had in court last week. Poor you, you must be feeling terrible.'

Our eyes met and we laughed. It felt easy, on a day like this, to laugh and be silly together – in fact, it had felt that way for some time. However busy we were, we'd regained the ability to connect with each other, to be in the moment, to remind each other how much we mattered – as individuals and as that vital, fragile 'us', which we'd so nearly lost.

'So where is this pub you were going on about?' Joe asked.

'The Winchmore Arms.' I checked my phone. 'It's on the corner of the park, just off the high street. I think if we cut down here we should get to it.'

We strolled on in silence, enjoying the growing warmth of the sun on our backs, listening to the rush of the wind through the trees and the chorus of birdsong, until the path led us to a gateway in the metal railings.

'Out here, I think.'

The pub was where my phone had told me it would be, on the corner at the end of a row of nondescript terraced houses. The street looked run-down and forlorn, paint peeling off the fronts of the houses, garden fences sagging at drunken angles. But the pub had hanging baskets of bright red and pink geraniums outside its door, and its windows sparkled in the sun.

'Apparently the refurb didn't cost too much,' I said. 'They reckon we could do something similar in a few months.'

'Never mind all that,' Joe said. 'What I want to know is, what's the beer like?'

'Only one way to find out.'

I pushed open the door and we stood on the threshold for a second. It was early, and the Winchmore Arms wouldn't have been open for more than half an hour or so. All the same, it was almost half full. I took in the group of people in running gear drinking coffee and eating muffins, the stack of board games on shelves, the enticing smell of eggs and bacon. It wasn't my pub, but it was so similar it could almost have been – like entering a parallel universe.

There was even, sitting at the bar, already three-quarters of the way down his first pint of the day, a lonely old man, this pub's version of Fat Don, who arrived every day and drank steadily until closing time. His wife had left him a couple of years back, Shirley had explained, and the Nag's Head was his home from home, and who were we to judge? At least it gave him some company, she'd said, which was better than festering at home alone, wasn't it?

This man wasn't Fat Don; he wasn't fat at all. But the slump of his shoulders was the same; the way he lifted his glass to his lips and sipped slowly – because being in the pub all day could get expensive at today's prices and you wanted to pace yourself – was the same. The way, when he heard the door open and felt the cool air on his neck, he turned to see who the new arrival was, and whether they might come over and give him some company for half an hour or so, was the same.

He was the same as Fat Don, but he wasn't him. He was Gordon. Jobless, friendless, alone, spending his days drinking on a bar stool.

'I've seen enough. Let's go.' I practically bundled Joe back out of the door.

We were back inside the park before he spoke.

'That was who I thought, wasn't it?'

I nodded. 'Sorry about your pint. I just couldn't…'

'I get it. Are you okay?'

Joe slipped his arm around my waist and pulled me close. I felt the warmth of his body through our coats, the comforting scratchiness of his scarf against my cheek. And I realised I was okay. Seeing Gordon had been a shock, that was all. I wasn't afraid of him any longer – why would I be? His power over me was all gone. He couldn't control me any more.

'Never been better,' I said. 'Honestly.'

'Sure?'

'Never been surer.'

We paused, halfway across the park, holding each other close against the breeze. Joe tilted my face up to his, looked down at me and kissed me.

'I hate that bastard for what he did to you.'

'I don't. There's no point hating him. It was a long time ago, and I got through it. I was lucky. But I've been thinking, Joe…'

An idea that had been barely beginning to form in my mind suddenly sprang to life.

'What have you been thinking?'

'I could start a thing. Like, a website at first. And then maybe a phone line. For women who've had stuff happen to them like happened to me. Sexual assault at work. It's a big problem in pubs and restaurants still. I could give people advice on what to do, what their rights are, stuff like that. Give them support if they go to court. Try and make the whole process a bit less daunting.'

'You know what? I think that's a fantastic idea. And you're the perfect person to do it.'

'As a lawyer-turned-landlady?'

'Exactly. If you'd just been appointed a high-court judge, I couldn't be more proud of you than I am right now.'

'You know what?' I smiled up into Joe's eyes, as blue as the March sky, but warmer. 'Me too.'

'We should get a move on. What time's the party starting? Two?'

'Half past. So I'll have time to get my hair into some sort of up-do and figure out how to attach that fascinator thing. Are you sure it's not totally over the top?'

'Don't be daft. It's a wedding, isn't it?'

'Well, a wedding reception. Still though. First one ever held at the pub, as far as I know. That's got to be a special occasion, right?'

'The most special.'

We hurried home and unlocked the flat. It was empty and silent, clean and orderly. The door to our spare bedroom stood open, the bed freshly made with white sheets. In the bathroom, Frazzle's litter tray no longer waited to trap unwary feet. When I'd opened the airing cupboard to turn the thermostat down a few days before, I'd thought something was wrong, and then realised the jars of fermenting kimchi had gone.

'It'll be really convenient for Zoë, living in the flat above the pub,' Joe said.

'And she's put a cat door in for Frazz, so he can get out onto the roof and then down to the garden.'

'I kind of miss them both, you know,' I said.

'Well, we'll see them often enough. And although we can't get a replacement for Zoë – unless you really want a flatmate – we could...'

'Get a cat? A cat of our own?'

'A rescue one. Maybe a black one. I read on the Cats Protection website that they're harder to rehome.'

'Funny you should mention that,' I said. 'I did, too.'

And we held each other close for the longest time, feeling the quietness of our home around us, until it was time to get ready.

The pub was as busy as it had been for the games night and the poetry evening – busier, even. Kelly and Freddie were whisking around from bar to tables and back, pouring drinks and carrying glasses. Shirley was behind the bar, dressed for the occasion in a fitted fuchsia-pink satin dress and a matching hat with enough feathers on it to supply an entire flamingo.

The kitchen door was closed, but from behind it I could hear chatter and laughter as Zoë and Juan prepared the curry goat, rice and peas. I'd worried about Juan being co-opted for this special occasion – it was too much for Zoë and her trainee sous-chef to manage on their own – but he'd immediately taken a massive fancy to her and clearly relished being both deferred to and bossed around by a much younger woman.

'Just look at the old git, poncing about like he's flipping Romeo,' Shirley had said fondly. 'As if she'd look at him twice, bless him.'

In order to keep the cash-flow situation under control and avoid eating too much into its limited funds, the committee had decided to keep to a bare-bones renovation, but still, the place was transformed. The sticky old carpet was gone, the parquet floor restored to glowing glory. The walls had been stripped of their faded flock wallpaper and freshly painted. New banquette seating, upholstered in reclaimed fabric, had joined the existing tables and chairs along two of the walls.

The luridly coloured portrait of Princess Diana was gone – it was Shirley's personal property, after all – and in its place was a vibrant street scene painted by students at a local art college. It had a whole lot more artistic merit, but I still found myself glancing up and expecting to see Diana looking down over the pub as she'd done for so long, and missing the chats I'd had with her inside my head. Above the bar was a chalkboard listing forthcoming events: the Woolly Wednesdays knitting group; the pay-what-you-can yoga drop-in sessions; the family fun day and lunch-for-a-fiver club for pensioners; the jazz nights and quiz nights and of course the next games and poetry evenings.

The entry for today read, 'Closed for a private function'. Not that it was particularly private – almost all the Nag's Head regulars were on the guest list anyway. Joe and I approached the bar and Shirley leaned over to greet us, not close enough for a kiss because her hat brim was so wide, but close enough for me to breathe in the familiar smell of her face powder and Obsession perfume.

'Hello, my lovelies. What can I get for you? Glass of Prosecco? Can't stand the stuff myself but everyone seems to be drinking it and you've got to move with the times, don't you?'

'Are you sure I can't help behind the bar? Or at least carry plates once the food's served?'

'Don't you dare, young lady! It's your day off. You might be general manager here now, but you'll still do as I tell you.'

I laughed. 'And it might be your last day here, but you're still the boss.'

Shirley leaned over the bar counter. 'I'm going to let you two into a little secret. No one knows except me and Juan. But when we talked about retiring, once we moved to Spain, we realised we just couldn't do it. I mean, imagine having him underfoot all day. I'd go mad. And there's only so many games of golf a man can play, aren't there?'

'But you were so looking forward to your life of leisure in the sun,' I said, amazed. 'And you've totally earned it. What will you do instead?'

'Have a look at this.' Shirley pulled out her phone and scrolled rapidly. 'Here we are.'

She passed it over to me. On the screen was a photograph of a sunny street, brilliant blue sky arching above it. There were palm trees, their fronds silhouetted against the light, and hanging baskets of cerise bougainvillea. On the pavement, under a green and white striped awning, were clusters of metal tables and chairs, each one bearing an ashtray and a dispenser for paper napkins. In between the hanging baskets, I could see a sign with something on it that I was pretty sure was a shamrock.

'O'Grady's Tavern, it's called,' Shirley said, her eyes shining with excitement. 'Oh, you won't believe the state of the place. Fights every night, shocking food and the owners have no more of an idea how to store beer than you did when you started here, Alice, no offence. But with a bit of TLC it'll be a real local gem in no time flat.'

'But it's an Irish bar,' I said. 'You'll change that, surely?'

'Oh yes. We've got big plans for the place. Juan's planning the menu already: fish and chips, steak and kidney pud, tomato soup – all the traditional things. We'll even do a veggie burger – see, we've learned something from her ladyship in there. That's the thing about this business – it gets in your blood, you know.'

I nodded. It had certainly got into mine. 'But what are you going to call it?'

'Oh, that was easy. We made that decision right away. It's going to be the People's Princess. I'll hang my portrait of her over the mantelpiece, and it'll feel like home straight away. Now, what can I get you two gentlemen? Been keeping you waiting, haven't I, rabbiting on?'

She put her phone away and turned to serve her next customer, and Joe and I moved away from the bar, drinks in hand, and looked around at the crowd.

Sitting at their usual table were Ray, Sadiq and Terry, all looking slightly uncomfortable in their smart suits and a bit like they weren't sure what to say to one another with no dominoes game under way. Their wives, in contrast, were dressed up to the nines and chatting animatedly.

Susan, Victoria and Jason from the pub steering committee were fussing anxiously around the room, Jason climbing up onto a table to secure a piece of bunting that had escaped from its drawing pin.

In another corner, a group of a dozen or so smartly dressed strangers were sipping soft drinks and looking ill at ease. The men were wearing suits and hats, the women elaborate, brightly coloured lace and satin frocks. One woman had her baby daughter on her hip, wearing a lime-green dress identical to her own.

'They must be from the church,' Joe said. 'Breaking rank or what?'

'I'm glad they came though.' I reached for his hand and squeezed it.

Near the door, Drew and Heather stood close together, glasses of Prosecco in their hands, his blond head and her dark one almost touching as they leaned in to talk, gaze at each other and finally exchange a brief but intense kiss. Drew caught my eye and waved, and we moved over to join them.

'I'm going to miss this place, you know,' Drew said.

'What will you miss most?' I asked. 'The twelve-hour shifts? Scraping Don off the floor at closing time? Or cleaning the bogs?'

'Oh, the bogs for sure. It's going to feel kind of weird, working a normal eight-hour day in an office.'

'But you've got this place to thank for turning you into a social-media marketing guru,' Heather reminded him.

'And you can move back to London,' Joe said.

Heather smiled, and I knew what she was thinking. *And move in with me.* My brother and best friend's relationship had proceeded at warp speed, hindered only slightly by Drew having to move back in with our parents. I knew it was wanting to see more of Heather that had motivated my brother to apply for normal, proper jobs for the first time in his life. It was strange, I thought, that just when I'd abandoned the corporate world, Drew had embraced it.

I just hoped that the corporate world was prepared for the shock to its system.

The kitchen door opened and Zoë hurried over to us, wiping her hands on her apron.

'God, this mass catering malarkey is hard,' she said. 'But I think we've got it under control. You should see the cake – it's a showstopper. I never knew Juan was a baker but he's nailed it.'

She gave me a quick hug, and Joe bent down to kiss her on the cheek. A few months back, I'd have bristled with alarm at that, but now I found I could see it for what it was – an affectionate gesture between old friends.

I remembered her telling me, just a few days before, that she was thinking about dating again.

'My horoscope said that this is going to be a good year for love. Apparently Venus is moving into Aquarius, and that alignment means my emotional side will be uppermost. Of course, being an Aquarian, I'm highly spiritual anyway and in touch with my inner self. So I've downloaded Tinder.'

It was a measure of our new-found friendship that I'd managed not to tell her to get a bloody grip.

I was about to ask if I could give her and Juan a hand in the kitchen, when the door swung open and the whole pub erupted.

There were cheers and whoops and applause, but soon everyone joined together and sang 'For They Are Jolly Good Fellows' so loudly I was amazed the roof stayed on.

Maurice and Wesley stood together in the doorway for a moment, hand in hand. They looked surprised, diffident at being the centre of attention – but also glowing with something that went beyond happiness. It might have been relief at being welcomed by a community they thought might cast them out. It might have been pride at being able to live honestly at last. Or it might just have been their love for each other, kept secret for so long and now shining as brightly as the sun.

Out in the street behind them, I could see the new sign swinging gently in the spring breeze, orange and black and gold and green: 'The Ginger Cat'.

A Letter from Sophie

Dear reader,

I want to say a huge thank you for choosing to read *Just Saying*. If you did enjoy it, and want to keep up to date with all my latest releases, just sign up at the following link. Your email address will never be shared and you can unsubscribe at any time.

www.bookouture.com/sophie-ranald

I started writing *Just Saying* in November 2019, and I am writing this note on Easter Sunday 2020, in what feels like a different world. While I was working on the first chapters of this novel, the first news about the Covid-19 pandemic had only just begun to spread out of China; today, it has changed – and ended – lives all over the world.

Here in London, we're entering our fourth week in lockdown. Many people have joked that for a writer, quarantine is not that different from normal life; we're used to spending long hours indoors, not talking to anyone. The worlds we create exist inside our computer screens, so for real life to suddenly become virtual, with

Zoom drinks taking the place of meeting friends in a bar, exercise sessions happening online and video calls replacing meetings with colleagues isn't too much of a shock to the system.

And yet, daily life has changed beyond recognition. People queue outside shops, their faces obscured by masks and their hands encased in gloves. On our daily exercise, we slalom across paths to preserve two metres of distance from others. We obsess over supermarket delivery slots. We read with horror about overstretched hospitals, doctors and nurses falling ill, funerals taking place without mourners.

I've been so humbled to have been contacted by readers telling me that my books have helped to keep you entertained, distracted, even smiling, in this strange time. Thank you all for reading – for living for a few hours in the lives of my characters. I hope that you and the people you love come out of this crisis safe and well.

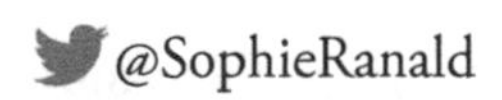

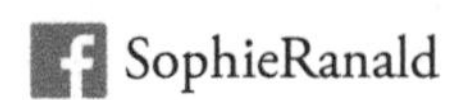

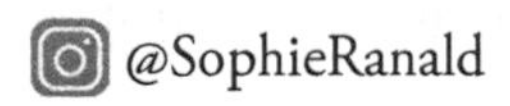

Acknowledgements

Although I've spent my fair share of time drinking in pubs, I've never had the experience of working in one. I expected researching this to be easy – after all, Britain is full of wonderful pubs that have been reinvented to meet the changing needs of the communities they serve. However, it quickly became apparent to me that I might as well have been trying to research the private life of international spies, so hard was it to find anyone who was willing to talk to me, or could spare the time! So I'm very grateful to Phil Harriss of the Plunkett Foundation, a worthy charity that restores disused pubs to community ownership, who generously shared his experience of saving the Kings Arms, which is now owned by the people of Shouldham in West Norfolk.

I also did some research the old-fashioned way, reading Mick Brown's *Running a Pub* and Malcolm Mant's brilliantly titled memoir *30 Years Behind Bars*.

Huge thanks to Mike Harris, who advised me on the intricacies of immigration law and how a person of the Windrush generation might be affected by the UK's often unjust 'hostile environment' policy. Dan Neidle and my dear friends Nikki Moulton and Louise

Mahon helped me with insights into the workings of City law firms – thank you all.

As ever, despite all the help and advice from these clever people, I may have got things wrong, and any errors are all my own.

Throughout my writing career, I've been represented by The Soho Agency, and I couldn't be more grateful for their expertise, wisdom and support. Thank you so very much Alice Saunders, Araminta Whitley and Niamh O'Grady.

I'm so fortunate to have the best publisher in the business. The team at Bookouture truly have the magic touch, making every aspect of my books as good as it can be. My ninja editor, Christina Demosthenous, takes my horrible first drafts and patiently and diligently transforms them into something I can be proud of. Noelle Holten, Kim Nash, Peta Nightingale, Alex Holmes and Alex Crowe have also provided invaluable support behind the scenes on publicity, production and promotion. Copy-editor Rhian McKay caught so many of my embarrassing glitches, and Lisa Horton came up with a totally gorgeous cover design. Thank you all.

While I was working on the edits for *Just Saying*, London and the world went into lockdown. During this deeply strange and worrying time, I've been kept sane by daily Facebook threads and weekly Zoom chats over wine with my wonderful friends, as well as killer online workouts with Henry Pinkrah and the amazing community at Base 13. There aren't enough words in the world to express how grateful I am to have such kind, inspiring and supportive people in my life.

Finally, all my love and thanks to my crew at home – my darling Hopi and Purrs and Hither the cats. You're the best.